The Long Watch

Also by Elizabeth Linington:

THE PROUD MAN

The
LONG WATCH

A NOVEL BY

Elizabeth Linington

NEW YORK

The Viking Press · 1956

Copyright © 1956 by Elizabeth Linington

First published by The Viking Press in September 1956

Published on the same day in the Dominion of Canada
by The Macmillan Company of Canada Limited

Library of Congress Catalog Card Number: 56-8563

Printed in U. S. A. by The Colonial Press Inc.

Author's Note

THIS IS not the story of the Revolutionary War, familiar to most Americans. It is the story of a man and his job, and in its essentials might have happened anywhere, at any time.

Perhaps it will seem that though this man lived in exciting times, he had few sensational adventures. We all live in exciting times, but the sensational, the melodramatic, seldom comes to any of us. There are always the many who leave adventures to others, and get on with the job.

The book is secondarily the story of a few years in the life of a city. Apologies are due the respectable and authentic Philip Livingston for presenting him with so graceless a godson as the fictional Darcy Trevelyan. The New York *Courier* is the only fictional newspaper in this story. The others, their editors where named, and quotations from them are authentic—as is the existence of Mr. Christopher Sower. Fictional license has been taken in predating the publication of the New York *Gazetteer* by a few years.

PART ONE

PART ONE

BETHUNE CONSIDERED the window. It was boarded up, but if he had something to pry out the nails, the old chestnut outside could help him down. Must be after midnight, he reckoned; dark enough in the box-room at any rate. He got out his pocket-knife, fumbled the blade open, and felt for the nails in the board. It was clumsy work in the dark. He had never been clever with tools; the knife kept slipping. And all the while Mr. Thurstan's ugly words sounded in his mind.

He stopped after a while to rest, wondering if it would be easier to try the door; the household must be asleep by now. As he moved toward it the knob rattled and a hoarse whisper came through the keyhole.

"Mr. Bethune? You awake, Mr. Bethune?"

It was suddenly queer to think that Shad had never called him anything else, even when Bethune was a little boy. Even now that he was grown—well, yes, you could say he was grown—Bethune was not sure it was proper. Gentry, Shad said: a meaningless word. Gentry were those on top, but Shad would say different. "Not all gentry got things, an' not ever'body that's got things is gentry—they's that Mr. Haines at Taggarts' Chance. But your pa, he was gentry even with the chains on, an' so is you." All very well to say. Bethune thought it had started a long time back, before he was born, with the man he'd never known, who was his father.

"Mr. Bethune? I got a key to let you out—an' I got some dinner for you." The door opened cautiously and the tall shadow of the old butler slipped in.

"You shouldn't come," said Bethune. "If Mr. Thurstan finds out—"

"He ain't goin' find out." Shad gave him a meat pasty on a plate. He had had nothing since the middle of the afternoon; it tasted good. "What they goin' do to you, Mr. Bethune, you goin' get whupped?" That was the worst Shad could think.

"He'll have me gaoled," said Bethune. "He said might be they'd hang me, Shad." It seemed to have nothing to do with him; he could say it almost casually.

"Lord! Mought be. They do that, times. Mr. Bethune? You do what he say?"

"Well," said Bethune. He finished the pie. He considered trying to explain to Shad, but he did not want to talk about it at all.

Shad waited and then said, "You got to git away, Mr. Bethune, an' never come back, if that's so. Git away far an' fast."

"I reckon," said Bethune.

"I c'n go fetch your things." Shad turned to the door and then added, "Lord. Hit's queer—queer. Once I fix to help your pa git away. He say, you all look atter Miss Reba an' the chile. Goin' git clear off to N'Yawk or Boston, he say, earn money to send for to git 'em away to him. 'Twasn't to be." He was an old man and rambling in his talk.

"I don't want you to get in trouble for me."

"You is the one in trouble, Mr. Bethune. Hit's no thing your pa woulda done, even when he were young like you. Hit's a wrong thing. But I don't reckon you oughta git hung for it. I go fetch your gear."

Bethune stood alone in the dark, waiting, and thought of what Shad had said, and about his father—the place it started, that was: James Andrew Bethune, like himself.

Shad and the rest could tell him little enough about his father. He knew all they could tell, and he had read in a few books and old pamphlets what they couldn't tell, about the Stuart claimant and his armies. And Culloden. Eighteen years back that was, in 1745. James Andrew Bethune was at Culloden. Some of the Scot officers were hanged, but he was one of those deported to the American colonies as lifetime indenturers, to be sold to the highest bidders. His son reflected that it must have come hard on him—a gentleman they said he was. "Not that he say much, Mr. Bethune, he were a quiet one like you is." Mr. Thurstan paid sixty guineas for him and set him to clerking for the factor here at Thurstan Hundred. He was twenty-two, Shad said. "You his spittin' image now, Mr. Bethune," so he had not been what you would call handsome: tall and gangling, sandy-haired, and gray-eyed. Perhaps the indentured girl, Reba, loved him because he was gentry, then. About his mother Bethune knew little. He went on thinking about it because his mind shied away from the other thing.

Mr. Thurstan had been kind to let them wed, but Shad said it was mostly because Mr. Thurstan was strait-laced and did not want a bastard born in his house, even to bound servants. "They was both Papist but that don't signify. Rector, he did it." Reba Downes her name was, and all they could tell him besides was that she was pretty, and gentle, and bound for seven years to pay her passage from England. The week after she was delivered of a son, James Bethune ran away from Thurstan Hundred, and the factor was late on his trail so an alarm went out. Mr. Philip Gerard of Twelvetrees, riding that morning with his sons, sighted the runaway and gave chase; he said afterward he meant only to wound him, but the ball struck too near his heart. "Hit come hard on Miss Reba—she don't have heart to fight when the fever git her. Jus' slip away like, an' you on'y a month borned." Sixteen and a half years ago.

Bethune reckoned it had been kind of Mr. Thurstan to raise him: no claim on him for it. But that was behind the way he'd come to be, he knew. Or would it have been the same if Mr. Thurstan had put him in the charity orphanage in Williamsburg— was it something in himself? For he was an in-between at Thurstan Hundred, Shad and Flora and Azalea and the other house slaves treating him like gentry, and the Thurstans like a bound boy. Never quite knowing where he was, except always by himself. Yes, that was the start of it.

Shad came back. He had a leather saddlebag filled with Bethune's clothes. "I didn't take your ole shoes, Mr. Bethune, or some other gear not good 'nough. I put in the Good Book Mr.

Thurstan give you, I reckon you in need of it. An' they's a packet o' victuals on top. I ain't no money."

Shad was taking an almighty risk for him. He wanted to say something about it; after this he could never come back to Thurstan Hundred, never see any of them again, and there were things he should say—about the time he had the fever and Flora sat up by his bed; about the times Shad had saved delicacies for him when there were guests. It was queer to think—they were Negroes but you could say they had raised him, as much as anyone had. He could not find the words.

"You better go, Mr. Bethune. Three-four hours to dawn."

"Yes," he said. He took the bag and followed Shad out, down the rear stair. He expected the old man to leave him at the door; instead Shad went with him round the house, ghost-white in the dark, and down the broad carriageway to the stone pillars and the iron gate Mr. Thurstan had sent for all the way to England.

There he stopped. "Mr. Bethune. Things I like to say. I can't rightly."

"Yes. I know." The strange, painful thing was, he'd have been leaving next month anyway, in June, leaving properly. Mr. Thurstan had said he would write to Mr. Wyeth, and there was a new life all laid out for him. He had not thought to be leaving this way.

Shad shifted uneasily. "Mr. Bethune. You know it were a wrong thing."

He could not talk about it.

"Your pa, he'd be mighty angerish at it." It was the worst reproach Shad could utter. "You better git far off, where Mr. Thurstan can't know. Like your pa say then, N'Yawk or Boston. You git to the ocean an' fin' a boat goin' north. That's the way."

Shad, if found out, would likely be whipped, valued house servant though he was. Bethune said, "You'd better get back, Shad." Nothing else of what he ought to say; if he had known the right words they would have stopped in his throat.

"I reckon. I pray the Lord for you, Mr. Bethune. You walk in the Lord's way an' ever'thing be right for you."

Bethune said, "Thank you, Shad. Good-by."

"Good-by, Mr. Bethune."

He turned left and started to walk down the road, away from the only home he had ever known, though never his home. But he did not go alone; Margaret went at his side. The words Mr. Thurstan had said were bad, but they had not hurt so sharp, like a knife in his chest, as the need to leave Margaret. He walked fast to escape her, but she stayed with him; he thought she would stay with him the rest of his life.

That was why it had happened, because he had never known that he was lonely. There were no Thurstan boys, and Miss Caroline and Miss Honor were older, so boys never came to Thurstan Hundred—not that he would have been allowed to play with gentlemen's sons. He had always been sufficient to Bethune: he had to be. Their attitude showed in the way they had always called him by the one name, so that he almost forgot he had others. Mr. Thurstan had done a duty by him: had the rector give him lessons until he was twelve, when it was apparent that whatever he might be good for it would not be a trade, unskillful as he was with his hands. But he wrote a better script than the factor.

Mr. Thurstan had talked to him about it. He would provide until Bethune was sixteen, in return for his work. Bethune was to help the factor, Mr. Bolt, at making up accounts, and then if he wished he could go to Williamsburg, where the lawyer, Mr. Wyeth, would be asked to find work for him as a clerk. Mr. Thurstan made it clear Bethune had no claim, that he'd been given a home from charity.

Since he had learned to read he had spent most of his free time going through Mr. Thurstan's library; no one else was greatly interested in it. He found a certain difficulty discussing what he read with the slaves, and had never been on intimate terms with anyone else. He did the work Mr. Holt set him to, in the office room. His amusements were all of necessity solitary: visiting the stable, walking the boundaries of the plantation, coming cautiously halfway down the stair to watch when there were guests. It was a revelation when he made a friend.

He had never paid much attention to the youngest Thurstan girl. Margaret was almost two years younger, and for three years she had been living in Williamsburg with her aunt, to attend a fashionable young ladies' academy. All that time ago he had scorned girls, but when she came home last Christmas she seemed so changed, and he was so changed—because of Zena?—that he had felt shy with her.

Margaret was friendly; she was as much interested in him as he in her, but able to show it as he was not. She would come into the office room, in the mornings, and then he got little work done, and it made him nervous, for he knew that if Mr. Thurstan or Mr. Bolt found them talking the devil would be in it. Margaret asked why, and he could not explain, though he knew. But he liked to have her come. After a while he was more at ease with Margaret than with anyone he had ever known. It was fine to be admired; no one had ever deferred to him before, but she was younger and a girl, so looked up to him. She listened to him, and all his defenses were down with her because she understood. He could say anything to Margaret.

It was hard to say when it came to be another kind of feeling. Margaret and Zena: the one had bearing on the other, but he could not say how or why.

That was no new knowledge in him. He had grown up near slave quarters; he could not remember a time he had been ignorant about that, but up to a couple of years ago it had been meaningless fact to him. Now it was a new, exciting feeling to be explored. And there was Zena keeping it in his mind.

Shad and Flora looked down on Zena: yellow trash. No one had to tell him why. What they called a lightskirt, the way she swung her hips when she walked, and painted her mouth. She liked Bethune: always smiling at him, hinting at him. Once he had met her in the dark kitchen passage and she had leaned against him like a cat, murmuring, "You want Zena be nice t' you, honey? You jus' say." And he wanted her, hot and hard, but what made him draw back was, mysteriously, the mere fact that she had offered. He should be the one to say. But he knew sooner or later he would say, despite the black looks that Shad gave her. She was there to his hand, and this wasn't the sort of thing you said no to.

He had a clear picture of it: Zena was half the way it was and the other half was how he came to feel about Margaret, the part you read about in stories, the polite part. He knew the difference, and that was what kept him from approaching Zena. He knew right from wrong: Mr. Thurstan was strict about the household's attending church.

The plans they made, he and Margaret! Often it seemed to him a foolish children's dream, that he would go away and make a deal of money, so much Mr. Thurstan would be glad to let him marry Margaret. "I'd rather marry you than anyone, Bethune, if I've got to, and there's nothing else for a girl. Even if it takes you years and years, I'd wait."

He did not know how it might be done.

"But you could be anything, Bethune! A lawyer like Mr. Wyeth, or—"

"Oh, yes," he said with the unsmiling humor that always made her giggle, "I've a fine chance of that, plenty of money to pay for schooling and keep me meanwhile. I don't know that I'd want to be a lawyer."

"But you must know what you want! Isn't there anything you want to do?"

He looked down at the column of figures he was copying for Mr. Bolt. Just as well he was only copying; figures had a way of slipping out from under him, meaningless squiggles. He said haltingly, "I don't know, I want—to find out, that's all."

"Find out what?" She did not understand, but neither did he, entirely. Find out? The why and wherefore of it, of himself, Bethune, insignificant but important on a crowded planet; of Thurstan Hundred, and the continent entire; of every man, the thing inside making each what he was, the reason and the beginning and the center force—the answer. He could not use those words, and it made little sense. He smiled at her.

"I don't suppose I'll earn much money clerking."

"There must be something. Don't you want it, Bethune? I mean—"

It was not in him to show what he felt.

Perhaps that was the way, to think what he wanted, and that would tell him how to have it. Well, one day he wanted a horse like Bay Brandy, fine and light-paced and lovely as the dawn; but he would have to learn to ride a bit first. He wanted fine clothes, the kind the young gentlemen wore who used to call on Miss Caroline and Miss Honor, satin breeches and embroidered waistcoats, lace frills to his shirts, elegant beaver hats, silver-chased buckles on leather shoes, and the things gentlemen owned: a gold snuffbox, a pocket watch, a seal ring, a silver-handled pistol. Like Oliver Gerard—he had come oftenest, and married Miss Honor last year; for Bethune he symbolized all of them. Bethune did not like Gerard, but envied him—not his dark good looks or self-confidence, but what he was and what he had. But to have those things you needed money, so the problem was only that—only! And the way to have it was more important than the things themselves, for it might take a year, say, to earn enough for the fine clothes, and would they balance a year of doing something you hated? But if money meant he could marry Margaret some day—

He had never asked to kiss her, never touched her hand. Later she would understand that part of it. He was still shy with her. He thought she was the prettiest girl he had ever known, and it did not occur to him that he had known no others at all. She had dark-brown shining curls, pink-and-white skin, and earnest blue eyes, and he loved her.

He never meant what happened. Afterward he felt it was a thing like thunder or fire, outside his controlling.

It was a Sunday afternoon. Mr. Thurstan had ridden over to Twelvetrees, Mistress Thurstan was napping in her chamber. A changeable February day it was. He and Margaret had gone out to the stables to see the new foal. No one was about, not Billy or Nego, the coachman, or Abed or the stable boys. Then he heard Billy coming up from the quarters, singing tunelessly to himself, and Margaret seized Bethune's arm and whispered, "Let's hide and scare him—the loft!" That was like youngsters playing; they scrambled up the ladder and lay in the fragrant hay, Margaret smothering giggles. He knew just when it changed and how, and it was nothing she said or did.

Only suddenly he touched her arm beside him; it was cool and soft. He put his hand on it, and something in his touch made her stop giggling and whisper, "What is it? Bethune——"

He did not remember consciously touching any other flesh; he looked at the plump white swell of her arm, smoothing his fingers over it, feeling a brief mad impulse to set his teeth in it. He did not know he would say it until he heard the words. "Margaret, I want to kiss you—let me——"

She gave a little gasp, not expecting it. Queerly he was sorry for her in the midst of loving; she did not understand this as yet. He must not frighten her, but all the same he wanted—he wanted only to tell her he loved her, and could not say the words, the silly, embarrassing words. He kissed her clumsily, knowing it was clumsy, wishing it to be better to make her understand. And that was all he ever meant.

But if she had struggled he would have let her go at once. She only lay quiet; she never spoke even his name. And afterward he felt nothing, only a blank of surprise and then embarrassment. Appallingly, he found he was wishing she would disappear, not be there so close, to let him think about this. Then he was afraid she would cry.

She did not cry. After a while they got up and climbed down the ladder and went back to the house, all without exchanging a word. He was relieved to be alone again.

And then he was afraid she would hate him. But the next time they were alone, with constraint between them now, she said, not looking at him, stumbling over the words, "I—it's all right, Bethune. I mean—I didn't mind. Really." That was the only mention of it between them. He was ashamed, but he felt easier about it then.

There was so little conscious memory in him of what had happened, it seemed nothing that could have consequences. She did not tell him; it was possible she did not wholly know. He was never to know how the Thurstans found out, questioned her; and he never blamed her for naming him. He had always known it was wrong.

His chief feeling was surprise that Mr. Thurstan knew all the obscene names to call him, words he had thought only the Nigras and common folk used.

"Little bastard, ungrateful, sly little bastard!" Tamely, after all the rest: "What've you to say for yourself?" Mr. Thurstan was white and shaking and deadly.

"I don't know—what you want me—to say, sir," Bethune faltered.

"You don't know! By God—I ought to kill you—" And then the ugly word.

"No, it wasn't like that," he had to say. "You don't understand—" No one ever did.

But he could not blame Mr. Thurstan either for not listening. There were more words, bad ones. Gaol. Hanging. "Ought to kill you myself." Something about despoilers, and, "Fifteen she is. Fifteen. My God. The law will deal with you!" He took Bethune up to the box-room to be locked in overnight. "In the morning you'll be taken to Williamsburg to the justices." His words went on sounding in Bethune's mind a long time when he was left alone.

But however frightened or angry or bewildered he was, there was always one place in his mind that stayed clear and cold. He did not try to justify himself; he had done wrong, and it might be he deserved to be hanged for it, but that would do no one any good now. He was not going to let them take him to Williamsburg for trial and hanging. It was wrong, yes, but not as wrong as Mr. Thurstan's word for it.

Not as if he did not know right from wrong. Running away, that made it worse. He could not delude himself over that. Twice that night he stopped in the road and turned to go back; each time he went on. All of it was bad: the heavy weight of guilt on him—he reckoned he would never be rid of it. But he wasn't going to hang. He thought again about his father, and felt queer kinship with him, a man running away, only he would escape where his father had failed.

After a while he forced himself to stop thinking about it, to fix his mind on where he would make for, what he should do. He supposed Margaret would be there at the back of his mind forever until he died, but he must stop thinking of her and of what he had done.

He must go on from here as best he could, that was all. No use, either, to wish, If I could go back, make it never to have happened—make it Zena instead. And he hurried his pace away from home, walking fast through the dark, fast for a man with such a burden of black guilt weighing him down.

CHAPTER 2

WILLIAMSBURG WAS twelve miles from Thurstan Hundred. It was a long way on foot; by morning they would find he was gone, and Mr. Bolt would come after him on Bay Brandy, and be up to him in an hour if he knew the way Bethune took. Bethune had, however, some cause to be grateful to Bay Brandy, the fastest thing in the stables. He still had the five shillings he had won from a wager on him in the race last fall, the second time he had been to Williamsburg. He hadn't decided what to spend it on, the largest sum he had ever owned, and it was in his pocket now with a threepenny bit Mr. Thurstan had given him on his birthday in November and a penny he had found in the road last week. Five shillings fourpence: not much, but better than nothing.

In early morning he stopped to rest and ate one of the biscuits Shad had given him; he had just started on when a wagon came up behind him. The driver pulled up his mules and called, "You like a ride a piece, boy?"

Bethune looked at him and saw he was only being neighborly. He said, "Thanks, sir," and climbed up to the seat. But the wagoner made him uneasy with questions. He wanted to know where Bethune was from, where he was going, and why. Bethune never liked questions: at the most casual query he felt like the yard dog rearing up to resent the stranger. He did not think he was secretive, but he liked his affairs to himself. He saw Mr. Bolt asking questions in town and the driver speaking up, Yes, sir, I met up with a young chap like that. He was glad of the ride into Williamsburg, but afraid to stop there long. He left the wagoner in Duke of Gloucester Street and walked on out of the town eastward toward the sea.

He walked all that day, another fifteen or eighteen miles, and at dusk came to another town, Yorktown, across the York River from Gloucester Point. It was a much smaller place, with only a few shops, but it was on water and he could see the masts of ships at the quay.

He thought what he had best do was slip aboard a ship. It was another wrong thing, but five shillings would not pay passage anywhere. He made out two ships anchored offshore—large ones, and presumably the larger the ship the longer its projected voyage; but there was no possibility of getting out to them. Of those moored at quayside only one was of any size. It looked almost too easy: there was a broad plank laid from deck to quay, and no sign of life aboard. He crossed the plank, quelling the slight uneasiness in his stomach, and stepped to the deck, aware of unfamiliar smells—wet boards and salt—sea scents vaguely exciting. He stumbled over an open hatchway, stopped in panic at the noise. When no one challenged, he peered at the dark hole, at last let himself down, hung a moment, and dropped.

The fall jarred him and the sound was loud in the quiet, but no one came. It was black dark and this was the first ship he had seen in his life; he had no idea where he was. He felt about among stacked boxes and barrels until he found a clear space, and sat down. Propped against the ship's side he finished the last of the food in his bag and wondered whether he would be found soon and what would happen when he was. Presently, surprisingly, he slept. When he woke the ship was swaying and creaking beneath him; they had cast off.

He was very hungry by the middle of the morning, when he was discovered and hauled up before the captain. After the hours in the dark hold the light hurt his eyes, and all he saw of Captain Marple at first was a large outline in the center of which was a black beard.

The voice was deep and astonishingly mild. "Now, young man, thee knows thee has done wrong in stealing aboard my ship." Bethune's vision cleared a trifle and he saw a stout benign-faced man who looked more like a farmer than a ship captain. His sharp blue eyes raked Bethune. "You may leave the young man to me, Jared, I will deal with him. The first time such a thing has happened on my ship—very strange. Well, fellow, what is thy name?"

Bethune massaged his wrist where the sailor had gripped him. "I don't know I'd best say, sir," he said woodenly. "I'm willing to work my passage, but I've no money to pay." That was fair enough, if they would let him work out the cost.

"Is thee running off from thy home? How old is thee?"

"No, I'm not. Eighteen," said Bethune laconically, aware that he might pass for that and rather nettled by the captain's solicitous glance.

"Is thee a bound man?"

"No, I'm not. I've the right to go where I please—"

"In my ship? Where does thee want to go?"

"Where are you sailing, sir?"

"I am bound for New York."

"Then I reckon that's where I want to go," said Bethune unsmilingly.

The captain cocked his head. "Yes, I see thee is older than I thought at first."

Bethune had never met a Quaker; the captain's language should have been laughable, but was not.

"Thee does not look to be a villain. Will thee tell the truth? Is there a law warrant out for thee, that thee must hide in my ship?"

"No, nothing like that." It was the strict truth.

"Thee runs away from thy family, then."

"I've no family, sir."

"I am John Marple, friend, thee need not call me sir. It is not good that one man should defer to another with worldly terms. Thee is an orphan, then. Very sad."

Bethune liked Captain Marple. He smiled at the man. "I'm willing to work my passage."

"It seems I have no choice. Certainly I shall not put back to Virginia for thee, and thee looks an honest enough young man. Does thee know anything of sailing?"

Bethune shook his head.

The captain sighed. "Well, I will find somewhat for thee to do."

They let Bethune sleep in the forecastle space with the sailors, and even found a blanket for him; he was put to helping the cook in the galley. As it would be only this short while he found it tolerable, but thought he would not care for a sailor's life (and remembered how Mr. Bolt used to say he was lazy, fancying himself a gentleman and too finicking to dirty his hands). The *Delaware Star* was an old sloop, battered but stout; she was carrying hides, rum, and cloth to New York on this voyage. Bethune was largely ignored by the small crew, save for the gregarious second mate. He asked the mate if the crew were all Quakers.

"By God, no, boy, not by a long way. But you don't want to let the old man fool you with his Sunday face an' Bible talk. Clever as be-damned an' outlie any skipper on the Cape. I was with him in the old *Queen Louise* an' many's the time I see him trick the hull British fleet." The mate grinned. "Runnin' contraband, same like seven o' ten New England skippers—to France. The old man, it's anything for profit with him—honest, o' course. To his way o' thinkin' England were all wrong goin' to war with France, so it were still honest to sell in France. Some handsome profit he had, too."

"Was he ever caught at it?"

"God save us, not him!" said the mate cheerfully.

Amused, Bethune tried to connect the bold smuggler with Captain Marple and his "thees" and "thys." He remembered reading about the war with France in Mr. Thurstan's newspapers.

On the third day at sea he had his second encounter with the captain. The old Quaker came up behind him on the deck. "What does thee think of the sea, young man?"

"I was wondering if this was as big as the Red Sea in the Bible and what it looked like when it rolled back for the Israelites," said Bethune truthfully—and without design.

Marple beamed on him. "I see thee has had a decent upbringing. What will thee do in New York? Has thee a trade?"

"No. I was to—that is, I've been a clerk." This was not a lie; he had been—for the factor.

"Ah? Thee is educated. Thy speech is gentle—but curiosity is a sin, I must not pry into thy affairs. I could have fears for thee in the city—thee is young, and New York a godless place. But I see there is strength and determination in thee, and no frivolity."

Bethune thought he would not exactly call that a compliment.

"Thee is not talkative," said Marple, making it another compliment.

"I reckon not," said Bethune.

"Foolish talk makes much harm. Do thee read in the Bible often?"

"Well—" said Bethune, who found the Scriptures dull save for portions of the Old Testament.

"It is a beneficial exercise for thy spare time." At that moment the lookout yelped, "Sail ho!" and the captain spun about and strained his eyes to the horizon. "Jared!"

"Aye, Cap'n."

"Do that appear to thee to be the rigging of a revenue patroller?"

"Could be, Cap'n. Looks some like the *Gloucester.*"

"Silas, we will make a point or two easterly, to keep well off."

"Ayeh, Cap'n."

Bethune wondered what contraband was in the hold.

On the morning the *Delaware Star* made New York Harbor, he was at the port side watching the motley collection of shipping they had begun to pass, watching for his first glimpse of this great-

est city in the colonies. The mate came beside him. "Ever been
to N'York afore?" Bethune shook his head. "She be quite a place,"
said the mate, spitting thoughtfully.

As the shore line drew nearer Bethune made out row on hap-
hazard row of the greatest number of buildings he had ever seen
together, and more ships—at anchor, and passing in both directions. There was so much to see he felt confused, so many men
on the water front, so many buildings and quays and ships of all
shapes and sizes. He was hardly aware when the mate went away,
when the *Star* turned for shore and slid neatly into the slot of
water between two long docks. He heard the thump of hawser on
deck, the rattle and splash of anchor, the shouts of men on deck
and quay.

Presently Captain Marple passed. "Thee can go ashore now,
friend, and I wish thee good fortune."

"Thanks, sir, I'm grateful for the way you took me." He went
to the forecastle, collected his bag, and crossed the plank to the
quay. Odor assailed him, exciting, new, marvelous: the smell of
land after sea—manure, grass, a tanyard not far off, sewerage,
and a thousand others—the smell of city.

He walked down the quay into New York, and almost immediately fell in love for the second time in his life.

The stout man in the pink-dyed breeches had a powerful voice,
rasping like a file on boards. He waved his hands at the little
crowd, standing on a box the better to command their notice.
"A perfectly genuwine monster, friends, must be seen to be
credited! The curiousest sight ever seen by man, woman, or child
in these colonies, and well wuth the paltry sum of one penny asked
for its exhibition! A genuwine North American monster—captured by the brave men of General Braddock's army in the Alle-
gheny Mountains—now preserved for the edification of the populace! It is thirty feet long, friends, with horns and a spiked tail,
and I may tell you, when it was opened to be stuffed, in its tree-
mendous belly was found the skelingtons of several dogs and a little
child!" A thrill of pleasurable horror swayed the crowd. "One
penny, friends, will admit you—"

A boy and a girl near Bethune were tugging at their mother's skirts, pleading to see the monster. Two young men passing gave the orator supercilious stares. Directly in front of Bethune stood an immensely fat citizen in black broadcloth; an urchin pressed up beside Bethune, jostled the fat fellow, dipped a couple of fingers swift as lightning, and came up with the man's purse. Bethune opened his mouth to call notice to it, as the man turned with a scowl; but the urchin had already slipped out of sight in the crowd. It occurred to Bethune that he was likely to be accused if the loss were discovered, and he moved off down the street, thinking with a grin of the monster, scarcely minded to waste a penny on it.

He had been walking and standing for hours, unaware of time; he thought a man might spend the rest of his life looking at New York. He did not know the names of half the places he had seen. The *Delaware Star* had come into Murray's Wharf on the East River, near the shabby old warehouses on Water Street and the narrow tenements up the streets so grandly named, he was to learn, Duke and Princess and Pearl. But he had walked on past those, fascinated by the size of the city, the occasional sections where the very buildings did not look English and the people passing spoke foreign tongues. He came to what no one need tell him was the Fish Market, and beyond that to a street where a sign proclaimed a rickety-looking building the John Street Theatre; but it was closed. Down past that he came to a great wide street with imposing shops on each side, taverns, a wide footpath. A street equally grand bisected it; he wandered up that past several churches, and presently came to another water front. It was incredible that so many buildings and people should exist in one place, the former so big, the latter so busy. The place was a hive of activity, a warren of streets and shops, a babble of noise, and all of it entirely marvelous. He could spend his life here and never see it all, never tire of looking.

But after a time he began to realize that he was tired, hungry, and homeless; he fingered the coins in his pocket, where he had kept a hand on them since seeing the fat merchant robbed. He would need to find work, a place to stay, begin building a life for himself. The money would not go far in a place like this. The most immediate need was food; he saw a man hawking tarts from a tray, two a penny, and bought a penny's worth; they were dry and tasteless, but he scarcely noticed it. He was wandering with a purpose now; he walked up several streets of houses, all of them too elegant to approach. At last he came to a shabbier street where the houses looked down-at-heel, as if they would welcome the paying guest. He knew better than to try a tavern; the cost would be high.

At the first house the woman snapped, "I take no lodgers," and banged the door smartly. At the second, the woman said, *"Wie ist? Nein, nein!"* and waved him on. He went to the end of the street and tried the last house, smaller and shabbier.

The man who opened to his knock was as thin and shabby as the house, and smiled sadly at Bethune's query. His English was thick with another tongue. "You enter, yes. A bed we have, yes. To stay, perhaps the night *oder* week?" There was a woman with a distinct mustache and a great deal of black hair, who stared at Bethune and at last pronounced, *"Nebuk*. No trouble. *Gut."* The man said sadly, "Would be the shilling for one week?"

Bethune paid him the shilling and was led to a room with three beds in it, where various belongings strewn about testified that the other two beds were also paid for. It was not until then that his host introduced himself as Mr. Isaacson. Bethune's companions, when they arrived, proved to be a pair of carpenters, brothers of the name of Cassidy; any bed would have seemed soft to him that night, and he slept soundly.

Next morning Mrs. Isaacson encountered him in the passage, where he had hesitated, debating whether to leave his bag in his room, possibly to be rifled. "You go out?" she said. "Work?"

"I want to find some. Do you know where they might be wanting a clerk?"

She regarded him with interest. "Writing," she said with more respect. "You do not eat breakfas'?"

"I do generally," said Bethune. That drew a wide smile.

"You come eat firs', then look. Not goot on emptiness, yes? Nice boy." She nudged him down the stairs to a dark cubbyhole of a kitchen and fed him fried bread, coffee, and a small, sweet, solid tart with icing that she called *Kaffeekuchen*. Mr. Isaacson sat by the window reading a newspaper; he smiled sadly at Bethune. His wife announced vigorously, *"Not* always, no money, no? But the one time, nice boy."

"You must forgive," said Mr. Isaacson softly. "She does not speak good. You understand?"

Bethune nodded, smiling back: this breakfast was not a precedent, only a kindness for once. "Would you know some place they'd be hiring clerks, sir?"

"Ah," said Mr. Isaacson. He ruminated, and then got up laboriously and came to the table. He laid his newspaper down before Bethune and put a finger on it.

Bethune read with interest: "Wanted by the publisher—reliable boys. Apply R. MacDonald, offices of the New York *Courier* in Maiden Street."

"Well." Bethune was pleased. Perhaps it would be easier than he had thought. The four shillings threepence in his pocket felt very slender; whatever the publisher might want of reliable boys, he need not stay at it forever, but at the moment it would serve to support him.

Before he got to Maiden Street he saw more of the city, for directions proved confusing. A British private sent him down William Street, but when he came to the broad thoroughfare he had seen yesterday a hawker told him he had come too far and sent him back up Stone Street to New. When he came to Maiden Street he reflected that in a place the size of New York it would be useful to have street names posted up where strangers could see them—which admittedly would be little good to those who did not know their letters.

The offices of the newspaper bore a sign over the entrance: THE NEW YORK COURIER, PUB. G. SHIELDS. It was an old building, narrow, of one story between two taller structures, one looking like a private residence, the other housing a milliner. Beyond the door it was plank-floored. A narrow counter ran half across the front, and an open door behind gave a glimpse of another room, barely furnished.

A harried-looking bald man was bent over the counter, ruffling a pile of papers. He glanced up irritably at Bethune's entrance. "Yes, yes, yes?"

"I'd like to see Mr. MacDonald, sir."

"Never here this time o' day," said the bald man—as if anyone should know that. "Try the coffee house. Where? The Merchants', o' course." He did not ask what was wanted of Mr. MacDonald or appear to connect Bethune with the advertisement.

Bethune set off to find the Merchants' Coffee House. This he discovered to be in Wall Street, only a couple of squares away; after even this short while he began to have some knowledge of the city's general plan. It lay in an elongated triangle, with water on two sides, and thus some streets ran straight while others crossed at odd angles or curved to meet still others. Wall Street was a street of shops and taverns, running toward the water; at the end of it he found the Merchants' Coffee House, but paused outside to orient himself. Not far off was the wide throughfare running away at a slant; and over to the left he saw the roofs of taller buildings, one with a standard and colors over it to identify a military garrison.

The Merchants' House was a fairly new structure of stone and brick. Its wide, welcoming door gave on a square room with a large hearth, wooden tables, settles against the wall, high windows making pools of light and deep corners pools of shadow. It seemed a friendly place. A dozen men in groups sat about at the tables, waiters wandered to and fro, and there was a buzz of talk in the background. Bethune hesitated on the threshold, wondering if he would be expected to order something if he entered. He got the notice of a waiter.

"I'm looking for Mr. MacDonald. Is he here?"

The waiter scarcely glanced at him, jerked his head. " 'Is reg'lar table, by the fust window."

The man sitting alone at that table, with a pewter pot and cup before him and a pile of newspapers at his elbow, was perhaps forty. He was a small man, with lank black hair which had partly escaped from its queue ribbon, and thin, sardonic features. He was carelessly dressed in ill-fitting tan broadcloth, breeches and long coat, black hose wrinkled on thin legs, and neckcloth wrapped loosely; there was no hat beside him. He looked anything but prosperous—or approachable.

Bethune went over and stood beside the table. "Mr. Mac-Donald?"

The man looked up from his newspaper. "Well?"

"They told me at the newspaper you'd be here. I came—that is, I saw your advertisement in the paper, sir, I—"

"Advertisement!" said MacDonald as if the word were new to him.

"Yes, sir, for boys. I—"

"Oh, that." He turned lively dark eyes on Bethune; they traveled up and down him, from the shabby shoes fresh-coated with New York dust to the cheaply tailored homespun breeches, plain shirt, and the coat beginning to be too tight across the shoulders. "The advertisement!" MacDonald ejaculated, and grinned. "God's teeth, I advertised for a boy, not the steeple of Trinity Church!"

Bethune felt himself reddening. "I beg pardon, sir, I thought—"

"Here," said MacDonald. "No matter, sit down. When did any last call me sir? You're no New Yorker. Southerner by your talk. Describe yourself as a reliable boy?"

"Well—" said Bethune. At the other's imperative gesture he sat down in the chair opposite.

"Don't look much like it to me. Have some coffee? Ben! More coffee. May I know your name, sir?" It was only faint mockery of Virginia manners.

"My name's Bethune."

MacDonald abruptly put down the pewter pot. "Bethune! Now this is marvelous—this is portentous! But what does it portend?"

CHAPTER 3

A WAITER came up with a fresh cup and poured coffee for Bethune. MacDonald looked at him and grinned. "I'm paying for it. There is somewhat about you interests me, Mr. Bethune. Mark you, my grandsire came across fifty-odd years ago and the nearest I've ever been to Scotland is the edge of New York Harbor. But a Scot I am, and proud of it—and something of a student as well. Irrelevant information, sir—the only sort worth having. You never know when it will prove to be relevant. D'you know anything about Scottish clans, Mr. Bethune?"

"No, sir."

"Well, 'tis a fact that the Bethunes are an old sept-clan to Clan MacDonald. And mark you, Mr. Bethune, a clansman is responsible for his sept-men. A case of empty pockets, is it?"

Bethune liked MacDonald better than anyone he had seen in New York thus far. "Four shillings thruppence, sir."

"It might be less. What misfortune brings you to this state?"

"I've only come to New York—"

"From?"

"Virginia. To find work."

"And what have you been working at?" A darted glance at his uncalloused hands.

"Clerking, sir."

"Yes, he is educated," said MacDonald dreamily, leaning back and regarding the ceiling. "Gentle speech and such elegant manners, if he has grown a foot too high. I am devoured by curiosity about him. I have it. He has fought a duel—notoriously hot-tempered, Virginians—and killed his man, and now flees from vengeance."

Bethune shook his head. "I don't reckon I'm that hot-tempered."

"God's teeth, one of the untalkative Scots. Drink your coffee, Mr. Bethune. Cold coffee is an abomination. How old are you? Sixteen? Virginia may reckon that a boy; in New York it's a man. What I'm advertising for is youngsters, for delivery work. What newspaper do you read?"

"I've seen the *Virginia Review*."

"Oh, God!" said MacDonald. "Lessons in London politics, monthly! Monthly! Is your education otherwise respectable?"

"You could say I know a lot of irrelevant information."

"Ah, a reader. Good. I take a notion to you, Mr. Bethune. I've a fancy there is a story to you, and one day I'll have it out of you, my close-mouthed friend. Meanwhile, do you come along with me and I shall start you on your duties. Yes, yes, I believe I've a place for you." MacDonald rose; he was even smaller than Bethune had thought. He looked up at Bethune, a good eight inches over him, with a kind of weary resignation. "There was a time I affected tall hats to give myself more inches. A vain delusion! Except rarely, I am not even sure providence compensates by allowing me more brains. Sixteen? God's fingerbones, let us hope you have your growth!" He flung a couple of shillings on the table and marched for the door.

At the threshold they met a customer entering, a tall, nondescript man near MacDonald's age, elegantly dressed. He gave MacDonald a glance of faint contempt; in the street, MacDonald spat deliberately. "You might remember that face, Mr. Bethune. It belongs to the blackest villain in New York."

"Why, who is he?"

"His name is James Rivington," said MacDonald. He turned and led Bethune up Wall Street. "How do you like New York, Mr. Bethune? The great monster of the colonies," and his tone was affectionate. "Look at her—listen to her—smell her! It is a peculiar circumstance that if a hundred individuals or a thousand make a crowd, the temper of which may itself be individual, a

hundred crowds which make a city create a monstrous individual, which has a heart, brains, spirit of its own. No two
cities are alike, but New York—what an error we made in naming her! New she is, compared to the cities in Europe, but no
copy of any place that ever existed before. The Dutch we may
forgive—insensitive merchants. New Amsterdam was all they
deserved. But we should have given her some wild strange name
none had ever heard, to match her character."

"It's quite a place," said Bethune.

"It is a thousand places! An island bearing many islands.
There are islands of Dutch among us," said MacDonald, "aye,
and Germans, too, and a black island of Negroes. And others—
islands of sailor men, and merchants, and the leather-aproned
tribe of laborers and craftsmen—each with its own dialect and
passwords. And then the smallest, Mr. Bethune, the smallest but
the most obtrusive—the elegant island of the wealthy."

"I've seen some fine houses."

"And streets of hovels. The elegant island has no civic conscience as yet. Its inhabitants are not aware of the fact, but
the monster is a bourgeois monster. New York is not a city of
the rich, but of rich merchants—a different thing entirely. As
one day they will discover. Do you," asked MacDonald abruptly,
"write a fair hand?"

"A very fine hand," said Bethune, touched in one of his vani-
ties.

"I trust a rudimentary knowledge of grammar?"

"Yes, sir."

"Latin or Greek is not needful." MacDonald swung along
briskly, continually glancing about alertly, as if on the search,
and Bethune's longer legs had to lengthen stride to keep up.
They had followed Wall Street on its way up into the city, and
turned toward Maiden Street; now MacDonald plunged toward
the *Courier* office, a rabbit turning for its burrow. The fore-room
was deserted; he banged on the counter with his fist and shouted,
"Tacy!"

The harried bald man emerged from the rear room. "Yes,
Mr. MacDonald?"

"I have found an assistant for you. Has that butcher of both bodies and the King's English brought in his copy?"

"If you mean Doctor French," said Tacy with a glance at Bethune, "yes, he has, but I'm afeared it's a line or two too long to fit, sir. If we was to put the paid-for bits in the margin—"

MacDonald seemed to swell. "I have never in my entire career sanctioned the printing of advertisements in margins, and I've no intention of starting now."

"Mr. Shields—"

"Mr. Shields and I are as one in regard to that. A niggardly, squeeze-penny trick and most inartistic. Let Doctor French go hang. No, stop, let me see the copy." Tacy rummaged among the bits and pieces of paper which seemed permanently attached to him and produced one. MacDonald read and clapped a palm to his brow. "God's teeth and toes! 'Sufferers from palpitations, lung-congestions, stoppage of the bowels, boils, impotency, racking cough, stomach disorders, female disorders, pimples, rheumatism, gout—' Is the man reciting a medical textbook? 'Stiffness of the limbs, painful swelling of any part, excessive weakness, and other discomfortable symptoms, will find friendly Doctor French's pills and powders—' Here, the thing is easy enough settled. We'll cut out all that and substitute 'any and every physical disorder,' eh? That makes up two lines at least—"

"But he's paid eight shillings sixpence for it as it stands, Mr. MacDonald."

"Am I to corrupt public service for eight shillings?" demanded MacDonald bitterly. "Must I bow before Mammon? Very well, I dare say you're right. What is above? The story on the mayor— I can cut a line of that with luck, and take somewhat out of Cato's letter in the left column, and begin the mayor at the bottom, that should just do it."

"There was a woman with a runaway indenturer—"

"Let us be correct, Tacy. Without a runaway indenturer. All good fortune to him—or her. I dislike to advertise for such. In any case, it is Wednesday."

"I told her the *Courier* can accept no advertisements after Tuesday."

"Good. Now let me introduce to you Mr. Bethune, who will be your new assistant."

Bethune had translated the other man's glance as unfriendly, but Tacy gave him a warm grip, dropping a few pages as he did so, and exclaimed fervently, "You're very welcome, Mr. Bethune!"

"We have been shorthanded," said MacDonald. "Three men to publish a newspaper—not counting the printers, of course. I believe you will do excellent well, Mr. Bethune. Come in here." He walked round the counter to the second room.

Following, Bethune found this room scarcely more office-like, containing only a plain, scarred deal table, two or three chairs, and a tall cupboard upright between windows that looked out on a yard and alley. MacDonald opened the cupboard, which seemed to contain only stacks of old newspapers, and from the litter took down a squat brown bottle and two tumblers; with one foot he hooked a chair from under the table and sat down.

"French brandy." MacDonald nodded at the bottle. "The only spirit I will drink. You'll join me. But no drinking in business hours, Mr. Bethune! That, both Mr. Shields and I insist upon." He poured each glass half full. "I take it you've no experience of work upon a newspaper. So long as you write a legible hand it is no matter. We are in need of some reliable person to perform the routine duties. You will be here from seven o'clock till six each day, and will also have the responsibility of carrying the copy to the print shop."

Bethune discovered the French brandy to be quite different from the raw-grain spirit which was all he had tasted before now. This was smooth and insidious; he eyed it with respect, reckoning a man would need to take care with it. He said, "Is that what you were advertising for, sir? I thought—"

"No, it is not. But I'm in need of a clerk and for the moment at least you're in need of the wages, eh? Ten shillings a week and an extra sixpence on Sundays."

At the moment it sounded like largesse. "Thank you very much, sir."

"We shall see," said MacDonald cryptically. He finished his brandy.

Tacy put his head round the door. "Word's out the *Portsmouth Queen's* tacking through the Narrows."

MacDonald sprang up and bounded for the door. "A fortnight overdue! God's teeth, if there is somewhat of import to go on the first page 'twill mean an entire remaking of the edition! I rely on you, let not a single page of copy fall into Brady's hands till I'm back!" He flung out the front door and off down the street at a trot.

Bethune spent the rest of the day at the office, learning about his new duties. He was to take down advertisements to be printed, answer enquiries, and deal with all the sundry routine matters, leaving Tacy free to do the copying for the printer. Each Wednesday evening he would carry the copy to the print shop. It seemed to him he had had great luck to find such a good situation so soon; he knew, however, that MacDonald had for some reason taken a notion to him, favored him on impulse. He must do his best to give satisfaction, or he might be as summarily dismissed. Ten shillings a week was no mean wage merely for work such as he'd been doing for nothing but his keep.

He had told MacDonald he had read the *Virginia Review,* and so he had a few times, finding a copy in Mr. Thurstan's library; he had seen perhaps half a dozen newspapers in his life, and felt little interest in them up to now. As for guessing anything about their production, he had clearer notions of mathematics, which was not saying much; but because he was grateful to MacDonald, he found himself interested in this place and what was done here.

Tacy left him in the front room, to get on with his copying, instructing Bethune only to explain to would-be advertisers that their messages could not appear in the *Courier* until next week's edition. On this understanding Bethune copied down several insertions dictated to him, Tacy stepping out each time to accept payment. Most of the notices concerned runaway slaves or items offered for sale. As he wrote down the particulars of one of the former, taking pains with his hand—"A male Negro of thirty years, near six feet tall, some pox-fretten, may be known by the marks of the whip about his shoulders, named Jud"—MacDonald returned, and after hastening into the rear room could be heard in vigorous comment to Tacy.

"Nought worth changing type for, but the report on Parliament must go in. We will leave out one of the letters—the one about street-refuse. Let me see it. News? Parliament never makes news, except now and then bad news, eh? They are in endless debate, but decide nothing. By God, I will not give the stiff-necked bastards more than a quarter-column!"

He came out presently, took up the page Bethune had just finished and glanced at it. "Very good—an elegant style, Mr. Bethune." He paid Bethune a subtler compliment by not again mentioning money or offering him some in advance. True, he knew Bethune had four shillings odd, which would keep him a week, after a fashion, but Bethune appreciated the assumption that he would look to himself.

At one o'clock Tacy intimated that Bethune might go out for a meal. He hesitated to enter a tavern, but saw a hawker with fresh oysters, cheap at three for twopence, and foresightedly bought a loaf of bread and a quarter-pound of cheese, which decimated his money by ninepence but would guarantee meals of a sort for two or three days.

He did not see MacDonald again, but Tacy complimented him on his writing at the end of the day. " 'Twill be a godsend to have someone here, Mr. Bethune. Since the last clerk left I've had it all to do, and the accounts alone'd keep one man busy. Mr. MacDonald is partic'lar about the accounts. Seven sharp in the morning you be here. Mr. MacDonald will take the copy tonight, as he's orders to give Brady, the printer. They've a standing quarrel and hates the sight of each other, and I've had the delibery to do as well. 'Tis a relief to have you, and I hope as you'll stay at the *Courier*."

On his way back to the Isaacsons' house in Cherry Street Bethune wondered at Tacy's unhopeful tone on that. Why should he not stay in such an excellent position? He had not thought it would be so easy; it seemed part of the magic of New York, all that was happening to him equally strange and pleasant.

He met Mr. Shields, the majority-owner and publisher of the
Courier—MacDonald owned a one-third share in the paper, he
was to learn—the following morning.

Because Bethune had grown among gentlefolk, if not of them,
absorbing their speech and manners scarcely aware he did so, he
knew the subtle differences of gentry and new gentry. Not that
there was anything subtle about George Shields. He was not like
Mr. Haines at Taggarts' Chance—men of that stamp in Virginia
had acquired money and sought to acquire gentility with it. Mr.
Shields occasionally boasted that he had begun life as a carpenter's
apprentice, and it did not trouble him a whit that his enemies were
wont to recall the fact. If he had got his first capital by wedding a
merchant's daughter, it was his shrewdness that told him what to
do with it. Business was a game to him, but his dearest ambition
led him toward intellectual pursuits, and it was not incongruous
that he should spend some of his money educating himself and
founding his own newspaper. He had a finger in many financial pies
in New York, but the *Courier* was his truest love.

Shields and MacDonald came in together in midmorning; somewhat to Bethune's surprise, MacDonald introduced him to the
owner.

"Hah!" said Shields, examining him. "Likely-looking, likely!
Robert tells me you are a Southerner."

"Yes, sir."

Shields was a stout, bounceful little man with thinning ginger
hair and lively blue eyes that looked on life with enormous enjoyment; his elegant clothes sat oddly on him and there remained a
trace of his native Yorkshire in his speech. It was evident he
wasted no time or effort pretending to be anything but what he
was, a likable and energetic self-made merchant.

He shook Bethune's hand heartily. "What are your political
persuasions, young fellow?"

"I don't know that I have any, sir."

"You will, you will. Listen to Robert," advised Shields with a
broad wink. He carried MacDonald off to the inner room where

presently they were heard disagreeing profanely about the disposition of columns.

Bethune returned to his copying of advertisements; Tacy came over to approve, and grew confidential. "You may think Mr. Shields is lucky to have Mr. MacDonald for the *Courier*, but the truth is I believe he'd like nought better than to do it all himself. And he'd not do too bad, either. He writes most of the lead-articles as 'tis, but he's not the time to see to everything, of course."

"Which are the lead-articles?"

"Oh, the reports on political matters and such. The *Courier* has very independent policies along of that, you see, and some of the other papers says as we're radical, but Mr. Shields don't pay that no notice, and Mr. MacDonald"—Tacy grinned—"he eats it up, as you might say. A very violent gentleman in his politics, Mr. MacDonald is. I was afeared we'd lose him over the last election. He near came to blows with Mr. Rivington of the *Gazetteer* a time or two, and after 'twas all over we never laid eye on him two-three days. He went to brooding on it—the election went against his side. It's a fortunate thing as he and Mr. Shields generally agrees on politics."

Presently the inner door was flung open violently and Shields came out. He called over his shoulder, "Dine with me tonight, Robert—I'll have something ready on Grenville by then. By God, I will smite him hip and thigh! Ruinous, we'll all starve, I'll swear! Ah, young man, industrious, industrious." He marched out briskly.

Bethune did not know about being industrious; he wanted to keep the promise of ten shillings a week.

He was free each evening at six, but rarely went directly to his room in Cherry Street. He was still in the throes of his first fascination, and wandered the city exploring. He had been lonely all his life, save for one brief interlude, seeming almost a dream, that he could not now think about; among the crowds he was still lonely, but that he did not know any more than he'd known it before. Here it amused him to consider himself an entity apart, watching. He had found a new life, and was only beginning to realize he had a new love as well for this monstrous, marvelous place. It was not for some time that he awoke to another fact:

that his ten shillings a week meant, in truth, less to him than the place where he earned it. Later, he thought that his professional life dated from his first visit to the printing shop.

CHAPTER 4

JOHN BRADY'S printing shop was in Pearl Street. Even by the time he first had occasion to visit it, the Wednesday after he had been employed, it was a section of the city Bethune knew tolerably well, for among the other "islands" MacDonald had spoken of, the little island around Fort George and the Battery, at the narrow tip of the city, interested him. The fort and garrison were surrounded by small streets of old houses, filled mostly by soldiers' families (with the exception of Whore Lane); but it was a section also of guildsmen, and one of the oldest in the city. The printing shop stood by itself on a corner where a street crossed and Pearl Street began. Bethune came there first one dusk; he caught a glimpse of the last sun on the waters of the North River a street or two ahead, and thought that after delivering the copy to the printer he would go down to the water front.

The first room of the shop was little more than a cubbyhole, and deserted; but he had waited only a moment when a boy came from the door at the back. "From the *Courier*? Da says you're to come in to him." Bethune followed into a large square place where a dozen men and boys were busy as beavers at incomprehensible activities.

A portly, red-faced man in what looked like a butcher's smock came up to him. "Well, a new face is a welcome change from old

Tacy. MacDonald's new clerk, eh? You have the copy? Will you wait over a bit? I must give you a message for MacDonald."

Bethune nodded, half-hearing in the din. Set up across the side of the room where two high windows gave light and brackets for candles were set on each side, ranged four square wooden boxlike objects of mysterious skeletal structure. A man and a boy manned each. An immensely long table served all four machines; not much could be seen of what went on behind it, for not only did it contain tall stacks of paper, but the entire room was confused by the seemingly aimless scurryings of a dozen small boys who darted to and fro with single pages. At regular intervals each machine made a heavy dull thump. When, presently, Brady drew him into the foreroom where they need not raise their voices, Bethune was almost disappointed.

"Look you, you're to tell MacDonald he should buy a better grade of paper. This last lot takes the ink very bad. Doubtless he'll argue, but let him," said Brady fiercely. "I've only a few reams of that left, and I want no more of it, but a higher quality. The price is none of my concern. You needn't add that."

"Yes, I'll tell him."

"He may have his usual sampler copy in the morning."

"Yes. Do you print the edition tonight, then?"

"Bless you, we're busy night *and* day," said Brady. "Not all the *Courier,* o' course." He cocked his head at Bethune. "Interested in printing, young fellow?"

"I've never seen any done before. D'you mind if I watch in there?"

"So long as you mind where you stand and keep out of the way, you're welcome."

Bethune did not get to the water front that evening; he was absorbed in watching the printers at work. Very shortly the frenzied activity ceased and most of the men and boys departed. Brady and two others set to work on the presses, putting up the type for the *Courier*. Brady was good-natured; he had a genuine love of his trade and answered questions happily.

"The type-face's got to be wrong side to, so it will print rightly, don't you see? How? The paper goes there, and the lid, as you call it, comes down—that's why we name it a press, eh, Mr. Bethune? And there's your side printed."

"But a newspaper—or a book—is printed both sides. You do only one at a time?"

"God save us, now there would be something, a press that printed both sides at once! That's right. We'll have the type set for this edition of the *Courier* tonight, and print it tomorrow. How long? Well, I generally reckon twelve hours to an edition—that's fifteen hundred copies at the present rate; your news-sheet has a respectable following. The best we can do is somewhere about one hundred sides an hour, each press. All four sheets must be done separately, see you. Each of these presses here is set up for a page, and off we go. As soon as the sheets are dry, back they come to be printed t'other side. We'll have the lot, fifteen hundred copies, at the *Courier*'s office say eight o'clock tomorrow evening."

Bethune watched his fingers fly over the type. It was a sobering thing, suddenly, to think about—MacDonald scribbling away at his table, Mr. Shields at his, presumably in a fine house somewhere, the advertisers bringing in their scraps of copy, the subscribers writing letters indignant or complimentary, the quotations from other newspapers penned by other men, all copied neatly in Tacy's clerkly hand and brought here to be translated into this meaning-less looking-glass stuff under the typesetter's fingers. Tomorrow these rows of inverted iron type would somehow produce the *Courier*, and what had been mere bundles of manuscript would take on awesome dignity; and all those messages, solemn, humor-ous, satiric, informative, or ridiculous, become available to any citizen in New York. He had the sudden absurd notion that friendly Mr. Brady was a magician, bending over his type-castings. Information in script was only opinion: you believed or disbelieved as you chose. But print, that was something else again: you would think twice about disregarding a thing you saw in print.

He wished he could come here tomorrow and watch the actual printing. "How does a press work, sir?"

Brady left off his work a moment. "Note the lever there? Just you take hold and try to fetch her down. Go on, you'll do no harm." Bethune gripped the heavy wood handle and pulled. The top of the press began to fall only when he exerted all his strength. Brady smiled and heaved it up again. "Stoutish pulling, eh? Takes a strong man to operate a press. The boy inks the type and inserts the blank pages, the man pulls down the press to print it, see you? Like that. Hard work? Indeed. A really good team can print upwards of two hundred sides an hour, thus, but only at maximum effort. All we can ask is a hundred, ordinarily." He showed Bethune the implement used to ink the type, a stick to the end of which was nailed a ball of deerskin stuffed with wool for absorbency.

When Bethune came away he had established friendly relations with the printer, who had invited hospitably, "Come any time you've a mind to, Mr. Bethune. I see you're interested. A bit over-age for an apprentice, but it's never too late to learn!"

"Well, I don't know I'd want to take on such a job, Mr. Brady. It's almighty hard work. But I'm interested enough."

Although it was not at first apparent, there was a routine at the *Courier* office. Bethune came at seven, meeting Tacy just opening the premises. MacDonald came in at nine or half after each day except Wednesdays and Thursdays, but never remained long before going out to the coffeehouse or one of the taverns where news might be heard. On Wednesdays he came in at noon to collect the completed copy and spent the afternoon checking over it with Mr. Shields. The *Courier* came out on Fridays, so Thursdays were always slack and the office seldom saw him. Mr. Shields came by most days, sometimes staying an hour or more.

MacDonald entered one midmorning during the fifth week of Bethune's employment to find him poring over a page of Tacy's copy. "Shirking your work, Mr. Bethune?"

"I was reading some of the next edition, sir."

"So I see." MacDonald twisted his neck to look at the item. "The letter from Vox Populi. These tedious subscribers. What do you think of it, Mr. Bethune?"

"Not for me to say, is it, sir?"

"Certainly it is for you to say. I divine by your caution you are somewhat less than enthusiastic. A mild enough piece it is, to fill up a column. What's your objection?"

Bethune looked at him, saw he did not mock, and smiled. "Well, I was thinking of the presses."

"The presses. At the printing shop?"

"Yes, sir. I expect you know it needs all a man's strength to pull the type down for one imprint. They do upwards of a hundred imprints an hour, Mr. Brady says. All I thought was, it looks an almighty waste of hard work, to print a letter about hogs running loose in Duke Street."

MacDonald leaned on the counter and laughed; but the interest in his eyes sharpened. "Damme, Mr. Bethune, that's frank! I'd a notion there was somewhat to you, and what I see of it I like. You've been hanging about Brady's, eh?"

"Only when I take in the copy, I—"

"Yes, it's damnable hard work," said MacDonald. He looked down at his hands. "I used to fancy I should never get these clean. A certain amount of the ink stays, you know. There was a time I'd back myself to set type against the fastest in the trade. Surprised, Mr. Bethune? I never had the reach for the rest of the job. Does it interest you?"

"Not to work at, sir."

"My very sentiments. Do you curtail your interest in printing for the evening and join me for dinner, Mr. Bethune. You will? Excellent. At the Merchants' House, seven o'clock."

Bethune was surprised at the abrupt invitation. He was unsure how to take it. Though it pleased him, the prospect of dining at the coffeehouse caused him anxiety of another sort: he had no suitable clothes. He appeared to have his growth lengthwise, and the blue broadcloth breeches that had been nearly new when he left Thurstan Hundred would do, but the coat to match had been binding his shoulders the last month. He had worn his only other clothes—the old homespun—for work, but donned the broadcloth each Sunday for services at Trinity Church; it must do again this evening.

He had stayed on with the Isaacsons, finding it convenient and comfortable. He saw his chambermates only briefly night and morning; for another shilling a week, Mrs. Isaacson fed him breakfast and washed his linen. He now had five shillings saved from his wages; he had found that ten shillings a week was not, after all, such a vast sum to live on, and wondered when he might afford a new coat. But thinking of MacDonald's perennially careless dress, he reckoned that it did not matter a great deal.

When he came to the Merchants' House he felt shy of entering alone, so went in boldly, to his relief seeing MacDonald before him, at the same table by the window. He thought MacDonald, rising to greet him, was aware of his uncertainty.

"Sit down, Mr. Bethune. I have already selected our meal. I trust you'll be satisfied with my judgment. Ah, damn providence!" said MacDonald, eying him. "Why could I not have another four or six inches to my legs? The lordly way you enter a room—" His eyes said, And none suspecting you are unsure of yourself; but it was friendly. "You do interest me, which is why I asked you here tonight." A waiter came with a plate of raw oysters and a bottle of wine; he filled two glasses and departed discreetly. "D'you know the first requirement for a newsman, Mr. Bethune? Curiosity. I've a deal of it. I'm almighty curious about you, God's teeth, I am! But I'll not pry—I'm only frank with you. Tacy, now, is a competent clerk, but he's not gentle-born. Nor am I, but I know a gentleman when I see one."

"I don't know you'd call me that either, sir."

"Or your father?"

Bethune did not mind telling MacDonald something about himself. "I wouldn't know that," he said. "My father was captured at Culloden."

"Ah," said MacDonald, sitting up. "I see. One of the unlucky ones who were not hanged." He took up his glass, smiling his crooked sardonic smile, and said, "The King," passing his other hand over the glass—the old toast to the King over the water. He drank, set the glass down. "The devil—that is as far as my politics go in that direction. I'm no Jacobite. The Stuarts make great stories and damned bad kings. Your father was indentured."

"Yes."

"And ran away."

"How did you know?"

"You cannot," said MacDonald, "judge men by race, Mr. Bethune, except in one or two universal matters. There never was a Scot could withstand fenced pasture. Good, bad, or indifferent, we must have space to be independent."

"That might be," agreed Bethune, thinking of himself and taking a cautious sip of wine.

"Did he get away?"

"No, sir. He was shot. They reckoned my mother died of it. I was just born."

"An orphanage never spawned you, Mr. Bethune."

"No, sir. Mr.—my father's master kept me."

"And in your time you ran away," murmured MacDonald. "I see, I see."

The waiter brought a platter of beef, side dishes of French peas with pork, sliced white bread, a fillet of whitefish, a bottle of different wine, an enormous round mold of butter. "That German in Whitehall." Then or thereafter, Bethune never heard Mac-Donald refer to King George in any other terms. "They tell me there are a good many different sins, but I'm inclined to believe more harm is made by sheer stupidity than any evil intentions. I'll not pry further. You have the makings of as competent a clerk as Tacy, Mr. Bethune. I fear we shall lose you shortly."

"I like being at the *Courier*."

MacDonald was watching him alertly. "You use your eyes and ears, and I fancy your brain as well. The one thing I cannot forgive in a man is slow-wittedness. I don't suppose I give you any news when I tell you that a good clerk can pick up twelve or fourteen shillings a week at any of several different concerns here."

"No," said Bethune. He had begun to suspect that, from casual conversations about the city. The clerks employed at merchandise warehouses, in the shipyards, at the city offices, earned an average wage of several shillings more than his.

"The *Courier*—or any other newspaper—cannot afford to offer higher wages. We operate on a relatively small margin of profit as it is."

Bethune said again, "I like being at the *Courier,* Mr. Mac-Donald."

"You would not prefer the twelve or fourteen shillings?"

He hesitated. "I wouldn't say. I reckon it's easier work than some other places."

"Not always."

"But I like it."

"However," said MacDonald, "you cannot intend to stay a clerk all your life, like Tacy. You're young, Mr. Bethune, you've a chance to make of your life what you wish. What would you like to do?"

Bethune looked down at the pale wine trembling in his glass. What would he like to do? He thought, but did not say, To right a wrong: undo a wrong thing I did, and that is impossible. Too late. For the rest, he seemed to have no burning ambition. He supposed there were men who always knew what they wanted, and had the perseverance to attain it. For himself, he did not know; he knew he had a mind, he liked to use it, but as for law or medicine or finance, any specified career, he could not say it appealed to him. Doubtless he was lazy, as Mr. Bolt said. The one ambition that was growing in him, which he would not tell to MacDonald, was that of one day seeing words he had penned himself set up in Mr. Brady's type and emerge neatly printed on a page of the *Courier.*

MacDonald was waiting for an answer. Bethune said, "Well, I don't know, sir. I'm not clever with my hands, I reckon I'd best stay with clerking."

"But you would not leave the *Courier* to clerk elsewhere for higher wages?"

Because it was clear in his mind now Bethune said, "No, I wouldn't. I like being with the *Courier.* It's"—he hesitated and finished—"different from anything I ever thought, a newspaper."

"I will tell you, Mr. Bethune," said MacDonald, "I think you may have the makings of a newsman. The first requirement I believe you have at least—an inquiring mind. And perhaps"—he grinned—"the passion for irrelevant information as well. Good newsmen are not to be found on any street corner. We shall

see how you come on, but I believe it may be in you." He poured
more wine; he had eaten little, and now produced a long segar,
then motioned to a waiter, who reached a spill to the hearth to
light it for him. "There is another requirement for the journalist,"
he went on, looking at the segar, "and that is absolute integrity.
We carry great responsibility, Mr. Bethune, though it is not
perhaps apparent. It is easy to tell lies in print and be believed.
Print is the most powerful factor in the modern world."

"Would there be aught else, sir?" asked the hovering waiter.

"No, no, that is all. —The most powerful factor," repeated
MacDonald intensely. "Far more powerful than guns and powder,
for they affect only men's bodies, while print influences their
minds. A trifle less than a hundred years ago, Sir William Berkeley
said a thing we should always keep in mind." He leaned back
and stared at the ceiling reflectively, emitting a blue cloud of
smoke. "In his report to the Lords of the Committee for these
colonies it was. He said, 'I thank God we have not free schools
nor printing, and I hope we shall not have this hundred years. For
learning has brought disobedience, and heresy, and sects into
the world, and printing has divulged them, and libels against
the government. God keep us from both.' A statement to remember, Mr. Bethune. For he was quite right. And it behooves all who
have aught to do with anything in print to make certain that the
heresies they preach are healthy ones, the learning truthful learning, and the disobedience righteous disobedience. For the synonym
for all those words is the same—doubt, my friend, doubt and
questioning. I say, God continue to put among us the doubters,
who will go against the current when it flows the wrong way. Do
you attend a church?"

"I've attended the service at Trinity Church here."

"Cease to do so," said MacDonald. "Go out among men and
use your eyes and ears and mind. You will learn more. I apologize for lecturing you. But I've a fancy something can be made
of you, Mr. Bethune—under my tutelage! Further, I have a suspicion, young as you are, you will prove malleable only so far."
He sighed and smiled. "Well, we shall see, we shall see."

CHAPTER 5

LOOKING BACK afterward, Bethune thought his first couple of years in New York seemed to fly by like as many months. There were times when his old life filled his mind, and in the midst of copying an advertisement, or alone in the street-crowds, there would be Margaret before him, and the sick memory. He had nothing at Thurstan Hundred reasonably to be homesick for, though he'd grown up there; but it was guilt more than home-sickness that made him remember. He felt immeasurably older than the Bethune who had run away that night; he looked back to Margaret with more than guilt, with sober amusement at that young love. The only girl he had spoken to, nearly: of course he had fancied himself in love with her. But there was nothing to do for it now. The guilt would be on him all his life; but gradually the rest of it faded, until it was an effort to recall her features, and memories of Virginia faded, too, and the quiet plantation life. It was fanciful, but he felt that in a sense he was born anew when he came to New York, began a new existence, with all that had gone before discounted.

They gave him more responsibility at the office after a time, and MacDonald's interest extended to a rise of wages until Bethune had twelve shillings a week. He had charge of the dozen boys who delivered the *Courier* to subscribers, and of seeing off by the Royal Mail the copies for subscribers in other places. A great part of him was devoted to the *Courier;* he took as much interest in it

as if he had been its publisher. Most of his free time he spent
exploring the city.

At the end of his first year he knew New York better than
many born there. He knew it from the Battery and Fort George
to the foundry up the North River, from the Point Hook ferry to
the shipyards on the Sound, and up to Arundel Street northeast.
He knew all its corners: the Old Slip Market; Whore Lane and
Horse and Cart Street; the taverns—City Tavern on Broad Street
(which the English called that or Bloomingdale Road, and the
Dutch called Broadway), Burns City Arms, the De Lancey Arms,
Hull's, the York Arms, the Queen's Head at Broad Street and
Dock Street, and Fraunces' Tavern at Broad Street and Pearl; the
Common and the Bowling Green; and the churches. Suddenly one
Sunday he rebelled against Trinity; he began a round of churches
that took him to the Dutch church in Nassau Street, the new
Moravian church in Fair Street, the Friends' meetinghouse, the
new Presbyterian chapel near the Common. He asked to visit the
Jewish temple, and because Mr. Isaacson was proud of sheltering
a newspaper employee, he found Bethune a hat to wear and took
him there. Bethune found the Jewish cemetery tucked away in a
corner of the city, and visited the old Dutch city hall on the water
front in Pearl Street.

He was fascinated as well with the people, the conglomerate
masses that had flocked to populate the city: people from everywhere. The Dutch, Irish, Germans, Scots, and Negroes formed the
largest groups; the English-born were among the smallest. There
were Catholics, Protestants, and Jews from various nations. A
city of *bourgeoisie,* as MacDonald had said—of prosperous merchants, shipmen, builders, dealers in everything from wheat to
slaves. The rich men of old family, the Livingstons, Stevenses,
Van Cortlandts, Kennedys, De Lanceys, were a minority in the
city: if they wielded influence, and even MacDonald must admit
they did, it was subject to the will of the rich merchants. New
York was a city of commerce, and no citizen was likely to forget
it.

But Bethune learned, too, that that commerce was hampered

by law. The statute taxing imported sugar had been in effect for thirty years but never enforced; now the new Prime Minister, George Grenville, had decided to collect that revenue. Since the merchants paid England with sugar and other produce from the West Indies for manufactured goods imported to the colonies, they felt themselves badly used by the Crown and were not backward in saying so. Very nearly all the political talk one heard in the taverns was complaint against the new taxes.

"Your ordinary citizen," said MacDonald sardonically, "never takes great interest in politics until they commence to squeeze his purse. Then he calls foul play, whatever the law be. They are saying in this case that the Crown has no right to impose taxes on the colonies, you are aware. What is your opinion on the subject, Mr. Bethune?"

"Well, there are points to both sides, aren't there? The colonies belong to the Crown, it's the Crown's right to do as it pleases here. On the other hand, you can't blame the merchants for complaining—they're losing a deal of money over it. The talk is, if the colonies can't afford to pay in produce for the imports from England, we'll have none. But I've heard men talking about setting up manufactories here in America, and I don't see a reason there shouldn't be."

"True. In time we might produce even more than England, who knows? But that means equipment to buy, and years of trial and effort. And do you fancy that German in Whitehall, or his shrewd ministers, would sit by and not interfere in that, if they saw a market to be denied England?"

"He's king," said Bethune, "and Grenville is prime minister. They've a right to do as they think best. It's up to the American merchants to get round it, or get the law changed."

"Then you think it's a right law."

"I didn't say so. Maybe it's fair to tax the foreign trade, but it seems an almighty high tax."

"You've little opinion at all," said MacDonald.

He and Shields were wholeheartedly against the Crown, and both wrote lead-articles which argued the merchants' side vigorously, not to say violently. It was one of those Bethune was reading one morning when MacDonald came in and greeted him, asking at once what he thought of this latest diatribe. He had fallen into the habit of forcing opinions from Bethune, though he said it was somewhat like pulling teeth. Bethune, knowing that his meticulous formality toward himself was half mockery, yet appreciated the other half.

He answered dubiously, "Well, Mr. MacDonald, it seems a little strong, if you don't mind my saying it. This bit where you compare the Prime Minister to Satan—"

"You don't care for it?"

"It isn't whether I care for it," pointed out Bethune reasonably. "It's the King's authorities. You could go to gaol for saying some of this, I should think."

MacDonald looked at him. A couple of men came in, stood waiting for attention, and Bethune would have turned to them; MacDonald rapped on the counter and called, "Tacy! Come here and look to the office. Mr. Bethune and I have an errand."

He took Bethune's arm and led him out. "I want to show you something, my friend." In silence he led the way down to Broad Street, turned up it. They walked all the way up to St. Paul's, where MacDonald went into the churchyard. The city had grown since St. Paul's was new, and the ground was filled with grave-plots; no one had been buried here for years, but the stones were thick all about. MacDonald seemed to know his way among them; he stopped before one near the corner of the yard. "There you are, Mr. Bethune."

It was a plain white headstone, with little cut on it. *John Peter Zenger, 1697–1746,* Bethune read, then looked at MacDonald enquiringly.

"Mr. Zenger was a journalist, not an especially good one. He was a German, and his English grammar was weak—also his judgment. He founded the New York *Weekly Journal,* having, like so many newsmen, begun life as a printer. His opinions were radical, and he expressed them freely in his articles. And so, Mr. Bethune, the governor's justices arrested him on a charge of seditious libel against the government."

"Yes?" said Bethune.

"There were men who agreed with Mr. Zenger, who was a poor man—he did not manage his *Journal*'s finances very well. One of them, a Quaker lawyer by the name of Hamilton, came from Philadelphia to defend him. You should read the account of the trial—a masterly speech, masterly. The jury were common-sensible, plain men, and they returned a unanimous acquittal. They said that a man's opinions are his own, even those of an editor, and that he is entitled freely to express them by whatever method he choose, and that if he does not advocate actual treason he cannot be prosecuted for publishing opinions in disapproval of governmental authorities or actions. It was an American jury, Mr. Bethune."

"I see."

"It established precedent. Because of John Zenger, I or George Shields or any publisher or news-writer—even, God help us, James Rivington—can cause to be printed any opinion he damned well pleases, in any newspaper of these colonies. Let us remember John Zenger occasionally, and give thanks." Suddenly MacDonald grinned, clapped him on the shoulder. "You annoyed me, Mr. Bethune—implying I cannot say what I choose—so polite about disagreeing with me! Never mind, I am lecturing again. Only do not forget it. At least our newspapers are free—owing partly to old Zenger—and God grant they remain so."

There were times when Bethune felt he might be clerking in another sense in a shop, for among the routine duties at the *Courier* was that of taking charge of advertisers' merchandise. Sometimes the fore-room was nearly filled with items offered for sale in the paper, for many of the advertisers had no place of business. Doctor French's pills and powders, in neat packets; miscellaneous books and pamphlets on consignment from Brady and other printers; cosmetic prescriptions; once a set of silver-mounted harness, a pair of cherry-wood chairs—one never knew what might come in, offered for sale with the direction, "To be seen at the publishers' office." It irritated MacDonald, but Bethune found it entertaining.

In those two years, though Bethune learned a good deal about the city and about the newspaper business, he made no close friends at all. He grew acquainted with many in his wanderings, but had not the money to frequent taverns or places of entertainment. His amusement was watching—the people, the places, the activities. In the late evenings he liked to stand outside one of the theaters to see the audience emerge: the common folk first, decently clad, talking loudly of what they had seen, going off on foot or ahorse; then the fashionable young ladies and gentlemen in their fine clothes and hair-powder, the ladies' hoops thrice as wide as themselves, shimmering pale colors, the carriages waiting in line to receive them. The American Company was playing at the Chapel Street Theatre and once or twice he paid his fourpence for a seat in the gallery; he would like to attend oftener than he could afford.

He settled into his new life so that in time it seemed he had known no other. Never having had confidants he did not feel the lack of them; but that was not to say he was entirely satisfied. That first winter, when the weather kept him indoors most evenings, he began to know he was lonely. The most of his attention, however, went to his work, or rather what he conceived should one day be his work: for at last his ambition was sure—he would write for a newspaper, and preferably the *Courier*.

With that in mind, he read every word of every edition, and other papers too: the *Post-Boy,* the *Weekly Mercury,* the *American Chronicle,* comparing styles and subjects. He came to realize that MacDonald was a more than competent editor; he noted Mac-Donald's tricks of phrase, his unerring judgment of the amount of space an article deserved. He determined to be as good a newsman one day.

By the middle of that first winter he found the long evenings lonely; sometimes despite the cold he would go out to be among people. Occasionally MacDonald again invited him to dinner, questioned and lectured him; for the most part, where he went he went alone. On the last night of the Chapel Street Theatre's current season, he indulged himself by attending. The company was not a large one and he had seen the dark, pretty girl in other plays, but this night her part was more prominent and he learned her name: Mrs. Gay Lamont. He wondered if she was married; all actresses, for dignity, were called Mrs. in the bills. She could not be much older than himself; she was very small, plumply curved, and he admired her intensely.

After the performance he stood outside to watch the crowds, and was rewarded presently by seeing her come out. She was even prettier at close quarters, a dark, laughing little thing, in a white gown cut low to reveal part of her bosom; she clung to the arm of a tall young man, who smiled down at her.

When they got into a carriage and were driven off, Bethune walked home to Cherry Street low in spirits and sorry for himself. He wondered where they were going: to some elegant restaurant, or just as likely to some discreet apartment where they would be alone. Actresses—his room seemed chill and too large, and he thought about the girl until he slept; he could nearly feel, in imagination, how warm and soft she would be.

He had exchanged talk with Mr. Shields on only a few occasions. The little man bounced in and out frequently, but left the routine business for MacDonald to manage. Twice he came accompanied by his daughter. Mistress Susan was a tall girl with plain features, no beauty; Shields seemed to dote on her, and Tacy, something of a gossip, told Bethune she was his only child. "Set on a fine marriage for her he was—he said he'd no care for money, he'd enough to provide for her, but a real gentleman of good family it had to be. Pleased as a dog with two tails he was when young Mr. Van Steen offered to address her. They're to be wed next summer."

The second occasion Mistress Susan came with her father, she spoke to him. "You must be Mr. Bethune, I've heard Father and Mr. MacDonald mention you." She was a trifle older than he, one of the few young women and the only lady he'd had speech with here. "Mr. MacDonald thinks a deal of your abilities."

He was too surprised at that to make any reply; but in the few minutes while Shields was closeted with MacDonald they talked. He thought her uninteresting and plain. "You're from Virginia, Mr. Bethune? That sounds very distinguished."

"Oh—does it?"

"But of course! I do admire southern manners! Do you not find New York crude and cold? It must be dull for you, working here. Well, that is, it's not difficult to see you are a gentleman. I would think—"

"Well, I wouldn't say I find it dull."

"I'm sure you must be lonely for company. Would you care to come to a dinner one evening, and meet some of my friends?" Her eyes were busy—a little puzzled—on his height, his ill-tailored garments. He thought perhaps she imagined all Southerners to be gentlemen and wealthy plantation owners. He was entirely confounded by the casual invitation, and at first suspected she was mocking him. He was so astonished, in fact, that he mentioned it later to MacDonald, who laughed.

"Will you accept?"

"Well, I don't know that she—that Mistress Susan meant it. She said—"

"I'm afraid your drawl and elegant manners are to blame, Mr. Bethune. George likes you, but he tells me you're too serious a young man. Moreover, you're a gentleman."

"It seems to me New Yorkers are almighty concerned with breeding," said Bethune.

"Possibly. Only a handful of real gentry among us, you know. You had better accept the invitation. You needn't fear they intend to be patronizing. You may even enjoy it."

Bethune was unsure of that. However, a few weeks later Shields one afternoon reiterated the invitation. "We've company dining tonight, young man, my daughter's friends—do you come if you're free. Nonsense, of course I'm serious! No disgrace for a man to earn his living, and my daughter was impressed with you. Not that you're to expect any favors, mind! But you're by way of being a valued member of our staff here. Robert says—well, no matter. Eight o'clock, we shall expect you."

Bethune had no notion where Shields' house was; he would like to avoid this invitation, but could not.

"Greenwich Road, up the river," MacDonald told him laconically. "You'll likely enjoy yourself once you're there."

Bethune did not think so. He was unhappy about it, but also a little excited.

CHAPTER 6

THE SHIELDS HOUSE was in the fashionable section, uncrowded as yet, along Greenwich Road on the way out of the city north. It was a large house, new, set back in a quiet garden. When he came to it, after a long and tiring walk (for he could not afford a hackney), Bethune was reluctant to enter, having visions of an embarrassing evening among supercilious strangers. But he was welcomed hospitably by Mistress Susan in the parlor.

"Good evening, Mr. Bethune, I am so pleased you have come. Do let me make you known." She introduced him to a dozen young men and ladies, and if some of them looked a trifle askance at his clothes, they seemed to find nothing laughable about him.

Mistress Susan's mother was dead. The Shields did not move in the first class of society, but associated with the wealthy burghers' families that made up the large and rich middle class of New York fashion. The only member of New York aristocracy present was Mistress Susan's betrothed, Mr. Edward Van Steen. Mistress Susan, Bethune thought, displayed him like a prize she might have won at whist. Aside from his breeding, Van Steen had little to commend him, being stout and slow-witted. Bethune, younger than the rest by several years, felt old and staid among them, their party games, their frivolity; but he enjoyed the evening after all. It was flattering that they accepted him, and pleasant to find himself part of a group. It was pleasant, too, to be among the young ladies and their automatic coy glances and giggles, their pretty colored gowns. They seemed to think it nothing odd that Mistress Susan should entertain a clerk of her fathers, when he was also well bred; New York was not Virginia in such matters, he realized. Not least among the evening's pleasures was the elegant meal served by servants in a profusion of china and silver.

He rather looked forward to being invited there again, but he received only two more invitations from Mistress Susan. It was not a large or an altogether young company on the third evening he spent at the Shields house. MacDonald was present, and Van Steen and his remarkably plain sister, among four or five others. After dinner, MacDonald and his host went off to the library, excusing themselves to discuss business, and had just rejoined the company when the butler, looking agitated, appeared in the doorway of the parlor.

"I beg your pardon, sir—" Two men brushed past him without waiting to be announced.

"Mr. George Shields?"

"I'm Shields, yes. And you?"

Both men were commonly clad, but wore also an air of authority. They came forward in step to confront Shields. "We are from the governor's police, sir, and hold a warrant for your arrest," said the first with great courtesy. There was dead silence for a moment, and then Susan uttered a small shriek.

Shields began to splutter. "Arrest? What nonsense is this, what d'you mean? By God—"

"The matter of the *Norfolk*, sir," added the man gently.

"Oh, my God," ejaculated Shields. He cast a wild glance about the room. His daughter was weeping, Van Steen staring at him indignantly.

MacDonald laughed. "Are you caught fair, George? Bad luck! You'd best go quietly and not make trouble or they'll raise the fine on you."

Shields was swearing at his captors, who now had him by the arms. "Damme, Robert, you needn't sound so pleased!"

Bethune had to admire the girl for the way she rushed to her father's side and ordered the men to release him; but the officers paid her no mind, or Shields either, and he was led out stuttering over his shoulder to MacDonald, "For the love of God, do you locate Carruthers—dispatch him—damme, fellow, not so fast, allow me—" Mistress Susan promptly burst into tears anew.

MacDonald was tactfully the first to depart, taking Bethune's arm. "What's it about?" he echoed in the street, still chuckling, but ruefully. "This cursed tax. George is hardly the only merchant who is in league with smugglers bringing in sugar and whatever from the West Indies. But as luck has it, I happen to know, he is part owner of the *Norfolk*. Evidently she's been taken by a revenue patroller."

"But—will Mr. Shields be prisoned?"

"I doubt it, but they'll clap a painful fine on him!"

His prediction proved true; Shields, haled up before the court, upon his lawyer's advice pleaded guilty, received a tongue-lashing from the justice and the imposition of a fine of two thousand pounds. "Which," said MacDonald amusedly, "hurt him more than a month in New Gaol, at that!" As he said, there were many merchants secretly subsidizing the vessels in the smuggling trade, but when those ships were taken, the merchants were not legally responsible if no proof existed that they would be the recipients of the cargo. Shields, being a majority owner of the frigate *Norfolk* taken on her way into the harbor with a full cargo of sugar and indigo, was indeed caught fair, one of the few merchants arrested for what was universal practice.

That was what made him most indignant, Bethune gathered: he was punished on a legal technicality, almost alone of all the men in New York who were guilty of the same offense. "Damme, it's too bad! If they prisoned every man who bought smuggled goods, some of these damnation holy-talking gentry'd be rubbing elbows with them they look down on!"

What caused Shields most pain was that the aristocratic Van Steens, dismayed at the prospect of a connection with such notoriety, caused their scion to withdraw from his betrothal. It was ungracious, but the engagement was not of long standing. Shields was furious at the insult to his daughter. Mistress Susan, Bethune heard, retired from all social affairs in humiliation; no longer were any bid to dine at the fine house in Greenwich Road, and she did not appear again at the *Courier* office with her father.

Six weeks afterward the official news arrived that His Majesty's Government had seen fit to reduce the taxes on foreign imports.

But it was not a sizable reduction, and the merchants continued to complain; the times were poor and grew poorer, over that next eight or nine months. At the same time that the Crown reduced the tax (an empty gesture of appeasement, since the new rate was still prohibitive) it took steps to enforce a control of smuggling. Not so many vessels as before managed to slip into the harbor with contraband cargo. Prices rose and then fell as earnings fell; money was short, actual coinage scarce. The Crown had some time since forbidden any issue of paper money, and the coins in circulation were as likely to be French or Spanish, as English.

The *Courier,* like the other newspapers, felt the depression of business early. A newspaper was among the first luxuries to be given up. The subscription list dwindled; then the remaining subscribers commenced to offer goods instead of money in payment.

Tacy was outraged; this was New York, not an outlying farm village. But MacDonald accepted conditions with equanimity. "Take it? There may come a time we'll be glad to have a dozen eggs or a half-cord of firewood instead of ten shillings coin—as soon now as later." And presently Bethune was living on seven shillings a week, but somewhat better than on his previous twelve, since prices were not so high except for luxuries. But many workmen and their families lacked money even for necessities.

The newspapers were soon in bad case, being caught at both ends of the situation. Themselves luxury items, they needed, for production, materials of that class which had risen greatly in price. Most of the paper and all ink and type had to be imported from England, and fewer and fewer imports were coming into the colonies. English paper, which had been two pounds the ream, rose to four, six, at last ten.

"Damme," said Shields, "we'll publish the *Courier* if there is none to read it but ourselves!" Though hard hit by the depression, he had still a fortune. The *Courier* had been operating at a loss for three months when another blow fell, a blow that was to have far-reaching consequences.

"They have attempted it before," said MacDonald grimly. He had unprecedentedly shut the front premises and called Bethune and Tacy into the rear office. Bethune knew he was upset because he offered Tacy, who liked his drink too well, a glass of brandy along with himself. "You remember the act of 'fifty-seven. Now they are trying again. They're out to ruin us, drive every paper out of business! A new tax? God's teeth, with a vengeance! I had it direct from the captain of the official mail packet. George will come galloping back from Boston when he hears this." He drank brandy and made a grimace as if at a foul taste.

"But what is it?"

"Parliament has passed a new act to be in effect the first of November next. All newspapers are to be taxed from that date. He could not tell me the rate, but we shall hear soon enough. But if I know George, it will but increase his obstinacy. And mine. We're losing a ha'penny a copy now. This will mean more, but"—and his jaw set—"you needn't fear for your wages. We shall continue publication." He added, half to himself, "George will carry me. May God damn them all! It's not only Grenville, but all those stiffnecked tyrants in the Commons—trying to pay for their last war, and damn where the money comes from! One day they'll go too far."

For a time it appeared they had already done so.

Shields indeed hastened back from his business in Boston, arriving on the day the new tax rates were officially announced by Lieutenant Governor Cadwallader Colden. Colden was acting governor of New York since the departure of Governor Monckton, until the expected arrival of the newly appointed governor. Upon Colden's relatively blameless person fell the wrath of New York, which delighted MacDonald.

"I've nought against Colden," he remarked to Bethune, "but it is encouraging to see the common run of men so stirred over this. It is proof that they have concern for a free press."

"There you're wrong, Robert," said Shields. He was looking gray and tired; Bethune wondered if his daughter held him to blame for her intended husband's defection, or if his worry was all for politics and money. "They don't give a farthing for the fact that the Stamp Tax affects newspapers. It is because there's a new tax, and the revenue to go three thousand miles to London. The colonies send no lords to Parliament—'twouldn't matter if they did—and that's the issue, taxes imposed without a by-your-leave."

"You may be right, but all the same it's one cheering aspect of it. The devil of a rate they make it too—it could put many a paper out of business. There's no journal in any of the colonies runs to less than a sheet every edition, the ha'penny-a-half-sheet nonsense is meaningless. We'll all be paying the full rate, a penny a copy—God's teeth!—but the two shillings duty for advertisers will hit hardest. Who will pay such an exorbitant rate? We'll be filling our columns with something other than advertisements—if there remains a *Courier* to be filled each week."

"I'll not go back on that," said Shields. "There is such feeling over this the act's bound to be repealed soon or late."

Whatever the reason in their minds, the majority of New Yorkers, always excepting the wealthy gentlemen and more conservative merchants, were bitterly resentful of the new tax. With the example of the tax on foreign imports still before them, businessmen in all the colonies had premonitions of trade made so unprofitable that it must cease and the colonies be bankrupt, as many individuals were now. In those months the *Courier,* like every other newspaper, was devoted principally to political news and opinions. If it made dull reading for those who preferred more sensational news stories, there was a deal of violent feeling about. Bethune considered that the violence seemed not always sure of its direction.

He assisted Tacy with the copying on occasion, and found the reports tedious writing, save for one article, a quotation from the *Virginia Review* which contained some stirring phrases from a speech made in the House of Burgesses. "There is a bold man, Mr. Bethune!" MacDonald exclaimed. "God grant we have others of the same stamp among us. 'If this be treason, make the most of it!' By all means!" For the most part Bethune failed to make head or tail of what was done or why: it was all talk. But for all their indignation the New York merchants at least were cautious men. They had other visions than those of bankruptcy— visions of a British fleet patrolling their harbor, and of chastise- ment from their lawful king. They acquiesced to the request of the Massachusetts General Court to convene a congress from the colonies, but only nine colonies sent delegates, who debated at length and decided nothing. In the end the only action they took was to draw up a petition to the Crown. That drew a snort from MacDonald.

" 'If you please, sir!' " he said, with a plainer oath than he generally used. "A deal of action *that* will induce!"

Toward the end of the summer, as the sweltering heat irritated already frayed nerves, the news had grown more exciting. Led by a core of radicals, a motley group of small merchants formed to offer more active resistance to what they termed the tyranny of taxation.

"Sears I know," said MacDonald; he had attended their latest meeting and come into the office looking as excited as Bethune had ever seen him. "A radical, a firebrand, but that's no matter. It would be no matter what he advocated, he'd rally half the city to join him just by ranting at them, he is that kind of man. Hardly a polished speaker, but persuasive—damned persuasive. Isaac Sears and John Lamb, they are the bear-masters. Sears' reputation does him no harm either. He distinguished himself as a privateer captain—pirate to you, Mr. Bethune—in the French war."

"Are they," asked Bethune, "decided to draw up another petition?"

"Sarcastic! They are not! The merchants have entered into a pact to refuse to purchase aught from England after the New Year, unless the tax is repealed. It shows you Sears' stamp," added MacDonald, "how he took up the name-calling of old Barre. He—Barre—was being sarcastic himself when he termed the radicals among us Sons of Liberty. Now Sears has seized on it, and names his followers so—with a somewhat different inflection. They will make trouble."

"You sound pleased about it, sir."

"God's teeth, trouble is a newsman's meat and drink, Mr. Bethune! Have you not learned that yet? And it may mean the repeal of the tax before it goes into effect. There's a Scot tangled in it, too, one Alexander McDougall, and he a bolder rascal than Sears. There's bound to be trouble."

CHAPTER 7

MAC DONALD CAME rushing in on a November afternoon. "Leave that, we'll have little advertising space this next edition! There is trouble brewing—come along and see it!"

Bethune took up his coat, for the afternoon was chill, and followed obediently. "What's happening?"

MacDonald led him up the street briskly. "The *Edward* is in carrying the stamps of the new tax, and a crowd is gathering at the water front to prevent their being landed—a crowd in ugly temper—they mean trouble. Whatever occurs I want a full report of it, and I cannot be everywhere at once. We'll separate and watch. I heard Sears ranting at a mob in Pearl Street, he—"

The rest of his words were lost in the growing confusion. The stream of traffic, all heading for the water front, was thicker than usual; voices were raised all about. Near the quays the crowds grew even denser, and at the wharf where the packet *Edward* lay a mob was collecting. Almost at once Bethune was separated from

MacDonald, pushed into the packed crowd by new arrivals behind; not for the first time, he was grateful for his height, which gave him a view over most of the heads.

In the center of the crowd a man mounted on a box was shouting in a powerful, deep voice—a stocky barrel of a man: "Do we submit tamely to tyranny? Are we slaves to the Crown, to be robbed of our rights and our hope of livelihood? Are you behind me, friends, will we show these—" The roared "Aye!" of the mob cut him off. Sears, or one of the other firebrands? He leaped down and was lost in the forest of bodies, which began to push forward to the end of the quay.

A ship's cutter drew up there. Bethune saw it slide along the quayside, the white faces of the oarsmen staring up; there was a ship's officer, all brass buttons, in the stern. A disturbance in the crowd ahead, a man's voice trying to make itself heard, and after a moment a long howl of disappointed rage from the crowd. People all about were asking excitedly of each other, "What is it? What's happened?"

Suddenly MacDonald was at his elbow. He had to shout to make himself heard. "A trick—damnation clever. That was the captain of the *Edward*! He slipped in last night covered by a warship and landed the stamps at the fort. Just telling the crowd—disperse quietly—"

The crowd had no such intention. It swayed and muttered angrily, a monster robbed of its prey. Bethune was frightened of it, the violence of its temper pressing him on all sides as tangibly as its physical mass; he was in, not of it, its mood communicated to nerve and muscle, and something MacDonald had said was in his mind, that a mob is an individual rather than so many humans in one place. This individual was angry. It was surging in another direction now, up the quay, dispersing and not dispersing; it took him along, and he lost MacDonald again. It pushed along the quayside toward the fort and battery, and its mutter grew louder. Round him in its mass was a ferret-faced man in the apron of a butcher, a stout matron clutching a basket of fish, a wagoner with his coiled whip, a little fellow in decent homespun who looked like a small tradesman, a burly sailor with his tarred queue dangling behind. They shouted with the rest; their faces were ugly with emotion; there was a smell in Bethune's nostrils of unwashed bodies, and a smell of violence almost as sharp.

At the fort the stocky man and a couple of others commenced more harangue, but were soon drowned out by the chant of the crowd: "The stamps! The stamps! Give us the stamps!" They swayed and jostled at the garrison gate. Bethune was being swallowed by the monster: he must have air. He began to fight his way out. Then a different shout rose: the garrison gate was opening to emit a double line of regular troops, and the chant turned to a howl; if they wanted battle, let them come on!

But the sight of fixed bayonets made even the bolder spirits hesitate; the howl died, and after a few aimless minutes the mob shifted back. Bethune had struggled out to one side where it did not press him in so close; he saw it turn, like a great sluggish serpent, and straggle back toward Dock Street. He looked for MacDonald, but the little man was lost in the mob. It was not dispersing, only moving; it flowed slowly up Dock Street, talking loudly to itself. At the corner by Whitehall it hesitated and at last began to break up into groups.

He thought it was ended, quelled by the glint of last light on bayonets. He thought, Like the petition—when it comes to the point, they cannot decide to risk all!

MacDonald ran up behind him. "There's more to come," he panted; his eyes were dancing with exhilaration. "I follow Sears, you go along with Lamb's mob and see what he's up to," and he gestured at forty or fifty men who were marching purposefully up Dock Street in a body. Without further words he was gone, and Bethune stretched his legs to catch up to his own quarry.

The little crowd apparently was making for the Golden Hill district, but never got there; a few streets away they met and were engulfed by a new mob fully as large as the one at the quay. So densely packed was the press of men it was a few minutes before Bethune saw that the new crowd was formed around a large object which they trundled along the center of the street. He could not see—yes, it was a coach, a gentleman's carriage, and a fine new one; the crowd was pulling and pushing at it.

"Colden's coach! It's Colden's coach!" went up the cry from a dozen men round about. A man hoisted himself up to the driver's box, lifted both hands for silence. What he shouted was lost in the din; this was a crowd rowdier than the first, and possessed of more definite purpose. The jam nearest the stolen coach now raised a jeering laugh; a couple of men got up on the box, busy with ropes. When they leaped down a hastily manufactured straw man was lashed there—an effigy in someone's long coat, with a beaver hat set rakishly on its head. The coach started to move again down Dock Street.

This was an angry crowd, but it was taking some action; there was not the pent violence he had felt at the quayside. Back across Whitehall they dragged the coach, chanting, "Colden—Tyrant Colden!" But they made no move toward Fort George; instead, they turned onto the Bowling Green opposite and mingled with the remnants of the first crowd. They smashed through the fencing, trampling it underfoot, and milled about; there was no attempt at speech-making, such was the confusion and size of the gathering.

"By God—by God!" The low exclamation pulled Bethune's head round, perhaps because the voice was soft among so many loud voices. It was a young man—and a gentleman, to judge by his clothes—who spoke. In the falling dusk there was something familiar about him. "By God, this will show them! There must be three thousand—" He met Bethune's eyes; in that instant, both recognized a kinship, that of all here they two were watchers, not engaged with these angry men. He smiled quickly. "What is it they've got there? I can't make it out."

"The lieutenant governor's carriage, I heard someone say. I expect they stole it from his house."

"By God, won't he be furious! He had warning of some demonstration. He's gone aboard the *Coventry* to be out of harm's way. Look there—I swear they've set up a gallows!"

It was a rude, knocked-together affair near the center of the green, and they were holding a mock hanging. A howl went up as the effigy of Colden dangled in mid-air; the next minute a louder yell followed as someone set a torch to it, and a dozen men caught up brands, thrust them into the flames, and ran to set the carriage alight. The straw man blazed up and was gone, but the coach burned a long time. It was full dark now and the black moving shadows of men against the flame were grotesque, primitive. Bethune thought of accounts he had read of Africa and the blacks dancing round their tribal fires.

The young man beside him drew a long breath. "Magnificent! A modern tribal ceremony!"

"I was thinking that. The lieutenant governor's got nothing to do with it."

His companion laughed. "Not one damned thing, friend. They must needs have a scapegoat, and the old man represents the Crown's authority, is all. But let's keep our voices low when we say so, or they'll have the two of us on their gallows instead of a scarecrow!"

"That might be," said Bethune.

"They're in that mood." He gave Bethune another swift glance. "I believe the excitement's over; this has satisfied them for the moment. Will you come and join me at—what's the nearest?— the Queen's Head, isn't it?"

"I'll do that." He had learned not to append "sir" so often; it marked him as a stranger in the north.

They came across the smashed fence to the road, walked up toward Broad Street. The other was as tall as he, and he thought not much older; when they entered the tavern the light showed him dark, handsome, with a humorous, mobile mouth. He was clad expensively in dark blue sateen breeches and a well-tailored coat with a velvet collar, but, after the fashion of younger New York gentlemen, had no lace to his shirt, only a plain neckcloth. And Bethune had seen him before—he was the young man who had been with the pretty actress, Gay Lamont, that night.

He had given Bethune a similar quick look; he smiled and held out his hand. "Remiss of me—I'm Darcy Trevelyan."

"My name's Bethune."

Most never enquire further than that; no one had ever called him by his first name. But Darcy Trevelyan raised his brows, his smile broadening. "First, last, or center?"

It was impossible not to like him. Bethune said, "The rest of it is James Andrew; you may take your choice."

"And I envy you," said Trevelyan vigorously. "Good solid names, both. You've no notion how that Darcy plagues me—sounding like a Frenchified finicking London beau! The devil of it is, my mother had a dozen decent ones to pick from in the family, but nothing would do but I must commemorate her own name. I had to defend myself on account of it twice a week regular at school. By God, I'm dry. Jem! Service, man! What is yours? Brandy for me."

"I'll join you."

"That was a farce," went on Trevelyan, leading the way to a table; the tavern was all but deserted. "But all the same, it shows 'em—these fogying old reactionaries—they'll have to do something about it soon or late."

Bethune was busy placing him. Trevelyan was one of the first names in New York society. Rafe Trevelyan, who was Darcy's uncle, he was to learn, was a close friend of Philip Livingston, who had been among the delegates to that abortive Stamp Act Congress in October. Trevelyan, like the Livingstons, was wealthy and of old family.

"My politics?" Bethune roused to answer the question. "I don't know I have any. A lot of talk is all."

"They made some action tonight. Don't tell me you're a Tory?"

"I wouldn't say that. But I expect you'd say I have a stake in the thing; I work at the *Courier*."

"You don't say! Famous! A newsman! And the best paper in New York. Your health, James." Evidently Trevelyan was a man of discrimination. "D'you know, that's an ambition of my own—family wouldn't hear of it, of course, but I fancy I'd acquit myself at it. It must be damned exciting, eh?"

"Well, I don't think you'd find it so—on seven shillings a week."

"Good God! I wonder you don't starve!"

"That's small danger. Of late we get payment in eggs and flour mostly." The brandy was good; he'd had no dinner, and it loosened his tongue a trifle. "I'm only a clerk, though I've charge of the delivery as well. All the same—" He found himself talking of his feeling about the print shop and the *Courier;* he stumbled a little, searching for words.

Trevelyan listened flatteringly. "I've never seen any printing. I'd like to. You're right, it's more of a factor than most people realize." He laughed. "My Uncle Rafe disapproves of the *Courier* —he says your MacDonald is a worse radical than Isaac Sears. He's between your paper and the *Gazetteer* in politics, say somewhere round the temper of the *Journal.*" He finished his brandy. "But what the devil are we doing, talking politics like two merchants? Have another."

"No, thanks, I've had no dinner."

"Nor have I. That damned mob prevented me from reaching home." Rafe Trevelyan's mansion, Bethune remembered, faced on the north side of the Bowling Green. "We'll dine here, shall we?"

For some reason he felt no embarrassment at saying it. "I'd remind you, seven shillings a week. I'd rather not—"

"But I meant to invite you!"

"No, I'd prefer not, it's kind of you, but—"

"Oh, damnation!" said Trevelyan. "Don't be so stiffnecked, man! What does it signify?"

"About ten shillings, I'd reckon," said Bethune.

"Under the mark. A decent dinner, here, nearer a pound. I'll tell you. Come out to New Market with me tomorrow and I'll put you in the way of a sure bet, one of De Lancey's nags, certain to win."

Bethune liked him very much; he was amused. "I've only Sundays off and sometimes not those."

"Oh, damnation! Well, Sunday, then. At all events, let me give you dinner now. I'm starving and I can't abide eating alone."

Bethune laughed and gave in.

"You had the better vantage point." MacDonald grimaced. "They call me a radical, but I can't say I love the common man *en masse.* I am Scot enough to hate wanton destruction."

"I heard the damage was considerable."

"Small word for it." MacDonald had been with the first mob,

which had marched up to Vauxhall to the house leased by Major
James, commander of Fort George, and, in aimless violence, had
demolished furniture, smashed china, and—as a last gesture of
defiance—walked off with the regimental colors of the Royal Artillery. "And mark it, there's more trouble coming. The city's
roused to showing five years' worth of resentment against the
Crown. And time—time we were."

"The lieutenant governor didn't pass the law," said Bethune, "or
Major James, either."

"Oh, I grant you that. But angry men never stop to think.
They're not in a reasonable state. And Colden at least is about to
be relieved of his duty. The new governor arrived on the *Edward*.
God's fingerbones! He walked into trouble when he set foot on
the dock. I wonder how he'll manage it."

The new governor, Sir Henry Moore, managed very well. The
garrison was alerted to cope with new mobs, but Moore was wise
enough to strike in the lull of that next day, while the citizenry
was, for the moment, satiated with its own violence. Opening the
fort gates and admitting the lackadaisical crowd milling about
there, he faced them with a line of troops and read a proclamation,
meaning little of itself, but his firm manner and the gesture showed
he was ready and willing to deal decisively with further violence.

But a day or so later, when another ship made port with more
of the new stamps, it was greeted by a mob which swarmed
aboard, surrounded the officers in the captain's own cabin, and demanded custody of the cargo. With little choice, the captain
surrendered, and the boxes were carried up to the Merchants'
Coffee House and ceremoniously burned while a crowd of merchants watched, too cautious to take such action themselves but
pleased enough that Sears and his rabble had taken it for them.

In the general uproar the principal victims of the new tax—
the one group that joined no overt action—were largely overlooked. The *Journal* came out before any other that week, with
its first page bordered in black and headed with—instead of its
customary device of the city's arms—the announcement in bold-
face type, NO STAMPED PAPER TO BE HAD. This ruse was eagerly
imitated by every other newspaper published in the city. The

Journal's lead article announced that this was in all likelihood the final edition, since under the prohibitive tax no publication could prove profitable. "It can only be concluded that Parliament means to tax us from existence." Even Rivington's *Gazetteer* resorted to the same subterfuge to avoid using the new stamps, and threatened to cease publication. All the newspapers were devoted almost entirely to the disastrous effect of the tax on publication, and the *Courier* was the only one which did not announce imminent cessation.

"We'll not be intimidated by Parliament," Shields said viciously. "If every other paper in the colonies is forced out of business I'll continue the *Courier* at my own expense." His article on the first page proclaimed that, and added a violent denunciation of the Commons, which was responsible for the act.

But in fact, after their dismal threats, all the papers continued to publish, though they carried fewer advertisements, the public being generally unwilling to pay the two-shilling tax as well as the fee. Most of them had been operating upon a smaller margin of profit for a year in any case, since the depression of business had been felt.

CHAPTER 8

BETHUNE WENT to New Market with Darcy Trevelyan that Sunday. He had been there alone, to watch the racing; Darcy said it was a rude course, nothing like its English namesake, but several wealthy men in the city kept amateur racing stables and there was usually a good crowd. Bethune found more pleasure in

Darcy's company than in the racing. It seemed they would be friends; they were on first-name terms that day. Enough alike and enough opposite to harmonize easily, they enjoyed one another.

It was at Darcy's insistence that Bethune was persuaded, against his own better judgment, to risk a shilling on a horse Darcy said was sure to win; to Bethune's surprise, it did, paying him five for one. But no argument would prevail on him to bet again. He meant to keep the five shillings, which had appeared as it were out of the blue, and having seen Darcy lose five pounds in as many minutes, he reckoned the safest place for them was in his pocket. It was his nineteenth birthday; the money, in a way, was a present.

But it was Darcy who unwittingly assisted him to a means of occasionally augmenting his resources. Darcy dropped in at the *Courier* office often in late afternoon, to accompany Bethune to dinner. He was quite willing to forego his usual exclusive haunts to accommodate his friend's purse; there was no snobbery in Darcy. He was easy with MacDonald, who liked him and in private jeered gently at Bethune's rich friends. But Rafe Trevelyan was respected in New York as an honest man, and even the most radical-minded in politics had respect, too, for his friend, Philip Livingston, who was Darcy's godfather.

On Thursdays Bethune was free earlier; the first Thursday Darcy chanced to seek him they wandered into a water-front tavern long before the dinner hour, against Bethune's argument, for he disliked to spend money on drink, even the cheapest of which was ruinously expensive on account of the import taxes. "Well, then," said Darcy casually, "I'll play you a hand for the cost, and ten to one have to pay anyway. I always lose at cards." He brought out a well-worn pack from his pocket and commenced to shuffle it.

"You'd likely win from me. I've never handled cards in my life."

Darcy stared. "Good God, James! That I can't believe. But no time like the present to improve your education." He insisted on teaching Bethune a couple of popular games then and there.

Bethune was not astonished to win a few times from Darcy, who told him it was beginners' luck, but he found that it continued, that for some reason he had cards sense. He never especially enjoyed cards games, and had no unholy thrill at winning or matching wits with the shrewdest opponent, but he won oftener than he lost at any game, be it piquet or whist or loo. Darcy, who was a reckless plunger, blamed luck; Bethune seldom took chances, for some cold intuition told him what to play and when, and informed him whether his opponent was up to trickery or did hold a better hand. After a time he refused to play with Darcy, who always lost to him.

Darcy had induced him a few times to accompany him to the more exclusive taverns; one cold February evening found them at Fraunces', haunt of the wealthier merchants. Bethune had never been to Fraunces' before; it was the best-known tavern in the city, with prices to match its elegant red brick, its English-made furniture, and, he thought, its flamboyant proprietor, a French Creole from Jamaica. They had just come in when Darcy said, "There's my uncle, I'd best speak with him." Bethune would have waited, but Darcy took his arm and led him across to a table near the enormous hearth where four men sat together over cards. "Evening, uncle."

The man who glanced up was much like Darcy, tall and dark, with humorous eyes; he was about fifty. "Ah, Darcy. Mr. Bethune? You must be the lad from the *Courier* I've heard my nephew mention."

"Servant, sir." One man at the table Bethune did not know, but the second was Philip Livingston, stout, pleasantly ugly; and the third was James Rivington. They had evidently just finished a game; the cards were scattered on the table. Darcy, having satisfied convention, turned away, but Rivington made a remark that kept Bethune where he was, awkward as he felt before these important middle-aged men.

"The *Courier*! Do not tell me any kinsman of yours runs in a pack like that, sir!" He raked Bethune with one swift stare, gathering up the cards. "I had no notion Shields was hiring six-shilling clerks to write under his name these days, but judging from the quality of his articles, I can't say I'm surprised."

You would not say that to Robert MacDonald, Bethune reflected. He said, "Mr. Shields writes his own articles, sir. He is under no obligation to any man." He was rather pleased with that retort, where Shields would have blustered and MacDonald cursed—a retort recalling Rivington's connection with Oliver De Lancey, other conservatives in the Assembly, and the favors he had of them. Rivington flushed a dull red; perhaps he had not expected any retort at all.

"The child has a tongue." He rose, and his eyes were furious as he realized Bethune topped him by several inches. He smiled. "What do they give you at the *Courier*?" he said. "I'll offer a shilling more."

Yes, thought Bethune, keep me a week and dismiss me, knowing that MacDonald would never take me on again. He was surprised that Rivington should take so much trouble for a mere clerk; Rivington was, evidently, one of those who could not withstand defeat in the smallest way. He said politely, "Thank you, sir, I prefer to stay with the *Courier*."

"More fool you," said Rivington. He looked down at the cards in his hand; he tried flattery. "I fancy you're too clever to stay by a tuppenny-ha'penny sheet like that long, Mr. Clerk. When I offer you, say, fifteen shillings a week?"

Bethune seldom found himself disliking a man; he disliked Rivington quite violently. "Not for fifteen guineas, Mr. Rivington," he said, and turned away.

"Here, wait," called Rivington after him. "It's no matter to me, one clerk's as bad as another, but I don't like being bested, my young cockerel. I'll play you a hand for it—*Gazetteer* or *Courier*."

Bethune turned back. For the first time in his life he knew the awful thrill of superiority to another man; it warmed him like a double of brandy. He had seen little sense to Darcy's frippery cards games; now he was grateful for the knowledge. It was a skill he had not courted or thought much of, but it was a skill he had.

"If you can handle the cards?" said Rivington with something like a sneer.

Bethune grinned at him cheerfully. "Whatever game you choose, Mr. Rivington."

Rafe Trevelyan was looking from one to the other. He said quietly, "Don't fleece the boy, Rivington. Let it be."

Rivington did not glance at him. "Piquet," he snapped.

"Piquet," agreed Bethune. Philip Livingston got up, relinquishing his chair.

"This is farce," he said. "I pray, do not—"

Darcy caught Bethune's eye; he was longing, Bethune knew, to reassure the other two, but could not speak to warn Rivington. He gave his uncle a nudge; Trevelyan glanced at him and subsided.

They cut the pack; Bethune won the deal. He settled down to play happily, and within ten minutes took the game from Rivington. "I think I'll be staying with the *Courier,* sir," he said, smiling.

Rivington stared at him across the cards. "I can't be beat twice by a pup like you. Another game for a guinea, clerk."

At any other time Bethune would have hesitated; he had two shillings fourpence in his pocket. But he disliked Rivington so intensely it made him reckless. "Done. It is your deal." Rivington concentrated on that game, but he lost it; and the next. In forty minutes Bethune took ten guineas from him, and that was the only time in his life he truly enjoyed a cards game.

Livingston and Trevelyan had watched the play; near the end Livingston began to laugh. "You'd best stop, Rivington, he'll have your watch and ring! Neat-played, young man!" He patted Bethune's shoulder; Bethune thought he was not ill-pleased to see the toad-eating Rivington beaten.

Rivington got up without a word and walked out of the room. Darcy said, "Whom did you ask not to fleece whom, uncle?"

The next morning when MacDonald came into the office Bethune followed him into the rear room and laid the ten guineas in a golden row on his table.

"You've taken up whoremastering," said MacDonald.

"I only thought you'd like to see the color of Rivington's money."

"Rivington?"

"I took that from him at cards."

"You don't move in such circles," said MacDonald incredulously.

Bethune recounted the story to him.

"God and all his archangels," said MacDonald. "I'd have given five years of life to see it. If I were a Frenchman you'd be kissed soundly, Mr. Bethune!" And he added characteristically, "I was beginning to wonder what you were good for. Now we know!"

Darcy had introduced Bethune among a good many young men of New York society; though Darcy had catholic acquaintance and paid no notice to a man's position or wealth, naturally he had a number of rich friends. Several times Bethune let himself be drawn into a cards game with this one or that, and seldom did he fail to rise heavier in pocket. He asked himself, cynically, why should he not take their money if they were bound on getting rid of it? There was no relief in the depression of business; because of the merchants' pact to refuse purchase from England until repeal of the Stamp Tax, the port was virtually closed, money shorter than ever. But with the wealthy it was a degree of shortness only; these young bloods frequenting Hull's and the York Arms were making do with five pounds where they'd had twenty. When they could gamble a pound or five on one game, why should he not win it?

But he never felt the money was come by honestly; it seemed too easy. He was not by nature a gambler, and when he lost, as occasionally happened, it was unpleasant to hand over the coins. He did not mind winning from any man he disliked. One evening he met Edward Van Steen at the York and deliberately challenged him to play, then took fourteen pounds from him with nothing but satisfaction. He gave three pounds ten of that to the Isaacsons for firewood.

He was still in the house in Cherry Street, but for an extra shilling a week got a small chamber to himself, where he might read as late as he pleased by his own candles.

Since their first meeting he had wanted to ask Darcy about the actress. He scarcely knew why he hesitated; Darcy, so free with confidences, would not mind.

When Bethune at last mentioned her name, Darcy only looked a trifle surprised. "Gay? You're not acquainted with her?"

"No, I saw her at the theater once or twice last year. You were with—with Mrs. Lamont when she came out one evening, I remember."

"Oh, yes," said Darcy. Bethune knew he had far more experience among women than himself; no reason a young man with plenty of money should not have. He shrugged and smiled. "I'll introduce you if you like."

"But I thought—the theaters are closed, and the players—"

"Oh, yes, but most of them take odd jobs in the off-season, you know—it's needful. Gay is at some milliner's, or was the last I heard."

Belatedly Bethune regretted the subject; if Darcy had a liaison with the girl he'd not welcome interference. But Darcy, catching his eye, said with a laugh, "You won't be making a third, James—with me at any rate. Gay's a dear little thing, but I never had her favor that way. One of my failures. I don't mean she's virtuous, but she is particular."

"You're not usually so modest."

"Not me," said Darcy with a grin. "I think her taste poor where I'm concerned! I don't believe she has any protector now. Maybe you'd have better luck. Married? Gay? Good God, no, I'd pity her husband."

Gay Lamont lived at the top of one of the oldest houses in Stone Street, in two cluttered rooms whose windows gave a view over the rooftops of the North River. Darcy appeared to know the house, walked in without knocking, and made up the stair. At the top of three flights he banged on the nearest door. "She's likely in at this hour, if only dressing to go out."

Bethune waited, outwardly calm, angry at himself for feeling embarrassment. This girl, an actress—but, by what Darcy said, expensive—was only for rich protectors. But it would be pleasant only to be close to a pretty girl a little.

He had forgotten how very pretty she was. The door opened and she gave a little cry of welcome at Darcy. *"Mon cher!* How good to see you after so long the time. You neglect me, Dar-cee!" She kissed him on both cheeks, taking his arm affectionately. "And who is this handsome one you bring to call upon me?"—narrowing brown eyes at Bethune.

Darcy gave her a shake. "Drop the curtain, Gay! He's no money at all and besides he's a friend. She's half French," he said to Bethune, "and plays it for every farthing's worth, but born in Boston if you want to know. How do you, Gay?"

"It's too bad of you, Darcy," she said, making a face at him. "I'm dull. I'm being slave-driven at Madame Fortuna's, and most of the company's as bad off. Poor Jeremy driving a wagon and Nicholas—but you're not concerned with it. And your friend? Mm, a nice name, do you come in and sit down." Her natural manner was far more charming, Bethune thought.

"All alone, Gay?"

She laughed. She could not be more than twenty, a dark, quick little thing. Bethune felt large and shy, so maintained calm silence, taking the indicated place beside her on an ancient sagging divan. The room was poorly furnished; she was anything but grandly dressed, in faded muslin. "No fault of mine," she told them impishly. "There was a nice fat major, I expect I was silly not to take him, but there, I'm particular as you call it. I wish I felt different about you, Darcy—you'd be nice to me—but I can't change it, you're more like a brother. Wouldn't your grand relations be cross to hear me say it! —But I can't call you Mr. Bethune." She whisked round to him suddenly. "And you've not said a word, are you tongue-tied or only shy? What shall I call you?"

"You've given him no chance, chatterbox."

Bethune said, "I was sympathizing with the major." She threw up her head to laugh, slipped a hand through his arm and leaned against him a moment like a cat. She was like a little black kitten—all eyes and warmth and softness.

"Oooh, I am going to like you! But I won't call you James,

it reminds me of that horrid manager at the John Theatre. I shall call you—I shall call you Jemmy, how is that?"

"You may call me anything."

"But I've nothing to give you—not even ratafia! That awful woman pays me only five shillings a week—"

"I knew I'd let myself in for expense when I came to see you," said Darcy resignedly. "I'll go and fetch something. You two seem to be getting on famously, you needn't come, James. What d'you want, Gay? Wine, biscuits, cake?"

"Anything, sweetest! Only not sherry wine, I don't like it."

"And besides, port is more expensive," said Darcy, and went off laughing.

Bethune felt awkward alone with her; he was also curious. He had never had any small talk, and was silent; she fidgeted about the room, getting out three glasses, a cracked plate. At last she whirled on him. "You're making me nervous, staring so! What are you thinking?"

"That you're very pretty."

"Oh, that! It's only luck, being born pretty or handsome. I lied when I said you were—but I don't much like handsome men. Vain, they are—awful. What else were you thinking, Jemmy?" She sat down beside him again.

"Wondering. I saw you last year at the theater. You looked— well, I thought an actress would have grand clothes, and—that is, I don't mean—"

"You're nice," she said, smiling. "Does it look that way from the house? I suppose so. The managers're the ones have the money. We don't earn much, mostly, specially in bad times like now. I'm the youngest one in the company anyway. Nick doesn't give me good parts account of Mrs. Jealous Lacy. She's his doxy, and gets all the best bits to do. You should've seen her as Portia— awful—but nobody wants Shakespeare now, too dreary, isn't it? I like being in the theater. Even when we're off like this it feels nice to think I'm an actress. But there's no fortune in it, you know." She had the readiness to confide, the careless candor, of many in her profession. "What do you do, Jemmy? Most Darcy's friends have money. A newspaper? That does sound dull. But you're nice." And as they heard Darcy's step on the stair she leaned closer and added, "You'll come see me again, won't you? Maybe by yourself?"

CHAPTER 9

BETHUNE WENT to see her again, and alone. Quite aside from her prettiness, she fascinated him with her lack of reticence. He had lived nineteen years all to himself; now he knew that he was often lonely, but some quality inside him was a fence all round to keep out prying eyes. About confiding his privacies of emotion, even to Darcy, who was the closest friend he'd ever had, he felt much as he would about bathing naked in public. Gay was so opposite that he wondered if she felt anything deeply, able to voice it so frankly.

Only twenty, she had been an actress with the American Company for five years, since her mother had died. "Of drink mostly, poor dear, but she would do it. I shall never start on that, at least!" She'd had lovers at various times. "But the only one I really loved was Adam. Such a nice boy, I'm glad he was the first. We were playing in Philadelphia then." She chose lovers naturally, for what they could give. "One must have this and that, you know. But it's not so much the money, I'm not like that. Adam never gave me a farthing, and I'd never have taken on Lieutenant Colville or Johnny Van Cortland if I hadn't really liked them."

He could not name her bad. She knew no other standards, and she faced life with a certain courage, a life not always easy and never luxurious. The first time he went alone to see her he went hesitantly, but she welcomed him. He fell into the habit of calling there two or three times a week, and Darcy looked at him quizzically when he excused himself from some meeting.

"Gay, is it? Well, I can't blame you. I wish you better luck than I had!"

He came to Stone Street one spring evening, after delivering the copy to the print shop. He thought that Gay welcomed him for someone to talk to when she was there alone (but she was out a good deal), that she was mercenary if innocently so, and that he was a fool to come laden with any gift for her. But she exclaimed delightedly over the box of little cakes, the bottle of cheap Burgundy wine.

"You *are* sweet to me, Jemmy, but you oughtn't to spend money on me. I know you're as poor as me, or nearly. It's a pity."

"Yes," he agreed, "but why d'you say so just now?"

"If you weren't I shouldn't feel wrong taking things," she said simply. "Besides, I think I've decided to love you for a little while. It'd be nice if you had money, but 'twon't matter, not really. Let's have a feast, Jemmy." She was struggling with the bottle; he came and opened it for her.

"Gay—" He was unsure what she meant by that.

"You would want it, Jemmy? I don't know, I dare say I do because you're different—I never know what you're thinking. Mostly I do know with a man, but I don't with you. You don't talk about yourself." She whirled round the table and kissed him quickly. "Do fetch the plates, that's a dear." He backed away from her and she laughed. "You're not shy?"

It was only, he thought, anything might happen if she did that again. He made no move to the cupboards. He said, "Gay— you don't mean that, I—? I never thought—"

"Of course I mean it, Jemmy." She came close to him again, leaned on him, hands on his shoulders. "You've got to please yourself sometimes, have a little fun. That's all it is, loving, just for a little while, but it's nice when it's there. But maybe you don't want me?"

"Yes," he said, staring down at her, almost afraid to move.

She giggled. "Funny way to show it, Jemmy." He did not realize how hard he was holding her until she gasped and protested.

Some time in the night he woke and lay listening to her slow breath beside him, and Margaret came into his mind. He looked back on that and it was a man looking back on a boy; and the black guilt was still in him too, but more sad than sharp now. No man had not done something he would regret all his life. They had been children. Margaret: he wondered about her.

Gay stirred and murmured his name sleepily. "Jemmy—nice Jemmy. 'S the best part, really, like this—talking, after, mm?"

For a moment it was, and enough to have her close, the female warm scent of her; then it was not and he drew her closer. "I wouldn't say—about the best part." She made a small laughing sound, turning to him willingly.

But Gay had set him thinking about himself. Not by what she said or did, or being there for him. That part of it was as simple as they all took it—any who knew about it—Darcy, or MacDonald (who always knew everything and had said to him only a cynical "Don't go falling in love with her"), or Gay's casual easy-living friends of the theater, to whom he was Gay's new man. Himself—he was troubled these days about himself. He felt all was not right with him.

He was still standing a little way off watching life. There must be something wrong in him when he could not feel close to any, or ever have any certainty of standard. Despite his lack of small talk he grew acquainted easily enough; people seemed to like him. But he knew he gave the impression of being standoffish; Darcy said so frankly. He was no recluse; he liked people, but part of him was both shy and wary of them. He'd matured these years, he knew what he wanted to do; but he was still apart, and he had still not—found out.

Found out? Some clear personal creed to tell him with confidence what he was, why he was here; some answer. Churches offered none; they had a glib answer for multitudes, never the individual. That one cold place in his mind was always talking reason, so he could not be excited over any controversy, seeing all sides whatever his first opinion. Darcy, now, had some radical notions in politics, and was forever (he said) having hot arguments with his uncle. Bethune thought in his place he'd have kept his notions to himself for the sake of peace; but perhaps if he had some strong convictions he would defend them as obstinately. Perhaps until and unless he acquired some one thing for which he'd fight to the death, he would always be floundering in a sea of uncertainty, the watcher, standing apart.

Had he a thing like that? Half-smiling, he reflected that he might do strenuous battle on behalf of the *Courier,* as you might say he had that night against James Rivington.

Sometimes he stayed the night with Gay; he did so that Wednesday. He was tired with a week's work more exacting than usual, and at first, with returning consciousness, he thought he had slept late, that the bells rang for morning service. Then he woke a little further, remembering it was Thursday, not Sunday; he sat up listening to the clamor of the bells, and beginning shouts in the street. It was just past dawn.

Gay stirred and yawned. "What is it? What's all the noise?" she murmured drowsily.

"I don't know. A fire, likely." He went to the window, but saw no hand engines, nothing but people running and shouting excitedly. The curiosity that MacDonald lauded so highly prompted him, cold and sleepy as he was; he said, "I'm going out to see," and reached for his clothes.

Stone Street showed unprecedented traffic for an early hour, and everyone seemed in a hurry. He caught a passing man by the arm. "Here, friend, what's all the excitement?"

"The tax—the Stamp Tax! Parliament's repealed at last! A ship just in—"

"My God!" said Bethune involuntarily. "And it is Thursday!"

The men stared as if he were mad and ran on. Bethune turned
and ran for Maiden Street. It occurred to him then that he had
no idea where MacDonald lived; but he'd be coming in soon
enough. He had a key to the premises now; old Tacy disliked
early rising. But Bethune did not arrive at the office five minutes
before MacDonald.

"Good morning, Mr. Bethune." As if it were nine o'clock
instead of six. "I see you've beat me, but you were closer, I
take it. Commendable! To leave a warm bed—it was warm?"

"Yes, sir, it was."

"And obey the call of duty. I could wish it were yesterday
morning, with time to remake the edition. But it cannot be helped.
I'd hoped to find you here. Do you go and knock Brady up and
tell him to stand to for an extra edition."

"An *extra edition?*"

"Why not? In the form of handbills, sold at a penny each.
We got one out for the big fire of 'fifty-eight, I recall, and this
most certainly warrants another—if it is true. I'm on my way to
the water front to try to trace the rumor and learn the facts.
I will meet you back here in an hour, and we'll set to work.
Make haste."

Brady, invaded at his breakfast, was bitter. "An extra edition!
Does MacDonald think I keep a corps of men at his beck and
call? Very well, very well, but I cannot possibly get to it afore
tomorrow, with the presses all set up for tomorrow's edition.
One page only—I might manage that."

Bethune hared back to the *Courier* office and met MacDonald
on the doorstep, who said, "I saw the captain of the *Duke*—it
seems fairly well substantiated. A great day, Mr. Bethune! That
German in Whitehall bested for once—all bullies are alike—
stand up to them and they back off! Did you see Brady? Just
so." He eyed Bethune with a broad grin. "How would you like to
draft this extra edition?"

"I? To write—" He was overwhelmed.

"Say two columns. You know our policy as to political stands,
but it will be principally a straightforward report, of course."

For more than one reason he would never forget that day.

His first extra edition, and his first article written for the *Courier*. He was disappointed, but not surprised, that Gay was entirely uninterested; it was Darcy who satisfied him with excited congratulations.

The news acted like strong spirits on the New York citizenry. There was a celebration on the Common that evening—fireworks and the military band from the fort. The crowds were nearly hysterical with joy. The repeal would mean the resumption of imports from England, the return of trade into the harbor, the end of this dreary while of stalemate, of waiting for Parliament to take up the glove or refuse the challenge.

They waited three weeks for official confirmation, and when it arrived it made an excuse for another celebration. Among all else there was talk that the theaters would reopen, which was all the interest Gay took in the matter.

New York was experiencing an ardent return to loyalty, and had—aside from the King—another new hero, William Pitt, who had fought for the repeal in the Commons. A group of citizens petitioned the governor for permission to erect statues of the two in the Bowling Green, which was promptly granted; but it would be months before the statues could be executed and set up, and the instigators were impatient. A crowd of volunteers assembled and, in lieu of the statues, planted a stout pole in the Green, to which was affixed a board with the bold inscription: *Geo. III Pitt and Liberty*.

Bethune stopped to watch them at work on his way to dinner. It was there Darcy came on him. "Mr. MacDonald said you'd only left, I hoped to catch you. That's a happy little crowd down there."

"Everyone is certain good times are coming now. Surely there'll be trade again. But what a senseless-looking thing it is, that bare pole. They're calling it the Liberty Pole."

"Now you mention it, 'tis rather ridiculous. Come and have a meal with me. How is Gay, by the way?"

"She's well, thanks."

"Dear thing," said Darcy, smiling. "I needn't say I envy you. The devil of it is," he added frankly, "you'd never think to look at you a girl would think twice about you, James! Dare say it's that awful calmness—still waters, you know—they can't help wondering what's beneath it. If the truth was out, maybe you could outboast me in your conquests. What is it?"

"Nothing." As they started on, he was tempted to tell Darcy how wrong he was. Only one other, only one. Damnation, would he never be rid of it, and of her ghost? He was appalled by his half-impulse to confidence. Margaret was one of the things buried deepest in him; he had thought, all that time ago, she would stay with him, and he had not been wrong. Of late he found himself wondering about her, wondering if all was well with her. Margaret—she was a cipher to him now; he could scarcely recall her features. All that remained of her was her youngness and softness and the terrible trust in her eyes looking up at him. He knew better now what it would have meant for her. They would have got one of the local midwives to do it, likely: kept it secret from everyone, of course. Margaret—she would be eighteen now. He wondered about her.

CHAPTER 10

MARGARET THURSTAN sat motionless before her dressing mirror, staring unseeingly at her reflection, to make a decision. But all that came into her mind was the thing she tried never to think of.

It was long past. She could pretend to forget, but her whole life changed for it, five minutes five years ago. She thought of the day the end finally came, in pain and fright and at last blessed darkness, and the hour she woke alone. She knew and felt more than they guessed. She heard it stirring there, in a corner of the room: the thing all this was about and for. And suddenly, desperately, it was the only thing, and she had somehow got down from the bed and tried to reach it. They found her there on the floor, and scolded and put her back to bed, and the old woman with kind hands and rough voice whisked out of the room with a bundle. Before she even saw, or knew if—

Do not think about it ever again: no use now. But it stayed with her, she thought it would stay until she died. Something of hers, and they had stolen it away. As simple and primitive as that.

She had been obedient; she had seen the reason. By then she knew he was not coming back for her. Foolish, childish—how she had thought that. Reason telling her, later, and never blaming him: how could he come back, a boy, with himself to look to?

She looked over those five years, weighing them, feeling the resentment, the panic, the bitterness all again, yet seeing it all as inevitable. It was not a thing possible to keep secret; her father had done his best, taken the only course, blamed Bethune. But she found that people would always hold the woman more culpable—even at fifteen. And there was inevitably some human satisfaction that the strait-laced Richard Thurstan of Thurstan Hundred should have a daughter who—

The ball at Taggarts' Chance. Such a lovely gown, her first grown-up gown, pale pink taffeta with a sarsenet overskirt and tiny sleeves, all sewn with pearls. Possibly Mama had something to do with that evening's outcome, keeping the other thing in her daughter's mind, so that Margaret expected to be treated so. "My poor darling, when I think how I'd have anticipated this occasion, before! Not that you would ever be as handsome as Honor, but she is somewhat quite extraordinary, and you are truly a pretty child, Margaret, I do not mean to say— People are bound to recall—and the only way we shall ever find a husband for you is to send you away; your aunt has said she's agreeable to be your chaperon, but it is scarce the time to discuss that now. You must only remember to take no notice of any odd looks or remarks, dearest, for you must make some social appearance, however meaningless it may be, here where everyone knows. Simply do not think about it, forget it."

"Yes, Mama." Colorless, obedient, and thinking: Does she really believe it is possible to forget? Could she have forgot one of us if, and only because, she and Papa had not been wed?

That evening—that terrible evening. The *sotto voce* comment she overhead from one of the chaperons: "At least Mistress Thurstan had the taste not to dress her in white!" The older Haines boy pawing at her on the balcony. The other girls' glances, and the way they avoided her in the cloakroom and between dances.

She never made what Mama called a social appearance after that. They could not force her. And they should not force her either to go away with Aunt Belle, to Maryland or the Carolinas, to play the innocent society miss and snare a husband who knew nothing of her past. She did not want to marry, ever. But what else was there for a woman? Nothing. The woman unmarried was a failure, a disgrace to her family. There was nothing anywhere for her. She could bury herself in books to pass the time— what matter if she turned intellectual? She could keep to herself with her solitary walks, or stay shut up in her chamber, but she could not escape the fact that she was constant embarrassment to her family and that there would be, for all the years of her life to come, nothing, nothing, nothing but this.

Better to marry anyone and escape—anyone who would offer for her—and have a life of her own, outside. Anyone, anywhere, away from here.

She looked at the mirror intently now. I am twenty, she thought: not very old; surely I am not so very plain? The serious-looking girl facing her in the glass was perhaps a trifle tall for the fashion, but with a fine figure; she rated her dispassionately. Her best feature was her fine white complexion, needing no cosmetic art; her face was too square for beauty, her nose too short, her eyes too widely spaced. She must do something about her hair—the dark brown curls seemed lifeless. No, not ugly, if no beauty. She thought about Oliver Gerard.

It was the first time she had seen Oliver since Honor died, that morning he came on her walking alone.

"Damme if 'tisn't little Margaret." He reined in the tall chestnut, staring down at her. She stopped because there was nothing else to do, and despite the cool stare she gave him in return, she was conscious of her muddied shoes, her old gown, her carelessly dressed hair.

"Good morning, Mr. Gerard." He was a handsome man: he and Honor had looked so well together, he so dark, she so fair. He was tall and slim, always in elegant clothes, and had dark saturnine features like the profile on a coin; his voice was like cream. He had never lacked anything; his only defeat had been the loss of Honor, when Honor died with her baby last year.

"You're too pretty a girl to be walking alone," he said. She looked him in the eye because she was embarrassed and uncertain.

"Perhaps I prefer to walk alone, Mr. Gerard."

"Maybe so," he said. "Maybe so, Mistress Margaret." He smiled and rode on. The week after that he came to the house for the first time since he had been back in Virginia.

It was, of course, not the usual thing; how could it be? She had never laid eye on him again until Papa told her, embarrassed, as incredulous, she thought, as she was herself.

"You can't have understood him," she said. "He couldn't—"

"Damnation, I know plain English, girl. He had to say it twice before I believed it. I told him it was to be your choice." He looked at her ruefully. "God knows I've never been able to do aught with you." He had used, when she was a child, to love her and pet her, but since she'd been what he called stubborn about going away, about staying shut up over books and making no effort to do something with herself, he was impatient with her. "If you want my advice, which I dare say you don't, you'll take him. Likely never get another chance at a husband, would you?" And with remembered rage, clenching his fists, "God, I wish I'd killed him—that pup, that common little bastard!"

"You'd like me off your hands," she said, not bitterly.

"Damnation, Margaret, it's not that. You're my daughter, child, I'm some fond of you after all. Want to see you happier than you've been, than you might be here. No life for you, mewed up—no friends. You see what I'm getting at."

"I don't understand," she said. "I can't believe that Oliver—"

"Honor is eighteen months dead," he broke in harshly. Honor had always been Papa's favorite; it was painful for him to speak of her. "As to that, I'm no fool, Margaret, nor are you. You might think I'd be angered at it, but I'm not. I'm a practical man myself. Oliver was mad in love with your sister, but she's gone, and he's a young man, only thirty-three. He's the third son, with little expectation, which is why they bought him a commission in the British Army. They've connections in England. And not many girls of any expectation would consider a younger son. He hasn't so wide a choice either. I don't deny he's likely got his eye on Thurstan Hundred—your sister Caroline has no family and won't have now, and her husband's a wealthy man. Oliver knows you'll come in for half the property."

"I don't want it," she said lowly.

"That don't signify either. You're my daughter. Oliver is of good family, a gentleman. There'd be some talk, of course, but he is on leave, and he'll be posted to some station, maybe England, where none would know about you, and be sure he'd never talk! I don't say it's a romantic match, but damme, how many marriages are? And I admit it, you'd be off my mind. I've worried about you. Your mother—" He passed a hand across his face. "Well, that's the matter. I realize it's a surprise to you—was to me, an almighty surprise. But he would not offer unless he liked you, girl, you can depend on that, even if it's no great romance with him. It'd be the best match you could contrive. Will you come and speak with him?"

"No, please, I—I couldn't. I must think about it."

Well, she had been thinking about it for a week, and all of them were growing impatient with her. She must decide sooner or later. Mama: "I must say, Margaret, I cannot understand why you hesitate. I own I may not care for the idea—your sister's husband—but we cannot bring poor Honor back. Twenty is a trifle old to be joining the other *jeunes filles* husband-hunting, and you'd certainly never be offered such a suitable match elsewhere. Oliver is of such good family. And you would be living away, among society who'd accept you."

Yes, living away from Virginia was the strongest inducement. Anything different from her life here—her sterile, meaningless life.

She had told herself she must decide here and now, but she knew it was decided already, that all her hesitation was reluctance to commit herself. She tried to count the times she had seen Oliver Gerard. In Williamsburg when he and Honor were married, but that hardly counted. Afterward he had been stationed up north somewhere. They had been home only twice.

He must be surprised that she hesitated at his offer. Practical: Thurstan Hundred he wanted, the money her father would settle on her; but it was as good a bargain on either side, was it not?

She rose from the mirror, went across the passage to her mother's chamber. Mistress Thurstan's querulous voice came at her from the half-dark. "Who is it? Oh, Margaret, I've one of my headaches. Pray do not raise the curtains."

"Very well, Mama. I've come to tell you I've decided to accept Oliver." Committed now.

"Oh, my love! You do make me happy with this, my dear; I could not understand your hesitation. Much the best choice for you, I'm so happy you have come to see it. We must plan—"

"Yes, Mama." She did not care about the gown, the date, the flowers, but she listened and nodded obediently.

They were married two weeks later, on the first day of the new year 1768, in the village church near Thurstan Hundred. None attended but the two families. The Gerards, she thought, disapproved; their faces were stiff. She felt nothing herself; she had made a bargain, she must keep her side of it.

She had never been alone with him. The day she gave him his answer, in the parlor, both her parents had been there. Stiff, rehearsed words. "I shall be very happy to accept your proposal, sir. . . . You're kind to say so. . . . I am sensible of the honor," and she felt herself flush at the unwitting slip. He had not appeared to notice.

"I believe we'll deal excellently, my dear." He kissed her hand formally. In odd cold panic she thought, But I do not know this man, this strange, dark man I have agreed to marry. He smiled a crooked smile. "Shall you like England, Margaret? Yes, the regiment is ordered home. We shall have to be married very soon."

"That is—quite agreeable."

She was not alone with him until the night. They set out at once for Norfolk where they were to take ship, and stopped the night at an inn. She had made a bargain—but all that next day she struggled with a tide of panic rising in her. Bethune, she thought numbly—but that had been different. She remembered very little of that time, mostly surprise, embarrassment. But it had not been shock and pain like this.

They stopped another night before boarding the ship, and that was as bad; there was something wrong in her, there must be. She was almost grateful for the seasickness that kept him away. But he came in later, when she began to recover. The man she did not know, this stranger who was Lieutenant Gerard of the Royal Artillery, so much more a stranger now in uniform, and her husband, standing over her bed.

"I'm sorry, Oliver—" Even a little effort to speak his name.

He looked down at her, a muscle twitching irritably in his jaw. "They told me you are better."

"Yes, some, but I—"

"But not all that much, hm? I can see you'll be little use to me that way." He laughed. "Evidently Thurstan's tale was true that 'twas rape on the indenturer's part. Somehow I fancied—" he shrugged. "But it's no matter, that's not the reason I wed you. What is it?"

"Nothing," she whispered. So long ago, that first childish romantic feeling! She had nearly forgotten Bethune's features, but she had to bite the retort off: He was not indentured, but a free man.

"So long as you behave yourself and act as hostess for me, that's all I care for. I shan't bother you," he said with another shrug. "I like a trifle more warmth in my bed!" He did not come again to her cabin room.

When she was recovered a little they said she must go up to the deck for air. She dressed carefully, caring once again how she looked, and dispirited as she was could not help loving the russet gown, its soft autumn color, its warmth, the velvet-lined cape to match.

She met him at the head of the companionway. He said, "Well, up and about again! Let us hope you stay that way. But you're pale, and you must learn to dress better, Margaret. That's the wrong color for you, all wrong. When we are in London I'll see you have expert advice on dressing."

He knew it was a new gown, one of those in her wedding gift.

She walked blindly to the rail, clinging to it against the strong salt wind. She thought, it is not I, but he. Small comfort to know it was not her blame.

He was a man who liked to give pain, found some strange pleasure in it, and that was partly the reason he had married her, for the power it gave him. She could never love him; she could never like him. But she had made the bargain, and his part was kept: she was away, traveling toward a new life. She must keep her part as best she might, however difficult it should be: she must be a dutiful wife to him.

PART TWO

CHAPTER 11

B ETHUNE THOUGHT very likely the controversial Assembly election of this year of 1768 had done much to bring on George
Shields' apoplexy. Coupled with the furor of political events of
the last couple of years, it most certainly had not been beneficial,
at any rate. As he waited on the doorstep of the Shields house he
was, however, not thinking so much of its master as of Mistress
Susan. He had not been here since those few evenings four years
ago before Van Steen had cried off and, by what MacDonald
said, set her feeling so sorry for herself she lived like a recluse
in the gloomy mansion.

He would not be here now save that MacDonald was busy
over the making of the week's edition and wanted Shields to see
a copy of his article on the election results. Which would likely
stir up his mind again, but, as MacDonald had said, "They might
as well save their breath, telling George to relax and not argue.
He'll do it to his dying day—he can't help himself."

Bethune fingered his jaw, straightened his neckcloth; he'd come
away in a hurry. "I'm from the *Courier*," he told the manservant
who opened the door. "I'd like to see Mr. Shields."

"I'm not perfectly sure, sir—I'll take you to Mistress Susan."

She received him in the parlor. "Will you not sit down, Mr.
Bethune? I'm afraid I mustn't let you see Father if you've come
to disturb him with politics. The surgeon *told* Mr. MacDonald—"

"Mr. Shields said especially he wished to see Mr. MacDonald's
lead article this week." She had changed little: a plain girl, too
prim. "How is Mr. Shields?"

She frowned. "He is still confined to his chamber. He will
grow so disturbed over politics—do you not think it absurd, Mr.
Bethune? But perhaps you're of like mind, working at the news-

paper. As if it mattered at all!" Her hands were nervous, preening her hair, fingering her rings; she gave him an absent smile. "Talking so about Mr. De Lancey—one of the oldest families in the colony!"

"It's been an exciting election," he said noncommittally, which was an understatement. A wonder MacDonald hadn't had an apoplexy as well; himself, he had leaned to MacDonald's opinion, but there had been trickery on both sides, though most of it by De Lancey's arch-reactionaries, now the strongest party in the New York Assembly. With Rivington's help: stirring up racial jealousies, spreading wild rumors. The odd part was that few of those who grew so hot over the issues had a franchise to cast the vote—though this colony was more lenient than some others, granting the franchise to any man who owned forty pounds' worth of assets.

She sighed. "I dare say he will be ranting at me if I turn you away. But you will try to say nought to excite him?"

He agreed; she rose to take him up to Shields' chamber. Over her shoulder she said, "Naturally I've no knowledge of politics, Mr. Bethune, but what I say is, if a fine gentleman like Mr. De Lancey cannot manage the colony's affairs to the best advantage, indeed who could? Father calls me a Tory."

Bethune made some polite answer.

Shields, propped in bed with a tasseled nightcap on, shook Bethune's hand and seized the manuscript sheets eagerly. "How do I feel? Never better, my boy, never better! Surgeons are all damned fools. Case of indigestion is all. Let's see what Robert's giving them. Ah, good, splendid, that's the business! 'This blow to the hearts of our hopes for a firm stand against the tyrant—'" At the thought of the De Lancey party in control of the Assembly his face purpled and he pounded a fist on the blankets. "Damned bastardly King's men—they'll have us under the heel of Parliament yet!"

"You'd best not get so excited, sir."

"Damme, who's excited? Damme, Mr. Bethune, what man with red blood in him would not be excited at such crooked work? A foul election, I am positive, but try to prove it! What beats me is

how a fair-minded liberal like Philip Livingston could go over
to De Lancey—class prejudice, and I never thought he would
stoop so low—tchah! Only fear of the rich merchants controlling
the Assembly! And a damnation better job they'd do! Now we
shall have these bootlicking Tories appeasing Parliament all down
the line. Tchah!" said Shields violently. "Reach me my snuffbox,
Mr. Bethune—thankee." He took snuff, sneezed less violently,
and employed his handkerchief. "I'd never've thought it of Philip
Livingston. The entire damned Assembly gone Tory."

"Well, it's rather an empty victory, sir. The Assembly is suspended from authority."

"Tchah! You're not thinking it'll stay suspended?" said
Shields. "It was a good liberal-minded firm-handed Assembly
that got itself suspended; the governor will soon enough restore
this one to favor." He sat back, looking tired. "Very well, tell
Robert I approve it. He might have made it stronger yet, but
it'll do, it'll do. And tell him—Mr. Bethune, you're still here?—
tell him if he requires any money—he may call on me for a
bank order at any time."

"Yes, sir, I will." As he came away Bethune reflected that
Shields had aged; the man must fancy this was a couple of years
back when the *Courier* was barely supporting itself. The merchants
might complain that even with the repeal of the Stamp Tax and
resumption of commerce with England and the West Indies, the
new import taxes held profits down. But there was no denying that
business was better, and the political controversies meant new life
for the newspapers. Even though expenses had risen, on account
of the new higher tax on paper, rising subscription lists balanced
it. Everyone was concerned with the news these days.

He looked back to that joyous celebration over the Stamp
Tax repeal: everyone so certain their troubles were settled! It
had been one thing after another ever since, all making news for
writing. Parliament had levied new import taxes, perhaps as
punishment for that insurrection, and issued a proclamation in-
sisting on the King's right to tax his colonies. The furor over that
had no sooner died down than several regiments of British regulars arrived and the Assembly flatly refused to subsidize their

quartering in the city: which was what led to its suspension. The new Tory Assembly would probably have its power restored fast enough. Then more uproar over the taxes: the new revenue was intended to pay the royal officials of the colonies, and the Sons of Liberty (both actual and spiritual) cried indignantly, "Bind our rulers, will you! A deal of impartial justice we'll have if the justices owe allegiance to a paymaster!" To Bethune's cautious thought, that was needless suspicion. But the Boston men, who seemed to carry chips on their shoulders anyway, had again argued for a nonimportation pact, and a limited one was in effect now.

Well, his opinion mattered little; his work was to report the news. For himself, he could look back on the past two years with some satisfaction. Materially, he reflected, he was in an enviable position for a man of twenty-two.

He'd nominal charge of the office now; Tacy's sight was failing, and he had been pensioned off, Shields feeling sorry for the old man. MacDonald had hired two clerks to handle the volume of business Bethune had once managed alone; Bethune did all the copying, and was occasionally allowed to write an article himself. He had three pounds a week, plus extra pay for the writing he did; he picked up more than that at the cards tables. He had invitations from a good class of society by virtue of Darcy's introduction, and he'd made a few friends: Hector Kennedy, John MacNamara, Francis Walden, others. He was not, of course, favored as a guest by any matron with daughters to marry off, being an impecunious clerk, but he found formal society events dull in any case.

In fact, the only regret he might have was Gay. He smiled a little, thinking of her. He supposed four months was about as long as Gay could stay by anyone. He had never been in love with her, and they had parted cheerfully enough when the company moved on to Boston that summer.

To Darcy's suggestion Bethune had replied, "Thanks very much, Darcy, I don't care to risk a professional house, and if I did I know where to find one as well as you."

"Not this one, you wouldn't. Very exclusive place, I assure you! You'll find no French pox at Mrs. Wise's house."

"But what an appropriate name for the madam of a whorehouse! The commercial transaction doesn't appeal."

Glancing at the sun now, he hastened his stride back to the city. It was Wednesday noon, and he'd still to make a fair copy of MacDonald's lead article. He would stop and have luncheon at the Queen's Head before returning to Maiden Street.

CHAPTER 12

IT WAS a few days after that he had indirect news of Susan Shields, from Darcy. Dropping into the office in late afternoon to seek Bethune's company at dinner, Darcy showed him a scented sheet of lady's note paper with a few lines of angular script in its center—an invitation to a dinner party.

"She's evidently entering society again, having come to her senses to realize she's no chance of getting a husband while she mopes alone at home."

"Evidently," agreed Bethune. He was uninterested, beyond his abstract pity for the girl, and that made him add, "I'll wish her luck. She's had small chance at happiness despite Shields' fortune. Will you go?"

"I may as well," said Darcy, giving him a curious look. "But surely it was her own false pride that—"

Bethune had turned to the clerks, dismissing the subject. "If there should be applications for delivery work, remember the new ruling—none under eight years, preferably nearer ten. We need at least five more boys, but reliable ones." Which was just what most of them were not, even at two shillings a week.

Haagen grinned cheerfully and said, "Aye, Mr. Bethune, we keep de eye to de office so it don't run off."

Haagen admired Bethune, who was his own age. The other clerk, Ingalls, was older and inclined to resent a young man as superior.

Whatever the cause, Mistress Susan, over the next few months, indeed showed evidence of regaining her social senses. Bethune seldom went out in a social way; as with most newsmen, his favorite haunts were the coffeehouses, and he had no invitations from her, nor did he see her elsewhere. It was Darcy, as always popular among society matrons, who gave him news of Susan's successful relaunching into a round of entertainments.

"Unless I miss my guess she's waging a campaign for a certain wealthy widower."

"Good luck to it," said Bethune, not looking up from his work.

Darcy, perched on the corner of the table and idly leafing through the advertising copy for the next edition, grinned at him. "She's setting her sights high, being a snob; doubtless we couldn't compete. All the same, there's a tidy little fortune, James. Not interested?"

"I? God forbid."

"Nor I. Both of us too fastidious, perhaps, to seize the main chance! So some middle-aged merchant wanting to renew his youth will add Shields' wealth to his coffers. Ah, well. What in heaven's name are shaloons?"

"I've no idea, why?"

"It's this advertisement. It's in Greek or somewhat, just listen. 'Boiled and common camblets, single and double alopeens, broad and narrow shaloons, durants, florettas, hair grazets, ducapes, stay galloon and twist—' I must say that sounds like a dance step, don't it? Oh, of course, it is female stuffs, I do know what calimanco is. Are you not nearly finished with that? I'm starving."

Bethune laughed and put down his pen. "I'll get my coat."

He heard veiled mention from other sources of Mistress Susan's ladylike pursuit of the widower. He thought she had chosen well; there would be little chance of her acquiring a younger, more romantic husband, at her age. After which, hearing nothing of her for some time, he forgot the whole matter.

Shields did not appear at the office the rest of that year. MacDonald reported his condition now aggravated by a severe attack of gout. One morning early in the new year of 1769 MacDonald came in looking preoccupied, nodded a short good-morning to the clerks, and announced, "Mr. Bethune, I will see you, please." He went into the rear room; Bethune followed. "Shut the door." He stood before the window, back to Bethune, hands in pockets, as if absorbed in the outlook on the dreary yard. "I have just come from seeing George."

"How is Mr. Shields?"

"He is not well," said MacDonald. He turned and fetched out the bottle of French brandy always in the cupboard. "Sit down, Mr. Bethune, I've somewhat serious to say." He had never in all these years dropped formality; perhaps he'd begun it half-mocking to the boy, maintained it, of habit, with the man. Bethune liked MacDonald, admired him, respected him. Affection? MacDonald was another like himself, who was always at arm's length: the fence all round. Likely MacDonald was as lonely behind his fence as Bethune, but there it was.

"Yes sir?" He accepted the glass, sat down.

"George—" MacDonald sighed and shrugged. "He's failed. I saw Dr. Humphries. Apoplectic stroke, they know all too little about it, I gather. His mind is slowed, he is not the man he was."

"I rather thought when I saw him—"

"Yes. I doubt very much if he will be contributing actively to the *Courier* again." MacDonald looked at him over the glass thoughtfully. "You and I will be managing the *Courier,* Mr. Bethune. Odd how matters come out. I scarce thought, all those years back—nearly six, is it not?—but you have done well, you've justified my predictions. I said you had it in you. Unseasoned, of course—but you're shaping, you're shaping. In time you will be a competent editor. That is what you'd wish?"

"Yes. Yes, it is."

"I take it you're serious about that. The *Courier* was founded sixteen years ago, and in that time Shields and I have hired a good many underlings—none with us as long as you, except old Tacy, of course. You've been quick to learn, and interested. You've some talent."

"Thank you, sir."

"We'll get in another clerk to take over the copying, and you will assume some of the routine responsibilities. You feel capable?"

"Yes, certainly, I'll do my best."

"It's not my choice to take in a managerial assistant so young, but you I know. I think I can count on you more than some strange lawyer, say. It is all good experience for you. And you need not expect any rise of wages at once," he added sardonically.

"I hadn't," lied Bethune equably. "I'll do my best for you, Mr. MacDonald."

He was kept too occupied from that time on to give much thought to anything but the *Courier*. He had not suspected there were so many finicking small details to publishing a newspaper. Much of his new responsibility lay with the accounts; he had never been quick at figures but was forced to practice mathematics now in making up the accounts for MacDonald.

The printer contracted so far in advance to print so many editions; he furnished his equipment, but the paper was supplied by the publisher. Several headaches were spared the publishers who hired printing done, for all printing tools—presses, type, and ink—were English-made, and since cost and tax prevented the importation of new presses, most of those in use were old, the type badly worn; ink had risen in price because of the new tax on dyes. Brady told Bethune most printers had experimented with locally made ink, concocted of berry juices, but it was unsatisfactory, being inclined to fade. Paper came under the new tax also; English paper now was priced at ten pounds the ream, and like other items under the Townshend tax must all be smuggled in because of the nonimportation pact the Boston men had forced on the colonies. There were paper mills in New York colony; the *Journal* maintained one of its own across the Hudson River; but rags were scarce for their supply and the paper made in them was only slightly less costly than that imported.

Then there was the carrying tax to keep straight. The attempt to levy a direct tax on newspapers had ceased with the Stamp Tax repeal. Now each subscriber must pay the carrier an extra sum: ninepence a year for a distance of fifty miles or less, one and six up to one hundred miles. It was a policy of the *Courier* to pay the carriage in New York and charge it to the subscribers in addition to the fee; of its eighteen-hundred-odd regular subscribers nearly a hundred resided outside the city, a few as far away as Maryland and Delaware.

The yearly subscription fee was eighty shillings, and all the subscribers' accounts needed to be kept separately; some were paid monthly, some quarterly, some annually. The *Courier's* printing contract with Brady guaranteed a weekly edition at eight pounds each, and a year's editions required some seven hundred reams of paper. The advertising fees brought up the profits considerably, however bitterly MacDonald complained of the space that advertising robbed them of. All told, even with its increased expenses under the new tax, the *Courier* earned a comfortable profit, upwards of six hundred pounds a year after expenses; but that was dependent mainly on its subscription list.

Bethune struggled with the accounts grimly, wishing he had paid more attention to the rector's teaching of mathematics. It was not unusual for him to sit in the office past midnight over the monthly totals, hunting for the lost halfpenny or twopence which spoiled the balance of the accounts. On the first of every month, when he presented the journal for the critical inspection of MacDonald—who understood mathematics as clearly as he did the English tongue—Bethune felt he had accomplished a minor miracle. Eventually it grew easier for him, but it was never a task he approached with any enthusiasm.

His closer connection with the inner mechanisms of the *Courier* gave him a deeper sense of identification with the paper and with MacDonald. Since his first days as a clerk in this office he had known this work was what he wanted to do; he felt now he was nearer his ambition. In a sense he was still a clerk, even though allowed to draft copy now and then, but there were times he felt—sitting alone there late, with the one candle casting a pool of shadow round the table—that the *Courier* was his paper; and he did not begrudge the extra time and effort he gave to it at no increase in wages. He was content as never before in his life; perhaps by reason of hard work, his vague personal dissatisfaction grew less as time went on.

MacDonald came in, laid off his coat, went purposefully to the cupboard and poured himself a stiff tot of brandy. "Will you take a guess, Mr. Bethune, what those whoresonly Tories of the Assembly have done now? Colden!" he exclaimed violently, making an imprecation of it. "When this is known—"

"Why, what's occurred?"

"Not that it is all Colden—Moore would likely have done the same." Sir Henry Moore had died a few weeks before, and the lieutenant governor filled his office. "Colden met with them today—I picked up the news just now—and requested funds for the garrisons, and they have voted him two thousand pounds! Two—thousand—pounds!"

Bethune sat back, chewing the end of his quill thoughtfully. "You don't say. There are a good many will cavil at that, right enough."

"Willful blindness! They refuse to admit they cannot act for the majority. There'll be trouble, we can depend on that. With the new troops arriving—"

"Likely they'll have the pole down again," said Bethune. MacDonald laughed, pouring more brandy.

"That would be the least of it! We shall have some uproar over this. I mean to flay them with my lead this week, I tell you!" He looked at Bethune sharply. "You're never excited, but this—"

"Oh, I quite agree, sir. They'd no business to do such a thing. But it's understandable. The Assembly is made up of men who all their lives have merely discounted any of the lower classes. God Himself could not make them see that common men have aught to say that's worthwhile hearing. And they could never be brought to believe, either, that the common groups have any power to force opinion." He shrugged. "Blindness, yes, but there's little use in swearing or naming it intentional malice."

In protest of the Assembly's action, mobs milled about the City Hall, accomplished some aimless destruction; as Bethune had foretold, there was another attempt to fell the Liberty Pole.

The fact that the pole had been raised in honor of the King and Parliament was all but forgotten; it had instigated a bitter feud between the troops and citizens. The very August after it was first raised, some unknown hand cut it down, and the rumor spread that the destroyers were soldiers from the garrison across the way. Indignant hands raised a second pole, which stood three weeks before being felled; the feud was open now, and the third pole planted stout. It stood six months, but eventually came under the (alleged) ax of the mischievous troops. Whereupon the Sons of Liberty had set up the present pole, girded with iron and surrounded with iron palings, which had thus far defied the destroyers' hand. In consequence of this latest enormity of the Assembly, there was an abortive attempt on the pole, but it stood firm.

Despite the general temper of the populace, however, which implied support of the nonimportation pact, that support continued largely theoretical; many goods were smuggled in and found ready buyers. There had been rumors that the latest tax was to be repealed soon in any case, so what harm? It was too much to expect that New Yorkers (or residents of the other colonies) should do without their tea, their fine stuffs for stylish clothes, glass for their windows, other luxuries—all that they were accustomed to. It annoyed Bethune—who had come cautiously round to acceptance of most of the patriots' views—that such double-dealing should exist; MacDonald cynically referred him to human nature.

"They're ardent as you please about ideological rights, but when the theory touches their pocketbooks or their animal appetites, theory will go hang. There's Scriptural precedence, is there not? I forget the exact wording—let not the right hand know what the left doeth, is it? As you grow older and, let us hope, wiser, Mr. Bethune, you will discover that men are seldom as virtuous as they should be—but never as venal as they might be, either. Surprising veins of good and bad in the worst and best of us."

CHAPTER 13

O N NEW YEAR'S DAY of 1770 Shields suffered another stroke
which resulted in partial paralysis of one side and confined him to his chamber indefinitely. MacDonald, returning from
a visit there, said to Bethune with an actual shudder, "God's
fingerbones, I can imagine no worse hell on earth than to be confined prisoner by one's own body! He's to have a man-nurse to
look to him. I do not think he is capable of understanding aught
to do with business, no. Carruthers was there." He added thoughtfully, "The girl seems to have a head on her shoulders for business,
she spoke up quite sharp once or twice."

Bethune said absently, "I heard Mistress Susan missed her aim
with that widower she was after. Darcy said—"

"Let us not be so common," said MacDonald with a grin. "She
did indeed. I dare say she was too eager, and frightened him off."

Bethune might not have remembered that little exchange but
for what occurred the following week. He had dined with Darcy
at Hull's, and accepted an invitation to join a game with Francis
Walden and two others afterward; Darcy sat by confusing the
play with humorous talk. Bethune had wone a guinea from Walden,
and their second hand was just played when several new customers entered, talking loudly of a riot in progress.

"It's the Liberty Pole again—the redcoats had no notion Sears
had set a guard. There was a pitched battle an hour since, and
I heard one man killed. Damnation nonsense, I call it, all over
a bare pole."

"Did the soldiers get it down?"

"I did not hear," answered another of the newcomers, "but by all accounts they tried strenuous."

"Nonsense is the word for it," agreed someone else, and Bethune had his mouth open to opine mildly that it was only a symbol of larger issues when the house door opened again and the clerk, Haagen, entered, looking about anxiously.

"Mr. Bethune—Gott be thanked I am finding you! It is de *baas,* sir, you must come—"

"What is it?" He'd never seen the normally stolid Dutchman so excited.

"De *baas,*" repeated Haagen, "Mr. MacDonald, sir, he is hurt bad. I didt not know what to do—he says to get you—"

"Tell me as we go." He dropped the cards, got up, reached for his coat. Not until they were in the street did he realize he had said no word of apology to his companions. But they would understand, Darcy would explain. And then he saw Darcy was at his side, struggling into his own coat.

"What has happened?"

"Oh, Mr. Bethune, it is bad, in de fighting at de Liberty Pole it was, I didt not know he was dere, but he would be—" Yes; MacDonald seemed to know of any newsworthy event intuitively, and was on the scene as quick as his legs could carry him. "I come up, hear all de noise, and dere is men fighting on de green— two, t'ree hundred, and some have clubs." Haagen's English was sliding under agitation. "Den I see a man on de ground, and dey say he is hurt—and I look, and it is de *baas,* sir. At first he look dead, I didt not know—at de office I have tooken—"

"Have you got a surgeon? Darcy, make haste and fetch one— Dr. Humphries, in Arundel Street. God, it's across the city! If you know one closer—"

"Yes, I'll do so." Darcy vanished down Wall Street at a run; Bethune turned into Maiden Street with fear knocking at his ribs.

The Samaritans who had carried MacDonald up from the Bowling Green had laid him on the counter in the fore-office; Haagen had found a blanket to spread over him. At first Bethune's apprehension receded; MacDonald's eyes were open and he greeted

him in his usual tone. "You missed a warm little riot, Mr. Bethune. As you see, I ventured a trifle too close to it. Had my
legs knocked from under me by an excited citizen with a club
near the size of the Liberty Pole itself."

"I've sent for a surgeon, sir. Have you any pain? Is there
aught I—"

"You may fetch me some brandy if you will." MacDonald was
pale, but otherwise looked quite himself. "Oddly enough, I've no
pain at all, though it was the devil of a blow, God's teeth it was!"

Bethune went for the brandy, but when he came back Mac-
Donald had lost consciousness. They hung over him anxiously
until a breathless Darcy arrived with one Doctor Vickers, somewhat irritated at being haled out on such a cold night. When he
saw MacDonald he was all gravity, and set about an examination
at once. At last he straightened, replaced the blanket, and came
to where they waited across the room.

"It is difficult to say, Mr.—Bethune? Yes—servant, sir. He's
no bones broken, but there appears to be a deadness in the lower
limbs. For the moment he should be put to bed and kept warm.
I'd advise you secure a hackney and convey him to his home, if
the distance is not too great. I will make another examination
there."

Bethune had no idea where MacDonald lived. It was curious
how little he knew of MacDonald's personal life, after working
so close with him for seven years. MacDonald had never mentioned
a wife, never volunteered any personal talk about himself. He
hesitated. "Well—"

"Mr. Bethune." He went to MacDonald at the faint voice.
Sweat glistened on MacDonald's brow, where the lank black hair
beginning to streak with gray fell away from its confining ribbon.
"Ann Street," said MacDonald, shutting his eyes. "The fifth house
in from William." Bethune got a hackney from the nearest stable;
they found a board and carried him out on it.

The indicated house was one of the oldest in the old street,
narrow; a knock brought a woman to the door.

"Mr. MacDonald resides here?"

"Yes, but he's not home—"

"No, there has been an accident, I—" But she had seen the others lifting MacDonald from the carriage; she brushed by Bethune and ran down the step. They brought MacDonald in and she indicated the nearest room silently. An oddly comfortable room, with a carpet, a couple of paintings on the wall, two doors leading to other rooms.

"Mrs. MacDonald—"

"I'm Mrs. Hicks," she said in a flat voice. She was a plain woman of forty-odd, slim as a girl, decently dressed in modest gray, her one charm a mass of light brown hair curling about her thin face. "What happened to Robert?" Her accent was faintly common, with overtones of London.

It was MacDonald who answered. "A slight accident, Dorcas. I think, Mr. Bethune, you and Mr. Trevelyan had best take me into the bedchamber where Doctor Vickers may get about his work. The first door. I apologize for the nuisance, I shall have the use of my legs shortly, but meanwhile—"

The woman darted before them to turn down the coverlet; she leaned over MacDonald, fear in her eyes.

"Pray do not be frightened, Dorcas, I am quite all right. A slight accident only."

"If you will all wait in the other room," said the physician, opening his bag.

"I'm staying," said the woman.

"My dear madam, I—"

"I'm staying."

It was some while before Bethune found out anything about the woman Dorcas; neither she nor MacDonald was given to confidences. It was only of the necessity to explain her presence that MacDonald told him the bare fact: that she was wed, but had left her husband. Bethune gathered that their liaison was of many years' duration. With everyone but MacDonald she was a silent, wary creature; Bethune never heard any exchange of endearments between them—those were in her eyes when she looked at him. And that was all he ever knew of Dorcas. He never asked; she was MacDonald's property.

She did not emerge from the chamber with the physician. Doctor Vickers came out clasping his bag. He asked, "You are members of the family?" Bethune explained; the physician raised his brows, looking as if he considered the radical MacDonald of the radical *Courier* better out of commission. "I see. Well, I can tell you little enough, and that not pleasant. The blow was across the lower spine. I do not believe it is fractured, but I fear some damage has been done. At the moment there is complete paralysis below the waist. That may pass; we cannot tell. I've seen a few similar cases where the paralysis was permanent, and only time will show whether Mr. MacDonald will recover of that or not."

"What is your opinion?"

"I do not think you had best count on it. I will see him again. Of course you are at liberty to call in a consulting surgeon. We must only wait and see."

When he was gone the woman came out. Bethune said he would remain the night.

"There's no need, I'll look to Robert."

"I think I had best—"

"There's no need." She opened the door; they were all but pushed out. They started in silence down Ann Street.

After a time Darcy asked, "Where are we going?"

"The nearest tavern. This is one time I need a drink. It will kill him, Darcy, it will kill him. Always so active a man. He cannot bear to be dependent on anyone for anything." He remembered then what MacDonald had said about Shields.

The paper— He thought, It is Tuesday. He would think about the paper tomorrow.

He went to Ann Street first in the morning; the woman refused to admit him. "Robert doesn't want to see anyone." He could not move her from that. He went to the office; there was the edition to get out. Fortunately most of the actual writing was done. He corrected some of the copy; Darcy came in and told him that damned woman was letting no one in to see MacDonald. "I know," said Bethune. "She'll let me in next time or I'll know why." He went back to Ann Street in the afternoon.

"You can't see him, sir." She did tell him that the physician had come, bringing a colleague with him.

"Mrs.—Mrs. Hicks," he said patiently, "Mr. MacDonald will want to see me, he will be anxious about the edition, I must—"

"No." She looked at him; her mouth worked. "He told me I wasn't to come near, nor let anyone. He asked the doctors—and no lies, he said, the truth, good or bad. I wanted to stay, but he wouldn't let me. I'll call when I want you, he says, leave me alone. He looked— But I can't let you in, sir."

He was defeated; he was frightened. He knew MacDonald. MacDonald with his fence to shut out anyone coming too close: MacDonald touchy as a cat about the hand on his shoulder, even of a friend; MacDonald the wanderer of the city, to whom news-gathering was the breath of life, and the busyness of the coffee-houses, the streets, the crowds. The woman looked at him dumbly. He wanted to ask her plainly, was there anything in that room MacDonald might use as a means to—? But the words stopped in his throat; he came away without speaking.

On Thursday morning he returned to the house, afraid of the news he might hear. The woman let him in. "Excuse me, sir, would you be Mr. Bethune?"

"Yes—"

"He wants to see you. I was to send to the office. None other, he said." She indicated the door.

MacDonald was in bed, propped against the pillow. He looked older, thinner, and tired; the streaks of gray in his hair seemed to have grown wider overnight. But his eyes were clear and cold, and he nodded at Bethune in his usual curt manner. "Good morning, Mr. Bethune. Sit down."

"Good morning, sir." He took the chair by the bed. "The edition is out, sir."

"Good." A glint of humor in the eyes. "Any other man I know would first have asked for my health. Thank you, Mr. Bethune."

"I knew you would want to know. How do you, sir?"

"I am told," said MacDonald, "that it's not likely I'll ever be on my feet again. One would not think a single blow—no pain or sickness—but there it is. They have gone over me a dozen times and given me long Latin phrases to impress me, and they say there have been cases when the paralysis passed off gradually." His tone was quite without emotion; he reached to the bedside table, selected a segar from a box, and struck fire from the tinderbox. "But I am not to hope for it. The spine, they tell me, is a delicate thing. Otherwise, for a man of forty-nine years I am in excellent health." He smiled. "I mean to remain that way."

"Yes," said Bethune meaninglessly.

"When I received this intelligence, I realized there was some planning to be done. Therefore I had everyone turned away while I shut myself up here to think."

Not only that, thought Bethune. He wanted no prying eyes to witness his Gethsemane. He had lain here in the darkened room alone and passed his purgatory in decent solitude; fought the battle, taken the decision.

"Is there anything I can fetch you, sir?" he asked suddenly.

"You will oblige me by not treating me as an invalid," said MacDonald. "If there is anything I want I will tell you. Yes, you may fetch me a dish for these ashes—there on the chest. It is, after all, the least important part of my body that is affected; I have still my faculties and my writing hand. I apologize for the extra annoyance I must make you henceforward."

"That's quite all right, sir."

"I will tell you what you must do. You will get in another clerk at once, to replace Haagen. Rather a mistake, Haagen—willing and cheerful enough, but his English is apt to be weak. He is receiving nine shillings a week. You will offer him twelve to come to me. He will attend me during the day, wherever I may be. You will go at once to a good carpenter and commission him to build me a chair upon wheels. Also a writing board without legs, which will be more convenient for me to use. With a drawer in it. Perhaps you had best take notes of these, Mr. Bethune."

"I'll remember."

"You will next take steps to inform Mr. Shields of this development—if he is able to see and understand you. Send Haagen to me here at once. You will inform me as to the carpenter's bill. I will give you a bank order, also a note to the bank manager. You will be attending to the banking from now on."

"Yes, sir."

"When you return here, bring me a sampler copy of this edition."

"Yes, certainly." There was dismissal in MacDonald's tone; Bethune rose.

"Just one moment, Mr. Bethune."

"Yes?"

"You will be responsible for a deal more of managerial affairs now. Do not suppose you are either indispensable or cleverer than you are. I am still the *Courier*—and I mean to remain that too."

"Yes, sir. I never thought otherwise. I'll attend to all that and be back here this afternoon."

"Just one moment," said MacDonald again when he was at the door.

"Yes?" He turned. MacDonald was not looking at him, but at the half-smoked segar in his fingers.

"Thank you, Mr. Bethune," he said softly, "for not reviling me with your sympathy."

CHAPTER 14

IT SEEMED genuinely to surprise MacDonald that so many sought him out to express sympathy. He hated condolence, but he had not thought, Bethune guessed, that he was so well known or well liked in New York. Sears came to see him. The *Journal* carried a long indignant article about MacDonald's injury. A great many subscribers called personally or wrote letters, and brought gifts—some useless or absurd, but showing good will.

Bethune did not think Shields had taken in what he told him about MacDonald; the old man's mind wandered. He had kept muttering, "Robert, Robert—what did you say? What's happened to Robert?" until Bethune came away.

Haagen was content with his new duties; he had great admiration for MacDonald. Except in the most inclement weather, he got MacDonald out, in the heavy wheeled chair, every day to the Merchants' House or some other, later to the office; he learned to anticipate his charge's desires and excuse MacDonald from the necessity of asking for attention. Except for the chair, Bethune found it difficult to realize that MacDonald was incapacitated; he was so much still MacDonald of the *Courier*. But it put more responsibility on himself, though MacDonald still did most of the writing.

MacDonald did not for some time accept the permanence of his state. The physicians advised now daily massage, now a succession of medicines, now elevating the extremities; he followed their advice faithfully, however tedious or futile it seemed. Never did he descend to self-pity, but he frequently grew irritable at his inability to be out mingling with the crowds when any newsworthy event occurred. Reports of facts were dry; but he made do with them.

"The true irony is that it was in a fight over the Liberty Pole," he said to Bethune. "Liberty!" In that affair the pole had stood; but a fortnight later the soldiers succeeded in cutting it down. Sears promptly purchased a lot of ground near the Bowling Green and caused a new pole to be erected, surrounded with a stout iron fence and girded with iron itself, a great tower of a pole nearly sixty feet high, with a twenty-foot mast at the top. This bid fair to stand indefinitely; not that it gave MacDonald any satisfaction for his injury.

Perhaps because they were alike Bethune understood MacDonald; and however he might admire his rigid will, his refusal to yield to what would be a crushing defeat for a weaker man, he never spoke any of that to MacDonald: it would have been intolerable effrontery. The relations between them were unchanged, as formal as before. Only once did Bethune fail to treat him with the respect due a senior and a brilliant man; that was in the March following the accident.

It was a Tuesday evening; Bethune was working late in the office over the monthly accounts. He had only finished and was in the act of donning his coat when Darcy came in. "I saw your light—I am just on the way home. Are you leaving?" They came out, and heard faint shouts, saw a glow in the sky to the north.

"That's a fire." Bethune quickened his steps; a fire was news. He could hear the rumble ahead of the hand-engines coming out, likely from the Hand-in-Hand Volunteer Company's place on Dock Street.

"And a bad one, by all the light. I've been at the Queen's Head, the other way, or I'd have passed it. Somewhere about the Golden Hill, it looks. Some fine houses up there. No, 'tis farther west than Golden Hill—"

"William Street," said Bethune. "Let's go up." They had walked another hundred yards, coming into a few excited groups hurrying in the same direction, before he exclaimed suddenly, "It's not William—it's Ann Street!" and he began to run.

Ann Street was one of the oldest in the city, narrow and lined with old wooden houses, a tinderbox. When they got to the mouth of the street on William, they found a crowd about two hand-engines manned by a few sweating volunteers who had pulled them up but were making no move toward the fire. The blaze had apparently started at the other end of the street, and had already engulfed three houses which were streaming flame to the night sky: the old wood burned fiercely. One of those alight, he saw, was but one house removed from MacDonald's. He seized hold of the nearest volunteer.

"In God's name, get the engines in! We will all help—"

The man shook his head. "Can't be done, sir, we've tried. The street's too narrow, we can't get 'em in and if we should we'd never get 'em turned to be any use. The captain's lining a brigade with buckets."

Residents of the nearer houses were bundling out, clutching

belongings; the men with the help of others in the crowd carried
out furniture. Many were in various states of undress. The din was
frightful—wailing children, barking dogs, shouts and screams from
the crowd as the first roof fell in. The house next to MacDonald's
had caught now. Haagen was not with MacDonald at night; he was
alone with the woman.

A brigade with buckets would be no use at all against fire so well
started. Bethune pushed through the crowd and ran down the
street; he heard Darcy shout to him to come back. Here he could
feel the heat; the street was no more than four yards wide, with
houses tightly packed on each side looming over it—and the
whole street was going. He got to the house just as the next roof
crashed in, and found the door bolted; but the warped wood gave
readily to his shoulder.

The woman Dorcas had got MacDonald into his chair, but it
was heavy for her to push; she had managed to get it as far as the
little parlor. She had a coat over her night rail and all that fine
brown hair fell in a mass about her shoulders. She looked at
Bethune and her mouth moved but he could not hear her words.

"Mr. Bethune," said MacDonald, raising his voice above the din
outside, "I wish you will remove Mrs. Hicks first, and return for
me. If there is time I should much appreciate your rescuing the
small walnut cabinet in the bed chamber, it contains—"

"To hell with the cabinet," said Bethune, and picked him up
from the chair; he was surprisingly light even for such a small
man. "Come along," he ordered the woman.

"The chair—"

"We can buy another chair," he told her irritably; arguing over
that! He got MacDonald over his shoulder in easier position and
went into the street again, the woman following. Already flame
was licking at the step, and the next house was a shell of fire.
Halfway up the street men met them, took MacDonald from him;
he saw him carried to the step of the nearest house on William,
the woman at his side. The futile bucket brigade was at work. He
saw that MacDonald was fully dressed but wore no coat, and the
night was chill; he started to remove his own, but Darcy came

up and offered his. "I am not," said MacDonald, "an invalid,
Mr. Trevelyan," but they got him into the coat.

Darcy asked in a low voice, "Are you hurt, James?"

"No, certainly not."

"I should have gone with you. I never thought I was a
coward—"

"Don't be a fool, Darcy."

The woman sat beside MacDonald; she had brought nothing
out, of clothes or any possessions. "All your manuscripts, Robert.
All your manuscripts."

Seventeen houses went up that night, half the street, and others
were damaged. A few of MacDonald's belongings were reclaim-
able; Bethune, Darcy, and Haagen settled him in a newer house,
half of which he leased, in John Street nearer the office.

For some reason the incident—in Bethune's mind it was no
more—had shaken Darcy, convincing him he was an arrant coward to have hung back. Bethune laughed at him; but he had
begun to realize that Darcy's confidence and perpetual high spirits
concealed a diffident nature. Darcy had been cosseted overlong by
a sentimental mother, and, when he commenced to assert his man-
hood, had been forced to an open break with her, which still
troubled him. Bethune thought Darcy was only now, at twenty-
four, beginning to leave childhood. Himself, he had never had
childhood, had perhaps been as adult at sixteen as now, and might
be no judge.

"I want something to do," Darcy said. "Of late it seems to me
an insane thing, all these grown men occupying time with sitting
about taverns gaming and drinking. I'm bored, James. And I that
was the leading light of the young city bloods! I feel a useless
creature."

"You must be growing to a man. Or bilious."

"No, I fear it's politics," said Darcy. "I've embraced the cause
of the common man and by birth I'm a Tory. Associating with
tradesmen and merchants even in spirit makes me realize I've
never done a tap of honest work in my life."

Privately Bethune thought his partisanship for the radical group was only another rebellion against his family, that if put to the wall Darcy would be less zealous in action than in talk. But that might be said of anyone. He said, "Well, I might offer you a situation, Darcy. We've not yet found a competent clerk to replace Haagen." He spoke in jest; to his surprise Darcy caught him up eagerly.

"I'd like it, James—d'you think MacDonald would take me on? I could certainly do that."

"You're joking—"

"No, I've a feeling I'd enjoy it." He insisted, and though Bethune expected him to tire of the tedious routine work, he stayed by it manfully and proved a reliable clerk in the office. MacDonald was amused at his serious endeavor.

Bethune came out to the fore-office one afternoon to find Darcy talking somewhat uneasily with Philip Livingston, who leaned on the counter quite at home. He nodded affably at Bethune.

"This will be the young man who administered such a sound defeat to Mr. Rivington, eh? How do you, Mr. Bethune? I dropped by to see how Darcy acquits himself at his new occupation."

"Quite well," said Darcy between defiance and sullenness. "You needn't worry for me, sir."

"Oh, I do not. Rafe only asked me to investigate. Your mother may"—the older man smiled slightly—"fuss over the indignity of work for a gentleman, but myself, I fancy a gentleman can hardly be aught less, whatever he may do, and in truth I'm happy to see you with some serious interest, Darcy. Possibly you've been good for him, Mr. Bethune."

"I scarcely think I've any influence, sir," said Bethune politely.

"So this is the *Courier*!" Livingston glanced about curiously. Bethune wondered if he expected to find Sears or John Lamb lurking under the counter with some of their seditious pamphlets. "I understand Mr. MacDonald suffered a serious accident several months ago. I hope he is recovered?"

Bethune explained. Considering that MacDonald had flayed Livingston unmercifully in print for joining the De Lancey party in the Assembly, he reckoned the visitor was only being polite; but when he said that MacDonald was even now in the rear room busy over an article, Livingston said, "There is a man to respect. May I interrupt him?" and went into the rear office, not waiting for reply. Bethune shrugged at Darcy and followed.

"Well, this is a surprise, sir," MacDonald was saying; and, sardonically: "You'll excuse my not rising."

"Indeed. I've heard of your misfortune, and you've my sympathy—and respect, Mr. MacDonald."

"I dare say you'd all hoped 'twould have me out of commission permanently," said MacDonald with a rather wolfish grin.

Livingston smiled, but his eyes were serious. "I would not say that, no. Every man's entitled to his opinion and the expression of it. I should think it a far more unhealthy thing for these colonies were all our newspapers of like mind, or all our citizens. We need always the dissenters."

MacDonald cocked his head at him. "You are very right—very right. Mr. Bethune, fetch the brandy, please. Will you be seated, Mr. Livingston? I hazard you came to rescue your innocent godson from the lions' den, but you seem to have retained some common sense at least."

Livingston only smiled the broader, taking the glass Bethune offered with a nod. "I trust so! As a matter of fact, I am pleased to see Darcy grown up a trifle and standing on his own feet. I may quarrel with a man's opinion, Mr. MacDonald, but never with his right to voice it. Even when it results in such a magnificent piece of satire against myself as appeared in your last edition but one."

MacDonald laughed. "Sportsmanship! Is it beneath your dignity to defend yourself in the opposite organ? The *Gazetteer* seems to be acquiring that distinction."

"I've more respect for you than for Mr. Rivington. Your opinion is honest."

"I had always supposed yours was, until last year."

Livingston said, "You make a hasty judgment. I've no objection to telling you that I'm no more in agreement with Oliver De

Lancey and his party, on certain issues, than I have ever been. But I have never embraced radical views either. That party grows too strong. I fear its influence, and the times are grave. Too grave to entrust weighty decision to impulsive rabble, Mr. MacDonald. I speak without prejudice—I hold myself no better essentially than merchants or guildsmen, but what I do say is that Isaac Sears and his party have no experience of statesmanship, the best of them, for managing public concerns. They speak out their first thought impulsively, like children, and, like children, they've no conception of compromise. The Crown has always left the individual colony governments to tax themselves; it's late in the day to levy taxes voted by Parliament where we've no representatives. But what sense does it make to cut off the nose to spite the face? That's what we are doing with this nonimportation pact, limited though it is. England can withstand the loss of trade indefinitely—she has other colonies. We cannot. It is only widening the rift between ourselves and the mother country."

"I know, I know, you advocate the sending of petitions and representation to London, and reasonable discussion. Have you any expectation that the German would listen, much less be convinced?"

"You are a Scot, of course—"

"I'm a Scot, Mr. Livingston, and we've known for long that given an inch an Englishman takes a yard. It's gone past reasonable discussion. All the Crown will understand now is force."

"I will say this, I'm not for a policy of blind obedience. But I may tell you in confidence—nay, the official news will be released tomorrow, so I tell you nothing your competitors will not have in their editions this week—the Townshend taxes are repealed, all save the tax upon tea. That should ease matters somewhat."

"Indeed? So it appears the pact had some effect after all, eh? And I'd remind you of the Stamp Tax too—nonimportation succeeded in getting that repealed. But it's gone beyond taxes, as well, sir—it is the spirit of Americans against the Crown, for any and all reason. I'll make a concession to you—at times I deplore the violence of the radicals. Sears is a crude Caesar of little reason, less patience, and no compassion. But men do not make the times, rather the other way about. And this you may say of the radicals —they are willing to try the new thing, where you sit back and refuse only because it's new."

"Experience—"

"Experience be damned," said MacDonald, pounding one fist on the arm of his chair. "I tell you what major mistake the Crown makes, Mr. Livingston, and perhaps you reactionaries as well, certainly De Lancey. These are British colonies, but not all peopled by Englishmen. The Crown tries to treat with us as if we were so, all Englishmen with inherent respect for the Crown and Parliament. Well, even Englishmen, the common ones, have a vein of independence. In the South it's true you have a little England in America, with the feudal system perpetuated. But look, for example, at New York! American, Mr. Livingston, American! Dutch, Germans, Scots, Irish—people from every corner of Europe outnumbering English stock. To them Parliament is but a nuisance at best, a tyrant at worst. And they will never take kindly to the Crown's attitude that it has any right over them whatsoever."

"I agree," said Livingston surprisingly. "It is the danger I see, and which some of us, I trust more far-seeing than the violent Mr. Sears, try to avoid. For we should be lost without England—if ever it should come to an open break. No, no," as MacDonald made to interrupt, "don't mistake me. Given time, enough capital, and willing work, we could establish manufactories of our own, become self-sufficient economically. But where is France while we are doing so, and Spain? We should be gobbled up by other tyrants, and far worse ones. It is madness to alienate the Crown further."

"I believe you're wrong not only about that, but in supposing that your minority party—for you are in a minority and cannot deny it—can indefinitely postpone action. There may come a time when you have to decide between England and America."

Livingston said gravely, "That would be a sad and difficult choice, but I think even you can doubt not which I should abide by." He rose smiling. "I must not interrupt your work more. I've enjoyed our talk, sir."

"And I. Each to his opinion, so it be honest—and I think we're both honest men."

"We shall leave it to time, Mr. MacDonald, to show which of us is nearer the truth."

CHAPTER 15

BETHUNE WAS to reflect later on the next year or so as the most contented period of his youth. There were times, with the months slipping by so swiftly, when he looked back to the boy who had come almost by accident to New York and here found a new life; it seemed impossible that was himself.

He remembered how that boy used to grope for some meaningful philosophy, an answer to all his doubts and questions: Where am I going, and why? Over-serious, foolish youngster! He still did not know, but he liked the direction he was going and that was all the importance.

"Do you never grow excited over anything?" Darcy asked him once, amusedly. Well, he did, but seldom showed it.

He was somewhat excited when the American Company returned to New York for the season. He bought a two-shilling seat and watched Gay pirouette through three acts of broad comedy. He thought she had grown even prettier—and probably no less scatter-witted. Afterward he went round to the players' entrance and asked for her.

She came scurrying down the dark passage to him. "Jemmy! It's nice to see you! Are you still with your dreary news sheet?" Disregarding the several persons about, she kissed him warmly.

"You're prettier than ever—but you've cut your hair!"

"Wait till I'm changed from this horrid thing they make me wear in the last act, Jemmy"—whispering in his ear—"or don't you care to take me home, hmm?"

"Need you ask?"

But he did not grow as excited as MacDonald over various political events. There was much indignation in all the newspapers about the massacre in Boston; himself, he would scarcely call it that with five casualties, and all too likely the mob had been violent, giving the troops no choice. There was more uproar when Preston, who'd commanded the troops to open fire, was acquitted. Bethune asked Darcy reasonably, "What else would you expect? He was judged by sympathizers, not the mob."

He derived some private amusement from the arrival, at last, of the long-commissioned statues of the King and William Pitt. New York had forgotten its fine flush of enthusiasm over the Stamp Tax repeal, and the statues were more embarrassment than anything else. But the subscription committee, headed by the mayor, formally unveiled them—the King in the Bowling Green, Pitt at the mouth of Wall Street.

Directly after that New York's new governor arrived, to create the precedent of bringing the *Gazetteer* into like opinion with the *Courier,* if only in one edition. John, Earl of Dunmore, impressed no one high or low in New York as anything but the drunkard, womanizer, and foul-mouth that he was; and it could be conjectured that even De Lancey, who worshiped nobility, was relieved when Dunmore was appointed instead governor of Virginia. MacDonald said, "There are too many Tories in the south—Dunmore will serve us well and turn them all patriots!" His successor was William Tryon of North Carolina, a sober, steadfast man at least honest in his conservatism.

The political controversy that was to rouse the bitterest feeling for some time to come was that over the pact with the other colonies. Parliament had repealed the Townshend taxes on all items but tea, and the New York Assembly saw little reason for quibbling further over the matter. It was anxious to end dissension, and urged that the colonies dissolve the nonimportation agreement.

The majority of citizens, however, stood by the pugnacious Boston men, and the equally belligerent, if more suave, Virginia House of Burgesses argued for all or nothing, refusing to purchase from England until this final tax was repealed.

The Assembly, perhaps hoping to create doubt among the opposing party, ostensibly conducted a poll of New York opinion upon the question, and not unnaturally discovered their own view the popular one—since the poll was taken of carefully selected citizens. In protest at this trickery the Sons of Liberty staged a mass demonstration, which of course turned to a riot. But the Assembly, pursuing its narrow way, proceeded to withdraw New York from the colonies' pact and resumed importation of all merchandise except tea. Massachusetts, in particular, was indignant at this desertion, and New York was vilified by all the other colony governments. But the flow of trade increased and once again the British merchant vessels crept in by the Narrows to anchor confidently in New York Harbor. It spoke volumes for the steadfast spirit of the radical party that they continued to revile the Assembly for its action, despite the fact that they, like the rest of New York, benefited enormously by the restored commerce.

Bethune thought afterward it was all a series of accidents—the thing that cut his life in New York into two parts, before and after.

He had a card for Mistress Whitefield's charity ball. It chanced to occur on a Thursday; he'd heard rumors that the new governor was to attend, and was curious to see Tryon at closer quarters. The card requested him to bring a partner; he asked Susan Shields to accompany him. He asked her because he knew very few young ladies, none other well enough to approach.

He thought she had improved herself by giving up her fashionable clothes, the painstaking curls over her brow. She looked like a sensible honest young woman, in an unfrilled gown of rose-colored taffeta silk. And the governor was not there after all; Bethune devoted somewhat more attention to her than he had planned.

"I do feel quite grand, Mr. Bethune, among all these social lions! Did you know you are somewhat of a lion yourself? Several people have mentioned to me your article upon poor Lord Dunmore."

"Really? And why poor, mistress?"

"Oh, everyone seems to have decided to dislike him before ever he arrived. I dare say he may have been a trifle objectionable, but such an old family—nobility is always inclined to be erratic, don't you think? Mr. Trevelyan—that is, the young Mr. Trevelyan —was telling me, by the way, that you are descended of nobility yourself."

"I? He must have been jesting."

"Oh, no, was not your father a Scottish nobleman captured at Culloden? Most romantic."

"I scarce suppose he was either noble or considered it romantic," said Bethune dryly.

"Are you to attend the governor's military review next week? I should so enjoy seeing it—I am able to come out so seldom now. You must tell me of it afterward."

It must be a bleak life the girl led, he thought: an invalid and a large house to manage, even with sufficient money. He said before he thought, "But I'd be pleased to escort you, Mistress Susan." She exclaimed in delight. He looked at her and reflected that she was not so ill-featured, and remembered that she was only twenty-six or twenty-seven, and had not had an easy time, what with Van Steen, her father, circumstances that labeled her spinster before youth was gone.

He escorted her to the military review, himself bored with it. A few evenings after that he was at Hull's with Darcy when John MacNamara came in and took a chair at their table. "Well, Bethune! I'm surprised to see you. By all accounts you're soon to leave our thinning ranks."

"Which are those?" asked Darcy.

"Oh, the liberty boys," said MacNamara with a wink. "The bachelors. Eh? Gossip has it you are dangling after your employer's daughter—and good luck to it, says I! Very sensible of you, man, marry into money!"

Bethune shook his head. "It's the first I've heard of it. Gossip—
and who built that tale of whole cloth?"

"Not so sly, Bethune! I saw you with her myself at that absurd
ball. Think to steal a march on the rest of us by denying it?
You've no rivals I know of. The Van Steens were never happy for
it, and took the first chance to rescue their blue-eyed boy. Plenty
of men in New York willing to relinquish a bit of freedom for a
wife with money, but there are larger fortunes than Shields', you
know, and with the other counts against her—a bit long-toothed
to say the least, and the blood's quite common for all she acts so
particular. Of course she's there under your hand. Can't say I
blame you."

"Just a moment, MacNamara," said Bethune. "Whether or not
I've any remote intention of marrying Mistress Susan, do you
think I'll bandy her name about a tavern?" Both the others glanced
at him curiously; there was unaccustomed hardness in his tone.

"Hoity-toity!" said MacNamara, raising his brows.

"It becomes you to mention good and bad blood when you're
so free with a lady's name!"

"Well, good God, man, I— Touchy, ain't you? Hardly likely
to be a love match. Your own choice, but you might as well
be honest for it, Bethune. Gossip—"

"Damn gossip," he said. He rose and stood over the other man.
"Some of you loose-tongued, loose-living, pox-ridden gentlemen,
MacNamara, might profit by a few lessons in manners! Goodnight,
sir." As soon as he was in the street he began to feel a fool.

Darcy caught him up. "That's the first time I've seen you lose
your temper."

"I did not lose my temper," said Bethune stiffly.

"James, don't tell me that's so? The way you took him up—"

"Oh, damnation, Darcy! I'm sorry for the girl, that's all. She's
not had much chance from life after all, even with her father's
money. Van Steen acted something less than a gentleman to her,
and it's not her fault she's no beauty. 'Twas the way he put it—
that I'd make up to the girl and wed for money."

"You'd scarce be the first man to do that."

"I'd not do it at all. And by the way, you've somewhat to

answer for—telling her I was noble-bred! What possessed you?"

Darcy chuckled. "Mentioned that, eh? It was a jest, James, I couldn't resist it. She's no sense of humor at all and accepts whatever wild tale you give her serious as bedamned."

"So it's a wild tale I'd be considered well-bred!" He laughed, restored to good humor. "Well, perhaps I needn't have taken such offense, but she's a lady, whatever MacNamara says."

"And you're sorry for her? 'Ware jumps ahead, James. That is fatal."

He'd no interest of that sort in Susan Shields, and certainly no intentions; MacNamara had annoyed him, was all. The evening was warm and in his chamber he raised the window. The nostalgic scent and sound of summer night drifted in, and perhaps turned him maudlin. He was suddenly remembering that night long ago when he'd stood outside the theater, lonely and sorry for himself, and seen Gay come out with Darcy. He knew something about loneliness; he had lived with it most of his life. Why the devil should MacNamara or any other carrier of gossip have the power to frighten him off a thing he wanted to do? There was no harm in giving the girl a little pleasure, and let the gossipers go hang.

He sat down at his table and penned a note to Susan Shields inviting her to accompany him to the dance assembly at the City Tavern the following week.

He had never thought of her like that, as a woman. That evening as he partnered her he found himself wondering about Susan. The primmest ladies were sometimes most ardent—or were they? He would not know about ladies. Her hand was light on his arm. He often noticed hands before other features: they could tell something about their owners. His own were long, thin, hard, fastidious-fingered: finicking hands for a man. Darcy's were oddly ungenteel, broad and strong hands; MacDonald's small for a man, with the shape of integrity. Susan's were small and square, at odds with her prim-lady manner: capable hands, blunt, no-nonsense. They rather amused him, giving her away; and they were well cared for, he saw, which he liked.

He had asked her out, he knew, directly to defy MacNamara's

gossip; he had thought less of the girl than the gossip. Now he was slightly ashamed of that; he enjoyed the evening more than he'd expected.

But he never meant more than that. He certainly had not meant to kiss her in the carriage on their way back to the Greenwich mansion. She openly invited him to do so. He had no lack of experience with women then, but he knew little of ladies.

She stiffened against him as if with sudden passion, and murmured, "James—oh, James." Simultaneously the alarm sounded in his mind. Long ago and far away—but take care: a thing like this happened before. He would have let her go, but she pressed closer; and the always reasonable part of his mind said amusedly, What the devil are you about, Bethune? Susan Shields!

"James—dear James! I do love you so much—did I show it so plainly? I should be ashamed, should I not? Tell me you love me—" He could not speak; but she did not seem to need an answer. He kissed her again because he did not know what else to do, panic rising in him then. What had he done already? In the ordinary way, a kiss or two, a girl would think nothing of it; but a primly raised, respectable girl, perhaps that was different. He had not thought. He put her away from him, but she had got her arms round his neck by then.

"James, I'm so happy," she murmured. "I did not dare hope you returned my love. I have been much too bold with you, I fear! But I knew—oh, you must forgive me!—I knew you could not approach my father formally, as he is. I'm so happy, my dear. We can be wed soon, very soon."

CHAPTER 16

WHY DID HE marry Susan Shields? At the time he had reasons, some honest, some ill defined; but essentially, he knew even then, it went back nearly ten years to Margaret. Was it that he felt this, in some mysterious way, to be atonement for a wrong he had done and never paid for? Or his greater pity for another girl, now mingled with this milder pity for Susan? Or reluctance (call it chivalrous) to cause her humiliation a second time? Or belief she loved him? A mixture of all those—and another thing. Margaret was gone from him. He did not think he remembered anything of her, but the lesson had stayed: dangerous to love too deep. And he did not love Susan.

He need not have felt obliged; brutal or not, he could have got free of her with a word. He never said it. He never knew which of those reasons was the strongest, or if he was simply a coward, unable to speak the necessary phrase as he would be incapable of striking her with his fist. He said, in fact, little to her at all. It was she decided the date—too close, he thought in panic, much too soon.

Not long after, he discovered he had been a fool as well. Too late he learned that. They were married at Trinity Church on the twentieth day of September in the year of 1772, two months before his twenty-sixth birthday, and he went to live in the gloomy Shields mansion on Greenwich Road.

He had not wanted to live in Shields' house; but he had no time to think of half the differences marriage would make to his

life, much less to reconcile them with Susan or himself. Before
the month was out he knew he would never be content in that
house, or with Susan anywhere. He had entered into marriage with
the expectation that it would be the usual humdrum, easy-enough
marriage most people had. And that it never was; how could it be?

It was his first experience of being at odds with a woman he had
made love to; he had not suspected how the intimacy would em-
phasize the irritation.

He had got out of bed and gone to the window.

"Please do not raise it, James, the night air is unhealthful."

He said, "It's stifling," and heard the edged anger in his tone,
not for the heat. He did not know what he wanted to say to her;
the words came out before he knew. "Damnation, you might at
least pretend to enjoy me!"

A small outraged gasp, her level voice chill. "You need not
curse, James. I cannot understand your meaning. Decent women
do not behave like—like others. I trust I know my duty as a wife."

After a moment he said wryly, "That is conducive to my enjoyment, isn't it? I don't understand you. You've changed. I
thought—"

"Yes?" Patient, exasperated.

"Never mind," he said. "No matter." He stood a long time at
the window, staring out to the black dark unseeingly; presently her
breathing told him she slept.

They'd had no wedding journey by reason of his responsibility
at the office; she commenced immediately on a round of entertainments. He would return in late afternoon to find he must
dress and go out with her, or play host to a party of guests he
hardly knew. He felt a guest himself in that house.

It was a waking nightmare, that first few months. All went
wrong that could go wrong, not only with himself and Susan—
all seemed to have changed with his friends. He might have expected that. He was in a trap, he had walked into it eyes open,
only too slow and stupid to see what he got into. Frank Walden

clapping him on the shoulder there in the Queen's Head. "Hand well played, Bethune! Set for life now, amn't you?" MacNamara eying him, still offended (and partly the cause of it, if he only knew). Kennedy a trifle embarrassed: "Seems odd to think of you wed—always a solitary dog, you were." Solitary—another word for lonely. He was twice as lonely now.

And he was unable to defend himself against them; there was nothing he could say. Feeling at times almost bewildered panic: This cannot be myself, Bethune, I never planned or wanted this, how am I here? All the reasons slid away now, it was incredible he had been caught so easily. Caught was the word. The odd part was, they did not think it particularly wrong in him, that he should marry for money; it was himself that was so sensitive to resent the charge.

He minded most of all about Darcy and MacDonald, both so unnaturally polite, withdrawn from him. And he was helpless to explain, show himself the fool and coward he was. There was also Susan. Whatever her lacks and notions, she meant well by him; he could not discuss her with others.

Everything wrong. Some of the difficulties had no remote connection with his marriage, but superstitiously he felt his bad luck was contagious. Brady was asking a new contract at a higher rate: prices were rising again. Subscribers complained that their deliveries were irregular. Accounts refused stubbornly to balance out. And always the house, and Susan—a nightmare round; he had strayed into someone else's life, an unhappy someone quite apart from himself.

He had not talked alone with Darcy since the wedding; they had never a chance now. Darcy did not seem to desire one. Bethune wanted desperately to make him understand, but what could he say? He did not plan to say what he did.

Darcy came into the rear office that morning as Bethune labored over a dull report of ship arrivals. The windows were streaming a dispirited November rain; Susan had more guests to come that evening; the second clerk had just left for a position with higher wages. Then Darcy came, with his new formality. "I'm sorry to interrupt you. That Doctor French has been in—he wants to withdraw his advertisement, he is leaving the city. It's several lines, isn't it? I'm afraid it will put you short, and on Wednesday too— I told him—"

It was the last straw. Bethune exclaimed, "Oh, damnation!" and flung his pen violently across the room. Immediately he was ashamed of childish temper; he got up, retrieved the pen, stood at the window, his back to Darcy. "Very well, I'll see to it." He thought Darcy had gone until he spoke.

"You're not looking well, James."

"I am quite all right."

"Well, that's a lie," said Darcy. He fidgeted about the table, uneasy, his eyes worried. "Damn it, James, I—! Oh, well, what's the good talking? Only—" For once he was inarticulate as Bethune.

"Only what?"

Darcy burst out, "In God's name, why did you do it—why? Oh, I've no right to interfere. Curse me and have done."

He did not, staring blindly into the rain outside. "Were you ever drunk, Darcy—so drunk you had to be told next day what you did and said?"

"Once, yes. A frightening feeling. Why?"

"Yes, isn't it?" he said. "Isn't it? An absolute blank. Some other man using your body, your voice, your hands. And then you are yourself again—and must cope with the consequences of what you did and said." He had not turned; his voice was dead.

Suddenly Darcy's hand fell warm on his shoulder. "All right, James, all right. I never believed the other—I know you too well. I'm sorry if I've appeared to—disapprove. If there is aught I can do—"

"Nothing anyone can do, Darcy." His eyes filled with absurd hot tears to have Darcy friendly again.

"I did not think you'd do that, only for the money."

"God damn the money," he said; and after a pause: "All right, Darcy—thanks. I'll see to the advertisement, fill up the space somehow. Will you take the copy to Brady tonight? I must be—home— for a dinner party."

Darcy's fingers tightened on his arm. "I'll do that, don't trouble for it."

The week after the wedding she was changed. All that month before sweetly affectionate, prettily deferring to him; his uneasiness soothed, he had thought they might deal well together after all. Then this: indifference at best, irritation at worst.

Overconscious of her parents' lack of breeding, she must be the eternal lady, never allow the manner to slip in the smallest particular. He could guess what marriage was to her; mere possession of a husband was the magic key admitting her to the social circle of matrons, the cards parties, the teas, the dinners, the balls. She had had one criterion for the husband, that he be gentleborn.

He'd been annoyed at it, that absurd jest of Darcy's somehow becoming common gossip. Several of Susan's acquaintances had mentioned it before him; he passed it off as inconsequential. But that evening of the day he and Darcy were reconciled, it irritated him more when one of Susan's guests, Mrs. Hardwick, began on it at the table.

"But, dear Mr. Bethune, how galling you must find it, that too dreary news writing! And when you are of noble stock! I vow, I said to dear Susan—"

He interrupted without apology. "You're quite mistaken on all counts, Mistress Hardwick. Indeed I'm not of noble stock, quite the opposite. I cannot imagine how that silly tale got about. And as for my work at the *Courier*—"

"Not? But—" Her eyes slid to Susan's. "I had certainly heard that your late father was younger son to a Scottish duke or somewhat."

"If he was this is the first I've known of it," he told her rather sharply. "For aught I know he was a croft farmer or a shepherd. I beg you'll scotch such gossip when you hear it."

She looked pleased; Susan flushed a slow crimson. One of the men made some noncommittal rejoinder; the subject veered, and the rest of the evening passed normally.

When the guests were departed Susan turned on him fiercely. "What possessed you to speak so to Mrs. Hardwick? You carry eccentricity too far, James, do you not? I'd not have you boast of breeding, but—"

"Eccentricity?" he returned, astonished. "I've had sufficient of that tale. I only told the woman the truth."

"The truth? I thought—Mr. Trevelyan said—"

"It was a jest of Darcy's," he said patiently. "You did not believe it?"

She stared at him. "So it is true," she said slowly, "what you said. Your father might have been—anything? Yes, and the way you put it—I was humiliated! So coarse, as if to imply you never knew your father, that you are a—a—"

"Bastard," he said. "And so I may be. For the love of God, Susan!" It was his contrariness made him take small pleasure in being vulgar before her everlasting damned prudery. "So it was you spread that little story? I see. Perhaps if you hadn't believed it you'd not have married me at all."

Queerly she said, "I don't know. I dare say—but it is no matter now. She will have it all among my acquaintance by next week. You might consider me on occasion, James."

He was too dispirited to make any retort to that.

CHAPTER 17

SINCE THE DAY Bethune had told him that he would marry Susan Shields, MacDonald had been distant; no more did he make friendly jests about the work, or even argue politics with him. Bethune had known, since that nightmarish time MacDonald was stricken down, how much he felt for the other man. Affection?

It was a poor word. He admired MacDonald as a man and writer more than any he had ever known, and he knew MacDonald had thought something of himself. He owed him a good deal; there had been a bond between them, even though it was a feeling unexpressed.

It was stupid of him, but the reason for MacDonald's unfriendliness had never occurred to him, not until the morning he came into the office to find MacDonald before him. Haagen had ensconced him comfortably in the inner office, a shawl round his legs; there was no hearth in the building and at times it was bitter cold.

"Good morning, sir. Is there any news of interest out?"

"Not to speak of, Mr. Bethune. All I can offer you is one Jacobus Roosevelt. He has a tannery in Whitehall, and his neighbors complain so loud of the stink the council has directed him to remove to a more isolated spot. Would you care to do a short column on Mr. Roosevelt?"

He laughed. "Scarce worth that, is it? I'll leave it to you."

"Kind of you," said MacDonald with something like a sneer in his voice. Bethune's spirits sank a trifle lower; he hoped each day they would take a step back toward their old relationship, hoped for the explanation that might destroy MacDonald's new, frightening enmity. He went to the second table. MacDonald added suddenly, and the bitterness of it almost made Bethune start, "Do you also allow that I compose the lead article this week, Mr. Bethune?"

He looked up. "What d'you mean, sir?"

"Yes, let us be careful of the formalities," rasped MacDonald. "Continue to sir me, will you not? I dare say I'll be asking you that question in all earnest one day—when George is gone and you are the nominal majority owner of the *Courier*. I have neglected to congratulate you. You played your cards well, Mr. Bethune."

He stared back at MacDonald. Shields had taken so little active interest in the paper of late that it was difficult to realize the *Courier* was not MacDonald's in fact as it was in spirit.

He did not even know what Shields' fortune was invested in;

he did not care. Of all Shields' investment, perhaps the smallest part, the *Courier,* was Bethune's only concern. And MacDonald's. One day the *Courier,* never mind the rest, would belong to Susan as the major investor. Except in rare instances a woman's finances fell to her husband to manage.

MacDonald had held his eyes; now he turned away with a shrug. Bethume said, "Just one moment." His voice sounded strange to his own hearing. He rose and went to MacDonald's table, stood over him, and small annoyance came to MacDonald's expression; he hated any reminder of his helplessness, in addition to the indignity of needing to tilt his head to look up at Bethune. "If there is any choice, Mr. MacDonald," said Bethune levelly, "I'd rather you thought me fool than villain. I don't suppose you'd believe that that had not occurred to me until just now. But I can tell you this. If the day ever comes I've any legal control of the *Courier* —and I should doubt it—I would rather make it over to you and be done than have any issue over it. If you think I'm not sensible of what I owe you—that I should ever in any circumstances presume to order you or forget my duty to you, it's better I should leave the *Courier* now."

MacDonald relaxed slowly in the chair. "Well, well," he said softly. "At last I succeed in rousing you to show emotion."

"I'll promise you this. If that day ever comes, so you are alive and able, you'd have a proxy to manage as you please as quick as I might get to a lawyer's office." He turned and went back to his own table; he was suddenly conscious that he was trembling violently with anger, surprise, the effort of speaking. "Do you desire me to leave now, Mr. MacDonald?"

"Sit down, Mr. Bethune," commanded the quiet voice behind him. "I'll apologize to you for giving way to, I fear, somewhat childish spite and jealousy. George Shields found most of the capital for the *Courier,* but it was I who built it to a newspaper, with the second highest circulation in this colony."

"I know," Bethune said. "I know that." His head had begun to ache.

"I am not apologizing to you for what I thought. You will agree I might find it galling that the untried boy to whom I gave a ten-shilling-a-week job barely ten years ago—it is just ten years, is it not?—"

"It's ten years next May, sir."

"—should by reason of a few words from a rector step into the position of my superior overnight."

"I quite agree," he said.

"You have said all you mean to say. I had believed I knew you; I had not thought you would be mercenary in marriage. I don't say there is aught wrong about that. I merely considered it a thing you would not do. But it was your choice."

Bethune's voice cut harshly across his. "I wouldn't say it was. Not in any particular. Unless you call it choosing to be a coward for action."

"I might say fool, for that."

"Oh, I'll agree with you there too," he said wearily. "I had best go." He got up to his feet again.

"But if every fool of that sort were to be penalized there'd not be enough innocent men to administer punishment. Fetch the brandy if you will." Unexpectedly MacDonald laughed. "It's an opportunity—I don't deny it—to be rid of you. In spite of the labor I expend on your education you've not always been satisfactory."

Bethune handed him the glass, filled one for himself. "Thinking of the time I miscopied your quotation from the mayor's speech and brought him down on us?" He attempted a smile.

"Oddly enough," said MacDonald, "my thoughts dwelt a trifle longer on the night of the fire in Ann Street."

"I was a coward then too. Frightened I'd be left to manage even one edition alone."

They both drank; there was a thoughtful silence.

"Very well, I'll name you a fool," said MacDonald amiably. And that was all he ever said on the subject of Bethune's marriage.

"I was a fool before you said it."

"You had best produce a few lines about Mr. Roosevelt. The edition's short—it will serve to fill up a quarter-column."

"Yes, sir," said Bethune. Already he was feeling surprised they had managed to be so articulate with each other. But as both took up their pens, settling to work at opposite tables, a current of peaceful understanding drew between them as of old.

He had said to MacDonald that he doubted any of Susan's potential wealth would ever concern him. He was coming to know Susan better. She might, though she no longer troubled with him, act the helpless, ignorant female; in actuality she was shrewd about money.

She had mentioned one morning that she must go into the city to visit Mr. Carruthers. Idly Bethune returned, "He manages Mr. Shields' investments, does he not?"

"As a matter of fact, James, he does not." That was the nearest to a genuinely amused smile he had ever seen her wear. "I was not altogether satisfied with Mr. Carruthers' management, and fortunately was able to induce Father to assign his proxies to me, before he became quite incapable."

"You are managing?" he exclaimed in surprise. "But surely that's tedious for you—"

"Not at all, I quite enjoy it! Of course Mr. Carruthers is of some help. Much of the investment is in shipping, the importation warehouses, and I can hardly visit the water front or deal with the seamen. But I make sure he informs me of the facts. I may say my judgment has never been at fault thus far." She smiled.

He thought probably she was more than capable. She was so utterly opposite, now he knew, from all he had thought she was, he wondered that he had been so blind. She had deliberately angled for him, as she had for others, just to have a husband; she cared nothing for him or any aspect of marriage save the satisfaction it afforded her socially.

She must think him a coward and weakling—and a fool. He had never desired her very ardently and her resigned submission killed any passion in him. After a little her presence irritated him beyond measure. One evening, when they were four months married, without speaking to her he transferred his possessions to a bedchamber across the passage. She came on him as he gave orders to one of the chambermaids that the bed be made up for him.

When the girl was dismissed Susan drew him into her chamber.

"What is this, James? Your wardrobe—you are—" Surprised, hurt, bewildered, like any abandoned wife.

"I'm sure you understand," he said, a trifle surprised himself. "I like to sit up reading. I'd not annoy you. It's better I should have my own chamber." If he had the courage he would leave this house entirely, go back to Cherry Street where at least he had been his own master.

"But I don't understand." She stared at him. "Husband and wife must share a chamber—"

"I don't think there's any law to that effect," he returned with a shrug, and repeated, "I'd not annoy you."

"But you do not. Or, rather, yes, you do—I wish to be honest with you, James—but that is part of marriage after all. You spoke to the maid, told her—I wish you had not, the servants will be talking, saying I'm an undutiful wife to you."

"Are you not? Well, no, not undutiful. What does it signify?"

"But it does matter! I've tried to please you, if you would tell me where I've failed—"

He saw, incredulously, she meant that. "Honest," he said slowly, "yes, let us be honest by all means."

"I have tried to be."

"Then tell me, you coerced me into marriage merely to have a husband, did you not?"

"Do you think I am the only woman ever to have done so?" She faced him rigidly. "Yes—yes, James. There's nothing in life for the spinster. A woman must marry. I am not so ill-looking, am I?"

"You played that little comedy of kisses guessing how I'd act."

She smiled briefly. "You're soft," she said almost wistfully. "Too kindhearted. I—yes, that's so. It was no more than many women have done, you know. But I am no cheat, James. I mean to be a good wife to you, believe me, I do! I—I have seen I do not always please you, but I try."

"What do you mean by a good wife, Susan?"

"Why—" she hesitated. "To—to fulfill my duty to you, and give you children, and act hostess—all a wife should—"

"In bed and out," he said. She flushed.

"You need not be vulgar. I only mean to be honest. I am sorry, I cannot pretend love where I don't feel it, but I find it hard to believe there is love between women and men, and that—it's nought to do with affection, only men and—and low women. I quite meant to make a good wife. And you had a reason too, James, you cannot deny it—the money."

"The money—God damn the money!" he said again. "Duty—" He was suddenly as fascinated by her as he'd been for Gay, for the same reason—groping to understand the way her mind worked, this literal mind, dealing only with tangibles. "Susan, would you desire children?"

She said at once, "Oh, yes. —No, I must be honest, mustn't I? I do not think I would, I'm not fond of children, but it is another thing one must expect of marriage, and I—"

"Would fulfill the duty. Willing to pay the price for the satisfaction of being a married woman. Is that a fair way to put it?"

"Oh, you put it crudely, but—" She turned away from his eyes. "I can tell you, James, nine of ten women feel the same, I'm positive, only they must make pretense about it even to one another. I am sorry I displease you, I will try—"

"You need not trouble," he said. He went out of the chamber, into the one opposite. Looking about it, he reflected he would need to find a small cabinet to hold his books; and he'd have the bed moved to the other wall, the wardrobe chest and perhaps an easy chair where the bed now stood, and another table for candles. She had followed him; she sounded irritated now.

"You will not truly—? I wish you will not, there'll be talk."

"But I thought you admired honesty. Only when it is not inconvenient? Yes, of course. You cannot pretend affection, you said. You managed that quite convincingly before we were wed."

"I—"

"Yes, I know, it was necessary then." He laughed. "Leave it, Susan. Fair exchange, no robbery. You've a married name and your precious matronly status. All I ask on my part is that you leave me my privacy."

"You are queer," she said. "I always thought so. I do not believe it's anything I've done or not done, that it's only because you are a solitary. You enjoy your privacy too greatly to relinquish it even for a wife. That must be the reason. Unnatural in you."

He stood at the window, with his back turned; he said, "Yes, of course that is it." He stood there not listening to her, not speaking further, until she tired of arguing and went away.

He had not visualized marriage except vaguely. He was not, he trusted, a sanctimonious prude; but some notions he had developed in his own mind—principles, perhaps. He had been in love once, and not again; perhaps he never would love again as he had loved Margaret at sixteen. It was dangerous, inviting too much hurt.

Solitary. He and MacDonald were alike some ways, but not that way. MacDonald disliked physical contact; he was interested in people in the abstract, the prophet watching from his mountain—except that he had a sense of humor, which prophets never possess. Bethune felt otherwise; he warmed to the friendly hand on his arm, but, self-contained, forever fearing rebuff, could not offer himself. He liked to be among people; with a party at some tavern, in the midst of talk, he knew an illusion that no longer was he the observer outside, that he belonged somewhere.

He thought of all that, standing motionless at the window of his new chamber then. He had only recently looked back with amusement to himself four, five years ago: the man who wanted so earnestly to—find out. Why am I here, Bethune, where do I go?

That no man ever found. He went through life blind, seeing his mistakes only long after they were made, and never any signpost pointing the way; he went alone in the dark, and, reaching hopeful hands to the dark, met nothing, heard no voice. Perhaps he went into nothing also, and always in the dark. He never found the answer to his wondering, because there was none, it was all blind, without meaning.

CHAPTER 18

IF THERE WAS gossip about them he did not hear of any. As time went on he sank himself more and more in his work, and because of the increasingly controversial political situation there was, that couple of years after his marriage, more than sufficient labor at the *Courier* to keep him occupied. MacDonald was fond of using the word "portentous."

"It's not unlikely this could lead to war," he said of the news about the King's latest act. "What a slow-witted blundering Teuton it is! And he thought to solve the problem that way!" The act gave Britain's East India Company monopoly of the tea trade with the colonies. Likely Parliament had expected the resulting drop in price would end all this picayune strife over tea; though in all probability they also had comfortable expectations of the enormous profit to England from that trade. Instead, the colony merchants almost in a body rose in alarm at the prospect of any monopoly, and where previously the dissension had been subsiding, a few of the colonies growing lukewarm over the issue and ready to accept a compromise, this Tea Act had the effect of starting the controversy all over again, more bitter than before.

"War!" Bethune repeated to that. "Rebellion, you mean. I should doubt it. That would be no way to settle differences, and an unequal struggle to say the least. Though I'll grant this seems to have accomplished one thing—the colony assemblies are holding together." Even the conservative, Tory-ridden New York Assembly was expressing indignation, and now wholeheartedly joined the more belligerent colonies in agreeing to refuse all shipments of tea, though not other merchandise.

The colony assemblies had named committees of correspondence to keep in touch with one another and agree upon concerted action, but aside from formal protest had done nothing as yet. It was the common citizens who talked loudest, and took action.

One of the broadsides in circulation, purportedly from a band of wilder spirits among the Sons of Liberty (if any could be said to be wilder than the rest) threatened revenge on any merchant or seaman who violated the nonimportation pact, and that it was no empty threat became evident when smugglers were caught; a few were tarred and feathered, others set on a mock gallows and made to swallow quantities of scalding tea or curse the King.

Aimless, vicious play it was; Bethune expressed that opinion to MacDonald. "They cannot accomplish aught by such show of force. It is childish. Oh, I agree, it's but a symptom of the whole trouble."

"As Livingston said," remarked MacDonald, "they are rabble— none of your dignified educated statesmen. Rabble is apt to express itself violently—but honestly, Mr. Bethune. They are in no doubt at least what they feel." He added, "speaking of Livingston, he turns out to be an honest man after all. I admire his resolution. Not many statesmen have the moral courage to admit it when they are wrong." Livingston, by his speeches in the Assembly during the last year, had come to see that radical opinion was too strong and too much in majority to be ruled now or henceforth by the liberal group, far less the Tories; he was again at odds with the conservatives. The *Gazetteer* vilified him as a weathercock; but only arch-Tories paid notice to the *Gazetteer*.

"Rivington is no Tory," said MacDonald bitterly. "He plays the side he thinks has most favors to give, is all."

"And plays foul," said Bethune. Rivington was without integrity as an editor. The wildest lies and rumors were deliberately inserted in the *Gazetteer* along with vicious attacks on the reputation of any man who spoke against the Tory view. Whatever their political policies, the other papers in New York used some discretion and decency in their expressions: John Holt of the *Journal* was closest to conservative in view, but a long way from Rivington; Loudon's New York *Packet* and the *Post-Boy* stood in the middle of the road, with Hugh Gaine's *Gazette* approaching nearest the radical *Courier*. Gaine had a standing grievance against Rivington for using a name for his paper so similar to the older *Gazette,* and had once haled him to court over it, but lost the case. Rivington, of course, had sympathy, private information, and probably financial aid from the Tories, and would print anything, lie or truth, in support of them. It was observable in that troubled time that the various editors, excepting Rivington, banded together, regardless of their views, where formerly they had been bitter rivals.

More than one paper carried articles on the freedom of the press; those of conservative policy had some cause to be disturbed, for the radical party grew more violent daily and there was rumor of an intention to mob the *Gazetteer* office. That rumor reached MacDonald one Wednesday through Haagen, who was an ardent Son of Liberty, though his devotion to his *baas* kept him from most of the meetings. "Dey are saying dey go into Mr. Rivington's office, break his presses and burn all his paper. Mr. Sears—"

"Do you tell me. Yes, I know there's high feeling about." All but the out-and-out Tories had become more incensed at Rivington, and at what was known as the *Lying Gazetteer,* as his accusations grew wilder. "God's teeth," said MacDonald, "it would serve him right! But it cannot be allowed. Mr. Bethune, drop what you are doing and scrap the lead for the first page. I want the first two columns, possibly half the third." They were the rest of the day remaking the edition, but the article was, Bethune thought, worth it.

"This lying toad-eater," MacDonald wrote, "who hesitates not to print unsubstantiated rumor so it be favorable to his chosen party, without all integrity himself must yet be suffered to protect the integrity of us all. It is no cause for surprise that many citizens are crying, Let us be rid of Rivington the liar! It is cause for alarm that any propose to accomplish that by violence. For as sure and as soon as the citizenry has the will to go in

violence against the editor of a newspaper which expresses un-
popular views, then indeed we shall have tyranny in these colonies.
Let us remember the case of John Zenger who fought and won the
issue of freedom for editorship. The press must remain free if
we are all to remain free. We denounce the pusillanimous policy
of the *Gazetteer* and the mishonest opinions of its editor, held only
for hope of reward from those they favor, and the *Courier* will
continue to oppose both with vigor, with dispatch, and with
honesty. But we say to James Rivington, as we say to all of
you, you editors, you news-writers, you publishers—Stand fast!
Hold to your individual expression, let none intimidate or coerce
you, but stay by your standard. If we speak of liberty but do not
practice it, we lose liberty before we gain it."

The morning that edition of the *Courier* came out, Isaac Sears
came to the office to see MacDonald. Bethune had met him once
before: a stocky barrel of a man, of personality so compelling
it was like a hot breath in a chill room. MacDonald called him
a crude Caesar. Whatever else he might be, Sears, the former
pirate, the rouser of rabble, was utterly sincere.

"I only came to tell you, Mr. MacDonald, that I saw what you
wrote in the *Courier* today. It set me thinking. True enough,
there's been talk of mobbing Rivington's premises—the bastardly
liar, he deserves it. But I never thought about how you put it—
losing liberty afore it's gained. You've the right of it, I reckon,
and so I'll tell the people. They'll not go for Rivington if I can
prevent it."

"Thank you, Mr. Sears," said MacDonald gravely. "I hope
you'll keep the principle in mind."

The furor over the tea continued to keep the colony seething.
A perplexed city council met with the Assembly to reach some
decision as to what should be done with several shipments of tea
expected in the harbor. Governor Tryon advocated that it be
stored, but the council maintained reasonably that that only
postponed decision.

The Boston men, never ones to shilly-shally, needed no council.
A day or so before that Christmas of 1773 a message rider by
the name of Revere arrived in New York with the news of a

bold stroke in Boston port. On the arrival of several ships carrying tea, a few Boston Sons of Liberty had gone aboard in disguise, by night, and consigned the cargoes to the bottom of the harbor. Their exploit was spread over the front pages of every paper in the city, and perhaps it stirred the New Yorkers to action; they would not allow Boston to outdo them, and by way of showing it outdid Boston. When a ship anchored off the Battery with a cargo of tea, the following April, the New York Sons of Liberty disdained to wait for darkness, but boarded her a hundred strong in broad daylight, held the crew at pistol point and sent the cargo over the side amidst triumphant yells. The city papers did some boasting about that as retaliation to the Boston men.

The results of those two rebellions against the act were to turn all topsy-turvy in colonial politics. Two weeks after the New York affair the official news came that the King, to punish Boston for insurrection, had ordered the port closed to trade until some repayment was made to the owners of the destroyed cargo. This was definite threat to the economic life of the colonies, for if Boston was closed to trade, so might New York be, or New Haven, Wilmington, Charleston—any and every port large and small. Overnight in all the colonies, but especially in New York as the greatest port, conservatives made a right-about-face to join with radicals; the whole structure of allegiances dissolved and changed.

"I said it before," commented MacDonald sardonically. "Touch them in their pocketbooks and they grow twice as rabid as about any elegant talk of rights and theories!"

All this had some effect on Bethune's life aside from the paper, and not entirely to his displeasure. He spent as little time as possible in the Greenwich Road house, but some lip service to convention he must pay—play host at Susan's dinners, Sunday teas. It bored him, and he could not help noting the character of those gatherings. Her everlasting penchant for associating herself with the highest society possible! Those she invited to the house were mainly Tories and wives of Tories. Naturally they would, on occasion, discuss politics, even the ladies; he refused to argue, but once or twice this man or that set out deliberately to provoke argument, knowing Bethune's connection with the *Courier*. It was an effort to reject all provocation smilingly, maintain courtesy.

Some of the more rabid Tories (and snobs) among Susan's acquaintances were Hardwick and Trumbull, both wealthy import-merchants. They and their wives were present the evening Bethune rebelled; it was Hardwick who precipitated it, at the dining table.

A big, hearty man, falsely genial, his eyes speculative on his host: "I've often wondered, Mr. Bethune—you connected with a rag of a news sheet like the *Courier*, and your good wife appears to retain some common sense in politics. Should think you'd find it awkward, eh?" He laughed without humor.

"You forget Mr. Shields has a large interest in the *Courier*," said Bethune politely. "The policy was his originally."

Hardwick shrugged. "That makes it all the more surprising Mistress Susan don't subscribe to his views. Or yours, sir. Eh? Come now"—another laugh—"don't tell me you never have an argument over it!"

"I never discuss politics with my wife."

Mrs. Trumbull, that militant female, challenged him. "Doubtless you are one of these men who believe women are too stupid to understand aught or have any opinions. Let me tell you, Mr. Bethune—"

"Everyone's entitled to opinion," he said without emphasis.

"Well, it's come to a pretty state," opined Hardwick, "when we must needs give any heed to the opinion of common laborers and tradesmen. Why, damme, the dock workers are talking of a strike from work unless we grant a rise in wages. Fivepence a day they're receiving now—fivepence! It's an outrage. And if the Assembly should agree to this damned nonimportation pact again—we'll all starve if that should pass. You take De Lancey now, he knows well enough—"

"That is just what I said to James when our present Assembly was elected," said Susan from the opposite end of the table. "If a gentleman of such old family is not qualified to order colony affairs, I am sure I do not know who might be."

"Exactly, dear lady! Of unquestionable breeding." All of them, Bethune thought, were snobs for the same reason she was: they were of middle-class merchant stock themselves, playing ladies and gentlemen by virtue of wealth.

Mrs. Hardwick echoed her husband: "Impeccable pedigree, all the De Lanceys"—as if she were personally responsible.

Bethune's patience slipped a trifle. He said in his driest tone, "So are my wife's carriage horses, but I should scarce care to elect any of them to the Assembly."

He should have known better than to tangle with a female. Mrs. Hardwick smiled at him and drawled, "Well, of course we realize that those without family background are always jealous of gentility. It is that element makes up the radical party. I am convinced it is mostly envy and greed with them, you know."

"Old family," said Bethune, raising his brows. "I believe we can all boast of that, can't we—being descended of Adam?"

Hardwick ventured a chuckle and was quelled by a glance from his wife, who continued, "I believe the editor of your newspaper, what is the name, MacDonald, is actually quite an underbred little man, is he not?"

Damnation, they were not even troubling to be polite to their nominal host. Bethune felt his temper rising.

"Oh, well, the *Courier!*" said Trumbull. "Dare say you stop there only to oversee some of your wife's potential investment, eh, Bethune? After all, any decent gentleman must agree there's but one sensible use for the paper—saving the ladies' presence—"

That was where his patience came to an end. He got up from the table. "I've a few other reasons for stopping with the *Courier,*" he told Trumbull, "but there's no point detailing them to you—I'm sure the ladies would find it dull. In any case, all of you at this table are of like mind, I appear to be odd man out. Likely you will all be more comfortably agreed without me. You'll excuse me—your pardon, Susan." He turned and came

out of the room, passing the butler, Sykes, in the doorway. The
man followed him out.

"Sir—"

"Well, yes?"

"Excuse me, sir, would you like me to fetch out your plate?"
The butler edged closer; he was trying to repress a grin.

Bethune saw him as a man, not a cipher, for the first time; he
smiled back. "Do that, please. You might cut me another slice of
the beef while you're about it."

"Yes sir!" Sykes could not help himself adding, "I just wish
Mr. Shields could o' heard you. Don't you nor Mr. MacDonald
pay no note to them." He jerked his head at the dining-salon.
"Just like Mr. Shields used to say, you smite 'em hip and thigh!
Excuse me, sir."

"We'll do that, Sykes," he said. "Fetch up a tray to my chamber, will you?"

"Right off, sir."

He had not expected to hear nothing from Susan about it. She
came up to him directly after the last guests departed; she was
flushed with anger. "Well, James! You made pretty work of
humiliating me before my guests, did you not? I never expected
such impossible behavior from you!"

"There was some provocation, wasn't there? And not the first
time. I came to the end of my patience, that's all."

"They were your guests as well. Such cavalier behavior!"

"Oh, no," he said, "not mine. I'll tell you now, Susan, don't
expect me to play host to a party like that again. It is bound to
create awkwardness. I apologize for the scene, but I think I was
justified."

Her lips thinned to a narrow line. "You and that absurd paper.
That odious Robert MacDonald. He has you under his thumb
just as he had Father before. James, why do you not leave the
Courier? I've been meaning to speak to you. It is not precisely
dignified work."

"Leave the *Courier*? Aside from any other consideration, I've
my living to earn. What put that in your mind, Susan?"

"I have always hated it," she said with sudden violence. "Everyone of any position and influence laughing at it. Shields' folly, they used to name it. It was only MacDonald's outrageous libels that made people buy it, only to see what lies he told! Mocking everything decent and established and right. Well, it may not always be so! When Father dies I shall own control of the *Courier*, shan't I? I can say what will be printed or not."

"You will own control of the *Courier*," he said, "but not of Robert MacDonald, Susan. Or of myself. So you want me to leave my work. Did you think to keep me about your house as you would a pet dog? Is that it?"

"There is plenty of money. I wish you would not be so difficult, James. I meant to be—"

"A good wife."

"—but you will not let me. I can't understand you."

"Then why try?" he asked. She looked at him a moment more in exasperation, sighed, and went away.

CHAPTER 19

AFTER THAT he ceased to render the marriage even lip service; he wished he had the courage to remove from the house entirely, and perhaps one day he would. He had said, Fair exchange. He could not now feel that he owed her any duty at all.

She seemed, after that episode, to accept the situation. She did not again ask him to head the table before guests, and a small fiction grew between them; she would tell him when guests were expected and he would plead extra work. "You will make my apologies, of course." "Of course, James." He spent no more time in the house than was needful; once again his evenings were given to the taverns and coffeehouses, most of his interest to his work. He was away from the house by half after eight most mornings, often did not return until midnight; he did not see her for days in succession, sometimes, for she accepted invitations without him now. He thought likely she was as content with the arrangement as himself. More, perhaps. A man could not find his work wholly sufficient. He had lost every trace of nice feeling about his marriage.

It was quite casually that he asked Darcy about the establishment he had mentioned, and equally casually that Darcy named the house and gave him a note to Mrs. Wise. There was nothing so wrong or rare about it; it was an accepted thing that husbands dissatisfied at home should find pleasure elsewhere.

But he frequented Mrs. Wise's house less for the wares offered than for the very atmosphere of the place. He had never been in a bawdy house before; he would have expected it to be just that. The dignified old house in Division Street might, with more accuracy, be called a bagnio, with its carpets, chandeliers, and velvet hangings. Mrs. Wise could easily pass for a respectable matron; and one found no vulgarities in her house such as face paint, slit-skirted gowns, or a communal parlor. Of the girls, he never met one who was not almost a lady in manner.

He grew quite friendly with Johanna in particular. She was a large, magnificently blonde German girl, and her only vice—aside from her profession—addiction to a pipe. "I hope you don't mind, Mr. Bethune. I do not usually indulge before patrons—Mrs. Wise is strict—but there, I feel you're a friend." A calm, slow smile. It was all very leisurely in that house; the list of patrons was limited, and you might stay as long as you pleased. "We're not encouraged to talk much," she added, "unless the customer wants. But I expect as you're with a newspaper you'd be interested. I mean, you'd be curious. I always read the *Courier* myself." He was surprised. "Oh, yes, I can read, Mr. Bethune. Isn't that De Lancey high-handed, I ask you. Fancying he runs the whole colony."

The novelty of discussing politics in such surroundings tickled his fancy; that, and interest in Johanna, was at least half of what took him back to Mrs. Wise's establishment.

The four to six months of his real marriage to Susan gradually faded to an unpleasant interlude. The tacit arrangement between them could make little difference to her social life. All her elegant acquaintances would politely accept the fiction that Mr. Bethune was occupied with his work, and probably were relieved to do without the presence of a *Courier* newsman. Very nearly the only difference his marriage made to his life now was that he lived in another house.

Massachusetts, bitter though her citizens felt toward New York for the refusal to join an unlimited pact, agreed to a proposal, made by the New York Assembly, of a Continental Congress; the other colonies, eager or reluctant, appointed delegates. But in New York there was contention even about that. The radical party objected to the roster of conservative delegates the Tory Assembly proposed, and organized what they called a Committee of Mechanics which threatened to appoint delegates of its own. Alarmed at the prospect of advertising dissension within the colony by inadvertently sending two groups of delegates to the Congress, the Assembly reluctantly agreed to include five liberal-to-radical members—John Jay, Isaac Low, James Duane, John Alsop, and Philip Livingston. But the radicals wanted all or nothing, and continued to threaten. There were mass meetings on the common, much oratory from Isaac Sears and Alexander McDougall, before any compromise was reached. The radicals pressed for an oath from the delegates promising that when it came to a vote all would cast for an unlimited nonimportation pact; when all but one of the contested delegates agreed, they approved the committee, and the business of the first Continental Congress might proceed.

In late August the New York delegation left for Philadelphia amid somewhat unenthusiastic cheers from a thin crowd; and then there were two weeks of waiting for official news.

There were more liberal minds than radical at that Congress, but it was the radicals who pushed it to the measures it took: a joint pact of all the colonies to cease all importation from England after December first of that year, a further agreement that if their grievances be not redressed by the Crown after September fifteenth of the following year, to cease all exports to England; and meanwhile to cease trade with the British West Indies. It satisfied most of the colonies only halfway; even the New Yorkers, not as belligerent as the Virginians or the Boston men, would have preferred more forceful action.

There began then to be open talk of war. Bethune could not conceive that the majority of colonials or their governments could show such temerity as to instigate open rebellion; nor could MacDonald. The formal cessation of trade had gained them redress before, not only once, and probably could do so again if the hotheads did not keep the citizens stirred to violence.

"Rebellion!" MacDonald shook his head. "That would be the sure way to invite more tyranny and lose all we've gained. What force have the colonies to put up against the British Army? And afterward the Crown could inflict what punishment it pleased for insurrection."

But through that long, sweltering summer before the Congress met, the tension had grown, and the spirit for open struggle. A great many small merchants and a number of wealthier ones moved to radical opinion, convinced that only force—or the threat of it—would win them their rights.

Bethune returned early one evening to the Greenwich Road house; it was too hot in the city for cards or talk at some tavern. As usual, he went directly to his chamber and settled down with that week's city papers; but before long Susan came in to him.

"James, I wanted to speak with you, I'm sorry to interrupt. You might be better informed. All this talk of open war—can it be that will happen?"

"I don't know," he said. "No one can know."

"Oh, but—" She fidgeted about the room in silence for a

little. "I can't believe they'd be such fools. This pact, it is ruining business. I can't understand the merchants who have joined the radicals—all against their own interests."

"They don't seem to think so."

"But what would happen if there were war? Trade—there'd be none, I suppose. No shipping at all. Would the colonies raise armies, I wonder? Oh, it's all such a tangle, I scarce know what to think. Mr. Carruthers advises that I sell some of the interests and put it in gold. I'd hesitate to do that—"

"And relinquish the yearly percentages," said Bethune rather dryly; he knew how fond she was of cold cash.

"I only wish all these absurd political quarrels would cease and everyone settle down again. No one is entertaining these days, and if one is invited out somewhere, all the company sit about with long faces and talk of nothing but politics!"

"It's a pity you're so bored. We must speak to the Assembly about it."

"Oh, you are impossible. I only—James. If there should be a war, what would you do?"

He laid down his paper for the first time. "I don't know. I really don't know. Go on getting out the *Courier* with MacDonald, I expect. I'm afraid I'd be little use as a soldier—and I'm not sure my heart would be in the fight."

If there was to be a rebellion, it had already begun in New York. By the beginning of that winter a known Tory was scarcely able to walk fifty yards down Broad Street without being the target for jeers and more tangible missiles. General Gage sent a routine request for supplies to the Assembly, but the merchants and tradesmen coolly refused to sell to the Army. This high-handed behavior further enraged the Assembly, which was also bewildered to find itself daily losing respect; perhaps the most bewildered were the cautious liberals who had tried all they knew to reconcile the Tories with the radicals, only to be called Tories themselves because they continued to distrust the radical group. Some, out of spite, turned true Tory. Others, like Livingston,

tried to stand firm by their tenets; but when such issues were at
stake a man must not hesitate in the middle of the road.

The Assembly next met at the summons of Lieutenant Governor
Colden, who harangued them powerfully despite his eighty-seven
years; a motion of approval on the proceedings of the Congress
was defeated, though by close vote. But the Assembly was no
longer in control of New York. Determined at any cost to avoid
being pulled into a similar binding agreement with the other
colonies, the Assembly refused to name delegates to the proposed
Second Congress which was to meet next May. This the Sons of
Liberty—and a majority of citizens were looking to them as the
ruling power, for at least they were vigorous for action—could
not withstand, and Sears called a public meeting at the Liberty
Pole to decide upon delegates to represent New York. The Assembly thereupon made its last and worst mistake, by causing
Sears and one of his lieutenants, Marinus Willett, to be arrested
on a charge of disturbing the peace. It was setting the match to the
magazine; the crowd converged upon the police, rescued the
prisoners, and proceeded to stage a riot resulting in much destruction. Several days afterward, at a second meeting, a public vote
was taken that the radicals' Committee of Mechanics should
choose delegates to the Congress; the Assembly, helpless to prevent it, agreed almost meekly.

But New York was not greatly concerned with the Congress;
that was a gesture. New York was, incredibly, preparing for war.
The *Courier* these days carried advertisements urgently querying
buyers and sellers of arms of all types—powder and shot; that
was one indication. A group of merchants had ordered an entire
shipload of arms and ammunition from England; arriving in New
York harbor with its cargo listed as hardware, the ship was
promptly seized by the port customs collector and the cargo
transferred to a British man-of-war. That made the first pages of
all the city papers; the patriots were furious and threatened reprisal, but nothing came of it immediately.

"I don't like it," MacDonald repeated. "It has all come too
quickly, overnight. If there'd been no dissension among the colo-

nies, if they'd all settled down at once to enforce the nonimportation pact, likely it would have been over by now. That was what
won the victory over the Stamp Tax."

"Do you think Sears and his rabble would actually—? It's
senseless, they must know they've no chance at all."

"It is no longer Sears and his rabble, you know. Seven-eighths
of New York is with them, and, by all accounts, a large majority
in the rest of the colonies. Well, by God, they're brave men,
I'll give them that—they don't mean to back down. You've seen
what happened with the liberals in the Assembly, and you know
Sears' battle cry—'Whoever is not for us is against us!' We had
best be choosing sides," and MacDonald laughed.

"You'd surprise a number of men in New York if they heard
you—MacDonald of the *Courier* unsure if he'll withdraw from
radical ranks."

"I may be a radical," said MacDonald, "but I've a good share
of Scots caution. It's always easy to get involved in war; the
difficulty is getting out again. And I'll tell you, with feeling as
high as it runs now any little incident might set off the charge.
At least it provides us with plenty of subject matter."

"But war—" Bethune shook his head, accepting the segar
MacDonald offered, lighting it absently. "Of course it would be
ended all too soon. They've nothing—"

"Don't be too sure of that either. I thought that once, but you
never know. There are good organizers with the patriots, and a
few wealthy men as well. You mind what I said that day to
Philip Livingston? The time's already come we must all choose
between America and England. It's that simple. No, in spite of
my political opinions, I can't say I'm wholeheartedly with the
notion of armed rebellion. But if the hotheads among us jump the
signal and precipitate violence, we'll have no choice."

"For once we agree, sir. I'm afraid the consequences of that
would be—but only time will show," and he shrugged.

The noise brought him out of the mists of sleep, reluctant; he
lay between the two states considering it, and memory stirred in
him and he thought, I have been through this before. A Thursday

morning almost exactly nine years back, it was. In a moment now
he would get up, and speak to Gay drowsy beside him, and go
out into the street to hear the news of the Stamp Tax repeal. All
the church bells in the city must be sounding.

Then he thought, But the edition came out yesterday, so this
is Saturday. He opened his eyes and the ceiling was not the rough-
plastered ceiling of the house in Stone Street, but the birch-paneled
one of Mrs. Wise's house. He had not meant to sleep, but he
had been tired. Johanna was sitting up.

"Whatever do you suppose that is, Mr. Bethune? It's just dawn.
Something's happening—"

"Sounds it," he grunted. He swung out of the bed, reaching
for his clothes, and stopped to laugh. "It seems when aught of
import occurs it finds me in bed with a doxy! But it's only the
second time after all." He dressed quickly, made his way down
through the stirring house, passed an agitated lieutenant of cavalry
buttoning his uniform as he hastened down the stair.

"What is it, man? All the bells—"

"I've no idea," said Bethune. "Let us go and find out."

They came into the street together; the lieutenant gabbled
something about his post and hurried off. Most of the excitement
appeared to be southwest of Division Street, in the city proper.
Bethune started down that way and met a few newly wakened
residents forming crowds, but none knew what the news might
be. He came down past the curve of Queen Street toward the
Common, and here the crowds were thicker. On the Common
musket shots sounded, and a swelling roar from many angry
throats. A man with a frightened white face came pounding up
from there on a dead run; it was not only Bethune who reached
to stop him, and in a moment he was surrounded by eager ques-
tioners.

"What is it? What's all the noise? What has happened?"

"Let me free—must get home," the man panted. "It's war
now—it's started now! Best you all go hunt up your arms—be
ready! There's been a battle—regulars fired on patriots—four
days since, the rider said—"

The first thing in Bethune's mind was, We must make an extra edition—it *would* be Saturday! The man was pulling away, starting on; he caught his arm. "Wait—did you hear any more, where it happened?"

The fellow jerked away; he ran on, but he cried back over his shoulder, "At Lexington 'twas—Lexington in Massachusetts!"

PART THREE

CHAPTER 20

THE STAGE from Boston set her down before the City Tavern, the limit of its journey. Her first sight of New York confused and almost frightened her; it was so big and so noisy. She wondered if the rattle of musketry was usual here, all the frenzied crowds, the shouting.

The stage driver noticed her confusion; when he lifted down her bags he said, "Your fust time in N'York, ma'am? It's not always like this—'tis the news of Lexington causes all the excitement."

"Oh, I see." That news had excited Boston two days ago, and she was too concerned with herself to be much disturbed over Lexington. There would be a war, everyone said; John Collard had been saying so for a year, and that his business—all business —would be ruined because of it. Like many Loyalists in Boston, he had made arrangements to remove to England. That had given Margaret her chance; and almost her only concern with the war was that indirectly, it freed her to make a life for herself.

Yes, she had heard about Lexington; her fellow passengers had talked of little else along the way, and from the stage they had all seen, along the countryside, the occasional marching troops, going to gather at Boston. But, in her weariness and her anxiety for what the future would bring her personally, she had given only surface attention to talk of the war.

Now she looked about; they had written that there would be someone to meet her. It proved to be a coachman in livery, who touched his cap to her.

"Would you be Mistress Thurstan, ma'am?"

She acknowledged it; when she left Oliver, she felt, she had relinquished any right to his name. It was better she use her own

157

here. The man carried her bags to the carriage, handed her in politely. On the long ride through a strange city, the teeming crowds giving way to green countryside, she leaned back in the seat, eyes closed, willing herself to relax, to recruit her forces for meeting her employer.

So you have done it, Margaret; you have freed yourself of them all. What life will you have now?

But all that mattered was that she was free. None of them could ever touch her again, not Oliver or Caroline or John, Caroline's friends, or any of the rest. They had no power over her. She could think that; in reality, she knew, she could escape them only in body; they stayed with her otherwise—as had Bethune. But Bethune she had loved, with all the inarticulate hero-worship of beginning womanhood. Long ago, far away, that did not matter now; and it was only when she was dispirited and frightened like this that he returned to her.

Could Caroline be blamed? She was a respectable, conventional matron. She had married and left Thurstan Hundred when Margaret was not quite eight years old, and they had met but twice since. That day, that nightmare day: still weak from the seasickness, explaining to a mistrustful maid that she was Mrs. Collard's sister, being admitted at last to await Caroline's return; Caroline, who was a stranger.

"You have *left your husband?*"

"Yes, I have. I'm sorry if you disapprove, Caroline—I can't expect anything else. Most people will. I simply could not withstand it longer. Please, may I have a glass of wine?"

Caroline ringing, ordering, waiting in rigid silence until the wine was fetched. "I dare say we should not have expected anything but awkwardness from you, Margaret. Father had sufficient trouble getting you wed at all; it was a great piece of luck that Oliver Gerard was taken with you. I will admit it was perhaps not quite the thing, Honor's husband—I could not blame you if you were a trifle squeamish for that. Still, a husband is a husband. What excuse do you offer for this outrageous behavior?"

"Perhaps none you'd think sufficient." Was Caroline thinking what Oliver had thought before, that she was a wanton?

Oliver openly flaunting a succession of mistresses, telling publicly it was because she was cold to him; making sure the gossip returned to her. Always finding fault: *You really must learn not to be so gauche with your guests, Margaret; you sound like a farmer's wife—and look like one, I swear!* Oliver coming in drunk, taking her in a brutal passion that she suffered silently, striking her a sudden childish blow: *But you're not Honor, why are you not Honor?* Herself unable even to feel sorry for him. Oliver with his wardrobe of elegant London garments refusing her ten pounds for a new gown—and she had had none in a year: *You'd likely choose something unsuitable as usual; we cannot afford it now.* Oliver, finally, with her dower money spent on his new commission, utterly ignoring her, going about without her. She had never got on with the other military wives; their interests seemed so senseless, their talk so silly and, at the same time, so sophisticated that it alarmed her. She had acquired a little cynicism since. But it had taken courage to run away.

She halted her inarticulate defense, seeing how Caroline's eyes never softened. "Most wives must withstand a little neglect and unfaithfulness in a husband. I'm inclined to think you're only a spoiled child, going into a tantrum the first time you're crossed."

"Very well, perhaps so," said Margaret. She faced her sister obstinately, knowing what would follow. "But you may as well spare yourself any argument, Caroline. I've left Oliver and I shall never go back to him."

"And what, pray, will you do instead?"

She had sold her betrothal ring and a necklace her mother had given her, to pay her passage from London; stolen away like a thief when Oliver was in Leicestershire for the hunting, leaving him the traditional note. She had four pounds ten in her purse; she had thought Caroline might take her in, and being known in Boston, aid her to find a position.

"A *position!* To earn your own living? Really, Margaret! You have not only disgraced yourself—a second time, I may remind you—by abandoning your husband, but you put your family in an extremely awkward situation. What had you thought you might do?"

"I could be a governess, I think. I didn't mean to go in a shop, or anything like that, you know."

"Surely you must see I could scarcely have my sister working as a governess," said Caroline thinly. "I think you had best return home to Virginia."

"I don't want to do that. I don't want to see Thurstan Hundred ever again. I haven't enough money to do that in any case." Better to be frank.

"I see. I would, of course, be happy to give you that. Whatever is decided, I suppose you must stay here for the time being. I've no notion what John will say, but we can hardly turn you away if you are destitute."

But what a fool she had been to stay almost a year. Not knowing what else to do, only stubbornly refusing to return to Virginia as they all wanted. She had been a coward, afraid to venture out on her own. Weakly her mind defended: I was not well, so tired all the while.

John Collard, that stern Boston merchant, the male counterpart of Caroline, bloodless, conventional, silently disapproving. Caroline's proper lady friends calling. Never mind, stop thinking of that; you are away and free now. Free. It was a relative term. The Collards had by now sailed for England. Caroline had pressed her to return to Virginia; and at last she had agreed, making plans of her own. No one knew of the New York newspapers she had bought, searching their advertisements, or of the letter she had sent in reply to the most promising. She had bade good-by to Caroline quite meekly, lying about having written their father; Caroline, when she learned the truth, might think what she pleased.

It might not be an easy or pleasant life she would make for herself—Margaret Gerard the erring wife—as a governess to Mrs. Kerr of Harlem Heights. But she would ask help of no one; it should be her life, to manage as she thought best.

She could not help, however, having a few qualms at telling Mrs. Kerr the lies she had devised: the deceased parents, the necessity to earn a living. One thing to write it, another to say it. But Mrs. Kerr scarcely listened; a kindly, talkative, youngish matron, she accepted Margaret at face value.

"I'm sure you will do splendidly, my dear, so long as you are not nervous. I don't mean the children, though heaven knows they are enough to make a saint nervous, but about the war. My best housemaid has just left with an hour's notice, if you will believe it, terrified of the British; she says the entire British Army will be coming to devour us! Such nonsense. As my husband says, now they have provoked us to war let us make it a good one! And we shall scarcely be having battles in New York. You look a sensible girl. How old did you say you are? Twenty-seven, a most suitable age. Not too old to be lacking in energy, not so young that you think only of making sheeps' eyes at young men. Though I vow I cannot understand why you missed getting a husband, pretty as you are."

Margaret wondered why Mrs. Kerr troubled to tell that polite lie. She was not pretty at all: too tall, and she had got too thin now.

She settled into the Kerrs' suburban home with some misgiving, but that was soon allayed; it was a friendly household, though she was left much alone by the adults of the house, because of her position between servants and gentry. Her two young charges kept her so occupied she had little time to think of herself. In this peaceful green suburb it was easy to imagine the city much farther off, and incredible that its inhabitants were preparing for war.

She was to have a free day once a fortnight; that day before her first holiday she found herself wishing for some excuse not to take it. She knew not a soul in New York; there would be nothing for her to do, for she had little money for shopping. Almost for the first time she felt lonely, and told herself sharply how fortunate she was, despite everything, to be away from the tangle that had been her life last year. This was the hour of the day she most disliked—between tea and dinner, when the children were free of lessons and she had nothing to do, time to feel sorry for herself. Here in New York the dinner hour was fashionably late, past eight o'clock sometimes.

After a little she came out of the rather bare small chamber they had given her, and went down the stair; there was to be a dinner party this evening, and perhaps Mrs. Kerr would like her to arrange flowers for the table, or have some other task to keep her busy. As she descended the last flight the butler was opening the front door to admit a caller. She heard his murmured greeting, the request to see Mr. Kerr.

"I know it is an inconvenient hour. I am from the New York *Courier.* If you'd tell him, it is about the articles we are printing regarding the franchise law. My editor was much impressed with Mr. Kerr's recent letter to him on the subject, and thought an interview would be of interest. If tomorrow would be more convenient, I can call again."

The butler bowed. "Certainly, sir, if you'd wait. I am not sure the master is free now, but I will ascertain. What name shall I say, sir?"

"Bethune—Mr. James Bethune of the *Courier.*"

Margaret stopped dead on the last stair. She clung to the newel post, suddenly giddy.

The butler glided away down the passage. The other was only a tall man, indistinct in the shadow of the entry hall, half turned from her, unaware of her presence. Desperately collecting her scattered wits, she took a cautious step on trembling legs; if she could only get past the stair, unheard, unseen, and hurry away toward the rear premises! It could not be—but if it was, she could not meet him, speak with him. And still, against her will, her eyes stayed on that turned figure. Only a tall man, fair hair above a dark coat. It could not be—

She was not quick enough. He heard, and turned. And it was; it was Bethune. As if in a blaze of light she saw him, recognized him; they might have met last only yesterday. He looked so much older, graver; but his eyes were the same, the steady gray eyes that said, Don't trouble, I am here to care for everything, only trust me. How odd that she had ever thought she had forgotten his features, his voice, his eyes. He looked prosperous; he was in sober blue broadcloth, with a plain neckcloth, and his darkened fair hair was tied neatly with a blue queue-ribbon. He looked

even a little taller; he had filled out a trifle from boyhood.
Bethune.

From a distance she heard his voice, sounding alarmed. "Are
you faint, mistress? Let me—" She found she could not stand,
and the giddiness increased. A strong arm took her weight, supported her to the nearest chair. A candle bracket stood on the
table nearby, and looking up she saw him more clearly. There
was no recognition in his eyes at all.

CHAPTER 21

ODDLY, that cleared her mind. The dizzy feeling passed, she
sat up and drew a long breath. She said distinctly, "Thank
you, I am quite all right." He was bent over her, concerned, and
their eyes met. That was when he knew. She saw the knowledge
come into his expression, the disbelief, the consternation. He
straightened quickly and moved away a few steps.

The little silence grew to tense embarrassment. If she could
get up and go right away from this— She began to say something, anything, but his voice cut across hers.

"Well, this is a little surprise, Margaret." His old whimsical
understatement. And, as if to himself, "Perhaps I always knew
you and I were not finished. Have you come to New York to seek
me out, is that it?" And that was cold, hard.

Stunned anger lent her strength and she got up from the chair
shakily, feeling disheveled, feeling absurdly fifteen again, a
child.

"Do you think—do you think I ever in my life wanted to see you again, Bethune? That I'd deliberately—" Incoherent as a child now. "Let me pass, let me get away, I—"

"Wait," he said. "Wait, Margaret, I ask pardon. That was a foolish thing to say—or think. No, you did not expect to see me, did you? I've grown too cynical since—we last met." He came nearer; belatedly she saw that this had been a shock to him too, of course. "What do you in New York?"

"Only coincidence," she fumbled, "that I—I'd never have come if I had known—" that he was anywhere here.

"Yes, I see. This is rather awkward, isn't it?" And almost at once it became more so, by the butler's soft-footed return.

"I'm sorry, sir, the master cannot see you now. He suggests you call at his law offices in Broad Street." Subtle indifference to the social standing of a newsman was in the deferential tone.

"Thank you. Mistress Thurstan is an old acquaintance," said Bethune easily. "I'd not expected to see her here, a pleasant surprise. May I escort you anywhere, mistress?" He assumed she was visiting the household.

The butler's supercilious glance put a little anger in her voice. "I've no free day until tomorrow." And that implied she would be pleased to see him then, which, God knew, could not be more false. Never again. She must leave here, she must. Always having to run away: from Virginia, from Oliver, from Caroline, and now from this!

Mrs. Kerr's little bell tinkled in the drawing room; the butler divided a glance between them and unwillingly Margaret said, "I will see the gentleman out, Barnes."

"Very good, miss."

And then there was another awkward time of silence. He was looking at her searchingly now, doubtless gauging the differences, the samenesses, just as she was. Twelve years was a long time. Changes in both, too, not to be seen on the surface.

She did not know what she would say until the words formed themselves. "We—I never knew where you went—"

"Here. First and—since. Did I err," he asked abruptly, "in calling you Mistress Thurstan just now? What are you here?"

There was no space for conventionality between them. "Yes, you did. I am Margaret Gerard now, but none here knows that; it is better I be called Thurstan. I have left my husband. I am nursery governess to Mrs. Kerr's children."

"I see." And now there came the sound of steps on the stair, Mrs. Kerr's voice calling directions to the maids. Bethune looked harried, as she felt. "We cannot talk here—I must talk with you, Margaret. When are you free, where can we meet?"

"I don't want—" she began, withdrawing.

"That is no matter," he said almost angrily. Bethune never used to be so autocratic. "I must see you again. You said you are free tomorrow? Meet me at—at the Bowling Green, by the Liberty Pole, at one o'clock. Anyone will direct you, or I can come here to fetch you—please, Margaret."

Mrs. Kerr was coming down the passage. In panic at being caught here, conversing with a caller—fearing sharp questions and perhaps suspicions—Margaret had no choice. "Very well, I will meet you. No, you are not to come here! Only go now, please!"

"Don't fail me," said Bethune. "I will see you tomorrow, then."

She shut the door after him just as Mrs. Kerr appeared. She pretended to be smoothing her hair before the hall mirror, but her hands trembled so she was sure the sharp eyes would see and wonder. As soon as possible she escaped to her little room, and now she was bitterly sorry at her easy capitulation. She did not want to see him again; but—

When they met that next afternoon, perhaps he too could bring to bear more reason than emotion. Margaret, during the night, had lived over the past agony and resentment and had reached a place of comparative peace. She could meet him almost as she might a stranger, and she did not mind it as she had thought to. Queerly, she felt as he had seemed to feel—there was unfinished business between them, and now or later they must meet again.

She came into the city that morning, and made her first acquaintance with the shops; Mrs. Kerr had generously advanced her a quarter of her yearly forty pounds' wages. On her initial drive to the Kerrs' house she had not noted how far it was from the city proper, a distance impossible to walk. The most fashionable residential areas, it seemed, were those suburbs farthest from the city. The Kerrs, like others, evidently thought nothing of driving eight or nine miles, he to his offices, Mrs. Kerr to social events and for shopping. But the Kerrs were kindly people, and she would be taken into the city by Mr. Kerr as he drove to his office, on her holidays; they assured her that she would find a hackney inexpensive when she returned. In London she had grown to like city life—the crowds and shops. She thought she would try to come to the city on her free days, for a change and to be alone; for nowhere is one so much alone as in a city crowd.

One o'clock found her on the footpath along the Bowling Green, which she had found without difficulty. She was not nearly so nervous as she had thought to be. But when he came, hurrying to join her, embarrassment rose in her throat to stiffen her expression and chill her voice.

"I apologize to ask you to meet me here—" Like, he might have added, any servant girl meeting a soldier. "I should have thought—I'm sorry. May I offer you luncheon somewhere?" He was the one who was nervous, now. She recognized the fact with obscure triumph, briefly felt, and accepted the invitation calmly. He brought her to the private parlor of a nearby coffeehouse, where he seemed to be known. Once there, the hesitancy left him; his tone was easy in orders to the waiter. She thought, He has grown to a man and this is his place. And when he began to speak to her, his voice was assured, if grave.

"We can talk here. It was a surprise to meet you again, Margaret—you don't mind that I call you that? I'm sorry, I should not. And perhaps you'll not want to answer questions, but"—he smiled slightly—"you'll agree it is but natural I am concerned."

"Yes, certainly." And now, even more obscurely, his sudden assurance annoyed her. "You may be sure, if I had known you were living in New York, nothing could have made me come here, Bethune!"

He smiled again; she remembered how seldom he had smiled,

and it lit his whole expression, made him look so much younger. "That sounds strange. You never called me anything else, did you? I am James or Mr. Bethune here, and under the circumstances I think the latter would be absurd, wouldn't it?"

"I don't think the need will rise to call you anything," she said to that.

"Please don't be angry." He was looking at his hands, folded on the table; his tone was quiet. "We are both adults, we can be reasonable about this. You are someone I—knew, and I did a great wrong to you. Now I find you, a lady, alone and in a position I would never expect, and isn't it natural I should feel some responsibility toward you?"

"I prefer to be responsible to myself, Mr. Bethune."

"No doubt. That does not change my feeling. I want to know how and why you are here, Margaret."

She said it in unadorned phrases. "I told you, I have left my husband. I went to my sister in Boston, I thought to find work to earn my living. But they disapproved. So when they were to go to England—she and her husband—I said I would return to Virginia as they all wanted, but I never meant to. I found this position myself, I mean to earn my own living and be free of all of them. Of everyone." She stopped; all that had nothing to do with him. She went on more quietly, "But they all disapproved my leaving Oliver, of course—"

"Oliver Gerard!" he said strangely. "But he was wed to—"

"To Honor, yes. She died. She died with her baby." And that made a tense silence between them; he looked away again.

"I used to envy Oliver Gerard," he said. "I'd nearly forgot his name. So you wed him!" There was something in his voice she translated as scorn, and sudden blind anger made her lash out at him.

"The other way about, Mr. Bethune! Do you suppose I had any choice of husbands? Everyone knew—about that. Of course everyone knew! My father was much relieved to have me off his hands, when Oliver offered for me—for my dower, that is—and I wed him to get away from Virginia where I was known. That is the whole of it. I keep thinking to escape. I thought I should be free here. I see I never will be. I'll go now, you'll not keep me here—"

"You'll go when I please," he said. He had gone very white. "Sit down, Margaret. Sit down and listen to me." But he took a moment to collect himself; she saw that his hands were shaking. "They have—misused you, I see. But it's no good running away, Margaret. I found that. I ran away from you, and you have haunted me ever since. All that was my fault, only my fault. I wondered—but I never thought it might be so bad for you. That everyone would know. Children, my God, just children. No one has brought you to these straits but myself; it is all my fault."

The little spite died in her as she looked at him. Twelve years was a long time but in a lifetime neither could be entirely free of what lay between them, or at least the consequences of what had been. They were strangers and not strangers; she had borne this man's child. She had loved him; ignorant, childish, shy, yes, but she had loved him once. She felt nothing for him now; he was an adult stranger.

She said a little dispiritedly, "I'll tell you something odd. I never held you to blame and I don't now. Yes, we were just children. It was—just a thing that happened, no one's fault. I'm only sorry we have had to meet again like this. I think I'd best go, and we won't meet again."

He said, in a tone equally quiet, "Do you think I can let you go, and forget it, to shirk my responsibility a second time?"

Margaret waited to answer while the waiter served them; when he took himself off, out of earshot, she found her mood had changed again to an easier one. The food looked inviting. She even summoned a smile for Bethune's pallor, his rigid expression opposite her there. "But it's not such a tragedy! It's absurd that you should feel that. You owe me nothing—now. We're both quite different people from those children, all that time ago. And you needn't feel sorry for me. It was my own choice to leave Oliver, and I've a good position. I'm quite content."

"Are you?" he said in a low voice. He looked at his plate as if the sight were distasteful. After a moment he picked up his fork;

silence held to the beginning of awkwardness before he added, almost savagely, "Perhaps I should bring you up to date on my own history. I am married too, Margaret—to a woman I never loved and never will love. A woman I loathe living with. And do not ask me why I married her, for I couldn't tell you, if to save my life."

In all the times she had thought of him she never imagined him married. It did not matter; but she was surprised and, inevitably, curious.

He made a gesture of anger at himself; he asked, "How long are you wed to Gerard?"

"Seven years." His silence suggested another question; she added, "I thought I would like children; it would help. Then I did not want Oliver's. No." This was none of his concern at all, and his life none of hers. Had his wife children?

He did not speak again until they had finished the meal, and the waiter had fetched them coffee. Then he took a breath and looked up to meet her eyes directly. "Margaret, I apologize for anything I've said to offend you. I understand how you feel; you've no desire to see me or speak with me, much less be under obligation. I can't blame you. But if I spent the rest of my life at it, I could never make amends for what I have done to you."

"But you mustn't feel that, please—" Yes, it would be ridiculous to call him Bethune, but she could not say James.

"How can I help it? No matter what you may think of me, I have some principles. I am sorry—" He stopped.

She took him up, understanding. "I know. You're as sorry as I am that we have met again."

"No!" he denied violently. "Reparation—my God, what an empty word it is! I've no wish to interfere, I don't want to annoy you. But whether you like it or not, I feel—responsible. If you are ever unhappy, if there is anything I can do, or give—"

"That is your guilt speaking," she said sharply. "I can hardly accept anything from you, you know that. I wish you will forget it."

"Then . . . can we make a pact, Margaret? To be two people

just met, no memories between us? I should like to see you again."

"Do you think we could do that?" she asked with a little smile. "I will not have you pouring commiseration over me, dwelling on your own guilt. Let us at any rate forget what's behind us. But I'm not sure—"

"That you would want to see me again. You don't surprise me."

She was not sure of that either, somewhat to her own surprise. He might have been a stranger indeed, opposite her here, and yet — She looked at him, this tall, fair, grave man with the troubled frown that made a line between his eyes. The thought moved slowly into her mind: I could like him very well—if he were not Bethune.

CHAPTER 22

Bethune wondered if he had done right in seeking her out, forcing a meeting. He had no rights over her. It troubled him to think of a lady's earning her living. She had sent a private devil to sit on his shoulder. He had not lied when he told her she had haunted him for twelve years, but the memory had faded, the guilt dropped to the bottom of his mind, no longer an intolerable weight on him. Now that he knew more of what she had suffered, the guilt had risen fourfold. Oh, Susan had not been enough punishment, nor youth the beginning of excuse. Margaret's very presence nearby, though he might not see her again, kept the guilt oppressive on him. But, now that he knew, would there be any difference if she were in England or Virginia?

There was also the war. But if it came, would Virginia be safer than New York? Likely less. Who could say?

Who could say there would be a war, even, in that first fortnight? Plenty of preparation for one, but not battles. The news of Lexington galvanized New York to frenzied and not all sensible action. The die was cast: war! And all in a hurry the hesitaters must choose sides, the attacks and defenses be prepared. On the evening of the very day the news arrived a crowd of patriots had converged at the wharves along Long Island Sound, where lay two ships loaded with provisions for the troops at Boston, and commandeered both cargoes; another mob invaded the City Hall, demanding admittance to the armory, and, upon being denied, broke in the door and carried off a great collection of muskets, powder and ball, and bayonets. Others had seized the powder store near Freshwater, northwest in the city, and set a guard over it.

Sears and a delegation of followers the next day forced the customs collector to hand over the keys of the custom house, and officially closed the port of New York to commerce. And then the first great exodus began. Any hope of conciliation on either side was dead; New York was in the hands of the patriots, and the Tories scrambled to get away from probable punishment, being in minority. The Assembly split as if at an ax blow, the most remaining Loyalist and fleeing almost in ignominy, while a few conservatives and liberals such as Philip Livingston promised support to the patriots. Fortunes changed hands overnight as Tories sold out their possessions, fearing that total loss would result from the war; some took ship for England, some only went inland expecting confidently that the British would hold New York eventually. Some of the younger Tories organized into volunteer Loyalist companies.

The patriots were not slow to organize, but almost the sum of their companies' defense at first was the military rank they parceled out. Alexander McDougall was styled colonel of the First Provincial Regiment; it was promised elegant uniforms and— more to the point—weapons, but had neither as yet. John Lamb gathered a company of artillery; there was also Colonel John Lasher's Minute Men, all lacking regulation dress, with a dozen fowling pieces among them. Since the British troops had several caches of stores in the city, not a few patriots were hot for commandeering them, but the Provincial Congress, which had taken the Assembly's place, held the leaders back from such action; New York was not officially at war.

After some backing and filling, however, the majority took the matter in their own hands, descended on the royal magazine at Turtle Bay, and carried away a great store of cartridges and powder, ignoring the Congress's order that it be returned. Other royal stores were plundered to outfit the new companies; it began to appear that the patriots were seriously succeeding in raising an army.

Awaiting definite orders, the British troops and their officers watched all this alertly; anchored off the Battery, the two warships *Kingfisher* and *Asia* kept their guns trained on the city, which was all that prevented the patriots' seizing the cannon at Fort George. To the dismay and no less the embarrassment of the fort commanders, a considerable number of British regular troops deserted to the Americans; half the Royal Irish regiment thus melted away. In order to save his command Major Hamilton ordered all troops aboard the warships; but even on the march to the wharves some men slid out of ranks to shed their red coats.

It was expected that the Second Continental Congress, which was to convene early in May, would formally organize a patriot army. Meanwhile, spirit was not lacking in individual readying throughout the colonies.

Darcy had been one of the first volunteers to join the new Provincial Regiment; the office saw little of him these days. He and his uncle were reconciled because of the war; Rafe Trevelyan was giving money generously to the volunteer American forces.

"Our bold soldier boy," MacDonald mocked gently. "We shall have to find a new clerk. And you, Mr. Bethune? You're not thinking of donning—or shall we say potentially donning—uniform?"

"No, I'm not. I'd make a poor soldier," said Bethune shortly

"If you consider the paper," said MacDonald, "I could spare you—or replace you."

That was half vanity; Bethune only grinned at him. "I've no doubt of that, sir." Actually he had grave doubt of it; MacDonald could not do everything. It was conjecturable what situations, financial and otherwise, they would have to meet. Panic was ruling the banks. In truth, he had no burning desire to join the patriots; he was still the watcher. Like MacDonald, his sympathy was more on their side than the others', far more; but he could not help thinking this sudden scramble for war foolhardy: children playing at soldiers. Time might show different. "I think I'm more useful where I am," he told MacDonald. "You remember once telling me that print is more powerful than powder and ball? This war will want writing about."

"Quite right. If there are any left to read the newspapers. But I tell you, Mr. Bethune, let us wish them luck. They stand for their rights. I don't believe it can be done, but what a facer for the German if we should give him a beating! And all the colonies joined—"

"If they remain joined," said Bethune. "If."

The demonstrations against loyalism in New York, the rush of volunteers to the patriots' cause, did much to change the reputation of Toryism that the colony had acquired; New York was solidly now with the most belligerent, Massachusetts and Virginia. The delegates to Congress were given an enthusiastic ovation at their departure for Philadelphia.

A few days later arrived news, and cheering news, of the first battle of the war. A volunteer company of New Englanders under Ethan Allen had attacked and captured the small but strategic British forts at Ticonderoga and Crown Point, thus making New York proper less vulnerable to attack from Canada. The news had the effect of steadying the city's pulse. There had been a battle now; with most of the Tories fled and others lying low or pretending sympathy, New York settled down to await official campaign orders, and the nominal government assumed more actual control.

In the middle of June those orders arrived. The troops at Boston had been named the official American Army; chosen as commanding general over them was Colonel Washington of the Virginia militia.

"A Southerner," said MacDonald.

"All I've heard of Washington is that he was with Braddock and supposedly organized the retreat after Braddock was killed. He's evidently well thought of."

"Well, we shall see how he does."

Bethune had enough to occupy him. But there was the devil on his shoulder. He did not want to see Margaret again now, he knew she would not want to see him; he did not need her presence to sharpen his remorse, and he would remind her of God knew what miseries suffered on his account. Yet he must see her, he was drawn to it; there was the uneasy sense of responsibility. Or was it the need to scourge himself with her?

He knew she had a free day once a fortnight; he wrote her, asking that she meet him where they had walked before, if she planned to come to the city on that day. She came; she was polite; she answered his questions. She was quite content with Mrs. Kerr, yes. But when she excused herself from his offer of refreshment, pleading necessary shopping, he thought the tension was eased between them. They were more natural together. Two different people, he thought; it is the past, it cannot be changed, I must forget it.

The next time they met it was by chance in the street, a month later. He thought she looked less strained; her thin face had filled out somewhat, so that the sharply arched, heavy brows seemed to dominate it less. Her full mouth had always a serious curve, only rarely lifting to a laugh, but he thought she looked more content than before. She acquiesced to his suggestion that they take coffee at the York Arms. There was a moment then, as they faced one another across the table in the empty private parlor, when it seemed impossible that they were here together.

Neither spoke until she said, "Yes, it is awkward," with a little smile, and suddenly there was no embarrassment.

"You don't mind?"

She understood him. "No—perhaps it's queer, but I don't. I used to think if we ever met again—but of course we should not, it was incredible."

"Yes, I know. But I am glad we have, Margaret. I'm not sure why." And by the time the waiter served them they were talking naturally. She asked him about his work at the paper; he found himself explaining at length, apologized. "I'm sorry to bore you." He thought, I could always talk to Margaret.

"But you don't. It's interesting. You think a deal of your Mr. MacDonald."

"I should never tell him so. He would be furious." They smiled together. But, as if impersonal talk had given them confidence, he asked abruptly, "I dare say you feel some curiosity about my marriage. Do you want to hear of my wife?"

"It's none of my concern, is it? I confess to curiosity, yes."

He shrugged, not looking at her. "She is heiress to a fortune. Most believe I wed her for it. I did not. I wed her because she set a little trap for me I was too great a coward to climb out of, that is all."

"That can't be fair," she said thoughtfully. "To herself or yourself. Did you say you'd grown cynical? If you were you would not sound so hurt over that. It is a very odd feeling, isn't it? We're really strangers, yet not quite—and talking so personally. You would like to know about Oliver?"

"I did not mean—"

"No, I know. Does any of it matter at all? We've no claims on each other."

"I've none on you, certainly. . . . I should not have asked to see you again."

"I'm glad you have. I don't know how it may be for you, but I was frightened of meeting you again, and then somehow—you were kind—it set me free of you. That's strange." She was stirring her coffee, staring at it abstractedly. "You said—haunted. Perhaps I was too. Now we have met again, it is two different people."

"I felt that too."

"Let us leave it so, then. Friends?"

"After all, we're not children. Friends." The constraint was not buried deep, however; how might it be? And it was not as she said, for him; he had been free of her, now he was in bondage again, only by reason of that gnawing sense of responsibility.

He learned she liked, on her free days, to walk on the Common, if she came to the city. He made opportunities to be there, hoping to see her. They could be natural together now, on the surface at least. And as he came to know her better, it was easier, for she was not the child he had known. She was a mature, intelligent woman. In an odd way it was provocative to him, to talk with this woman just met who was still not a stranger. It was more fantastic that they could attain such a relationship than that coincidence should bring their lives together again; but he had already learned that life is full both of queernesses and coincidence.

She had said that first day, I never blamed you. He found that more incredible than anything else; knowing Margaret as she was now, he believed it. It was not she who had put the devil of guilt in him, but his own conscience.

An excessively hot July thinned New York's population—that and the British warships' cannon trained on the city, which was probably the major cause of the citizens' flight. But the Kerrs, along with many prosperous families, remained.

"I'd thought your employers might be leaving," he said once.

"Oh, no, Mrs. Kerr thinks it all nonsense, you know. She says it is silly to suppose there'd be danger here; wars are not fought in cities, it is the safest place in all the colonies."

"I wonder. After all the excitement in April, the war seems slow in starting, doesn't it? Only one battle, at Bunker Hill, and that a defeat for us. What is your feeling about it?"

"Will it shock you as a newspaperman if I say I'm not much concerned? Oh, I feel as you do—I don't think I'd be considered Loyalist. But I'm afraid they—we—cannot possibly defeat the British. Everyone is so nervous about those warships; to tell you the truth, I can't understand why they have not bombarded the city long since."

He laughed. "They're hoping New York will be held, and it is the most valuable city in the colonies, after all."

She looked at him quickly. "Then you think there may be a battle over it?"

"I am beginning to think this may be a longer and bitterer war than anyone had guessed." It had been at first a little joke, Darcy and his new uniform. Yesterday Darcy had left with his regiment for Boston where the armies gathered: a sober Darcy, older, grimmer. There would be men killed in this war—had been; it was not a game of politics argued out between *Courier* and *Gazetteer* on their front pages. That was only just coming home to him.

She said, "Perhaps I'll be sorry I came to New York," and smiled.

"Have you been?" he said gravely.

She shook her head. "No. I've got free. Whatever happens, I'm dependent on no one."

Susan had refused to leave the city. Most Loyalists had fled to more congenial surroundings, for fear of reprisals or of being caught in the crossfire. Sears' new Association of Patriots had ordered the arrest of all known Tories. "They cannot mean women," she said incredulously. "I do not believe that! Only because most of my friends were Loyalist—"

"I scarcely think you'll be arrested," Bethune agreed.

"I intend to remain in my own home. They have done enough without forcing me to remove. All trade stopped—property devalued—and if you think they will succeed in holding New York, you'll find out how wrong you are! Common rabble, not soldiers. The troops will put them down in no time!"

He did not argue; he was not greatly interested in what she did or thought.

He soon was to be. On a steaming August night, the hulk that had been George Shields ceased to breathe at last; almost the last piece of legal business Mr. Carruthers accomplished before he left New York for England was to transfer the estate—drastically reduced in value—to Mistress Susan Bethune, under the terms of the will.

The funeral was hasty and makeshift; Susan was dry-eyed at

the grave. Bethune had not realized Susan hated her father; no, he was as yet no cynic.

"At last, at last. You do not know how glad I am. Would I not resent him, all he did to me? His stupidity over that smuggling cost me a match with the Van Steens! His vulgarities—that odious newspaper." She repeated that, looking at him. "I wish you will tell Mr. MacDonald I will have an interview with him. Concerning the policy of the *Courier*."

"I hope you won't create an issue," he said mildly.

"I will discuss with Mr. MacDonald, not you," she said tautly. "I will see him tomorrow."

That night the war started for New York. So slow had the hostilities been in beginning, so hesitant the British stationed roundabout, that even the Provincial Congress had grown bolder, and sanctioned the seizure of the cannon on the Battery at Fort George. An orderly troop of patriots marched down that night to accomplish the deed, and in the harbor *Asia* and *Kingfisher* kept an alert watch on them. Midway in the proceedings a musket was discharged, by chance or as signal, no one could guess. The Americans instantly opened fire, and after nearly five months of waiting, the warships commenced a cannonade against the city.

CHAPTER 23

"IT IS A PITY," observed MacDonald, "that you are such an independent young man. Half the reason your wife came here was to gain the hope of a little power over you."

Bethune said, "She does not like you too well either, sir. May I ask the situation?"

"I told her it is a trifle late in the day for the *Courier* to make right-about-face, and that if we did so, we should lose the half of our subscribers we've not already lost. I showed her the latest accounts. And I asked her," said MacDonald, "if she imagines it is of great import what any newspaper prints in times like these."

"She did not swallow that?"

"Whole, Mr. Bethune, whole. She is not a reader. The accounts surprised and worried her. They worry me. But your wife's legal control is the least we've to worry about. If it came to an open quarrel, how could she hope to begin litigation with no official government law operating? By God," said MacDonald, "I shall go on publishing until we're bankrupt! It may not be long—we're already in difficulties."

That was understatement. The bombardment of the city had thrown New York into panic. Little actual damage was done: a few houses near the fort destroyed, the roof of Fraunces' Tavern holed, a dozen men wounded; but New York had never expected to have the war on its doorstep. The expectation had been that the actual fighting would be elsewhere. A year ago a thriving city, largest in all America, of twenty thousand population, New York had dwindled at the start of the war when the Tories fled, and now overnight shrank more by some seven thousand who scurried out of the city as from an inferno. The most fled across the river to New Jersey, some to Long Island; the country reaches began to be dotted with the tents and rude huts they put up for shelter. The country folk supplied them food, but eventually the majority fled farther to escape. Business was at a standstill in the city; the American troops remaining in New York as safeguard halted their preparation for the Canadian campaign to arrange some defense for the harbor. They ran a *chevaux de frise,* a stout chain, under the surface of the North River between the two new hastily erected forts called Washington and Lee, opposite each other, which should keep out any attack by water from the north. The British ships still lay off the Battery; no new bombardment had come, but the threat was always there. Tryon and his government had fled to the *Duchess of Gordon* in the harbor, to be out of reach of the Americans, and the patriots held the city.

Like all businesses, the newspapers had suffered greatly. Many of their subscribers had fled the city; communications began to be difficult, with Boston besieged and troops everywhere, friendly and otherwise. Supplies would pose a problem as well as communications. Bethune considered what they had on hand, knowing Mac-Donald was reckoning too. They had two hundred reams of paper; the contract with Brady had two years to run, but who knew what might come in that time? The office was without clerks; Ingalls had fled. He and MacDonald alone were the *Courier*.

"I'll ask you again if you've any impulse to join the patriots."

"And I told you once, no," he answered. "I am a newswriter, not a soldier. Why should I? Do you think of quitting publication?"

"You just heard me say we'll continue. For one thing, we've a responsibility to paid subscribers. Those we can deliver to. What about the delivery?"

Bethune shrugged. The *Courier* had employed some two dozen boys to deliver papers about the city; most of those had simply vanished. "We can try to find more," he said. "Beyond another four or five editions, it may not matter—where are we to get more paper?"

"There are mills in New Jersey. I should like to lay in a good stock if possible. But you know, Mr. Bethune, one way or another, I may lose you. They're not looking kindly on young men who are slow to rally to the cause these days."

Bethune laughed. "Are you giving me any news? I had a little scene in the street with a few hooligans only yesterday." Jeering at him, crowding close: What's a strapping fellow like you a-doing without a musket, friend? Are you Tory or coward? A place for your sort, and that's New Gaol!

Well, it was his contrariness again: he was angry, but not for being called coward. "Damnation," he said, "no one will force me to anything! Rabble is a polite word for them. Let them go and fight their war. I'll cheer them on safe enough, but we cannot all be expected to drop responsibility and drill with broomsticks! Do you think it is any use to put out an advertisement for clerks?"

"We can try it." MacDonald swore, trying to maneuver the

heavy wheeled chair; the wooden wheels were out of true because of the rough streets, and it took all his strength now. "I'll do without clerks if I can save Haagen! He is wild to go. But we may have to make do without more than Haagen."

That afternoon Mr. Isaacson came to the office. On the heel of greeting he produced a large brass key and gave it to Bethune. "The house. You will see to it."

"What? But—"

"We go," said Isaacson simply. "Perhaps we come back when the fighting is stopped—perhaps not, *nicht wahr?* Perhaps we be killed. But not here. War is not good. I do not know where we go, but we go." He patted Bethune's arm. "The house you see is safe. If we do not come again, after, is your house."

"But, Mr. Isaacson—" The old man was already at the door. Bethune weighed the key in his hand, perplexed, at last dropped it in his pocket.

He had not seen Margaret in six weeks; he thought possibly the Kerrs had left New York. He had had one letter from Darcy, a hasty scrawl; the First Regiment was joining the Canadian campaign and likely by now Darcy was marching north with that army under Schuyler, to attack Montreal.

In November the patriots went on a drive to round up the Tories in hiding. Feeling ran so high that any man not in uniform and not obviously senile was suspect of Loyalism; fortunately for Bethune, his connection with a radical paper absolved him of that charge. But he thought the whole affair farcial; he remembered what Philip Livingston had called the Sears party: children. Any man who shouted praise of the patriots they accepted as a brother, never inquiring his record. Bethune knew several former Loyalists who were now fire-eating patriots, to judge from their talk; Sears' police never went near them, and there were a good many others of the same stamp.

It was in that month that there began to drift into New York the first official talk of independence. The hotheads had always talked it; but the more educated men, the liberals, had looked on such talk with dismay. Many colony governments still regarded the war as a show of force to bring the Crown into line; but the spirit for a permanent break was growing.

"Will you need more money?" MacDonald asked abruptly, seeing Bethune don his coat and tidy the papers on his table into the drawer.

"Have you any more?" Five hundred pounds in gold and paper in a belt round his waist felt heavy and conspicuous.

"A bit," said MacDonald. "I'm not keeping tabs these days on how much is spent on the *Courier*. You'll do the best you can for us. And one other thing, Mr. Bethune—"

"Yes?" He turned and shied away hastily. MacDonald had produced from under the shawl about his legs an ancient pistol with a barrel a foot long.

"It is a little comfort; I shall miss it. Take it along and buy some ball and powder for it, a good supply. It might not be amiss if you acquired a weapon also."

"I've never fired a gun in my life." Bethune took it gingerly. "I dare say you're right—one never knows." He stowed it away in his pocket and went out to arrange passage on the Point Hook ferry.

He crossed to New Jersey that night, with a hired nag, and rode to Newark to the one paper mill in operation there. They were inclined to argue with him, reluctant to sell so much stock to one purchaser; the manager was almost tearful.

"You don't know, sir—we've bare supplies of rags coming in, and commitments right and left. You know Mr. Holt of the New York *Journal* owns half the shares, and he is due two hundred reams this coming month."

"Several New York papers are making drives to collect rags, Mr. Van Eyck. You may not be in such bad case as you fear. And I'm offering—" It was the gold turned the trick; worth a dozen times as much as paper money. He got a signed agreement that one hundred reams would be delivered within a fortnight. In Newark he also bought a supply of powder and ball for MacDonald's pistol, and, feeling absurdly melodramatic, purchased a pistol for himself, smaller and more modern.

It was the week after he returned that he met Margaret in Broad

Street. He was surprised; he had thought the Kerrs had gone away
—so many had. "Oh, no, Mrs. Kerr was terrified at the bombardment, but it's not come again and she says in any case Harlem is
far enough out of the city to be safe. I have not been in to the
shops for some time, and all the deliveries are stopped now, you
know—Mrs. Kerr had some commissions for me to do for her."

"I see." They were near the City Tavern; he offered her refreshment there, and then remembered that the City was closed; many
taverns and other public places, all the theaters, were shut now.

"No matter, I must be starting back. It is already past four."

"A hackney—"

"Oh, I should not afford it. I am to meet Mr. Kerr at his office
and he will drive me back in his carriage."

"But I meant to escort you myself—"

"There is no obligation." The last word emphasized; but she
smiled slightly. "I keep telling you that, do I not? You will never
believe it."

"It is not a question of believing it." He looked at her helplessly. Even after this time, it was incredible that Margaret should
be here. He thought she looked older, more staid, in rather shabby
dark garments. "You are quite content, Margaret?"

"Oh, yes." But she was like himself, wary of confidence; it
might be truth or lie.

In January came the news of the failure of the Canadian expedition: Montgomery killed, Arnold and Lamb both wounded. New
York stirred uneasily, not at all confident of security from the
enemy; and after that news came action. Suddenly the city was
filled with American troops: Lord Stirling came in from New
Jersey with a thousand men; Colonel Waterbury with his New
Englanders, General Lee with an army of Southerners; other various troops. They quartered themselves on New York, many in
private homes, but these were patriots and the citizens welcomed
them. Their activities, however, filled New York with something
like consternation: they set about fortifying. They fired private
houses and put up barricades; they dug trenches, erected breast-
works, lined cannon at strategic points. Quite evidently battle was

expected here! Impossible, people said; the war is elsewhere. But the visible evidence was to the contrary, and once more the city dwindled, as those who had hesitated until now to abandon property took the decision and fled. The troops were all too pleased to take over the empty houses.

In New York harbor lay the British warships *Mercury, Phoenix, Asia,* and *Duchess of Gordon;* when the American troops came in, all four hoisted anchor and set sail to anchor again off Bedloe's Island. They did not wait there for nothing, New York knew; did they expect reinforcements?

In March they could guess the answer to that.

Hugh Gaine of the *Gazette* came to the office that morning; Bethune recognized him with surprise. The various editors were generally wary of consorting, but their rivalry was a game the war was changing; nevertheless he would not have expected to see Gaine at the *Courier.* He had met the editor of the *Gazette* once, several years back.

Gaine nodded at him affably. "Morning, Mr. Bethune. I see you're acting your own clerk. This war plays the devil with newspapers. Is MacDonald in?"

"I am," said MacDonald from the rear room. "Bring the villain Gaine in, Mr. Bethune." But he offered his hand amiably. "What is on your mind, Hugh?"

Gaine hoisted one hip over the corner of the table. His beaver hat rode on the back of his head; he did not trouble to remove it. He was running to stoutness in middle age, but his jaw was still pugnacious. "Have you heard the news, Robert?"

"Of Boston?" MacDonald grinned. "Don't think to get ahead of us. Mr. Bethune was at the wharf when the packet anchored."

"So. The British have lost Boston. They're evacuating at once. And where d'ye think they'll come?"

"I don't need three guesses for that. Here. I apologize we've no liquor to offer you. All one can buy now is the local product. Yes, there is going to be a battle for New York. Have you any predictions to make?"

"Damn all," said Gaine. "Suppose the British take it? What will you do?"

"What of yourself?" countered MacDonald.

Gaine fingered his jaw. "I've a business to think of. I'd not lay a wager on them letting any publisher carry on except he's a Loyalist. In other words, Rivington. I'm talking soft these days, Robert. I'd not have you think me a coward, but if we must live under them— I intend to go on putting out the *Gazette* if it's at all possible. If I avoid controversial opinion it may be they'd allow it."

MacDonald was lighting a segar. "I doubt it. Mr. Bethune and I have been discussing the matter. I consider it likely they would stop all publication by military law, but it's conjecturable. We can cross the bridge when we reach it."

Gaine said, "Never know, Robert. By the time we get there, might be there'd be no bridge."

"Let us wait and see."

When he had gone Bethune said, "Chary, were you not? Don't you trust him?"

"I trust no one," said MacDonald. "You cannot predict how men will behave under fire. And I think we will be under fire."

"But you'll not let it stop us publishing the *Courier*."

MacDonald said, "I let nothing stop the *Courier*. Not your lady-wife or our empty pockets or the whole British Army. And I shall publish what I please."

CHAPTER 24

BETHUNE DODGED DOWN a narrow alley, flattening himself
against the building as another roar of gunfire shook the city.
Fool—if there was a direct hit anywhere near that would do no
good. Where had he got to? He'd been in Cherry Street when it
started, and had run blind, swerving to avoid tangling with the
troops. He peered out, wincing involuntarily at the noise, and
swore: so many landmarks were gone, torn down to make space
for barricades or destroyed in the cannonade, that even old New
Yorkers lost themselves. That was Broadway—he had got half
across the city; he came out of the alley and ran south down this
street, came to the mouth of Fair. What looked to be a whole
company of American troops—Colonel Clinton's Third Regiment
in the smart gray faced with green—filled the street. They ran;
in the sweltering September heat their faces streamed sweat, the
gray uniforms were dark with it. A mounted officer was trying to
circle them, get them in some order; a big red-faced man on a
gray horse, he screamed oaths, naked sword lifted, and they scattered like chaff before him. Bethune turned and ran down William
Street.

A man pushing a wheelbarrow loaded with household gear
looked back at him, trying to run, and slowed. "Gord, I thought
you was a Britisher—they're comin'—'ave they landed?"

"Not till the guns stop, friend." Another thunder covered his
reply. He got to John Street; it was jammed with a crowd trying

to reach the wharves—people clutching the few belongings one might rescue from a fire; people screaming at each other: They're coming, oh, God, let me get away! The guns thundered again and somewhere close a shell hit with a crash of falling masonry. He'd never get through here; he turned. A troop of Holmes' cavalry, all unmounted, a dark brown tide marked by their scarlet facings, washed over the crowd from the other end of the street, trampling it down, pushing through. No officer there. Bethune ran through to Maiden Street by an alley; it was deserted.

A shell had sheered the roof of the *Courier* building. He burst in, shouting MacDonald's name. MacDonald was sitting at his table in the rear office with his pistol in his lap. Haagen, frightened to forgetting his English, gabbled in Dutch.

"What the devil are you doing here?" demanded MacDonald.

"The roof—"

"Damn the roof. What's happening?"

"They're running like rabbits. Civilians too. The whole fleet—"

"I can hear the whole fleet. Doubtless they're hearing it in Philadelphia."

"There's no hope they'll hold now." Bethune leaned on the wall; he was tired.

"Then in God's name," said MacDonald, "get you to Brady's!"

"Brady—"

"You heard me! God's teeth, will you move! God, if I—" It seemed he would lift himself by mere will; he was dead white. "Go and get those presses under cover, damn you! Now's the moment, in all the confusion!"

Bethune was ashamed, and surprised at himself for forgetting the presses—the precious presses, two of Brady's four, that MacDonald had bought for two thousand pounds a month ago. Brady, an obstinate man: Can't let you have 'em, I've my living to earn. MacDonald: You can't use them if you must let them rot here to save your own skin!

He went out to the street again. The heat was scorching; the very ground was hot to thin soles. The guns on the Battery thundered back at the British ships. He began to run again toward Pearl Street.

The beginning of the end had come—they all should have seen it, he thought as he ran—when the enemy arrived a month back. New York playing host to the American Army and its new General Washington, so arrogantly confident of British weakness! General Lee had pulled the lion's tail once too often. Those few men-of-war gathering so shyly round Staten Island, and then one morning New York waking to find itself in the middle of the British fleet, more than a hundred, all with guns trained on the city. That was the beginning.

The battle on Long Island was the end. How long ago? He tried to count the days, placed it only as recounted in last week's edition. Defeat? A rout. Washington retreating up to Harlem Heights, leaving five thousand troops as vanguard, and much use they'd been. They said ten thousand British had gone out against him—the army the fleet brought in—under Clinton and Cornwallis. The city had listened to the battle; and they had seen the beaten army straggle through the city northward, having been rescued off Long Island by a thousand patriots in every crazy craft available.

God, they'd have the whole city down. He stopped to catch his breath. It was not New York today, but some strange city unknown: this street deserted of life, its houses shut up, that street jammed with abjectly fleeing soldiers mad to get away and civilians equally desperate, battling each other for right of way. He leaned on the wall at the corner of Pearl Street and thought: Harlem Heights.

Probably the Kerrs had departed weeks ago, taking Margaret with them. All sensible people had left New York then, when the fleet gathered. Only the fools had stayed. And the newsmen. And today the fools were trying to get away too.

Brady, he saw, was joining the refugees. A wagon with sweating team stood before the shop. The oldest boy was on the box, watching over a half-load of household furnishings; others were carrying more from the second floor where the family resided. He went into the print shop, found it deserted, and as he shouted Brady's name remembered the first time he had come here as a boy, all those years ago, and, watching the presses fall, found his mission in life.

"I've expected you," said Brady. He came up from the yard; his normally genial face was white.

"You're leaving?"

"What d'you think, Mr. Bethune? If we can get out in time. To my brother in Poughkeepsie I'm bound." Brady shrugged. "God knows if I'll find work there. Be none here, that I know. I don't know what in God's name MacDonald thinks he will do with my presses."

"The *Courier*'s presses. We've the bill of sale at the office. You're taking the other two?"

"I am. Tell you the truth, I let MacDonald have the others because I knew 'twould be awkward to get more than two out."

"And you should have had penance from your confessor for the price you asked, the service they've seen." That hit was somewhere very near. Brady's wife came to the door and urged him in a frightened voice to hurry.

"Are you thinking to take them now?" Brady said. "If you've a wagon—"

"My God, man," said Bethune, "you'll be the rest of the day getting out to Broadway with your wagon—you don't know what the city's like." He found while he had been running and dodging that the cold piece of his mind had come up with a plan for the presses. He would need a wagon to take them, and he could not get a wagon through the city past fleeing American soldiers and civilians, and an invading British Army which would be landing very soon. "I want you to help me get them out to your stable—quick!" He gestured at Brady and the indentured man loading the wagon. They got the presses out to the small stable behind the shop, in one corner of the harness room. He worked quickly, raking up every wisp of hay from the floor, emptying the mangers, covering the presses over. He found a couple of old sacks and spread one over the precarious pile as further camouflage; the other he wrapped carefully about the heavy wooden box of type. He carried out the *Courier*'s boxes of paper to hide with the presses; the type he could take with him. It was hot work; he was streaming sweat when he finished. He came out; the Bradys were gone, the shop was deserted.

Somehow he got back to the office. The cannonade was dwindling. He said to MacDonald, "This isn't the best place to wait out an invasion."

"Let us go to John Street. If it is still there. How do you think to get those presses out?"

"I'll get them," he said. He looked at Haagen. "Well, Willem! Do you change your mind about staying by us?"

Haagen managed a grin. His round boyish face was still pale but he said, "Damn, Mr. Bethune, maybe I don't make such a goot soldier for de Americans anyway—de noise from guns I don't like! I stay by you and de *baas.*"

They got MacDonald's chair to the street. "God be thanked it isn't far." But the crowds were already thinning; most of the retreating troops were gone, and the civilians who had not succeeded in crowding aboard some, any, craft along the river were scurrying for shelter, warned, by the cessation of gunfire, of imminent invasion. The house in John Street still stood, and the woman Dorcas met them at the door.

"I was thinking you was killed," she said, her doglike eyes on MacDonald.

"Not so easy, Dorcas." In the little parlor, curiously prim, they sat, not speaking often. Presently the woman made some coffee, weak because there was little to be had. MacDonald primed and loaded his pistol, making a small jest at himself for it. "Surprising how much confidence a weapon engenders."

The thunder of cannon gradually ceased. They heard, even here in the middle of the city, the beginning of British invasion: marching columns in the streets, a bugle call in the distance, a troop of cavalry. Once there was a volley of closer cannon fire, then silence.

"That was the last word from Fort George if I don't mistake," said Bethune.

"Very likely."

Haagen said nervously, "Will dey come here, Mr. Bethune?"

MacDonald answered. "No, not at once, not tonight. They'll be too occupied taking possession and making bivouac to search private houses and smoke out patriots. Any who remain indoors should be safe." He looked at Bethune. "Will you be going out?"

"I imagine so. When they settle down a trifle they'll have more leisure to be suspicious. I think tonight is the time to get our presses hid permanently. Will you tell me," he added conversationally, "why we did not leave New York a month ago?"

MacDonald laughed. "It was a gamble. We've lost this throw, but it might have been the other way about."

"And just what use will it be to have those presses somewhere safe? We might print one edition of the *Courier* under the British. How would we do that without printers?"

It was growing toward dusk; MacDonald's voice came disembodied from the gloom. "It's a feeling you should understand, Mr. Bethune. I said a moment ago holding a weapon engenders confidence. A printing press is a far more powerful weapon than this pistol."

Bethune laughed. "I'll get them for us, sir."

Yes, it was too late now for parley on either side. It was more than a year since the first skirmishes provoked formal hostilities, and even then there was delay, reluctance on both sides to plunge into full-scale war—the liberals of both parties hoping for a last-minute reconciliation. Damnation, the patriots' own appointed Provincial Congress here in New York had persuaded the city to supply the British warships anchored in the harbor: for months they had done so. Waiting. Parliament indeed backed down at the last hour, offering generous terms: cessation of all taxes. Too late by that time: the Continental Congress had the bit in its teeth. Those men, liberal or radical, knew what they wanted and what they believed: some colonies would say they had been dragged in willy-nilly, but there they were now, committed irrevocably after the Congress voted for independence.

A stirring document; yes, it had stirred him. They had printed it in full in the *Courier,* including all the signatures, Philip Livingston's among them. But he had acquired enough of the newsman's cynicism to appreciate MacDonald's comment: "The key word, Mr. Bethune, in the entire document is none of the earnest passionate terms they've embellished it with—the liberties and rights and humanities. It is the innocent little word 'united.' If they can make that stay a fact, this brief document may be the cornerstone of a nation; if they cannot, it is a meaningless piece of grandiloquence. And I'll say something more. They say Jefferson had the upper hand in writing it, but even the Congress would not have taken such definite steps, to go all out for independence, if the whole spirit of the patriots had not been strengthened and defined by Paine's pamphlet." Which was the simple truth: no one event or man had had so much to do with unifying the patriots for independence as Thomas Paine's *Common Sense;* published in January of this year, it had sold over a hundred thousand copies within three months. Its message had spread through the colonies like wildfire. "Print," said MacDonald, nodding. "Always the most powerful factor."

But, committed, the patriots suffered only setbacks; the first and worst was the loss of New York, which followed on the heels of that belligerent decision of the Congress in July, as if the British too had been waiting. It was just six days after the Declaration was signed that the fleet opened fire on New York; and the only reason, evidently, that Washington succeeded in holding the city to this fourteenth day of September was that the fleet had been awaiting reinforcement and land troops that finally launched full-scale battle from across the East River.

Indignation over the reported—and later proven—hiring of Hessian mercenaries by the Crown had spurred the war spirit; but this first real flavor of British gunpowder had sent the Americans scuttling in disorderly retreat. And Bethune remembered what Darcy had written in the one letter he had had, a smudged, hastily written letter three months on the way, after the Canadian campaign last winter: "It was mainly poor management is all. Arnold is a fire-eater, damn the consequences, but erratic—and the routine arrangements were scamped, supplies and so on. I have been low with the flux several times, it is rife in the army. The entire spirit and confidence of the men has changed to see all this bungling and failure, and already we have had a good number of desertions, or should I say a bad number."

"United" was the word.

It was ten o'clock when Bethune left John Street with Haagen. It was a moonless night; he could have wished for some river fog, but either the British were all exhausted after their efforts in September heat or they were utterly contemptuous of the inhabitants remaining in the city. He had half-expected patrols, or at least bands of looters; they got to Pearl Street without encountering a soul.

There was a hiring stable round on Whitehall; Bethune knew the owner, a man named Jacoby, was a patriot; he would be safe to approach. No light showed anywhere, in any house they passed; there was no telling whether they were empty, or whether their inhabitants cowered inside in the dark. No light about the stable or the house at the side. He tapped at the door, calling Jacoby's name, but had no answer. They went to the stable. He was nervous at striking a light, but had several candles in his pocket in readiness; he lit one cautiously, saw two horses left in their stalls.

"Can you harness them?"

"Dat I can do, Mr. Bethune."

The only equipage left was an old carriage, its upholstery green with age, and the horses probably the poorest in the stable since they had been left. They drove round to the print shop without meeting anyone, and he began to think this would go easier than he had expected by a long way. "Drive right into the yard, we don't want far to carry them." But both were panting by the time they'd got the presses into the carriage, with every box of paper there had been in the print shop. This was no time to be nice about mine and thine; all the paper Brady had not been able to take, they could use.

"Where we tooken dem, Mr. Bethune?"

"Cherry Street, across the city. I never thought 'twould be done

so easy. There seems to be no one about at all—by God, I wonder
if they're here, or are we all frightened of shadows? Go up Whitehall and down Maiden to Wall, we'll avoid the water front as far
as possible, there'd doubtless be a watch there anyway."

"Right, sir."

Haagen drove. Bethune sat beside him on the box, and the
noise of their going seemed loud as the thunder of those cannon
this afternoon. Every minute he expected a challenge, even a
warning shot; but nothing happened. They turned down Maiden
Street; automatically, even in the dark, he glanced toward the
Courier office as they came by—and he reached to put a hand
over Haagen's on the reins.

"Look there." Alone, of all the buildings they passed on quiet
residential and commercial streets, the *Courier* office showed light.
A wisp of flickering, ghostly light, as insubstantial as the cold
finger down his spine.

"Mr. Bethune—you think it's dem?"

"British? Why should they be here and nowhere else?" He bit
his lip. "I shall have to investigate. Look you, if there's trouble,
or if I don't return at once, drive like the devil back to Mr.
MacDonald. Here is a key, don't lose it. It's for the house in
Cherry Street—Mr. MacDonald knows where it is." He swung
down off the box. Haagen protested, but Bethune crossed the
street to the office without hesitation. Now a certain cold resentment was growing in him. Who had the right to enter the *Courier*
office but himself or MacDonald?

Susan.

She had a right. That was absurd. He did not even know if she
was still in the house in Greenwich Road. She had obstinately
refused to leave, but so had others, who this day had fled in
panic. He had not seen her this morning before he left.

He entered quietly, but his step sounded on the planked floor
and he heard a sudden startled stir from the rear room. That was
where the candle was—he thought no more than one. He came to
the threshold and halted.

Seated at his table, her stare blank with fright, was Margaret.
She had lit one candle in its brass holder; as he came into the

wavering circle of light and she recognized him she gave a little involuntary sob of relief, caught control of herself instantly.

"I thought—you would have gone," she said.

CHAPTER 25

"WHAT ARE YOU doing here? I thought you had left the city weeks ago—"

"I could not," she said. "I could not." He saw there were two bags at her side. He was not sure if it was the candle flame made her seem to tremble. He came and laid a hand on her shoulder.

"What of the Kerrs?"

"They have left. Last week. They went to Mrs. Kerr's cousin in Williamsburg. So I could not go with them. She did not want to leave me alone." Yes, it was she trembling. This day cut all the formalities; he shook her slightly.

"You should not have stayed."

"What else would I do?" She looked up at him. "I stayed in their house—they left hurriedly, they thought I should go elsewhere. Then today, everyone said—and I was frightened, I thought I had best—I came to the city, I thought to cross the river—"

"Some thousands thought the same. You saw the retreat, the landing. How did you get down to the city?"

She nodded stiffly. "There is a great camp in Harlem. The general. They expect a battle there. I left the house early this morning—I've been all this time on the way, it was—dreadful. The crowds, and the noise—the fighting—"

She will be very tired, he thought, and frightened, and confused, after the exhausting day, all her struggle to achieve safety. He was tired himself, his mind fumbled for decision, but another unexpected feeling came to him and that was a kind of sly triumph: all her confidence gone, she needed someone now to take responsibility for her. He said, "You cannot stay here."

"I'm sorry, I did not know where to go—it was not that I was looking for you! I had to find shelter."

"Yes, very well. Come with me now." He took up her bags, snuffed the candle. She followed him out almost docilely and he was surprised at the savage satisfaction that gave him. "I'm sorry, there's no room inside, you must come on the box. It's all right, Willem—a friend."

"You hat me scared, Mr. Bethune. Where do we go?"

"Cherry Street. I must get these under cover before anything else." She was silent between them. He thought some of the explanation for the strangely quiet city was that the British had pursued the retreat north. Tomorrow would be different. They met only single ghost-shapes, not many, and those started at the carriage, scurried away in the dark. None of them spoke again until they came to the house in Cherry Street. "You'll have to tether the team."

"Not these, Mr. Bethune, they stand."

"Very well." He touched her arm. "Come along, you can hold the candle." She got down obediently. But he dared not light a candle until they were in the house. "The cellar—the door's along here." She held the candle while they struggled in with each press, strained to get them down the ladder-like stair to the earth-floored cellar. "You want to cover dem up, Mr. Bethune?"

"Nought to use. It's the safest place I can think of. Drive us back to John Street. Take the carriage to where we got it. Best hurry, there's no telling when—"

"Can I not stay here?" she asked.

He stared at her. "Here, alone? Certainly not."

"I can look to myself," she said.

He took her arm. "I see you're recovering of fright. You can't stay here."

"But I cannot—" She meant she would not stay in his house, his wife's house.

"I am not taking you to my home." He had no intention of trying to get there tonight.

Haagen let them out in John Street. He carried her bags in. MacDonald and the woman were just where he had left them in the parlor, and suddenly he realized the problem he ran into. MacDonald. The woman Dorcas—hardly a lady, and technically a fallen woman.

MacDonald gave one swift look at Margaret, but his first concern was the presses and he barked the question.

"They're safe in the cellar at Cherry Street. This is Mistress Thurstan—Mr. MacDonald. She's no place to stay, I—"

"The lady's welcome." His curious dark eyes devoured her.

"Mistress Thurstan—is an old acquaintance," he fumbled on, "and alone, I thought—"

Margaret said quietly, "How do you, sir? I'm sorry to intrude on you. I'd best explain, my employers have left New York, I'd thought to leave too but was prevented."

"There's no need for explanations today, young lady." Mac-Donald smiled. "What a fortunate circumstance Mr. Bethune rescued you! You're welcome to my house. Dorcas, take the young lady to a chamber, she'll be weary."

The woman rose silently and went off, nodding to Margaret to follow her. Bethune carried her bags into the chamber indicated, returned to MacDonald, expecting questions. MacDonald asked only, "You're not going home tonight?"

"No. I must—in the morning—find if Susan has stayed." He was too tired to think. He sat down in the nearest armchair, and never knew when he slept.

That next day it was more obvious that the city was occupied by the enemy. There were British everywhere; he was stopped fifty times on his way out to Greenwich Road. If New York had lost half its population in the last year, it had swelled to former size overnight with the British Army. There seemed to be no formal patrols, but everywhere soldiers stopped the few pedestrians venturing out, jeering, jesting, boasting. It was all oddly jocular, there was no least animosity on the part of the regular troops. Think yer little old amachoor army could hold, eh?—we show you different! Say this be the greatest city in the colonies? Gord, y' could set it dahn in East Lunnon and never know 'twas there! Here, friend, don't run away, we ain't off to shoot you yet! The officers were different; they maintained vigilant silence, stern; he was stopped by only one, who coldly inquired the way to Fort George.

He half-expected to find the house shut up; it was not. Susan was coming down the stair as he entered. "I thought you might have gone," he said.

"Why should I leave? Though in truth I cannot imagine how I will go on, all the servants have run off, stupid creatures. How do you think I should have gone, James? To leave all my clothes behind, everything I possess?" He looked at her for the first time in a year or more, really: it was an incredible thing that he was married to this woman, the narrow, discontented mouth, the little lines about the eyes, the sharp voice. She was thirty-one; she looked ten years older. She had not troubled to dress, and wore an old chamber robe trimmed in fraying velvet over her night rail.

"I told you the British would take the city," she said. "This won't be for long, things will settle down, everything be right again with the British here, you'll see. There'll be trade again and business. Why did you not come home last night?"

"I couldn't very well reach here."

"I thought I should go mad with the noise of the guns," she said. "It will all be different when the British have taken over definitely." She did not ask if he had been in danger, if he had trouble getting through the city to come here; she seemed uninterested in details of the invasion, the fighting, only dwelling pleasurably on the fact that the Americans had fled so ignominiously.

"They are only six or seven miles off," he reminded her mildly. "It is possible General Washington will retake the city."

"Never! They'll soon be chased farther than that."

He dropped the subject. "It will be difficult that I get back and forth every day, I'm sure you understand that. I'll take some gear into the city. If you want me for anything you may send to Mr. MacDonald's house in John Street, someone will take the message."

"So you propose to leave me alone here without a man in the house for protection? The troops—"

"I should not think you'd be frightened of British troops. I'm sorry, Susan, this is a difficult time. As you say, we must manage as best we can."

When he came back to John Street he found Hugh Gaine with MacDonald. The editor of the *Gazette* looked tired and worried.

"Of course there's the chance they'll retake the city. But if they try it we'll have battles in the streets—worse than the gunfire and retreat. I don't know. Ask me, it's a slim chance, the way they broke yesterday. Soldiers! They were scared children!"

"Inexperience," said MacDonald cheerfully. "They need to be shot over in the military term. Don't make rash predictions, Hugh! I am gambling on them—they'll steady down. Ah, Mr. Bethune. What is happening about the city?"

He gave them a brief description.

Gaine shook his head. "You'll call me a faintheart," he said, "but I'm getting out. I doubt if Washington can retake us, and even in the event the British allowed a free press—which I'd not wager on—it'll be poor business in New York for some time to come. Damnation, I should have seen the warning months ago and left then."

, "What will you do—abandon business?"

Gaine's jaw came forward; he grinned. "I'm fond of eating. No. I'm taking the *Gazette* up the river, behind the American lines. There's printers in Esopus, and I've some men of my own who'll go along. You're not staying?"

"I'm staying," said MacDonald coolly, "and what's more I'm publishing." He looked at Bethune and there was a dark devil in his eyes. "News is my business and a war is big news. I'm taking the gamble that Washington will recapture the city. Perhaps next week, perhaps next month. Meanwhile I bring out the *Courier*. We'll take an almighty loss on a few editions, but we must have some subscribers left in New York. I'll cut the edition, say a thousand copies, and by God, if we have to give them away I'll still be publishing—that is my business."

"Poor business," said Gaine.

"Oh, we'll take a loss. But if the city's retaken, once the Americans come back, we'll make it up. And add to the *Courier*'s reputation as well—the one paper to continue publication through the invasion!"

"How are you going to do that?"

"I'll do it," said MacDonald. "I take your viewpoint, Hugh—the better part of valor. I wish you luck in getting out."

Gaine swore, buttoning his coat, taking up his hat. "I'm beginning to think all the doubters were right—we've little hope of winning a war against England. I don't know—I don't know. Well, good fortune to you, Robert. I hope you'll not get yourself into difficulties."

Bethune said, "I think he will get us both into difficulties, Mr. Gaine."

"Like to come along of me?"

Bethune looked at MacDonald and smiled. "I'll stay a bit longer—maybe to get him out of the difficulties." Gaine laughed and went off. "Do you mean to bring out an edition this week?"

"Most certainly," said MacDonald. He leaned back in his chair. "Reach me my pipe, will you? Faugh—I'll never be used to it after a decent smoke." Segars were unobtainable in the last six months; even pipe tobacco was costly and adulterated with God knew what weeds. "I'm just beginning to realize, you know, what luxury it is to be incapacitated. I sit comfortably here and issue orders right and left, and you must scramble to carry them out. Or, no, you are never excited or in a hurry, are you? But I expect them to be carried out nonetheless."

"You'd have seen me in a hurry yesterday."

"Doubtless. We'll establish a print shop of our own in Cherry Street, eh? God's teeth, I believe I am enjoying this. I was growing bored by this war, but it provides some excitement after all."

"And how do you propose to print the edition? I ask only for information, sir."

MacDonald grinned. "Impudence. It will be a little job. I'll set the type; I earned my living at it some years. All we want is a couple of strong-arms to handle the presses. You'll find some; there must be laborers in the city out of employment after yesterday. A couple of men to pull the pages, and there we are."

"You do make it seem simple. I'll see what I can do," Bethune said. Against his reason, which told him this was foolhardy, MacDonald had fired him for the idea. But as he turned and took up his hat again, Margaret appeared in the doorway.

"I'd hoped you would be back." She wore a troubled expression. "It's very kind of Mr. MacDonald, but I can't remain here, you know. Do you know if any of the ferries are in operation?"

Bethune was irritated. Women, ignorant of so much! He said brusquely, "Don't be absurd, Margaret. Of course none of the ferries are running. We are bottled up here with the British Army—you recall they took the city yesterday. Doubtless anyone attempting to leave will be stopped, and prisoned, for aught I know."

"Oh. But I can't take advantage here. I've been trying to think what I can do. Surely even when the British are here there'll be employment, if I could find somewhat to do—a place to stay—"

He did not feel equal to going into detail: the abandoned houses, taken over by the military; others with doors left open, all the furnishings ready for looting; the shops deserted by their owners; the people homeless who had had houses destroyed under them yesterday, some appropriating houses whose owners had fled; all places of business shut up; the entire life of the city disrupted. He felt unreasonably that she should understand how it was. "You can't possibly—" he began.

"But we're fortunate in having you here," interrupted Mac-Donald smoothly. "Indeed you must not think you're unwelcome, Mistress Thurstan." He would be curious about her; he would know from their manner there was something deeper than acquaintanceship between them. "I understand you feel awkward at being

thrust among strangers—but, my dear young lady, there's no
question of allowing you to make your way alone, with the city
so disturbed. And if you feel you put us out, I'll say that unless
I'm mistaken, there will be sufficient work for us all to do, merely
to support the household. With the shops shut and so on, as Mr.
Bethune tells us is the case, it may be difficult even to locate food-
stuffs though we've the money to pay. We should be grateful—I
know I speak for Mrs. Hicks as well—if you stay and assist us in
such mundane matters. I should apologize to ask a lady, but these
are extraordinary times."

She hesitated, smiled at him. "That's not necessary, of course.
If I can be of any help—I did not expect—but I see it may be
difficult. I seem to have little choice. Thank you, I will—I will be
glad to stay."

CHAPTER 26

BETHUNE HIRED the men: six brawny fellows, none young
but all willing. Two were Dutch and spoke little English;
Haagen came useful as an interpreter. At the expense of much
hard work—MacDonald had not set type for twenty years and
none of the men had ever seen a press before—they brought out
a small edition of the *Courier* that following Friday.

There was sufficient material in the news for MacDonald's biting
wit. Had Bethune ever thought himself cynical? The events of that
week following the city's capture would have left him unmoved
had he not retained some illusions. He could not tell if Mac-

Donald was as shocked and disgusted; his article was filled with blistering sarcasm only.

Of its former population New York boasted no more than three or four thousand on the day the British captured the city. Many of the ardent patriots had delayed flight until the very day; but for months the Loyalists had been fleeing in droves: there were none left, or very few and those lying low. A large proportion of Dutch and Germans had stayed—the small merchants, tradesmen, guildsmen. Most of the population in April had greeted the Americans with joyful celebration, opened their homes to them, patriots to the core. These same citizens now proceeded to give the British a welcoming ovation, as if they turned Tory at the signal of a musket shot. Well, they had their lives, their homes, their businesses to think of; but they need not have been so enthusiastic.

The American retreat, he learned from talk with various soldiers, had been less disorderly than it appeared. The British had landed from across the East River, and the abject flight of the new volunteer militia there had caught the major American forces, under General Putnam, in the toe of Manhattan; but Putnam had organized a magnificent retreat with a fighting vanguard. It was the volunteer militia who ran. Bethune heard many tales of that day; one he could believe. He heard it from a British sergeant who claimed to have witnessed the affair: Washington and Putnam, at the last, attempting desperately to force the men to turn and hold, laying the whip to their backs, and Washington shouting, "Are these the men with which I'm to defend America?" before wheeling to charge the British alone, and an aide catching the rein to stay him.

There had been little warning; it came in twenty-four hours. The ferries had been crossing and recrossing to New Jersey all day, but even so, not all the American patriots who desired to leave could have succeeded; many were left in New York. It was these people—or had they always been Loyalist, talking like patriots from fear?—who met a boatload of British officers and carried them ashore on their shoulders, shouting praise and welcome; who broke into Fort George, tore down the new American flag from the standard, trampled it underfoot, and raised the British colors; who flung open their doors to the troops as to brothers.

"Disgusting spectacle?" said MacDonald. "I said you never know how men will behave under fire. They are human beings is all, and that last fight convinced them the American cause is lost."

But Bethune worked so hard in the next week that he had energy for few emotions. He had a makeshift bed in the Cherry Street house; he took his meals with MacDonald. Somewhat to his surprise, Margaret and Dorcas appeared to get on amicably. He supposed they worked as hard as he and MacDonald, over the housekeeping; Margaret mentioned once waiting in a queue several hours at a butcher's shop, one of the few open. The weather continued sweltering; the nights were breathless and humid. He got out to the house on Greenwich Road once, to find Susan helpless with no servants, all of them having fled; but she planned to come into town herself to find more, since the confusion was settling down a trifle.

The problem of delivery was the worst. There was no way of discovering at once how many of their subscribers had fled; in the end, the most of that first edition was scattered about the various shops commencing to reopen, to be sold over the counter.

Bethune came back to John Street in late afternoon of that day, to find MacDonald absent, presumably still at Cherry Street caring for the type. They had arranged quite a professional print shop in the little cellar there.

He thought the house empty; he sank down in a chair, shutting his eyes, and Margaret's voice startled him.

"Would you like something to eat? You look exhausted."

He sat up, passing a hand across his face. "I'm tired, yes. I've placed the whole edition. No, nothing to eat, but is there coffee?"

"I'll get you some." When she came back with it he noted her with more attention; she looked as tired as he felt, and as untidy, in a drab gown of unstylish cut. There was a smudge on the bridge of her nose, and he pointed it out in almost brotherly fashion. She scrubbed at it hurriedly. "But I'm not surprised—"

"You've worked hard these days too. I'm sorry."

"It's not your fault, is it? Actually, you know, I've enjoyed it. Yes, I have. It's—it's real," she said. "After all, most women have these things to do all their lives. It's only ladies who are waited upon. Dorcas—"

"Hmm?" he asked as she paused. He wondered what she made of Dorcas.

"Well, I respect her. She hasn't turned a hair once. She merely goes on to do what must be done, and knows how to do it too. I'm afraid I have been a trial to her, so helpless, but she's quite kind."

"Is she?" He was surprised. He caught himself yawning and apologized.

"You should rest—and I must get back to my washing."

"Washing!" He jerked upright in consternation. "You mean to say—?" She was laughing.

"My dear sir, do you suppose clothes remain clean forever or wash themselves? Though I'd no notion they took so much scrubbing, I confess. I am reminded that Dorcas says if you will fetch yours we will care for them."

"Well—" He really could not countenance the idea that a lady, Margaret, should wash his shirts and body linen. He realized all at once how dirty he felt, and was.

"Please do not look so embarrassed. It's quite all right. Someone must do it, you know."

"Well, you need not, it's outrageous, I never intended—surely we can find a woman to come in. Now you speak of it, I should much like a bath."

She said, "I'm not sure if there's enough water; I had one this morning. You could use the kitchen." It was quite absurd, standing here in MacDonald's parlor, talking so personally with Margaret.

But MacDonald came in before he considered the bath further, and presently Dorcas indicated that a meal of sorts was prepared. They were still at the table when the first alarms sounded, and he ran to the doorstep to see the glow in the darkening sky south-east.

"What is it?" The shouts, the bugles, might have meant any-thing—another battle. "What's happening?" Margaret came up behind him.

"It is a fire. As if we hadn't enough to worry over, a fire—and looks a bad one—toward the docks."

Since the fire in Ann Street six years ago, and the worse one that destroyed a hundred houses two years after that, New York had been fearful of fire, knowing how the city could burn—many streets too narrow for the hand-engines, many old wooden build-ings. The British troops turned out at the double to carry buckets, the war forgotten for those twelve hours. But a third of New York burned that night, and only the changing wind saved the rest. The fire started along Dock Street, and engulfed Bridge, Stone, and Marketfield streets before crossing Broadway to bring Trinity Church crashing in; it traveled up Partition Street like a ravaging army.

Bethune was at the mouth of Broadway in the midst of an excited crowd when he saw the wind swinging the flames about northeast; and John Street lay northeast. He ran back; by the grace of God they had stayed within. "We'll take no chances. It is a half-mile off, but will drive this way, the wind has changed. We'd best all get to the place in Cherry Street."

"God's teeth, adding insult to injury! Am I to be burned out a second time?"

"At least we've the chance to rescue some of your possessions tonight." Bethune managed to hire a coach from a nearby stable; he saw MacDonald and the two women off first, and worked with Haagen ferrying furnishings and miscellany across the city, all amongst the frenzied crowds, three journeys, before the first house on John Street caught and the rest were lost.

Nearly five hundred houses went up in the fire, a great number of shops and warehouses. Trinity was gone, leaving the sky oddly empty of its finger-pointing steeple. St. Paul's was damaged but it stood. Queerly, the fire burned all about the John Street

Theatre and left it lonely. A thousand were homeless; but there were plenty of abandoned houses for them to appropriate. MacDonald's house was a blackened shell. Some damage was done in Maiden Street but the office survived, though all that remained there was the sign over the door.

"I'll tell you one thing," he said to Margaret—they were alone in the Isaacsons' bare parlor—"the fire took notice away from this edition, for I'm afraid most of it went up in smoke before anyone had a chance to read it! I was not too easy about the consequences." MacDonald had not spared opinion in that edition; he stayed by his guns. Bethune had had visions of British wrath ordering their arrest, commandeering the presses. As a result of the fire, no one seemed to pay special note to the copies that escaped.

MacDonald gambled on Washington; it seemed a long chance. There was an abortive attempt a few days later to fire a warship in the harbor; but the real wonder was an ingenious device, a small raft bearing a charge of powder on a long fuse, which some foolhardy patriots towed against the *Phoenix* in attempt to explode her side. The only other noteworthy event that week—aside from the death of Colden on the night of the fire, at his estate on Long Island—was the execution of a spy by the British. There were a few genuine patriots left in New York (besides the prisoners taken, quartered in New Gaol and the garrison prison). On the morning after the fire several ardent Loyalists were found hanged, with placards accusing them of starting the blaze. It was from one of those patriots that Haagen heard about the spy. Simple Dutchman, he was almost tearful over it.

"Dey hang him, Mr. Bethune, de British hang him like he is a murderer! De man who tell me has heard it from a troopman who was dere. A young man, he said, just try to find out about de British a liddle for General Washington."

"A spy—that's news for the next edition—did you hear his name, his rank, what his regiment was?"

"No, sir. De fella didn't know. But just afore dey hang him, you know what he says? He says, I am so satisfied in de cause

I engage in, I regret only dat I have but de one life to give. A brave man, dat spy. I'm sorry I don't hear more, Mr. Bethune."

They mentioned the spy, however nameless, in the next week's edition. That edition attracted some attention of a sort Bethune had not expected. He thought MacDonald was surprised too, and disappointed; he thought that amusedly. MacDonald the fire eater! He had made the grand gesture, and if the British commanders of New York had gaoled him for sedition he would have been almighty pleased with himself, a martyr to the freedom of the press. With the next two editions of the *Courier*, the British indeed became aware of the second newspaper being published in New York—the first being the *Gazetteer*. They became aware of it with amused admiration, if the officers Bethune met hanging about the old office were anything to go by. He had been of two minds about taking to his heels when he saw them.

"Know aught about this fella prints the *Courier*?"

"No," he said. "No, I'm sorry, sir, I was just passing."

"Oh! Damme, that's a jape! Place shut up, eh? Must be doin' it somewhere else. Did you see the edition yesterday, man? I swear, I never saw the colonel so tickled!"

"Deuced cool," said the other officer. "I laughed m'self. Right under our noses. Spirit! Daresay it's nought of import, but shows spirit. These Americans!"

MacDonald snorted when he heard that. "Stupid idiots! They'll learn how powerful print can be! They did not say they'd been sent officially to the office?"

"No, sir, I think they were just curious."

MacDonald snorted again.

They brought out four editions of the *Courier* under British occupation. The fourth edition was set up and half printed when Haagen came in to tell them that the fleet had weighed anchor and was making up the North River. Well, if they missed the story this edition there would be plenty for the next, with that chain across the river, and the American Army waiting for the land troops marching north to attack. Washington's camp was still on Harlem Heights.

But, doubtless to the consternation of the Americans who had put it there, the chain failed to keep the British ships down-river; they sailed serenely across to lay a bombardment on the twin forts Washington and Lee, which held strongly. Meanwhile the Army, under command of Sir William Howe, marched to a point north of Harlem, ready to attack in full strength. Although initially driven back to retreat, they came on again. It might be conjectured that Washington, still unsure of the caliber of his army after the disastrous retreat from Manhattan, and fearful of being trapped between troops and fleet, chose discretion as the better part. The Americans retreated precipitately across the river to Jersey; the New York campaign was lost entirely.

There was great jubilation in New York over Washington's second retreat. The British were boastful, confident that the war was nearly ended; the *Gazetteer* came out with an extra edition hailing a truce expected to be asked. MacDonald would flay Rivington mercilessly for printing that rumor, in the *Courier*'s next edition.

"Do you think there is any chance at all, after this rout?" asked Bethune.

"I don't know. It is a blow for the patriots, loss of the greatest port, though they've still Boston. What I do know is that the Americans will not give up so easy. It's the last battle that counts, Mr. Bethune."

Now that they were certain of tenure, the British set about establishing law and order. One Major General Robertson was given command of the city; Bethune heard subdued grumblings about that from the troops. Robertson was nearing eighty, an old barracks officer who had reputedly feathered his nest lavishly by warm dealings in Army supply circles. But he was a martinet and an organizer, apparently. The casual looting of empty houses ceased; regular patrols appeared about the city to keep the peace; a curfew was enforced for all civilians. And Major General Robertson, whatever his good qualities, had no sense of humor.

Bethune left the house the afternoon they had that news, as Margaret also came out. "Dorcas says we must have some flour if I can buy any. Do you know she is shy of venturing out alone?

She is a queer little creature, but really I'm growing quite fond of her."

He wondered if she realized the relations between Dorcas and MacDonald. She must; they still shared a chamber, the woman tended him at night. But Margaret's tone was quite natural.

He said he would walk a way with her. "Where do you make for, can I not come to help you?"

"Oh, no, I can manage, thank you. The Old Market." That was across the city. He was disturbed at the thought of her walking so far to supply the household.

"We will find a servant to do all this. I should have seen to it long ago."

"Please don't," she smiled. "You know what Mr. MacDonald said. I am earning my keep. I shouldn't feel right about staying there, doing nothing."

Yes, it was a queer household when he came to think. In his remotest flight of imagination he would never have seen Margaret and himself sharing a roof, talking of baths and servants and flour. Absurd was no word; so absurd it suddenly overwhelmed all the grave constraint of remembered tragedy between them.

He laughed. "It has all been rather confused."

"Will you stay in New York?" she asked. "After this, I mean? I know you said, at the first, they'd make Mr. MacDonald stop publishing, in all likelihood."

"So I did. I don't know. They may do so yet. In that case, we should remove somewhere, I suppose—if we were allowed. There's money to think of too. We've made none to speak of on these last editions, you know, and we can't keep on publishing indefinitely on that basis. If we should be stopped publishing and not allowed to leave the city—" That would pose some problems, he reflected. He finished lightly, "I should likely have to take an honest job for a change."

She glanced at him quickly. "Yes, I see, it would be difficult. Mr. MacDonald is helpless, for all but his writing."

And that, of course, was the major reason he could not join the fighting ranks, if he had had strong impulse to it. Otherwise—

he did not know, he might have done that. But he had this responsibility; there was none other to take it.

He said, "I wish to God you had left with the Kerrs. But you never expected to be involved in all this, did you?"

"Please don't worry for me. I have not minded, really."

They had walked along Wall Street. He asked, "Do you mind if we turn down Maiden? It's as near as any. I want to see if the office is still standing."

"You are sentimental about it," she accused.

He laughed and shook his head. "I don't think so. It was—home—to me for a long time. Let us hope it will be again one day." He thought she would make some reply to that but changed her mind.

They passed down Maiden Street on the side opposite the office; it was still there, looking rather forlorn with its battered sign. They had never taken Shields' name from it; that should be done. A woman came round the side of the building and tried the door, tried it repeatedly; when she turned away there was a disconsolate droop to her shoulders. He stopped, frowning. "Now what—"

The woman saw him, and ran for him calling his name. "Jemmy—oh, Jemmy! Thank God I've found you!" It was Gay—as always, irrepressible, even in this dirty, decimated, pillaged city, wearing a stylish gown and velvet-collared cloak; her pretty face was pale under cosmetics. "I've been looking the city over, I couldn't think of a place you'd be, and then I remembered there was an office for your newspaper—" Words tumbling over one another; she had him by both arms, trying to shake him.

He was very powerfully embarrassed: Margaret, a lady, and Gay, who was— He did not know what to say; he said haltingly, "Well, this is a—Mistress Lamont, I did not think you'd still be in New York."

"Oh, don't be so stuffy, Jemmy!" She shook him again and then, suddenly stricken, stepped back, casting a look at Margaret. "Oh, Jemmy, it's not your wife!"

Very like Gay, coming out with that revealing little remark.

He shrugged. "No, Gay, not my wife. Mistress Thurstan, Mistress Lamont."

Gay flashed Margaret a smile. "I didn't think your wife would be so pretty. But, Jemmy, you must listen—you've got to get away, clear away from New York! There's a warrant out to arrest you—and that other man, the other one at the paper—just this morning, they don't know where but they're going to search for you and prison you, because of the paper. Jemmy, you've got to get away!"

CHAPTER 27

H E FORGOT his embarrassment. "Where did you hear that?"
"Archie Saunders, Jemmy, he's on the staff of the city commandant, it was last night he said—"

"You lost no time making liaison with the enemy," he said, but absently.

She shook his arm. "Archie's quite nice. When d'you suppose any of the theaters will be open? Don't be stupid, Jemmy."

"What did he say?"

"Oh, that the high officers have orders from whoever gives them orders—the King?—to shut down all the American newspapers, I mean all but those who're Loyalist, you see, and Archie said he—this Robertson—was very angry over your newspaper. Archie was amused himself—he only laughed—but they've put out a warrant for your arrest, you and the other man they know is doing it, on—on—"

"A charge of sedition."

"Yes, that's it, and—"

"Very well," he said. "Now be quiet and let me think." The first thought he had was how fortunate it was they had removed from the office. Margaret was standing quietly by, watching Gay with a tiny smile, but with a frown in her eyes. He turned to her. "No one knows you've any connection. You'd best go on and do your shopping, but don't purchase anything heavy and make haste back to the house."

She did not move. "You had best get back too. There must be dozens of people still here who know you by sight. And Mr. MacDonald—"

"Yes." MacDonald in his wheeled chair with his attendant was a landmark not to be missed. "Go on," he said. "Hurry. Get food easily carried, whatever you can find."

"Is there anything I can do, Jemmy?" Gay asked as Margaret hurried off obediently.

"No, thanks, Gay, you've done enough. Thank you for troubling—"

"Troubling! I don't care about all their politics—the war's an awful nuisance—I can help my friends, I hope, Jemmy! How'll you get away?"

"Leave that to me." He patted her shoulder. "Best not be seen with me, Gay—off with you." Yes, dozens who knew him by sight, and MacDonald. Possibly none who knew exactly where they lived now, save the laborers hired for the presses—simple men, anxious to keep out of trouble; at the first offer of reward they would go forward, one or all of them. He walked back to Cherry Street quickly and met MacDonald on the doorstep.

"I'm off for a jaunt about the city, Mr. Bethune, to collect material for the week's edition. Care to accompany me?"

"You are not," he said. "Willem, get the chair inside—quick." He told the facts, incisive, brief; his mind was working furiously.

"Well, well," said MacDonald. A slow smile grew on his mouth. "So they decide we are dangerous after all! We must get out of New York, and at once."

"A brilliant deduction. It may not be so easy as it sounds. We'll keep to the house today. I can do nothing until nightfall. I'll try to find a boat to ferry us across the river."

MacDonald said, "I don't stir one step, Mr. Bethune, without my presses and my paper. I must leave the arrangements to you, unhappily, but it would be little use to escape without the means to carry on the fight. Not one step without my presses."

Bethune said, "I had not considered leaving them, sir."

But it was farce: planning escape from under the noses of the enemy, and taking along two enormous presses, a hundred and twelve reams of paper, a cripple in a wheeled chair, two women— farce.

Two women. God, why had she not gone with the Kerrs? She could not be left here alone, to make her own way. She returned presently; he took her aside.

"I don't know what you've thought about this, Margaret, but I think you'd best come with us. It is a risk for you; if we are caught we'll likely all be prisoned. But you can't stay alone in New York."

She said tranquilly, "I could look to myself, find work. But I think it the lesser of two evils that I go with you. There is another outbreak of smallpox—I heard while I was out."

After a moment he said, "Then perhaps we get out only in time." There had been much sickness in the American ranks; the retreat had left hundreds of sick men in the new hospital, and the churches and abandoned mansions were pressed into service as sick-wards. The British had, incredibly, burned the one hospital deliberately. There were prisoners transferred to New Gaol who were dying off like flies, he had heard. The fire had not helped matters. There had been smallpox spreading in the British ranks for some time, and an attempt made to isolate those who contracted it; any man who had himself inoculated was summarily court-martialed, the opinion being that inoculation only spread the disease more quickly.

"What did you think of doing?" she said. "Can I help in any way? You might be known, and I would not be."

"That cannot be helped, I'll see to it myself," he said. She did not argue. He sought out MacDonald to talk about money. "I'm afraid this will cost something."

"That I had foreseen. Have you any money, Mr. Bethune?"

He turned out his pockets. "Five pounds ten and an odd copper. I've ninety pounds in the Merchants' Bank, if it ever opens its doors."

"You surprise me. I'd have thought you were shrewder than to leave money in a bank in times like these. You will find approximately two thousand pounds in gold and silver in the locked compartment of my bed table. Here is the key. It's all that remains, Mr. Bethune. If you think it would be any use to apply to your lady-wife for more wherewithal to rescue her investment in the *Courier*—well, I disagree with you."

"No, I daresay not." He had forgotten Susan.

He had luck in that affair. He could think of no other plan than to visit a water-front tavern, seek out a shipman, and offer a bribe to ferry them across the river. There must still be Americans who wanted to leave New York; it could not be too unusual a proceeding. But a delicate little business all the same; if he chanced to approach a definite Loyalist, he might be haled before a military judge and prisoned at once. He dared not risk starting out after curfew; it was just past dusk when he left the house and walked straight across the city to the North River water front. He chose a dingy tavern at random. He was inconspicuously dressed, and the place poorly lighted. The only drink the house offered was rum, and that liberally watered. Rum—so there must still be some smuggling going on.

At the table nearest him sat three men, none young, all bearded: the mark of ship captains. They leaned heads together, talking; he edged nearer. They were talking of trade.

"Almighty difficult. By God, when they commence asking a man's political opinion afore buying his cargo—! I'm landed with all that rum, damnation take it, Morris decamped the city and his warehouse's burned. I can't offer it to the British, can I? Clap me in gaol at the word."

"Risk you took, friend."

"I ne'er fancied the Americans'd run so easy and lose the city."

"War is always bad for commerce. As friend John says, thee knew the risk when thee loaded the contraband. If thee can obtain clearance papers—"

Something stirred in Bethune's mind; where had he heard that slow deep Quaker voice before? It was Captain John Marple of the *Delaware Star* that had brought him to New York. Speak of luck! He would wager on Marple any day. He stepped up to the table. "Captain Marple?"

"Aye, friend?" The Quaker looked up.

"I'd speak private with you if you will."

"I will listen." Bethune drew him out of the inn; it was too crowded to talk secrets. They strolled slowly up the water front; there was dim reflection off the river. "Well, friend?" He was peering at Bethune. "Do I know thee?"

"Perhaps you remember a young fellow stowed away in your ship at Yorktown, some years back."

"Well, friend, indeed. Let us see—yes, a tall lad he were, like thee, and fair. Thy name I never knew. This is curious. What is it thee wants of me?"

"Ferriage across the river. Not only myself. There's some luggage, four others."

The shipmaster was unsurprised. "There be British patrols in the river. Where would thee want to be landed?"

"I've no preference, so it's not any place held by British. Wherever is convenient in New Jersey."

"And how am I to know thee is not a Britisher who will report me do I agree?"

"That you'll have to chance. I'm not."

After a moment Marple said, "Thee has an honest voice. And how much do thee offer for passage? There is risk."

Bethune was of no mind to raise the price by letting him know two of the passengers fled from a military warrant. "How much would you ask?"

"Five of you and baggage. I must live, and this war is bad for shipmen. What do thee say to five hundred pounds?"

"I say too much. A hundred."

"Oh, no, friend, I'd not take the risk for less than five. They might impound my ship, thee understands." Marple was not to be moved from that, and Bethune was forced to agree. "Tomorrow night. I will show thee my ship, where she lies."

Bethune felt it only fair to say, "I said five passengers, two women. It might be there'd be another woman, I'm not sure. If so you would be paid."

Marple bent a grave gaze on him in the dark. He said, "Three women, friend? It do appear to me thee has spent thy years in New York to evil advantage."

He could not leave without offering Susan the chance to escape from a city perhaps to be plague-ridden. The curfew was near, it was dangerous to remain out, but he went up to the house; he had his key still.

She had retired, and came to him summoned by the one man-servant. "Leave? What are you talking of, James? Now the British hold New York it is the safest place in the colonies. . . . I've no care for the smallpox, I'm a way out of the city here, in small danger." Her eyes narrowed. "You are leaving?"

"Yes, MacDonald and I, both. Susan, are you provided for? I know shipping is at a standstill, your investments— I'm sorry, there is likely to be little return from the *Courier* for some time. And I don't know why I ask, I've no money myself. But—"

"I am quite well provided," she said stiffly. "I've a deal of gold. Where are you going?"

"Have you any concern?" he asked hardly. "I've no idea at the moment." God knew when, if ever, they would meet again. He rather hoped they would not.

"And why do you, and how? I understood it is forbid for civilians to leave—"

"Do you think to report me to the commandant? I should imagine you'd be relieved to be rid of me, with your friends the

British here—a husband with rebel sympathies some embarrassment. Well, I only wanted to give you the opportunity."

"You may have rebel sympathies," she said, "but I note you did not rush to join the volunteers." She did not trouble to wish him good fortune. He came away, and was lucky in avoiding patrols back through the city.

"We thought you'd been taken," said Margaret.

"You went to see your wife," hazarded MacDonald.

"I felt it a duty. I asked—" He shrugged, stopped there. "We are in luck about the passage."

He would not soon forget that night of leaving New York. They stayed indoors all that day, expecting arresting officers any hour; there was no knowing but that someone who knew their whereabouts had already given information. But darkness found the house still unmolested. He set off the first time with Haagen at eight o'clock; they had carried the presses up to the ground floor in readiness. He waited round the corner near a hiring stable while Haagen bargained for a hackney and pair; they came back to the house, got the presses in the carriage, the boxes of paper, and drove across to the river front. He was growing to be as much an old woman as MacDonald about those presses; when they had got them on board, he left Haagen standing guard while he went back for the others.

It was past the curfew then. He brought MacDonald out, lifted him into the coach; it took all his strength to get the chair in after him. Dorcas crowded in next MacDonald. "You'll have to come on the box," he told Margaret. She took his offered hand, climbed up to sit beside him. She had a large covered basket clutched in both hands.

"We thought it best to pack some food. There's no telling when we could get more or where we shall be, I suppose. Where are we making for?"

"I am going to think of that on the far side of the river." He drove north to avoid the main streets. They had got as far as Berkeley Street leading down to the river when they met the patrol. At the sharp command to halt he hesitated, half-minded to make a run for it; it was not far; but once they got to the dock, there was MacDonald to get out, the chair—

"It's past curfew, you've no business out. 'Ave you a pass to show?"

"No—I'm sorry, I did not realize the time, sergeant," he temporized.

"Let's 'ave a look hinside—down orf the box. Hif you please—sir!"

Margaret laid a hand on his arm to stay him. "We're dreadfully sorry, sergeant—is it truly after curfew? I told Major Hood —but he would press us to stay for dinner, you know! The least he could have done was offer us safe-conduct afterward, don't you think? Do overlook it this time, sergeant, won't you?"

"A lady it is. 'Ere—"

Her voice was coaxing, saccharine: the flutter-brained society miss. "You see, this horrid war, so difficult to find servants— and there was no space for all of us in the carriage, am I not a figure of fun up on the box, so? But, Archie, do tell the soldiers —it is all Major Hood's fault, we've been to dinner at his house, sergeant—Major Hood of the Hussars, surely you know him."

"Well, ma'am." The troop corporal sounded hesitant.

"You could ask him, he would tell you himself." A trifle fretful now. "Do let us pass, it is but a few squares on and we'll not stir out again, I promise you!"

"Well—orl right. Only make sure ye don't, ma'am! Get on, sir —this once."

When they were out of earshot he said, "I'd no notion you were such an accomplished actress."

"It was fright. I could only think of them pulling Mr. Mac-Donald out in the street."

"And I should complain to be christened Archie."

She actually giggled, there in the dark beside him. "I believe it must have been that girl yesterday morning. Did you say she is an actress?"

"I did not. She is."

"She is extremely pretty."

It was not the *Delaware Star*, but another smaller sloop. Marple, that canny man, did not weigh anchor until he had payment. "And when thee said baggage, young man, thee did not specify such a cargo as thee load on. By right I should ask another twenty pound, but I take pity on thy crippled companion." They cast off near midnight. Marple was genial to the patrol boat they met in midstream. "I am but changing my wharf to unship cargo, friend. Thee'd not suspect a Quaker of meddling with thy sinful wars?"

Bethune watched from the shadow of the cabin until the patrol boat sheered off. He went to lean on the rail. Presently a soft step sounded behind him: Margaret. "Are we safe, do you think?"

"Now, yes."

"You paid a great sum to this captain, did you not? I should have offered—I've nearly fifty pounds. I'd not be a charge on you."

"You paid your passage when you got us away from that British patrol."

"I should," she said, "be making plans for myself. I would not—"

"Be a charge. I know. You're not. Though I scarcely thought we should be refugees together." He laughed.

"Yes, it's strange." Her shoulder touched his as the ship swayed. After a silence: "Have you decided where you are making for?"

"I've been discussing with MacDonald. Marple is to land us on the Jersey shore as far north as he dares to go tonight. We've decided to go then to Esopus—Kingston—up-river. It's a good-sized town, there will be printers there, some market for the paper. I'll need to buy a wagon and team in Jersey, that will be easiest. I'd not countenance your going off alone," he added abruptly. "I'm sorry, Margaret, I don't mean to sound overbearing. Very well, I claim no responsibility for you, but you're a lady, and alone, and there is a war going on. You say you would not put us out, well, you do not. On the contrary, you've been of great help. I know I speak for MacDonald—"

"I've great admiration for Mr. MacDonald," she said as if to herself. "Yes, I know what you'd say. And in a town I should have a better chance to find work, of course. I expect I had best stay with you. All of you." And after another interval of silence she left him quietly, without further speech. He went on watching the water slide past; he began to think about all that must be done, trying to make alternate plans. He wondered how long this war would go on. Longer than a hundred and twelve reams of paper would last, very likely. He thought of Margaret and of Susan, of many things. He had not liked to leave New York—it was his city, dirty and deserted and ravaged as it was. He wondered when he might return. The dying moonlight on the water shone tranquilly back at him; it told him nothing at all.

CHAPTER 28

MARGARET THOUGHT it was strange what is in people and what is not. They said, As the twig is bent; but she did not suppose Bethune had had much moral teaching, in her father's house as a boy. Men were born with their own natures, the experience they met could change them only in surface ways.

Responsibility: it was a little mania in him. Absurd to say mania of Bethune, so quiet, so reasonable, but it was. He would never believe anything properly done unless he saw to it himself. Not that Mr. MacDonald took advantage; though he was an autocratic man she thought he had deep affection for Bethune. But so much fell on Bethune to do.

They came to Esopus that was later rechristened Kingston,

on the west bank of the Hudson, on the fifteenth day of November in that year of 1776. It had been an exhausting journey even for the men, save possibly Haagen, who was always cheerful and proved invaluable; Bethune was a townsman by nature and experience. The wagon he purchased was old and battered, though it had a canvas top providing a measure of privacy for herself and Dorcas. The team was old too, and the harness patched. Haagen drove most of the way, a hundred-odd miles, over a week of journeying, the roads bad and winter coming swiftly, the first snowfall the day before they came in. And much of the way was uphill, through rough country. It must have been cold for the men, sleeping on the ground. But at least she had found out something more about Dorcas, queer little Dorcas. . . . "Cannot you sleep? It is cold."

"Too cold, ma'am." Dorcas was always conscious of the difference in their stations. "It's bad for Robert. He'll sicken— not a young man—I'm afeared."

"Let us hope it won't be long. We'll be in a house soon. I don't believe there are any British about here, we shouldn't have difficulty."

"I'm not afraid of British, ma'am. I'm not afraid of aught save something happening to Robert." Simple, unanswerable. Perhaps in the dark, alone with another woman, the first she had talked with in long, she needed to speak. "Thirty year it's been. I was nineteen. It's hurtful to love that way. I never loved Will—he was bad to me. Wed him to get away from home, I did."

"You left your husband?"

"Yes, ma'am. It were wrong, but—"

Margaret put out her hand in the dark, touched the other woman's arm. "I don't know, Dorcas. I did that too."

"Oh. I didn't know you was wed. You would be, o' course. Is it Mr. Bethune you did it for—like Robert and me?"

"No," she said. "No. Not anyone. Only because—he was bad." Simple word for it—Dorcas's word.

"Oh. I wish we'd get where we're going. It's bad for Robert."

They talked, after that, a little each night before sleeping; perhaps both were shy in the light. Dorcas had never had a close woman-friend either. "He's been awful good, Mr. Bethune, the last years. What Robert'd do 'thout him I don't know. It's a pity that girl got hold on him. Robert says a-cause he's soft-hearted. I wouldn't doubt." So she heard all about Susan Shields.

"It's a kind of law, ma'am, I dunno why. Bad men getting good wives and bad women good men. Funny it is."

"But sometimes—"

"Oh, I reckon. Not often. I've tried to be good to Robert even if— I wouldn't know what to do without Robert." There was a note of panic even at the thought of it. "Might be if I'd had a family—"

"Didn't you ever, Dorcas?"

"No, ma'am. I wanted babies, but I never had. I thought maybe that was my punishment like. Did you ever have a baby, ma'am?"

And in the dark she whispered, "Yes—yes, I did. I had a baby, Dorcas." In the dark she felt the sudden hot wetness on her cheeks. And they stole it away, I never saw it, I can never forgive them for stealing it away, something of mine. She turned and pretended to sleep because she could not speak further.

They came to the town about midday; it was very small after New York, but larger than any town they had passed except Passaic. There had been rumors all up the road that the American Army was somewhere near, but they had seen none of it, or of any British. There might not have been a war at all, save for the high prices, the dearth of young men on the farms, the talk. This town had been larger too, had shrunk in population as the Loyalists fled, and those fearful to stay near the fighting; some were coming back now, seeing there was no fighting about here.

Bethune found a whole house to rent, a small one, but a house. The man had gone to join the rebel army and the wife was grateful for the money; she removed to her sister's to give them the entire house. There was a little furniture. It was good to be under a roof again, with a kitchen hearth to cook on. Margaret smiled at herself: Margaret Thurstan, the lady, cooking! There was a time she had scarcely known how a meal was prepared. Well, a war changed many things, she found, and she had no snobbery for it, rather it bolstered her pride to feel a little useful. When they were settled she meant to look about for work she might do to earn money. Bethune would not take what she offered to help pay for the house.

Men. She exchanged a secret smile with Dorcas that morning over their first breakfast. Bethune and MacDonald could think of nothing but the newspaper, making the most minute plans. All they need do was find a few printers. Men—no conception of what must be done to make a household go smoothly.

"It's none of their concern," Dorcas said when the men had gone out, Haagen wheeling MacDonald in the heavy chair, and left them in peace. "We'll go on better 'thout 'em, they're awful handless even when they're willing and I reckon 'tis natural."

But Bethune at least seemed vaguely to realize some work had to be done in the house; he sought Margaret out when they returned that late afternoon. "I'm afraid you have had much to do—the meals. I'm sorry."

"Oh, no, not a great deal," she told him, smiling. The house had been fairly clean. She had fetched in a supply of water from the well fifty feet away; carried in some wood already cut, while Dorcas made up the beds; gone out to find a butcher for fresh meat, while Dorcas washed down the dusty kitchen floor. They started a fire, with coal borrowed from a neighbor, set potatoes to roast in the ashes, and she heated water and thankfully washed herself all over after the long dirty journey, and put on a fresh gown, after setting the smoothing-irons in the hearth and pressing out the wrinkles. By then Dorcas had the table set and the rest of the meal ready. They would need to find more dishes, more cutlery. And already more water had to be fetched. "Oh, no," she said, "we've managed quite well. And you?"

"We've arranged with the printer, Mr. Corder. He's a pleasant fellow, and helpful. We'll bring out an edition next Friday. They are to use our presses, but only for the *Courier*, and our type; the contract is cheaper so. They seemed glad enough of the business. There's a little news—Fort Washington and Fort Lee have fallen. There was another battle a few days since. The Americans are in retreat again across the river into Jersey." He was frowning. "It seems this war may be over sooner than we thought. Well, there is still a deal to do. I've lost my penknife," he added. "Have we a small knife, Margaret? I should have brought more quills, and ink—God knows where I can find more ink—and for the presses too."

They settled in well enough; strange, strange, sharing a roof with Bethune again. Now, adult, seeing him more clearly, she could feel respect and liking. And she came to understand some of what he felt about the *Courier*.

"Do you think I'm a coward?" he asked abruptly once. "I've sympathy for the Americans, I'm on that side. Am I coward not to go and fight with them?"

His wife had said that to him, Margaret thought, never wondering how she knew. "Of course you're not. There are other things to a war besides fighting. How could you have left Mr. MacDonald, as he is? Of course you're not."

"I don't know. The paper—it seems most important to me that the newspapers should continue. Especially now. A part of what they are fighting for, do you see? Freedom, their Declaration says—that means for the press as well. And it's not easy now." No, she knew that; he was worried about obtaining more paper, more ink; and distribution was difficult. "It makes me feel that is all the more reason. But it sounds a little thing, against the fighting." That was just after they had the news of Washington's surprise victory at Trenton, the capture of the mercenaries.

She said thoughtfully, "I think perhaps it is more important." Trying to think what to say to him: "I remember your telling me what Mr. MacDonald wrote about the editor of the *Gazetteer*. Somewhat about it's being little use to speak of liberty or fight for it if it is not practiced at the same time."

"I don't feel a coward," he said. "I don't know. I feel we must keep on, not miss a single edition. I am going down-river to see if I can locate more paper. Most of the mills are burned or shut up, but I may have a little luck at Newark."

"I am going to find some work to do," she told him. "You may say what you please about my earning my way, I've not, you know, and I must. Very well, I've agreed to stay here, but I am no charge of yours or Mr. MacDonald's—I shall find work for myself." He did not like it; that was no matter. Bethune was nothing to do with her, only the fortunes of war bringing them together. She found work at the bakery. The baker had gone to war (so many gone) and his wife tried to keep the business; she was glad of help, a brisk, kind woman, and paid Margaret five shillings a week to serve the customers.

Bethune paid a pound a month for the house; she insisted on his taking five shillings from her toward that. He argued, but at last said resignedly, "I see you are determined. It is not right, you know we are happy to have you."

She did not know what profit the *Courier* might earn in normal times, but when she had first been in New York Bethune looked prosperous enough. He had good clothes—worn now, and his shirts needed mending, she had noticed. Here the *Courier* had a very small list of subscribers; they sold only a few copies of each edition in Kingston itself, though Bethune hired a boy to hawk copies about town, a shilling each. He said an edition in New York used to be eighteen hundred copies; now they printed only five hundred. It was impossible, of course, to supply those of their subscribers still in New York, but there were some in Newark, others in Philadelphia; he arranged carriage there. After the first few months, when they had managed to distribute enough editions to former subscribers to let them know the *Courier* was still in publication, some renewed subscriptions came in.

She remembered the old rector at home who had taught him, saying that Bethune was a promising boy; she had wondered what he might make of himself, but this had never occurred to her. It had come to be the largest part of his life, she saw: the one thing, to him. She had never seen him angry; he seldom swore; but he was coldly furious that day he came in to tell MacDonald about Hugh Gaine. The editor of the *Gazette* had been publishing here when they first came; he had come to see MacDonald once, complained that he was only losing money.

"The bastard," said Bethune coldly. "The bastard!" He strode up and down the little parlor, telling about Gaine. "He's going back—just for the money—plenty of money in New York now, he says, all the Loyalists flocking in, all the military. He'll let them dictate what he's to print. Worse, he says he'll choose to toad-eat them, print aught they want to read—just for the money. The bastard."

"Money is a thing I'm fond of too." MacDonald was dry as always. "But I draw the line a trifle higher than that."

"He is another Rivington—"

"No man so black as Rivington. I'd not thought Hugh Gaine would do such a thing. But money tempts the most honorable men."

"The bastard," said Bethune.

"He is worse than that, Mr. Bethune—he is a traitor," said MacDonald.

Margaret felt no burning patriotism for the American cause. Her sympathies lay on that side, but she thought vaguely there must be a better way to settle differences than by this destruction and killing. The war to her was important only because it brought such tremendous change to her life. She had told him meeting him again had set her free; so it had, some mysterious way. She had never have thought to find it tolerable that she should see him each day, that his presence should no longer remind her, taunt her. Once they were away from New York, safe, she had stayed with his little household, though working for herself, because it was more reputable that a lady be with others. It came not only to be tolerable, but pleasant: the strangest thing of all. She thought she had never known a real home, and this was that, perhaps because they all worked, in their own ways, to make a place for themselves—but he the hardest; so much fell on him to do.

A queer household: MacDonald had never asked her one question. He was curious, she knew, but he liked her, and a kind of delicate formality between him and Bethune kept him from questioning. There was never any intimacy among them, as in a family, however long they shared a house. The only time they gathered was at meals. Dorcas a silent little ghost save on the brief occasions she and Margaret were alone; MacDonald shut

up in the parlor, writing; Bethune with him or more often out
at the printer's while the edition was being set up and printed,
overseeing the delivery, even carrying copies himself to sell
about the countryside. She had a tiny bedroom to herself at the
back; MacDonald and Dorcas shared the larger chamber; Bethune
slept in the parlor on a makeshift pallet taken up during the day,
Haagen in the barn. She would not have thought people might
live so, reasonably content. War changed so much.

They had been there almost half a year when she made the
new gown—another thing she would never have thought she could
do. Dorcas and the baker's wife helped her. She had not had a
new gown in five years; there was little choice now in the shops,
but it was a charming color at least, a bright ombre, heavy corded
poplin. Had fashions changed in the cities? No way of knowing;
she made it in a style shown last year in New York, rather low-
cut, with side drapes and half-hoops, sleeves to the elbow with
a row of tiny buttons down from the shoulder. It was silly to feel
so excited for a gown, so triumphant at having produced it herself.

She wore it for the first time on a Sunday. She was in the
kitchen when Bethune returned in the afternoon; he came to ask
if there was wood to cut or water to fetch, as Haagen was sent
on another errand.

"No, thank you, we've enough till morning, I think. Do you
like my gown? I have finished it at last, I'd not like to earn my
living as a sempstress! But it is not too bad, do you think?"

"Indeed, it's charming," he said. "Charming. I'm sorry, Margaret; you should not need to—"

"But I didn't mean to sound complaining! You've no idea how
proud of myself I am that I accomplished it! It's satisfying in a
way to be able to do things for oneself."

His first response had been absent; now he was looking at her
with more attention. He said, "It's a lovely gown. Yes, I like the
color."

"I have pricked my fingers to pieces over it—" She laughed,
holding out her hands ruefully. "But I would not give up, however hopeless it seemed! Now if I only had a bonnet to match—
but that is beyond my ability, I fear." She stopped smiling, look-

ing up; she nearly stepped back away from him. He was staring at her hands; for one moment she thought he would reach to take them.

Then he said brusquely, "Is it? Well, I do approve the gown," and turned away.

"It does look lovely, ma'am," said Dorcas, when he had gone. "I wouldn't be surprised did Mr. Bethune just see how pretty you are. Busy and all, way he is, and single-minded." There was shy speculation in her eyes.

Margaret said, "That's absurd, Dorcas," but her voice sounded feeble. She went into her little box of a chamber and looked again in the cracked, wavery glass. The woman staring back at her said, I am nearly thirty, thirty, thirty, such a dreadful age. She tried to think when last someone had complimented her—a man, looking at her, smiling.

Oh, you do not know how absurd, Dorcas. Likely no man at all, ever again; but if so, any man in the entire world—except Bethune, except Bethune.

CHAPTER 29

BETHUNE WENT on for a long while telling himself it was not true, he did not love Margaret. There had been no woman in so long, she was young and lovely, and that was all the reason—nothing more. But he could not lie to himself forever. What he did not know was whether it was loving Margaret again, or still.

He had not been in love since he was sixteen, and loved her

before. With the few women since, it had been the one thing: the need satisfied, the woman had meant little. He had had amused affection for Gay, nothing to speak of for the few others.

He caught himself noticing everything about Margaret; it was effort not to look at her when she was in the same room. That was how it began. The day she wore the new gown, showing him her hands: her long slender hands, not a lady's now, roughened, but quick, delicate. He kept seeing her hands in his mind. Then it would be the sharp curve of her brows, one a little higher, the way the hairs grew to a point at the end. Watching the firm full shape of her mouth for its rare lift to a laugh. There was a tiny brown mole on the side of her white throat. And the time after that he would find himself caught by the slim line of her shoulder, a familiar gesture, the shape of her eyes, their widely spaced setting under the broad brow; small things of her.

It grew to be worse, living in the same house. There was a night he returned late, and she heard, and came to ask civilly if he wanted a hot drink or something to eat. She had an old robe about her, shapeless; but she had just unpinned her hair. Women's hair had always a fascination for him; one of the little sensualities of love-making to him was the look of a woman's hair loosened, spread on the pillow. He had been angry that Gay cut hers in the new shoulder-length style. Margaret's hair was very thick, very long, polished chestnut; it fell about her shoulders still rippled from its braids. He stood silent so long that she repeated her question.

"No," he said, "no, thank you, there's nothing I want." It sounded rude. That was a bad night; though he was tired, he did not sleep for a long while.

He knew the difference: wanting and loving. Both together the worst. He could lie to himself, say any woman would so arouse him. It was not true. It was Margaret herself. And he would never know if it was because of that earlier time or in spite of it. He knew only that it was as if the ability to love a woman deeper than the body had been blocked off in him since he ran away from Margaret; and now that they came together again the bond was cut and the love let out, a frightening torrent he could not, but must, control.

Where was the reason, the meaning, in a man's life? Any other woman, he thought; any other woman in the world except Margaret.

He drove himself grimly to use up the energy for emotion in him. God knew there was enough work—if little profit. They had few subscribers left, with so many patriots scattered in the Army. He arranged with a few shopkeepers in Newark and Philadelphia and Trenton to take copies on consignment each week; but the carriage fee was high in wartime, and the post apt to meet delays, so that by the time the papers arrived they were two or three weeks old. They managed barely to live on their publication, that was all. True, not so many newspapers were still published, but there was less demand, with the high prices of war making most people wary of buying luxuries and so many more occupied with fighting the war than reading about it. Every setback spurred him on to greater effort, even without MacDonald's obstinate determination. He had a private war to fight. They should not kill the *Courier;* he would keep it alive and in print if he must operate the presses himself, carry copies on foot one by one, go without food to buy paper and ink. Some of his blind stubbornness was Margaret's blame, to keep his mind from her.

Not so many papers now: but they were all stubborn about giving up. John Holt had brought the New York *Journal* here to Kingston before the *Courier;* Loudon had taken the New York *Packet* to Fishkill. Edes took the Boston *Gazette* to Watertown before the British evacuated, Thomas took the *Massachusetts Spy* to Worcester. All the papers were much smaller, irregular in editions, and few earned much profit. The case the *Courier* found itself in differed not much from that of the rest.

The presses had been old when MacDonald bought them; new presses were a rarity anywhere in the colonies, or new type. The *Courier* had two sets of type, one bold-face, both old and badly worn from long usage. With good paper and ink it might still produce a legible page; but both were in short supply. Only two or three mills were in operation, and those lacked rags to strengthen the paper; what they turned out was thin and shoddy, took ink unwillingly, and was all too easily torn. All the best ink was made abroad; in their extremity publishers and printers made do with the local product, but the dye was faulty, and a newspaper more than a couple of months printed was apt to become illegible as the ink faded.

"We don't print the *Courier* to be read a couple of months from now, Mr. Bethune, but this week—next week! So long as we print the news and get it to our readers reasonably fresh, that is all the importance." But the first time they brought out an edition of two pages instead of the customary four, MacDonald was unutterably depressed. It saved paper; but there was a good deal of news to write about.

The nominal New York Assembly, fleeing the British, brought the government here to Kingston. It amused Bethune somewhat that among the solemn businesses discussed and voted upon by this body was a "State Constitution" and the election of the first governor of the independent state. The war only begun, and no certainty of any kind that it would be won, yet the politicians already were planning thus confidently.

The British defeat at Bennington was cheering news; but rumor had it that the darling of the British Army, Gentleman Johnny Burgoyne, was sweeping toward New England from Canada, to meet Howe's forces in a pincers move against Washington near Philadelphia. The American Army was low in spirit by all report, and there were desertions; one could see why. This war had turned out to be longer, duller, and more dangerous than the patriots, in their first burst of belligerence, had expected. It went on and on. And there the British still were, confident, abundantly supplied. The Americans lost enthusiasm; those who only then joined, those who stayed, did so in a spirit of grim determination rather than that earlier up-boys-and-at-them attitude.

He was still telling himself it was only the physical need when he rode down-river to Poughkeepsie, hunting more paper, and met the tavern girl. He took what she offered, savage, eager, thinking, Now I will be released; and woke knowing how useless that was.

It was growing to dusk of the day after that he returned; he left the horse at the stable where he had hired it, walked to the house, and Margaret met him on the step. The instant he saw her he knew how futile the little passion with the inn girl was; this was a thing not only of the body, and the knowledge moved in him sickly.

"I saw you come past—James." The first time she had ever spoken his name; it would be this moment. "You had better know, Mr. Trevelyan is here. Did you hear me? I said—"

"Yes." He woke at that. "Mr. *Trevelyan?*"

"Your friend. You had best know, he—" But Bethune passed her, calling Darcy's name.

"Darcy, man! I thought the redcoats had got you a year ago!" It was good to feel Darcy's warm handclasp. He looked older, he had seen war, he was fully a man; his uniform was shabby, a different one than that he had worn before.

"I'm attached to General Greene's staff now—that is, I am to be after this leave. I've been in hospital, nought serious—a little wound at Princeton, and then the everlasting damned flux! Yes, yes, I know, you've a thousand questions—so have I! But I'd best tell you my news first. I'm wed, James—yes, caught at last!"

Bethune thought it jest; when he saw Jacquetta he knew it was anything but jest. He was not a good liar, but Darcy seemed to suspect nothing forced about his smile, his congratulation.

"Say you're pleased to meet Mr. Bethune, my sweet."

"I'm pleased to meet you, Mr. Bethune," she repeated, flat, obedient. She might have been sister to the tavern girl in Pough-keepsie: dark, not fair; younger. Quite obviously pregnant. He thought, caught is the word. Darcy was in love with the girl; that was obvious as her pregnancy. Darcy, the fastidious gentleman!

When they spoke privately Darcy dropped much of his false gaiety. "I know it's a deal to ask, James. And I'd not have you think it's the only reason I came! It's good to see you, know you get on reasonably well." Darcy at least saying never a word that he stayed by the *Courier,* had not joined the fighting ranks. "I am at my wits' end. A soldier is not his own master and I can't have her following the army with the camp women. She has been living near me in lodgings, but that's not suitable either. . . . Where? It was when we lay at Philadelphia, Jacquetta served in a shop there—look you, James, I know she's not a lady, but good God, what's that to say to anything?" He was defiant; he had the look he used to give his uncle, the belligerent little boy. "She is my wife, and that's that. I'll tell you straight, I took her to Uncle Rafe and my mother, but they refused to have her and she refused to stay. I can't blame her, the attitude they took." Rafe Trevelyan and Darcy's mother had removed from New York to Elizabeth-town, in New Jersey, sharing a house there with Philip Livingston. Both had contributed generously to the American cause. But Trevelyan was still of one of New York's first families, a gentle-man. No, he would not look kindly on Jacquetta as brood-mare to the Trevelyans! "I am due back at my post next week. I thought, when I knew you were here, behind the lines and still in business—" But Darcy bit his lip, looking about. "You do fairly well here? I'd expected—"

Something more like the old New York office. "We get on," said Bethune. He would not commit them rashly; it was unfair to the others. "I don't know, Darcy."

"I've money to leave for her care. It's only, with the child—oh, the devil! You understand, James. I've no one else to ask. You should have heard the fuss they all made at me—the way they talked of her! She is my wife," said Darcy hardly.

The girl Jacquetta flattered him, Bethune saw, deferred to him; that was why he fancied he loved her. He knew Darcy. Darcy at thirty-one, still the boy hedged in by a domineering mother. It occurred then to Bethune that Darcy was caught even worse than himself; at least he had never been in love with Susan and she was never a wanton. Was the child Darcy's even? No telling. Darcy—going back to war. And Bethune thought, a little grimly, that Darcy had been tactful in asking no questions about Mar-garet, as he might have. He accepted Bethune's lame expla-nation at face value: an old acquaintance fallen on unlucky times. And so, had Bethune a right to challenge Darcy about this girl? He shook his mind violently from the implied connection.

He found MacDonald unexpectedly indifferent. "Would you say it is our contribution to the war effort? Mr. Trevelyan will leave money for the girl's keep. It is for the women to say, what odds?" MacDonald was seemingly quite uncaring that the girl was—what she undoubtedly was, and would live here with Margaret, a lady. But it was Margaret who made the decision.

They made up beds for Darcy and the girl in the parlor; Bethune would sleep in the barn with Haagen tonight. When the visitors had retired he haled the women into the kitchen. "It would not be fair that I agree to it without consulting you."

"It's no matter to me, sir, so Mr. Trevelyan pays for her keep," said Dorcas in a colorless tone.

"Of course she may stay, you should have told him so at once."

"But, Margaret—" He was embarrassed. She faced him, surprised.

"You have nice notions. Only because she's not a lady?"

"Certainly not, you know it's not that! I only thought it would make difficulties, I—"

"She may share my chamber." And at that he was horrified.

"She'll do nothing of the kind! If you think I'd countenance—damn Darcy! Well, yes, I see how he's placed, but—"

"Had you thought to turn her away when his own family has refused her?"

He said, "I know Rafe Trevelyan. He is a gentleman, a good man. He would not have refused for no reason. He's not a fool."

"You will not tell me he's so fine a gentleman he never lay with a doxy," said Margaret. "Oh, for heaven's sake, James, don't look so shocked at me! I'm not a fool either, I can see what Jacquetta is as clear as you or your fine Rafe Trevelyan, and I'm as sorry for your friend as you. But I'm thinking of the child, don't you see? She'll need care, it's not far off. *Will* you cease looking so embarrassed! We are not children ourselves! Of course she must stay."

"I don't like the notion."

"If you refuse to have her," said Margaret, "I shall go and stay with her somewhere myself. Someone must think of the child."

"You cannot—"

"I can and I will. You've no rights over me. I shall do as I please."

"My God," he said. "You're only being stubborn over it." He looked at her in silence; he thought suddenly, But that is the reason. Again my fault. She was not quite a child; she knew; and hers they had killed. And the black guilt weighed on him again, an iron hand: Margaret, Margaret, I love you so and I can never tell it, never hope, because of five minutes fifteen years ago. Where was the reason in life when it played such ironic jest on a man?

"All right," he said. "All right. It's nothing to do with me." He sounded angry; he was angry. "She may stay."

Darcy gave him fifty pounds—all he had. "Even my uncle is lacking money now. Investments have gone to pieces, there's nothing of what my father left. I don't know, James—we're all two years and a bit wiser. They're not so easy beaten, but we don't mean to give up so easy either. I'm grateful, you know that. A letter care of the Continental Army, staff to General Greene, will catch up to me eventually. I've no notion where we'll be. We must see how it goes. You'll let me know—"

"Yes, of course. Good fortune, Darcy."

Darcy grinned a little forcedly. "That's all it is in war—fortune. If there's a ball with your name on it, nought you can do to prevent it being fired. I will try to write. And thanks, James."

Bethune did not like it; and it made difficulties, as he had expected. Jacquetta was not stupid; she knew well enough how to play up to a man. But she was indolent as a cat; he suspected she never lifted a hand in the house.

Margaret confirmed that readily enough. "She has no notion of how to boil water, and makes no effort at all. You would never guess what she said to me this morning." Her expression was between amusement and horror. "Dorcas and I gave her some stuffs, to make garments for the baby—she hasn't a thing. And she said she wouldn't trouble, she cannot sew and doubtless someone else will care for it as they did for the other. Yes, another child, heaven knows whose, if you can believe it. I think she is really stupid, you know—she might know we would tell her husband."

"Would you like the chore?" he asked.

"Oh, I know." She sighed. "Do you suppose they are really wed? Of course he thinks so, but from what she says—"

"No telling about that either." He was not really concerned with Jacquetta. He went about his work automatically these days, driving himself to create the need for sleep, to make the nights easier—and she twenty feet away beyond one door; but that was the least of loving her. He found himself watching her as if each time he saw her might be the last, storing up in him the look of her, the one woman. All he could do: watch. The man apart, as always. Thinking, Can it not somehow be possible, somehow? Have I the courage to try? No longer was she Margaret Thurstan of Thurstan Hundred, daughter to a gentry landowner; no longer he the boy suffered of charity, between the slaves and indentured servants. Everything was changed between them, except forever the one thing.

CHAPTER 30

THEY HAD the presses in the print shop, but MacDonald kept the type in the house except when it was carried there to be set for the edition, and oversaw the printing, and brought the type home in its box. It was too old and worn to risk Corder's using it for anything but the *Courier,* and new type, even if it could be had, was worth its weight in gold. Doubtless this had given faithful service before the *Courier* was founded.

So MacDonald was still at the print shop the afternoon Bethune came in to find Jacquetta in labor. It was not long, they told him later; she had been laboring several hours and he heard only the last of it. He did not like the girl, but he had never been near a woman in childbirth before and thought her screams would never stop. Yet he could not go, he paced distractedly, fearing she was dying, in cold sweat for the imagined pain, until Margaret came out of the room.

"Is it—is she—?"

"She is quite all right." How could they be so calm about it? "Dorcas thinks the baby will die—such a sweet little girl. It will not. Please, will you or someone bring more wood? It must be kept warm."

It was Dorcas who fetched the meal to the table that evening; Margaret sat by the kitchen hearth with the bundled infant, trying patiently to make it suck. She had a dish of warm sweetened milk, and was dipping a clean cloth in it, trying again and again to make the child take it. They had said the girl had no interest in the child, and no milk. MacDonald was imperturbable as always, but he thought Haagen felt as awkward and embarrassed as himself.

"You need not try to be quiet," Margaret said. "Jacquetta is sleeping sound, and it does not matter for the baby. I don't want her to sleep now, she must be fed."

Dorcas said timidly, "You can't, ma'am—I told you, poor mite, she's too little, I think it was early."

"I won't have her die, you'll see." She went on sitting there after the others had retired, Dorcas slipping off to tend the girl. Bethune had one brief look at the tiny, pinched, white face in the bundled shawl.

When he looked in very late, after Haagen had taken MacDonald to his chamber, she still sat there. She had put out the candles because they were expensive, and sat in the firelight; he came to her side, seeing how the quietly leaping flame made a nimbus round her head.

"Margaret—"

She did not look up. "You'll see, she won't die—I'll save her. I won't have her die."

He said, "You must be tired. It would be best for everyone, wouldn't it? She doesn't want it, and can you think it's Darcy's?"

She did look up then. "What does it matter whose it is? It is a baby! Is that how you think? Damn you then—I will not have her die, I'll—I'll do somewhat, I—"

"Margaret, this is foolish. I talked to Dorcas, she said— You must not—"

"I must," she said. "I must. Don't you know why, James, don't you guess why?" He might guess; he was stricken to silence. There had never been one word between them about that; neither had dared speak. He knew nothing of how that had been for her. All the ease, the new relationship they had achieved, one word of that would destroy in a moment; it lay too deep. She said, "Because they stole mine away. They took it from me, I never knew!"

And still he did not guess, he was moved but not wounded.

"Oh, Margaret, I know—I'm sorry, but don't you see—"

"They would not have killed it—oh, God, they wouldn't? I never knew, and I tried, I tried to forget, no use thinking—wondering. They stole it away that same hour, I never knew if it was boy or girl, I could not reach it—I only heard it crying, and tried. I tried. But they came—" She was bent over the bundle, not seeing she dealt him a blow as if with an ax handle.

He was, he found, kneeling beside her, holding her shoulders, and feeling nothing at touching her. "But you can't mean—Margaret, you can't mean—! I thought—"

She looked down at him, and some of the usual tranquillity came back to her eyes; she looked at him as if she too felt nothing, their faces near as lovers' in the dim intimacy of firelight. She said slowly, "Oh, I see. Of course. You would think that, of course."

"I never imagined— But why? Margaret—"

She did not stir under his hands. "Of course. I'm sorry—I did not mean to say all that. Why? They said it was too late. They brought old Mrs. Williams—perhaps you remember her, the midwife. She said it was too long, it would be dangerous. It was born in November. That's odd, your birthday is in November. And odd I should remember that just now."

"Oh, my God, Margaret. I never thought that. What can I say? I don't—I cannot—"

She looked at him curiously, dispassionately. "It does not make all that difference to what you feel? It was only natural you should think as you did, it was the first thing they thought of too. Does that make it worse, James? I've never known if it was worse or better for me—for I shall never know, and it was mine, I may have been a child but not that much a child. But it is so long ago, and no use expending agony over it now. Only sometimes—I can't help it. I'm sorry."

He got up and turned away from her. He said, "There's nothing I can say to you. If I had done nothing wrong before or since—if I spent a lifetime trying to pay—" And what was in his mind was that girl this afternoon, screaming.

"But that's foolish too," she said in a tired whisper. "Just children. Nothing you could have done. I said I never blamed you."

He said nothing; there was nothing more to say. After a time he heard her stir and she said, remote and sad, "Poor darling thing. She's gone. I tried—but she's gone. Would you go and call Dorcas, please, James? I wanted so much to keep her."

He could not have put it in words, the difference it was to him. Knowing that there had been, was, a child. It was not the mere knowledge that somewhere alive in the world was a child he had sired; there were, he thought wryly, few men could be sure they had not got a bastard or two. Perhaps it was partly that he learned it the same day he heard that girl screaming in labor. Perhaps it was that. He only knew he felt it to be a blacker wrong than he had ever thought: that the guilt increased a hundred times for this knowledge.

He was grateful for work, something to put his mind on. There was enough of it, and of news to write. Some of it filled his mind with uneasiness somewhat more personal than concern for the American troops. Burgoyne was moving southward, sweeping all before him. It was possible that if the Americans did not hold him, there would come a British threat to Kingston. Indeed, the New York Assembly, still resident here, was so alarmed that they were already planning removal to a safer place. Once again the doubts were descending on patriots—could they possibly hope to stand against the power of the British Army?

The *Courier* was dangerously low on paper; Bethune rode south, made the rounds of every mill he knew of now in operation. Only three were outside enemy territory, and the lowest price he was quoted was twelve pounds the ream. Fantastic, but they must have it. He signed a contract for fifty reams in September. He thought he could manage that, six hundred pounds. They had only a handful of regular subscribers left; he had six boys now to hawk the other copies about. He sent off a hundred copies each week to shopkeepers in Trenton, Philadelphia, Elizabethtown, Newark; but there was the carriage fee to come out of any profit, and always the printers to think of—a day's wages for four men and four boys, that was one pound eight shillings once a week, and another two pounds for the use of two of Corder's presses. Discounting any wages for himself or profits paid to MacDonald, they were lucky to realize an average take of ten pounds an edition, and an edition at the minimum cost of upwards of five pounds to produce —and that was not reckoning the cost of the remaining paper.

"Do you remember the depression of trade during the Stamp Tax business, Mr. Bethune? We were almighty indignant at first over being offered eggs and firewood in payment!" Well, these days, true enough, they took some payment of that sort, and gladly. He worried over that six hundred pounds to be paid in September. He had been riding all about the countryside, twenty miles every way, selling copies where he could each week. Now he set Haagen to doing that. He took work in the fields as an extra hand at the harvest; with so many men away at war wages had risen and he could ask five shillings a day—the wages a full printer had. That was thirty-five shillings a week, almost another two pounds. Hard work; he welcomed it; while he had his strength and MacDonald his wit they would bring out the *Courier*.

On the first day of September he had five hundred and seventy pounds, and three hundred and fifty of it was the last of the gold MacDonald had brought from New York. They must have the paper. He did not want to borrow, that would be mad; he must somehow get that thirty pounds. Harvest was almost over, but he could find other work; however, he needed the money now. He had never seen MacDonald so depressed as he was now; belatedly

Bethune realized it must have galled him that he sat by while another man sweated in the fields on his behalf. Not a personal thing, that way: this was their private war together, to keep the *Courier* alive—if we must give the copies away, MacDonald had said; Bethune echoed that now in his own mind.

There was an inn on the edge of Kingston called the Rebel Arms (formerly the King's House); he stopped there one afternoon on his way home from work, to find how many copies the publican had sold of last week's edition. Sitting at the sole table was a portly man in elegant clothes, who complained loudly of the regular stage. "Change here for Passaic, he says, be along in an hour, and by God I'm waiting three hours by my watch already! The war, they say, but by God—"

The publican leaned to Bethune. "Says he's in the employ of the governor's staff in New Jersey—but no good patriot's the kind of money he's wearing on his back, these times. Ask me, he's trading with the British out of New York." Bethune, looking at the fellow, thought that very likely.

"It's an outrage. Some way to pass the time—" And now the prosperous customer brought a pack of cards from his pocket and commenced to shuffle them as if to keep his hands occupied.

The same cold, superior thrill fingered down Bethune's spine that he had felt on that night when, scarcely more than a boy, he had faced James Rivington over the cards. Here was his thirty pounds, asking to be taken. He went over to the table.

"Afternoon, sir. I agree, it's an outrage about the stage into New Jersey, but it'll be coming. Can I oblige you with a little game to pass the time meanwhile? I'm at loose ends myself."

The man looked at him, suspicious at first, then relaxing to a smile at his obviously well-bred manner. "Why, thankee, sir, indeed, I'd be delighted. What shall it be?"

The Passaic stage came in three hours later. Bethune went home with thirty-eight pounds twelve shillings he had not earned by the sweat of his brow, and never the suspicion of guilt in him for it.

Four days later he hired a wagon, drove to Newark, paid the mill, and collected his paper. He also collected some news during his week's travel.

That Gentleman Johnny was in difficulties with his northern campaign had been obvious for a month or more, even if one discounted half the rumors. It was distinctly gratifying: the trustful professional soldier, Burgoyne, expecting support from his nearest brother-general who should have given it to him; and Howe sat there in New York amidst the most select regiments of the British Army, all armed to the teeth and impatient for action, Howe with his women and his banquets and plans to reopen the theaters. Burgoyne was too far from his supply base; unless Howe made haste he would surely be lost. What Bethune had not heard before was that Howe had at last moved—to lay attack on Philadelphia.

Philadelphia! Only a fortnight since, his informant confirmed. So Howe ignored Burgoyne completely! It was not only gratifying news to patriots, but comforting to him: for any supporting army going to join Burgoyne must probably come up the Hudson by way of Kingston.

MacDonald was as pleased, if as incredulous. "God's teeth, if the British have many generals of Howe's stamp, the war is as good as won! By all the rumor—and it appears much of it is founded on fact—Burgoyne cannot hold out much longer." And a week later news drifted in of a great battle on Bemis Heights, where General Gates administered Burgoyne a sound beating and a staggering loss in men, if rumor did not exaggerate. "When Burgoyne is taken"—it was surely "when" now, not "if"—"we're securely behind the lines, and a good way." Neither of them had said anything to the women, but the thought of Burgoyne's army sweeping down to cut off upper New York had not been a comfortable one.

"But it's a masterpiece," exclaimed MacDonald delightedly. "God's fingerbones, I never turned out such subtle irony in my life. I wonder who composed it."

The harvest was long over, it was a chill autumn day, the Indian summer late and just past. They had printed an edition yesterday, and he was sorry they had not had this to include in it—as well as a trifle indignant that official army sources had sent it to Holt to publish in the *Journal;* they discounted the *Courier* as a means of communication, did they?

"Paine for a bet, sir. He is serving as aide to General Washington, you know."

"What are you laughing at?" asked Margaret, coming to the door curiously. "I've not heard either of you so cheerful in weeks."

"A woman could not appreciate it, but you shall have the chance." MacDonald waved the page. "It is an official recruiting advertisement for the American Army. Just listen—masterly! 'The encouragement at this time to enlist is truly liberal and generous, namely a bounty of twelve dollars, an annual and fully sufficient supply of good and handsome clothing, a daily allowance of a large and ample ration of provisions, together with sixty dollars a year in gold and silver money on account of pay, the whole of which the soldier may lay up for himself and friends, as all articles proper for his subsistence and comfort are provided by law without any expense to him. Those who shall embrace the opportunity of spending a few happy years in viewing the different parts of this beautiful continent, in the honorable and truly respectable character of a soldier, may if he please return afterward to his home and friends with his pockets full of money and his head covered with laurels.' "

Margaret gave him the lie with laughter. "You cannot mean anyone's actually printed it? But how absurd—let me see."

"Can we suppose there are any dunderheads left so credulous to take it at face value? No, the only reason it might influence a man to enlist would be in appreciation of such irony. I'll keep this as a souvenir."

And that was the moment they heard the first shots. Bethune jerked round, but before he reached the door Haagen burst in, his face white.

"It is de British—a big fleet of dem—in de river! Dey've landed, dey're coming—"

MacDonald folded up the recruiting poster and tucked it away in his pocket, then fetched out his pistol and began to load it. Bethune snapped at Haagen, "Don't leave Mr. MacDonald an instant! Margaret, you and Dorcas run and fetch in water—there may be a siege. Fill everything in the house." His own pistol was buried at the bottom of his pile of clothes—dwindling now; no matter, likely he'd never hit anything with it anyway.

"Mr. Bethune," said MacDonald, "you are not company commander here. Pay no attention to him, Willem. I want the two of you to go at once to the printer's and fetch our presses. Get them on a wagon, bring them here. There seems to be a fight going on —the local militia is out, doubtless—that may hold them awhile. Go now, don't stand arguing at me! Get those presses!"

"I'll look to him, sir," said Dorcas in the doorway. Bethune knew an instant's agony of indecision: he could not be in two places at once. The presses, yes, but—

He was facing MacDonald, back to the house door; he did not at first understand the expressions on their faces. Margaret went white as death; Dorcas gave a little moan. MacDonald said, "Stand out of my way, Mr. Bethune," and then Bethune whirled. A British soldier stood in the open door, and his musket had bayonet fixed. Another soldier was behind him. MacDonald raised his pistol and shot the nearest man through the chest.

It did not take five seconds. The other soldier had his musket up. Bethune flung himself forward, between the gun and Mac-Donald, and crashed into the man as the gun went off into the ceiling. He got up to his knees, the soldier lying stunned beneath him, and Haagen took the third who ran up then. Haagen snatched the musket from Bethune, jammed the bayonet into that third man again and again. There were shots from all directions then, and yet oddly in this room for a moment it was still. Neither of the women had screamed.

MacDonald was looking out the window. He said, "They are firing the town. In God's name, Mr. Bethune, go and rescue our presses!"

CHAPTER 31

IT WAS no moment for indecision. But he felt almost that he tore himself in half as he snapped, "Margaret, Dorcas—look to Mr. MacDonald, barricade the doors after us and admit no one until we're back! Willem, come with me." He heard the bolt shot behind them as they ran into the street. Margaret would keep her head. . . .

There was a crowd of townsfolk at the end of this street, not running to or from the enemy, only frightened, confused people milling about. Bethune pushed through with Haagen after him, damning them for fools that they seemed of so little purpose; not a man he saw carried a weapon.

"The British—regular troops—" "God, they're firing the town!" "But there's no rebel soldiers here!" No soldiers! It would be small difference to the British, evidently. He saw not far off a house, set ablaze, streaming flame and smoke. And half of him was still back there with MacDonald—with Margaret. The British were not asking today, Soldier or civilian?

If he had stopped to think, he would have known his prime feeling was not (as it had never been) hate or fear of the enemy. (British, the enemy? A family quarrel, as it had been from the start!) It was more personal, an anxiety for what was his. Now it all fused in him toward one point—the *Courier*'s two presses in Jacob Corder's print shop. As he ran, jostled by the crowds, deafened by shouts and shots, everything else went from him.

He ran around a corner into the street, and did not hear

Haagen's whimper of profanity behind. The print shop was in flames, there were redcoats in the street ahead. There was no consciousness of danger in him; he pounded up to the blazing door and through it, and if the redcoats fired at him he did not hear. The presses, the precious presses— It was an inferno, the shop had been fired in several places. "Willem, help me—"

"I'm here, Mr. Bethune." No time to feel surprise that the frightened Dutchman had followed. The presses, God, were ablaze too—all but one, one of the *Courier*'s, in the corner. He wrestled it away from the wall, sobbing for breath. Not through the front, a wall of fire there now— "Back door, Willem! Hurry!" Two men could not carry that heavy machine; but they had before, that night in New York.

Somehow they got out the slit of blazing rear door, to what had been a lane. Fire all about now; the next house was going, the one beyond had gone—black and crumbling. No safety anywhere, now. Haagen gabbling at him. Thank God, the box of type safe, with MacDonald. But, Christ, the paper! And Haagen caught him, held him, as he flung back toward the fire.

"No, Mr. Bethune! You can't—burned up you would be, no—"

He could not get back; the whole building was falling in. The heat sent him staggering away. They were struggling with the press again, up the narrow lane, past more flames and a roaring and the breath of hell too close. His mind began to work again, slowly. He shouted to Haagen, "We must—get right away from the town— they will fire it all! Hurry!"

By the grace of God, Corder's place had been not far off the edge of town. The lane led into the countryside. Ten minutes of terrible effort saw them a safe distance from the nearest burning house, between hedges now bare in autumn. No cover, but it must serve. "In here, Willem—" They hid it as best they could under thin growth, off the path. "Stay and guard it, understand? I must —get back, see to the others—"

"Not alone, Mr. Bethune! Mr. MacDonald—I will go—"

"No! Someone must guard the press!" There was no breath or strength left to him, after that effort, to run; but he ran desperately, back into the streets—streets crowded now with panic-stricken, fleeing people, clutching belongings snatched at random from the flames. There was a din of shouting, screaming, but strangely, no shots. He fought his way through the crowds; when he came in sight of the house, it was licked by flame all up one wall. The breath was harsh in his throat; he could not do any more. He beat on the door, it gave to his hand, and he stumbled in.

Margaret called his name, in a frightened voice, from a back room. They had retreated to the kitchen; MacDonald, still clutching his pistol, asked at once, "The presses? Have you——?" The type, yes, MacDonald had the box on his lap.

He made two attempts before he could speak. "Must get out, they're firing every house. Hurry—right away from town, the hillside—only safe place. Help me, Margaret—" And MacDonald's chair seemed as heavy as the press. He was torn in two again now by all his urgency to herd his private importances together, get to the press with only Haagen, unarmed, to guard it. He was unaware of the women, of the noise all about, even of his own exhaustion.

"Firing the town!" echoed MacDonald, sounding stupefied. "My God, the whole street is going—see there—"

"And every other street. Not that way, we'll only run into the crowds—can't get through. The back lanes. What? Only one, only the one press—the others were burning when we went in. I would have tried—"

A little company of British were running down this lane, straight for them. The pistol shook in MacDonald's hand as he raised it; but they might have been invisible, for the redcoats ran past, uncaring. The high clear call of a bugle sounded from the distance. And now, ahead of them in the countryside, the crowds were straggling from the doomed town—crowds not noisy now, but almost silent with the aftermath of shock.

The girl Jacquetta said plaintively, "I'm hungry." Margaret told her sharply to be quiet.

"It is almost over," said MacDonald. "Look there, they are leaving." From their vantage point on this rise of hill behind the town they could see the ships' boats moving slowly in the river.

They were not alone on the little hill, crouched among tangle of undergrowth, watching. Most of the town was there. Somewhere a woman sobbed loudly, men cursed; helpless, disbelieving, they stared down at what had been Kingston.

They were to learn that a general with a modicum of wit remained in New York; Clinton had sent Vaughan up the river with a force to meet and support Burgoyne. Vaughan failed to make liaison, and, at the rumor of Gates' army north, was only too thankful to turn down-river to New York and safety. The only action he took on that expedition was his burning of Kingston.

They sat on the hillside and watched the town burn. When the British began to move down-river only one house was standing— the Van Steenbergh house, on the edge of town, and isolated. The British made no attempt to invade; aside from a first skirmish with the local defenders, there had been no fighting.

Bethune sat on the ground, a hand on the press beside him.

The girl said again, "But I'm hungry," and, unexpectedly, Margaret slapped her.

"Be quiet! I've never seen anything so wanton. What are these people to do? Everything burned—the harvest—"

Bethune did not give one damn for the harvest. He could have wept for the paper, the precious paper, six hundred pounds' worth of paper. Not only the money—paper was rare even if one had a million pounds to spend for it. All unused, boxes unopened, gone up in smoke.

MacDonald said, "We'd best be taking stock and thinking what to do. It appears we are out of commission for the time being, at least. One press. One. And all the paper gone."

Bethune stood up. "We are not out of commission, sir. We are going to publish."

MacDonald looked up at him with a little strained smile. "Cocky, Mr. Bethune, cocky!"

"Now they've made me angry," said Bethune. "Now they've touched me. Bold soldiers indeed, making war on civilians, are they not! I don't believe I was angry enough before, any time. They are not going to stop me now or next year. We go on publishing, by God."

"That's my man," said MacDonald softly. "Tell me how."

Dorcas said, "You and your newspaper—what difference is that? How are we going to live, what shall we do now? My hens— all the flour—just the clothes on our backs—"

"All these people," said Margaret. "What will they do? I suppose the countryfolk will help, but—"

"Let them look to themselves," said Bethune. He was watching the British ships moving off in irregular line. He did not curse them or shout threats after them, as other men on the hill were doing; he only watched with cold eyes. "I've sufficient to think about besides that. No quarter now, no quarter. Let them try to stop me, let them try. I think I've been overlong taking sides in this war." He looked at the others. "Turn out your pockets—what have we?" They took inventory; it was soon done. There was twelve pounds seven and fourpence among them in coin; Mac-Donald's gold watch, his own cheap silver one; the box of type; the clothes they stood in. Margaret had brought out three blankets, Dorcas a cloak of MacDonald's. Haagen had the bayoneted musket he had taken from the redcoat, MacDonald his pistol.

MacDonald was ignoring the fleet, watching him. "I'll relinquish command, Mr. Bethune. Where do we go from here?"

He took all the money but a pound, MacDonald's watch, and the musket, without powder or ball for it. He started south down-river in the darkness; he walked all that night and much of the next day, and found a raftman to ferry him across the river. He came to Poughkeepsie about sundown. They had heard of the disaster there, and had seen Vaughan's fleet pass; the townsfolk were collecting food and clothing for the victims. He sold Mac-Donald's watch and his own for ten pounds gold.

He was in Poughkeepsie two days; on the day he left he met John Holt in the street. The editor of the *Journal* had aged ten years in as many weeks; he was not a young man. But if he had lost much, he still had wealth left. He owned a paper in Virginia, Bethune knew, which his son edited; he had a half-interest in one of the few mills in operation. Bethune had met him once or twice in New York, but it was flattering that Holt hailed him, asked him into a tavern. "How goes it, Mr. Bethune? I'll not ask what you lost at Kingston, but what you saved—it makes shorter telling."

The boy brought them the usual watered-down rum. Bethune asked, "And you, sir?" He remembered seeing nothing of Holt the day the town burned; the *Journal* had had its own print shop there.

"Everything," said Holt. He brought one hand flat down on the table, a gesture of finality. "Everything. I've not been up-river as yet. I was here when it happened, one of my men came yesterday to tell me the news. The presses, all I had in Kingston, gone."

"May I ask your plans, then?"

Holt shook his head. "I don't know, I've not decided. I'd need to have more presses shipped up from Charleston. Very probably I shall do that, but at the moment I've no hesitation saying I'm low in spirit. Seems scarce worth the effort, does it?" He added, "I never saw quite eye to eye with Robert MacDonald, but these times a little difference in policy hardly counts. When I think of that traitor Gaine sitting smug in New York—! Have you many subscribers left?"

"That bastard," said Bethune. "Scarce two hundred. We'll have more."

Holt stared at him. "You're continuing publication? MacDonald —I should have asked you, he is safe?"

"Quite, sir. We're going on. I am not sure where, no. Jersey somewhere, likely. I've bought a cart and horse here to fetch the others down—and you can guess their quality, for fifteen pounds cash! Kingston is dead, God knows if they'll ever rebuild."

Holt eyed him. "What have you?" he asked curiously. Bethune laughed.

"We're scarce rivals any longer, as you say. I'll tell you, sir. Somewhere about one pound ten between us, one press, a box of type, the clothes on our backs, an old pistol, MacDonald's wit, and my strength. What had I thought to do? I'll settle us somewhere first—I thought of Tenafly. I'll need to find work, support ourselves and begin to save for more paper. It all went up—sixty, seventy reams—fifty I'd just paid for." It would be long before he forgot his grievance for that paper. May their souls burn in hell for it—fifty reams, six hundred pounds.

"You didn't complete the list," said Holt. "A plenty of guts, too, Mr. Bethune. By God, if you publish, so will I! I'll tell you what I'll do." He searched his pockets. "I will give you a note to the mill in Newark, they'll let you have ten reams on credit by my word. These times, all of us must help each other."

"I never expected—I can't thank you. I'll see it's paid." The unexpected windfall almost brought tears to his eyes. They could publish again at once.

"That I know," said Holt with a friendly nod. "Good fortune to you, Mr. Bethune, and my regards to MacDonald. I'm thinking he is lucky to have you by him."

"The other way about, sir. There'd be no *Courier* without him."

He drove the cart back up-river to Kingston, and was ferried across by an obliging farmer. Little had been done as yet, but here and there men poked about in the ruins, clearing ground to rebuild. MacDonald, his chair, and the press filled the cart; the others walked, taking turns in riding with the driver. They started for Tenafly along the Hudson, a little village the British were not likely to trouble. The cart and horse had cost all he had, save a few shillings which went for food to carry; both were aged and slow. They took ten days for the eighty-odd miles, sleeping along the road. He thought the first few days Jacquetta complained with every step. He was a patient man, and he had never laid hand to a woman in anger in his life. On the fourth morning when she commenced to lament that she was starving, she could not walk another yard, she didn't know why she had come with such unfeeling folk, he pulled up the horse, got down and shook her with all his strength.

"Now be quiet! I'll not hear another word the rest of the day! If you think it's any pleasure to us to have you along you're much mistaken. But you are Darcy Trevelyan's wife, and in my charge, and you will remain so."

She went deliberately limp against him, a sly smile in her eyes. "I don't mind being in your charge, Mr. Bethune. Only I am hungry, and I don't see why we got to travel so far. You wouldn't want I should die on you, would you, Mr. Bethune?" The black eyes made promises.

He resisted a strong impulse to slap her harder than Margaret had. "It's nought to do with me one way or the other," he said coldly. "You are Darcy's wife and I've contracted to look after you." It came to him that this girl was directly to blame for the new blacker guilt he carried. But for her, he would never have known, and he wished to God he had not found out. Of course, no sin a sin unless it is known: Jesuitical, Bethune! Damn Darcy for a fool and himself for another.

"Well, I dunno," she said with a shrug. "I been wed to some others, but it don't seem to make it any better. How much more do we go on like this, Mr. Bethune?"

So legally, in all probability, they were not married at all. He regarded her with exasperation. "Until we reach where we are going. And I want no more complaints from you. Margaret, you will like to ride a bit." He helped her up to the seat. She gave him a smile, and her voice was low.

"Thank you. Let's hope that takes some effect." She looked tired, but still to him lovely. He thought it was strange that intimate talk and new confidence between them had not made more constraint; but was there a time either of them forgot? He thought not. He thought, too, perhaps he would never see Margaret clear, as others saw her: memory and emotion blurring her a little for him, into beauty.

He nodded to Haagen that he might drive a way; he fell into step beside a silent Dorcas, a sullen Jacquetta.

They reached Tenafly the same day as bad news. Howe had occupied Philadelphia; the Americans were on the run again. They were all too depressed and tired to discuss it long. He found a sympathetic housewife—of course the man was away in the Army —who let them have an empty stable for the promise of rent. When he had seen them settled in, the loft making partial privacy for the women, he set off in the cart for Newark to get the paper from Holt's mill. On the return journey he met the first snowfall of winter, which promised to be early and severe. The war was at a standstill for it; the major American forces, he heard, were settled in winter camp at a place called Valley Forge.

In some ways that was the worst time: certainly in material ways. He knew this was a mad thing, this determination to continue the *Courier*. It was a thing he had to do. The only British he would like to kill were those who had burned his paper, and in any case, he could not leave MacDonald, who would be helpless —but he had a war to fight all the same. He thought eventually he would be forced to acknowledge defeat, find work to support them until the war should end, and God knew what would come then, if it ended the wrong way. But until he was forced, he would keep trying. No quarter now. The day after he came back to Tenafly they printed an edition, of one page only.

There were few men left in the village, and he had no money to pay those. Their erstwhile hostess had a young son who came to watch and stayed to help, fascinated; that was all the help they had. Haagen made a team with Dorcas, himself with Margaret, after MacDonald had set the type. They took it in turns of an hour's work at the one press. He was grateful for that field work in the summer which had hardened his townsman's muscles. The press was as heavy to pull as he remembered finding it that day at Brady's shop long ago.

"Another hour at it. Margaret, I'm sorry to ask you—" She looked tired, as tired as he felt; the perspiration stood on her brow, her hair clung wet along her temples. Hard work for amateurs at it, and not only for himself and Haagen who pulled the press down; the women, inserting the pages, removing them, spreading them to dry, had the more active job. And only the one press: when the front of the page was done, MacDonald took down the type, set it up for the back, and they'd as much to do over again.

"It's interesting," she said. "We're glad to help. Once you're established here you'll be able to hire men."

They printed five hundred copies. He sent most off to their former agents in Trenton, Newark, Elizabethtown; Philadelphia, a large market, was now lost, and the carriage to Boston was prohibitive for profit. The remainder, after the few regular subscribers left were sent copies, he managed to sell about the countryside. They took in seven pounds six and threepence on that edition.

The day before they would begin to print another edition he and MacDonald discussed it. He had been too occupied to notice the change in MacDonald this year; suddenly, that morning, he saw as if for the first time that MacDonald's hair was nearly all gray now, there were new lines in his face, his movements were more deliberate. Even his voice had aged.

"The grand gesture is all very well, Mr. Bethune, but we've our bellies to think of—and two women. Mistress Thurstan—" He stopped there, giving Bethune the chance to confide.

"I dare say she could look to herself, she stays only because she feels she's needed. As she is." How much, she would never know.

"You never had a head for figures. If it goes like this long—I need not tell you how bitterly I regret my incapacity," and Mac-Donald's mouth twisted. "If I could take other work—"

"Don't think of it, sir, it's no matter."

"How much do we owe the mill? Two hundred and twenty pounds. By June. I do not believe we can do it. Two days of back-breaking work to get out one small edition. We cannot continue that."

"I'll find men—"

"And pay them with what?" asked MacDonald harshly.

After a moment Bethune asked, "Are you saying we should give it up? Do you want to do that?"

MacDonald's hands opened and closed, white-knuckled. "I never in my life wanted aught so much as to keep on publishing now. But we can't go against figures—we could not publish at a loss indefinitely. I don't know, Mr. Bethune." He was silent, and then swore. "God! Just across the river there—New York. They say the city drips with money—all the Loyalists left in the colonies, all the British officers with their ladies. And for the need of a steady ten pounds a week we—"

Bethune said, "We'll publish. There'll be a way, I'll find it." He did not know how; it was only postponing defeat. He went off alone to think it out. He went almost by instinct to the little shed where they had been allowed to put the press. And he found young Will Clark there, fingering it—the fascinated boy.

"I bet I could pull it down, Mr. Bethune. Can I try?" He was not strong enough. "But I will be. Mr. Bethune? I'm going to learn to be a printer. I never saw a press before, I saw a couple other newspapers though. Mr. Bethune? You reckon there'll be newspapers after the war?"

He looked at the boy. Fourteen, fifteen, young Will. Fourteen. November that year—that made it about right, fourteen. Young Will, freckles, sandy hair, eager eyes. Something peculiar rose up in him, something savage and primal.

He said, "I reckon there'll be newspapers. You know why? Because you want to be a printer. I'll tell you, Will—we'll make a bargain. After the war you come to New York, to the *Courier* office. I'll be there. I'll help you learn to be a printer." He came out of the shed and started to walk, blind. He thought, It is not all the reasons we've given for it: any obstinate refusal to be stopped, any need for the profit however little, any partisanship for the American cause, that the *Courier* has to go on being published. It is because young Will Clark wants to print newspapers after the war. And by God, so he will and so will we.

Tell me how, MacDonald said softly.

He stopped. MacDonald's voice was saying something else to him: Across the river—all that money. And suddenly Bethune began to laugh quietly, excitedly to himself.

PART FOUR

CHAPTER 32

THERE WAS a large mirror on the wall of the main room in Fraunces' Tavern, opposite him here. Looking up, Bethune met his own gaze. He was absently pleased with the man in the glass, the elegant gentleman with a little smile slantwise on his mouth. He wore excellently tailored maroon coat and breeches of polished sateen broadcloth; his white linen shirting gleamed, and his linen stock; though the glass did not show it, no wrinkle was in his black hose, and his thin black city shoes were newly polished, their silver buckles gleaming.

"Your declaration, captain."

Captain Lieutenant Barr pouted vexedly at his hand. "Oh, damnation, so 'tis. Well, not much, but the best I can do. A trio, sir." He slapped the cards down in pettish triumph: queen, knave, and ten of diamonds.

Bethune's smile quivered slightly. "Not good," he said. "I've quatorze." He laid the cards down: ace, king, queen, and knave of spades.

"Oh, damnation," said Barr. "That gives you game again. Never saw such luck."

"It gives him more than that," crowed Hector Kennedy over the officer's shoulder; he had watched the play. "You've not made fifty points, you lose double."

"Good God, so I do." Barr did not seem greatly concerned; he frowned and laughed. "Damme, sir, talk of luck! What d'you make it?"

Bethune was shuffling the pack. He said indifferently, "I quite forget the stakes. Was it five guineas the game?"

"Right, right. That makes thirty guineas I owe you and five

259

you owe me. All square. No, no, I've had my fill," with a grin. "Find some other to take you on!"

Bethune smiled after him, scooping the twenty-five guineas from the table to his pocket. He was fond of Barr, who liked cards and was as handy at it as a ten-year-old in his first game. He decided his night's work was done; twenty-five guineas was a trifle more than his usual take. He invited Kennedy to join a game, knowing he would refuse. "Then let me give you a glass?"

Kennedy slid into Barr's vacated chair. "I wonder if your honest face belies your hands."

It was a pun; Bethune smiled. "Only luck, Hector. I was always lucky at cards."

"Damme, you puzzle me, Bethune." Kennedy studied him over the Madeira wine. "I told you before, I thought you a fool to go over to the rebels, but ask me, I'd never have said you'd change your mind in the middle of the road, so to speak."

"Who says I have?" asked Bethune. He began to lay out the cards for solitaire. "I'm like you, Hector—I find the war a damnation nuisance. A man must live. Where else is there any money now but New York? I'll pocket a little pride to eat regular." He smiled. "I may have sympathy for the rebels but not so much to carry a musket for them."

"Or write for one of their newspapers? Or is the *Courier* yet printed?"

"I've no idea." He said his little piece as he had said it to others, indifferent. "It was losing money. When my wages stopped I left it. And after all, my wife is here."

"Oh, yes," said Kennedy with a lift of his brows. He was only son to a wealthy city family. Like many young Loyalists, he had seemingly no impulse to support his opinion with action; let the regular army do the fighting. His life, that of so many others, had remained almost unchanged for the war since the British held New York. Bethune swept the cards to a pile, having brought out his game.

"And I think I'll go home to her. Good night, Hector." An attendant produced his gray beaver hat, his caped maroon cloak. He went out into New York, and even after these months felt again the pleasure at being here once more. His town, his place. He'd fallen in love with New York nearly fifteen years back; she held him as a mistress. Even as she was now.

He did not go to the house in Greenwich Road; he was not living there, though all who knew him took it for granted he was. He had furnished a room in the Cherry Street house, but he spent little time there. As he liked to do, he wandered the streets, looking at, listening to New York.

She had come in for a deal of vilification, the glittering mistress, playing eager host to the enemy. Well, New York (had not Mac-Donald told him so?) was a city of merchants, and merchants kept one eye always on their profits. Were there patriots left? Very likely a number of them; but they lay meek and quiet under the heel of the conqueror. It was a city of Tories now; they had come flocking in droves to the one safe haven in America. They, and the war, had at a stroke destroyed the great middle class of the city; now there were the very rich at the top, the very poor at the bottom, and nothing between. A prodigal city, a lavish city: you could buy any luxury you fancied, ships coming in every week from England. And the civilian Loyalists—most with investments here or in England still safe, still paying—spent extravagantly. The military officers did not stint themselves. At the bottom there was starvation, but who cared for those at the bottom? Prices were high, wages low; New York held perpetual holiday, and only the working people remembered and cursed the war.

It did not seem to care, New York, that many of its old rights had vanished; that citizens were subject to military trial without jury, that the franchise was ruthlessly denied. Despite all, it was still New York. He was glad to be home.

He had come back in mid-November, five months ago. It had been so easy; he had never thought it would be so easy. He felt guilty for it: living the life of an indolent gentleman—and why pretend it was not a deal pleasanter, even among Tories and British?—while others outside lacked so much of what he had. He'd crossed the river by Tenafly and walked down to the city; he heard there were patriot raids on military outposts on Long Island and

Staten Island, but evidently none here. The countryside was quite peaceful.

Uniforms were necessary for most things—fighting a war, tricking the enemy. He took thirty pounds in the first week, and spent ten on new clothes. Gradually the average take increased as his acquaintance widened. It was a poor week he did not average fifty pounds. British officers liked deep play.

Talk of luck! But it was—when one thought—natural. A great many who had known Bethune of the *Courier* before had left the city; he had never had a wide acquaintance among the first, and therefore Tory, society. In a week's evenings of haunting the more exclusive taverns, he had casually met two dozen officers and as many civilians, all apparently with money to burn; they accepted him without question, a gentleman. Those who had known him seemed unsurprised he forsook former sympathies; he was scarcely the only man who regretted siding with the rebels this last year. He had gambled on the possibility that the warrant against him and MacDonald would be forgotten; so it had been, for in that first few weeks of the occupation all had been confused.

It had been an almighty gamble; at times he went cold, thinking of the chances he took. He thought of that first evening when he sat down to play for guinea stakes with eight shillings in his pocket. But he had won twenty guineas and not looked back. He lost sometimes, of course: the run of luck. But he was satisfied to come out twenty or thirty pounds ahead in a week, that was enough; it was usually more. He had learned to stay clear of men like Major Canning, Percy Head, Bull King, who were shark cards players, as good as he. There were enough like Barr who never seemed to keep a record to see that they always came out at the wrong end of a deal, winning five pounds, losing twenty-five.

The only one who seemed surprised to see him had been Gay. He smiled, thinking of that, and frowned. The British had re-opened the theater in John Street, naming it the Theatre Royal now; he had attended the first night on invitation of Kennedy, and could hardly be missed, sitting in one of the boxes overhanging the stage. Seeing him, she had faltered in her lines one moment. After the play he excused himself to Kennedy with the truth: "The little dark girl in the second act—an old acquaintance I must renew." Kennedy laughed, dug him in the side. "And I don't blame you, man—but best find out if she's under contract elsewhere or you're like to be called out by one of these fire-eating officers!"

He went round to the players' entrance. Perhaps she had been expecting him; she hurried down the passage to him at the attendant's word. "Jemmy! What are you doing here? I couldn't believe my eyes—"

"Surely I may look up an old friend?" he parried for the attendant's benefit; he drew her from the door into the dark thread of alley. She kissed him absently.

"But I thought—why've you come back? Isn't it dangerous?"

Gay meant well, but she could no more guard a secret than she could guard her chastity. He said lightly, "Oh, perhaps I've decided I was mistaken in opinion about the war. It's no matter, I'm here, and I want no gossip about last year or the year before. How do you, Gay?"

"Oh, I'm all right, Jemmy. You can't see me home, there's an officer—"

"Not a fat major?"

She giggled. "Not fat, anyway. But he doesn't always come. It's nice to see you, Jemmy—I—well, I could let you know when you could come, if you want to see me."

"Something's the matter, what is it?"

She only shook her head; it was mainly of curiosity and concern he accepted her invitation. He had a note handed him ten days later, at the Queen's Head. Her childish scrawl said tonight, named the house: a quiet, dignified neighborhood along Chambers Street north. She was waiting, took him up to a room that was pleasantly furnished.

"It's awfully nice to see you, Jemmy. You were always so nice to me."

"That sounds as if the officer is not."

"Oh, well," she said, "we're not any younger, are we? You've got to live. I can't pick and choose as I used to, Jemmy." He saw now in the light, with a little sadness, that she looked older, harder. "I don't like him much for all he's handsome—but that's none of your concern. He won't be coming tonight."

He lay and thought with remote sadness how he had enjoyed Gay once. It was a little pleasure now, as a glass of wine might be, no more: soon done and forgotten. Margaret's blame. He was sick for Margaret and so shut off from any feeling for any other woman.

"Jemmy, what's the matter?"

Dear Gay—silly Gay. She had tried, but— He said, "You told me we're not any younger. It's a long time, Gay."

She murmured assent. After a while she sat up. "I expect you'd best not stay. He might come."

"Good God," he said mildly, "I thought you were certain. A fine thing if he should discover me here."

She giggled. "I don't really think so. He was drunk last night, I suppose he's still sleeping it off, but you never know."

"I won't take the chance." He was a little relieved at the excuse to leave her. Poor Gay.

On the evening after he had taken the twenty-five guineas from Barr, Mistress Caulfield gave a Military Euchre dinner. He had a card for it; the men he had met and been accepted by in the taverns had introduced him to more private social circles. There was a whirl of entertainment in the city now; hostesses vied with one another in capturing the most sought-after officers, in the number of guests, the novel amusements offered. Even in wartime New York the ladies outnumbered the men, and a well-bred gentleman was always sure of invitations, if only from hostesses who needed him to make an even number. He had intended to get away from the city early tomorrow, but another day was no matter and a Military Euchre evening not to be missed; it might mean another twenty pounds if he was lucky in partners.

Mrs. Caulfield had outdone herself in the size of the party; he thought there must be sixty guests. The dining salon was uncomfortably crowded. In such a mob they were not all made known to one another; when, after an interminable dinner (nine courses, nearly every dish an imported luxury of some kind—he stopped noting after the roasted capons and smoked eels) they were set down to play, the other three at his table were all strangers to him.

Military Euchre was a new device on an old game. Each table bore a standard of four miniature flags; after a game was played, those seated east and west rose and progressed to the next table, the winners bearing off a flag for each game won. When the players had made a circuit of the room and returned to their original tables, those with the largest number of flags were counted the grand winners. Strictly speaking, it was not expected that the players would make side wagers, but military men being what they were, some respectable sums changed hands at any such party.

To his disappointment he was placed north at his table, which meant he would be remaining here all evening with the man opposite him, an Army major. There was no partner-playing at euchre; it was each man for himself. The butler laid a new pack on the table; Bethune broke the seal and commenced to shuffle through rapidly, tossing out the low cards unused in this game. The major reached for the pack when he put it down, and re-examined it as if doubting its integrity. That irritated Bethune a trifle. The major was a lean, dark man in his forties, with the marks of the drinker on him: the network of red veins showing in the eye-whites, the very slightly unsteady hands, the nervous twitch of eyelid.

He said tersely to Bethune, "Shall we say a guinea the game?"

"Quite agreeable." Lower stakes than he had hoped. They started off easily enough; the major cut an ace which gave the deal to Bethune; the hand falling to him was good, and he took the game. As the ladies left to begin their circuit, the major produced four crowns and a shilling, and stacked them neatly on the cards before Bethune, without speaking a word. Bethune found he had taken active, instant dislike to the man; it increased as the evening went on. The major spoke only as it was needful to play; he attempted no pleasantries even when there were ladies at the table. And he was the devil of a cool player. Bethune lost two games to him, won three; lost a third; and he felt irritation rising at the terse, low-pitched phrases from across the table, never alleviated by a curse, a jest, or a comment on the weather. "Play, sir. . . . I cannot make trumps . . . the Left Bower, sir . . . a triplet. . . . I will declare a sequence. . . . My trick."

He came even on the eighth game; if it went on this way the evening was wasted, he would make no profit at all. He played grimly; he never enjoyed cards, one reason being that he was no gambler; of himself, he would not risk a shilling on the fastest horse, the best hand in existence.

He took the next two games and lost the third. He had made two guineas thus far. He concentrated savagely on the twelfth game they played, made more difficult by one of the newcomers, a chattering lady who scarcely knew king from ace. The major made trumps. The object of euchre being to prevent the trumps-maker from winning three tricks, Bethune dogged him at every turn. The major got a sequence, and then he betrayed himself. Like most military men, as a rule he would not play euchre; it was a lady's game; men preferred piquet or ecarte. For one moment he forgot they played euchre—he laid out a sequence: knave, queen, king, ace.

"Ooh!" exclaimed the chatterer. "However did you get all those at once, Major? Oh, gracious, I'll never be able—"

"Just one moment," said Bethune. "The sequence is not in order, sir. It's a triplet, not a sequence. The suit of diamonds is trumps."

The major had seen his error at once, but had been minded to leave it if it went unchallenged. In euchre the knave ranked above the ace in trumps-suit; the ace did not belong in that sequence at all. The major took it back; he shot Bethune a dark look across the cards. The lady chattered, finally produced a seven-eight-nine triplet. Bethune laid down a sequence, the best save one to be had at euchre: knave of the trump-color—the Left Bower—the jester card, queen and king of hearts. It gave him the game.

The others moved on. The major took out four half-crowns, a ten-shilling note, and a new silver shilling. His eyes smoldered on Bethune. He took the next two games; lost the next; and won the last. Their original table mates insisted on comparing flags; there was much confusion over the count, and a tie of four winners. The major rose and bowed.

"It was my pleasure, sir."

"And mine." He resisted an impulse to say it between clenched teeth. He had neither won nor lost a penny: the evening was wasted; and he had seldom met a man who irritated him more. "If you'd excuse the discourtesy—after we've spent the evening together—may I know who I've been playing? My name is Bethune."

The major bowed again. He'd had eight glasses of Madeira through the evening; it had not apparently reached him at all; he would be more used to brandy. "Certainly, sir. Gerard is the name—Oliver Gerard, First Royal Artillery." Perhaps it was the light of low-burning candles in the floor bracket behind him that made his eyes seem to hold a wolfish mockery.

CHAPTER 33

BETHUNE LEFT the city the next morning; he had his own horse now. There was a time he had listed his desires, envying young Oliver Gerard: a horse, elegant clothes. He had both, and both were means to an end.

Oliver Gerard. Likely he had forgotten Bethune's name, if he'd ever known it. All the way he was debating whether to tell Margaret her husband was in New York; and asking himself angrily, What difference is it?

He rode up-river as if he were going out to a suburban home in Harlem; a couple of miles out lived an incurious Dutch farmer with a raft, who ferried him across to Jersey, five shillings the trip. He was riding into Newark by four o'clock; when he came into the narrow street and saw the house he felt his heart lift as if he came home—he who had never had a home. A modest house, but sufficient for their needs, and inexpensive, though they had no need now to be so careful for that. They had removed here just before he returned to New York; it was not only a larger town but more convenient for his secret trips from the city. He dismounted at the door and Haagen came to take the horse, grinning widely.

"Goot to see you, Mr. Bethune—it's near t'ree weeks, we was wondering was you fighting a duel like dey tell gentlemen do in de city now!"

"Is everything right here?" She was gone, she had left. . . . She had come here with them only because in a larger town she might find better-paid, more congenial work. And at first she had intended to rent a room in some other house. She was not, she repeated to his argument, properly of their household at all, and now they did not need her help in any way. He had actually felt grateful for the war then, which had caused something of a housing shortage.

For while many housewives were eager enough to hire a room for a few extra shillings a month, with their husbands in the army and money short as it was, refugees were crowding most towns now. Some had fled from places destroyed in the fighting, or now held by one of the armies—there were Loyalist refugees from American-held towns, as well as rebels, among the displaced. Margaret had searched, but the few available rooms, she had reluctantly admitted, would not offer the comfort she had here with their little household. And she had, Bethune thought, grown fond of Dorcas.

Margaret had found work almost at once, and a more suitable occupation than she had had before; she was mistress at a dame-school for young children. The school was near the outskirts of town, and she had argued that she should live closer. But in the end, however reluctant, she had stayed with them. Now—perhaps she had found another place, perhaps she had left. Every time he came back he knew that fear, that they would tell him she was gone.

"Is everything all right?" he repeated anxiously.

"Oh, yes, sir, fine." Bethune looked up and she was there in the doorway; he wanted to run, hold her close, tell her—he could not tell her, not begin to. Margaret in a blue gown, smiling at him.

She said, "You're looking well, James." She said it easily, naturally, now.

"And you." He was glad of the saddle bag to keep his hands occupied. He came into the little parlor and clasped MacDonald's hand. "Largesse, sir. Yes, yes, I have your segars! And a pint of English ink. And even a bottle of brandy. And"—he reached into his pocket—"count it, sixty guineas. I kept five out, I need some new shirtings. Margaret, will you accept a gift?"

"That depends what it is, sir."

He brought out the length of silk. "The woman said 'twas enough for a gown." He thought she would refuse it; he did not say he had got it because it was the color of her eyes.

She fingered it almost tenderly. "Lovely. I should not—it's good of you, if you'd let me pay—"

"Nonsense, a fat city merchant paid for it, not I." He turned to Dorcas, to cut the subject off. "And will you accept somewhat? If Mr. MacDonald won't object." He had a length of silk for her too; she stammered shy thanks. "Now we begin to come on better times, we must look the part, don't you agree?"

Margaret said he would want to talk with MacDonald, and took Dorcas away with her. He doffed his coat, sat down, declined brandy—"I won't rob you, sir"—and lit his pipe; he'd come to prefer it to segars. "How did this edition go?"

"Quite well. Things are looking up indeed. We'll need more paper by June, I've ordered another two hundred reams. You'll find the accounts—"

"I'll leave the accounts to you," said Bethune. "Don't tell me we earn a profit."

"The last two months, a respectable one. Have you any news? How is it in New York? There's been great furor—"

"There too, yes." He took Margaret from his mind to give MacDonald news of their town. "They're like silly chattering children—society-mad women, the men not far behind. And the military—half of them old grannies of regular line-officers, you know the sort, still thinking in terms of the Hundred Years' War, and the other half beardless youngsters with brand-new commissions. They spend their time at whist parties, in the taverns—and the bawdy houses. There's quite a fad among the young officers for acting at the theater; I understand they're no end of nuisance to the regular company. They don't seem to recall there's a war going on. Howe is worse than an old granny—a coward and worse than that. Even some of his officers have little stomach for his liaison with the Loring woman—though her husband is twice as bad. No finesse about it, he exchanged her for his appointment as controller of prisons, and they say he makes a good thing of it too, withholding rations and selling them elsewhere, and damn the poor devils in the cells. You know all that, I meant to say it's from none of that ilk you hear any worried talk. They went into a flurry when Burgoyne surrendered, but forgot it. It's the merchants—and some other civilians—are uneasy about France—"

Furor? You could say that. There had been rumors for a year that France might enter the war on the American side. A number of French officers had volunteered for the rebel Army, and the Congress had sent envoys to the French court. Their best hope was in that shrewd old man Franklin, who had, probably by very contrast to the court company, come to be quite the darling of Paris—to the dismay of Parliament, which was confident of defeating the rebels alone but had no desire to have the war widened. Lord North held out promises of sweeping concessions for truce and armistice, but they were ignored. It seemed likely that Franklin yet would persuade the French into the fight. And in New York James Rivington reported in the *Gazetteer* that Franklin had been victim of an assassin and lay on his deathbed, that Washington had taken a mortal wound at Brandywine, that—there was no end to his lies.

"All the same, I believe the military is worried. For one thing, if France enters the war she'll send a fleet—there are rumors of that already. New York lives on shipping. A blockade—"

"Let us hope it comes to pass."

"Not for a bit," said Bethune. "We don't want all my easy marks to grow so poor they tighten their purses."

MacDonald laughed. "Your talent has come in mighty convenient. Cards I never understood or enjoyed."

"Oh, neither do I," said Bethune.

"But we're back on our feet now, inside the year we'll be more than solvent if it continues like this. Our subscription list is up near five hundred again, and the sales aside are rising. We printed a thousand copies last week and will from now on."

"Good," he replied absently, "excellent."

He approached Margaret at the well behind the house that evening for privacy.

"Margaret"—abruptly—"I've something to tell you. Your husband is in New York."

She stood very still for a moment. "Oliver. You met him? He did not—"

"He never knew me, and it was a long time ago. I didn't know how you'd feel for it."

"I don't know that I feel a great deal. I never hated him, you know. I just could not withstand him any longer."

There was so much he could not ask her about that; his imagination ran riot on it. He thought that man could be brutal with a woman and enjoy it.

She moved suddenly and said in a harsher tone than he had ever heard from her, "Oh, not that way. He never wanted me for that—it was the money. Only when none other was available. If you want to know, not a dozen times in six years." The moment she had spoken she was sorry, he felt that; she was embarrassed. "I don't mean to— Forgive me. Plain talk. Hardly ladylike." Mocking at herself, angry.

He tried to keep the incredulity from his voice; he said carefully, "He'll be stationed at Fort George, on the Battery, with the artillery. He's likely overdrinking, he looks it."

And she whispered remotely, "Poor Oliver. I think I can feel a little sorry for him now. He must have loved Honor—a queer, savage sort of love. It's strange, isn't it, James? Neither of us seems to have had great luck in marriage."

It took him unaware, her dispassionate tone. He said, "You know why—you know why, Margaret! We belong together, no one else for either of us—" He reached for her blindly, knowing it would be only an instant, knowing this would destroy all they had so carefully built.

She wrenched away. "Oh, my God, James, no—no! How could you? How could you?"

But of course he had to try. His voice sounded dull, expressionless. "I love you. Margaret, I—"

"To think I could—oh, damn you for a fool, James!"

"Fool—not liar. Margaret, please listen, let me tell you—" But he could not say it in words.

"You and your damned conscience," she said. She whirled and ran from him, stumbling once in the dark. The kitchen door banged.

Christ, yes, where was any reason in life? A man should be able to look back from the vantage of thirty-one years and see some pattern in it. Instead it was for him the hit-and-miss design on a crazy-quilt. He knew when it began to go wrong—fifteen years back when he had run away. A knot in the chain binding all men together, so he was set apart from any warm contact.

Margaret had said something about Susan once: he had told her more of Susan now. "But you know why she is like that, James. She cannot or will not love, and so she will never be loved herself. I don't mean only the one kind of love. Any kind. One must give it to have it."

But in himself, it was not that lack. He had given it, he gave it; there was a thing in him outward-going toward people. He had a superstitious conviction about it, the only conviction he owned about any pattern in life. You might not have too much: you could have only the one thing of all you wanted, by some esoteric law. He might have a *Courier* built up to a prosperous, popular paper again: or the desperately wanted sense of belonging, with friends and a place of his own: or—but not both, not all. And he could never have Margaret any way, any time.

She had said she could be sorry for Oliver. He could not say the same of Susan. He had gone to the house when he first returned, to find it locked, shut up, the curtains drawn; but a manservant let him in, intimated he would take a message to the mistress.

"But I want to see her. Damnation," said Bethune, "I am her husband, I've just returned. I'll go up and find her myself."

"Oh, please, sir, 'twould be worth my place if I was to let you—" The man darted before him. She came down presently to the parlor, which was darkened with pulled drapes; he could not see her clearly.

Her voice was the querulous, fretful one of a much older woman. "James? I'd not expected to see you here again! Why have you come back?"

"That is my business, isn't it? Why on earth do you keep the house so dark? I can scarce see you."

"I've a good reason! Would you care to see?" She came up to him, reached to pull the curtain. "A pretty sight, is it not?" she asked bitterly.

He looked at her in silence. She had taken the smallpox after all; it left her marked. Not bad; he had seen many worse; and smallpox was no respecter of persons, there were society ladies who kept a mark or two from it as well as beggars. "I'm sorry," he said, "but you needn't make so much of it, Susan."

"When I am disfigured for life? When none can look at me without shuddering?" She pulled the curtain again at once. "What do you want?" she asked him, disembodied again in the gloom. "Why have you come back?"

She'd become a recluse again, he found, just as she had that long time ago over the Van Steen affair. Her first instinct when life went against her—pull into herself, go to brooding alone. And he understood Susan better now. It was an excuse. She loved the social life, but it had increased her envy and bitterness and self-pity, for all she found in it was other women with prettier clothes, lovelier women men flattered and flirted with, more lavish dinners than she might give, rooms more grandly furnished than hers. She had never been a great success in society, and when she chose to fancy this a reason for hiding herself away, she need not compete with others.

New York had stirred with uneasiness that late spring, and the arrogant Loyalist society, the military, talked worriedly of France as the merchants had for six months. When the official news was out that France had declared war, the city lay under a pall of fear. There was a great fleet on the way to attack—an army of French coming—and people began to depart, not in droves as they had before from a patriot city, but almost ashamedly, creeping away. The most took ship for England, acknowledging discouragement for the war's outcome now.

Rivington pooh-poohed the danger of the French, but that was one time Loyalists did not wholly believe what they read in the *Gazetteer*. Bumbling old Robertson was relieved of command of the city and Major General Valentine Jones took over from him; if New York was to be in straits, it needed a commander of some force. What had they done to New York! What would they do under this new threat? The military had commandeered all the finest houses, abandoned when patriots fled at their conquest. They had quartered troops in Roger Morris's mansion that had been Washington's headquarters; for their own staff headquarters they had taken James Beekman's mansion at First Avenue. Fine old staircases chopped up for firewood, paintings burned and libraries; homes and churches used as hospitals— and there was need of them. And along with the British Army had come its perennial camp followers to be quartered, upwards of two thousand of them, harlots and regular soldiers' wives and families. They had taken over private homes willy-nilly. Under military law the soldiers and their officers could and did behave as they pleased without fear of reprisal. No worse than the Sons of Liberty when Washington occupied? They had plundered De Lancey's mansion, those of other Tories, destroyed Loyalist possessions right and left. But then, rabble was rabble, be it British or American.

Some of the uneasiness communicated itself to Bethune. If a French fleet should blockade the harbor, it might not be so simple to get in and out of New York, and not so much money there to be so easily taken. Perhaps his little venture was drawing to a close.

CHAPTER 34

IT ALL CAME ON in a rush, everything happening at once. And perhaps France had something to do with that, too, tightening tempers in the city with fear of the fleet. The news had come to New York in May; Howe, starting back across New Jersey after evacuating Philadelphia, ran into the Americans at Monmouth and suffered a sound defeat which did nothing to raise Loyalist spirits. New York expected to sight the French fleet any day now, and anxiety increased throughout June and early July. Howe had had his fill of the colonies and of this war, and his unpopularity was no secret to him. He asked relief from command, and as soon as Clinton was appointed in his place, sailed for England gladly.

Bethune was thinking seriously of quitting the city. He did not want to be caught here if there was a siege, and there would be no easy marks with easy money in that event; he had tided them over with this, the *Courier* was solvent and earning a profit again, if a modest one. And there was Margaret. He had been to Newark once since that time. He had feared she would be gone, and for good. But it was Jacquetta who was gone.

"She heard the American Army was nearby," said Margaret, exasperated and resigned. "She simply said, 'Soldiers are always good spenders and more excitement,' and off she went. I could not have stopped her."

"Good riddance. But what to tell Darcy—" Post in wartime was uncertain; he had left the direction with Mistress Clark in Tenafly, where Darcy would send a letter—if he had received Bethune's letter telling of their removal there; but there had been no word from him. A letter lost, or never sent?

She was still there—but she took care, the few hours he stayed, never to be alone with him; she did not again say his name. She was remotely polite when she spoke to him, and did that as little as possible. And that was more than he had expected. He had known how impossible it was that she listen or believe, or feel anything for him.

He betrayed himself; he could not help it. Since he had been in New York this time he had not met either of the editors publishing here. The week he intended to leave for good he ran into Hugh Gaine in the York Arms—ran into him literally, in the doorway. He apologized before he saw who it was.

"Well, Mr. Bethune, this is a surprise! What are you doing in New York?"

He told Gaine his little tale, but Gaine would not believe it and he could not keep the distaste from his own tone. Gaine, who knew his bond with MacDonald. Gaine, the traitor, who raised his brows and smiled and shook his head. "Don't pitch me a tale, Mr. Bethune. You've some reason for being here— you don't change sides so easy. But I'll not pry. Let me give you a drink."

"You'll excuse me, no."

"Hoity-toity. I'm not good enough to drink with?"

He said, "No, Mr. Gaine—and I'm not generally particular."

He brushed by and went on, knowing he should not have said that.

That was on Thursday evening; it was the next morning, as he dressed, that he heard someone enter the house, and froze, thinking for one moment that Gaine had followed him here, was curious enough to seek him alone for more questions. No one knew he was sleeping here; no one except—

Yes, it was Gay. And he could not remember how or why he had happened to tell her where he stayed.

"Jemmy?" Her steps light and sharp on the bare floors, her voice uncertain.

He came out to the passage tying his neckcloth. "Well, Gay. Nice of you to call, but an unconventional hour. What may I do for you?"

"You're always talking silly," she said a little forlornly. "Lord, this is a skeleton of a place, Jemmy! I nearly didn't come in. Funny place for you to stay." She shivered.

"I am not here a great deal." He thought she was looking strained and ill, and her clothes were shabbier than any he had ever seen her wear. "What may I do for you?" he repeated.

She took a little breath. "I don't know as you can do anything, Jemmy. But—you know Major Gerard, don't you? You asked so many questions, when I—"

Bethune's interest sharpened. "Gerard," he said. It had been no surprise to him that Gerard turned out to be Gay's present protector. He'd almost expected it, rounding out a tangle so neatly. He had seen Gerard meet her at the theater one night, his proprietary air unmistakable, and—remembering how Gay had said, I don't like him much—had gone to the trouble of making another assignation with her, to ask questions. "You never used to put money first," he had said. "If you don't care for him—"

"D'you know him, Jemmy?"

"Slightly. No. It's no matter, I only wondered." Know him? Well, it is a little bond between us, Gay: his wife.

"Oh, well," she'd said. "We're paid higher now, but everything's so dear—and a girl like me has to think of a time she can't earn any more, even at acting. You know. But he's not a spender, except when he's drunk. He's all right really, it's just that sometimes he—he seems to like hurting. I don't suppose I'll stay with him long."

None of his affair, except that he had mild affection for Gay. He had not seen her since. And now here she was, seeking him.

"Gerard?" he said again.

"Jemmy, I—I don't know what to do about it, I thought maybe you'd tell me. They were both drunk—crazy-like, you know—there wasn't any reason for them to fight."

"Who?"

"Oliver and this other officer. I never did hear his name proper, Captain Somebody. It happened all at once—last night it was, in my place. He came with Oliver. A big red-faced man, I didn't like him."

"You're babbling," he said patiently. "Tell it plain. There was a fight?"

"Oh, yes. An awful one, Jemmy—before I knew what was happening. Not just hitting each other. They got their swords out like in a duel. It was awful—and then the other man ran away. Because it *hadn't* been a duel after all, there wasn't anyone else there, and so it wasn't—what do you call it—a fair fight. And he'd run Oliver right through, I think."

He was startled into an expletive. "You don't mean—"

"Jemmy, I'm frightened!" She clutched at him. "Look, I didn't think he was bad at first, he was swearing awful, and there wasn't much blood. He *said* it wasn't bad, he'd be all right this morning—and he'd get back on this captain. I helped him get to bed, and he dropped right off, after I put a little bandage on. But now—I don't know—he isn't breathing right, and I can't rouse him. He's hurt bad, Jemmy, maybe it went into his lung, or something, do you think?"

"But, good God, why didn't you fetch a surgeon at once?"

"I told you, it didn't seem bad! Only a little cut in his side, high up, and not much blood—"

Yes, he thought absently: those thin rapiers some officers affected. A blade like that could slide in and out, lung-deep perhaps, and not bring much blood or rouse much alarm even in the victim. *Not so deep as a well, nor so wide as a church-door—*

"Jemmy, if—if he dies or—anything—he's there in my room. They'll say I did it! That captain'd never own up—Jemmy, if you'd come and see him—"

"Nonsense. Why should you be supposed to have done it? See here, Gay, I can't do anything to help you. What you must do at once is to go to Fort George where he's stationed, tell the whole story honestly. They'll send a surgeon to see him, and he'll be looked after. . . . Of course they'll believe you! Doubtless someone will be able to name the other officer—"

"I don't even know what the fight was about," she said irrelevantly. "I was cutting the cake. I'd be scared to do that, Jemmy. For all they know, I stabbed him."

"Don't be foolish." He said it all over again, repeating that he could not possibly be of help. He started her on her way with a pat on the shoulder. "Nothing to be afraid of, only hurry—the sooner a surgeon gets to him the better." Such concern for Gerard, who had hurt Margaret!

"I don't want to," she said miserably. "But, well, thanks, Jemmy. Maybe you're right."

"Of course I'm right, you should have gone at once! At times I think you've no sense at all, Gay!" The sooner her story was in the military records, the more readily she would be believed. He saw her off down the street, and, frowning a little, went up to finish dressing.

Hugh Gaine, for all his toad-eating of the British, looked down on Rivington and would not be friendly with him, so he would not have mentioned Bethune to the other editor. It was only coincidence that Rivington saw Bethune that evening at the Queen's Head.

He had just ended a game with a young officer, winning a couple of pounds. A man dropped into the vacated chair opposite, and he looked up from the pack, expecting to see an acquaintance. "Good evening, Mr. Bethune," said Rivington.

"And by heaven it *is* Mr. Bethune—I did not trust my eyes across the room. A surprise to see you in New York."

"Is it?" He gave the other man a half-smile. "Not the only man who changes his politics, am I?"

"Oh, have you? That, somehow, I doubt. How does Mac-Donald?"

He shrugged. "How would I know? I have left the *Courier*. I should think it was no longer in publication."

"You're wrong, Mr. Bethune." Rivington looked much the same as always. Years had changed him little: a lean, nondescript man with a narrow mouth and the eyes of a fanatic, and as always foppishly clad. "I have seen copies in the last month. The *Courier* is in publication from Newark."

"Is it?"

"As I think you very well know," said Rivington gently. "I recall how obstinately you once refused to leave MacDonald. I hardly think a war succeeds where I failed. Likely you slip across the river to pick up city news, eh?"

"That was a long time back. Men acquire a little sense— sometimes." He let Rivington see his contempt.

"I also recall something else, that there was a warrant issued against you just after the British took New York. I hazard it's still in effect, if forgotten."

Bethune went cold for an instant. Rivington was a man who nursed a grievance, small or large. He had not forgotten being bested by a boy, all those years ago, just as he had not forgotten what that cards game was about. It was in the cards now that Rivington would go straight to the military court and remind them of that warrant; if it had been lost in the files or marked off somehow, Rivington would trump up some charge against him. Rivington was well in with the British, their mouthpiece and confidant, and military justice in New York these days was a law to itself.

Bethune got up from the table. "You'll excuse me, sir, I have an appointment."

"But not so fast," said Rivington. "Yes, I could go to the court and ask them to locate that warrant. It would be much simpler to beckon the nearest officer—there is Major Canning over there by the hearth. One word from me that you may be a wanted man and you're caught, Mr. Bethune."

"But I doubt if I am, you know. I can swear I've officially turned Loyalist. What's to prove I ever thought different?"

"My word," said Rivington rather viciously. "The *Courier* calls me a liar, but my word is good enough for the British here. I can have you clapped in gaol in ten minutes, and pleased I'd be to do it. But I've a drop of sporting blood—have you?"

Bethune sat down again. "I am listening." He was caught fair —or unfair, Rivington still holding a grudge for him.

"I like to pay my debts, Mr. Bethune, even thirteen years after contracting them. I make a proposal. I'll play you a hand of ecarte, my word against your freedom. If I win, I'll call Canning on the instant and have you arrested. If you win, you walk out of here free."

"And how far down Broadway?" asked Bethune, smiling. "It's a toss of the coin—heads you win, tails I lose." He took up the cards. "I've no choice." The stakes would be five minutes' head start. But that would mean something; once he was out in the dark streets, let Rivington alert the officers, the officers alert the patrols. He would have time even to collect his clothes from Cherry Street, make his way out of the city by night. If Rivington won the game—

He shuffled the pack, gave it to Rivington, who shuffled it and laid it down in the center of the table. He cut the eight of diamonds, Rivington the king of spades. "My deal, Mr. Bethune." And, when the hand was dealt: "I play. . . . The trump suit is spades."

He had not a good hand. He concentrated grimly on the play; this was a little different from his first game with Rivington. He had the luck in the first draw to turn a king; he said quickly, "I mark the king." One point; but he failed to take a trick until Rivington had two. He must make three or give Rivington two points; the game was five. He got a sequence, two triplets; he would like to see the ace of hearts turn up, but it did not—until Rivington played it in sequence.

"Bad luck, Mr. Bethune. . . . I propose."

"I do not accept." Rivington had three tricks, one point. He was aiming for the vole, five tricks out of five, for another two. "I play." The best Bethune had was another triplet. Rivington hung back in the next few plays, and Bethune began to think the luck turned—Rivington wore a noncommittal look, but there was a frown in his eyes over his cards. Bethune drew, glancing swiftly over the cards down, reviewing what was already played; he was lucky, his card made up a sequence and he played it hastily.

"Point to me," said Rivington.

It had been the king of clubs—Bethune had seen only that it fitted his hand, and had not marked it to claim the point for turning a king. Fool! He was losing his shrewdness, growing nervous over this; he must take his time. Rivington had three points, he but one. But Rivington obviously did not like his hand; he was hesitant now.

"Cards! I propose."

"I do not accept." Once round again. "I propose."

"I will accept." And Rivington laid down two sequences to make his five tricks: the vole, the luckiest hand dealt through the game. Bethune stared at the cards; they blurred a little in his vision, red and black spots dancing. "My game," said Rivington. "You know ecarte, Mr. Bethune, but it is your misfortune you never learned a French-Canadian cards game called *poque*. It consists of misrepresenting one's hand in order to encourage reckless play from an opponent. Bad luck, Mr. Bethune."

He did not waste time exchanging elegant formalities. He stood and started for the door, not too hurriedly to call attention; there was no attendant in the passage and he did not wait to collect his hat. He heard some commotion behind, and ran down Broadway like fox after hare—only he was the hare; he doubled back through a few alleys before he was sure any pursuit was lost. He would make for Cherry Street at once, collect his clothes, get the horse he kept in a stable not far off, and be out of the city in an hour. Rivington did not know it was an empty victory, that he had intended to leave for good anyway. But damn Rivington all the same.

He knew the city so well it was easy to choose the back ways, working toward Cherry Street. Despite the darkness and a circuitous route, it was scarcely twenty minutes later he reached the house. It would not take long to tumble his belongings together.

Then, in the entry with the door shut behind, he went cold. There was a light, flickering faint in the first of the downstairs rooms. Someone was here—someone had known where to come, perhaps? He took one step back in wary retreat.

"Jemmy?" said Gay.

"Oh, my God," said Bethune. She was in the doorway ahead, peering at him in the dim circle of light cast by a single candle. And after her visit this morning he had given some thought to Gay, but this business with Rivington had put that out of his head. He controlled his breathing with effort; he said, "I'm sorry, Gay, I cannot stop to talk now, I'm in some haste."

"Oh, Jemmy," she said limply. "I didn't know if it was you. I've been waiting here hours, hoping you'd—Jemmy, please help me, please—I don't know what to do, I'm so frightened—"

He shut his teeth on impatient anger. "What is it, Gay?"

The candle flame was trembling as if it caught fear from her hand. She came up close to him, and he saw her face pinched with fright, tear-stained, pale. She caught her breath with a little sob. "Hours, I've waited—didn't know anywhere else to come. Jemmy —he's dead. He's dead, there in my room—for all I could do. He—"

"Gerard," said Bethune softly, and that scene this morning recurred vividly to him. So Gerard was dead, of a careless sword-thrust in a careless drunken brawl, and likely over nothing that mattered ha'pence.

"I've got to get away, right away. They'll hang me." She was half-crying. He scarcely took that in.

"The surgeon was too late, then. What did—"

"Oh, God, Jemmy, I know what you said was sense, this morning, but I couldn't do it. I was afraid! I should've done that, but I was too afraid how they'd take it—a girl like me, and waiting all that time after, and all. I never did, I just—went back to see how he was, then. He was bad all day, a lot of fever—I did what I could for him, really, Jemmy—"

Gerard, appropriately, dying slowly, with only the frightened ministrations of a bought woman to ease his passing. "My God in heaven, Gay," began Bethune angrily, and then stopped himself. No use to rant at her for folly, any more than at a child. That was Gay. She was weeping in earnest now.

"It's easy to say what I should've done! You ought to know how they are—a pound to a penny they'd never listen to what I said at all! Everybody knew he was bedding with me—and only my word there'd ever been that other man there! You can't tell me I was silly to be afraid—"

Reluctantly his mind said yes to that. Even this morning, say eight hours after the event, they might have heard her story with suspicion; it would have depended on the officer who listened. Perhaps his well-meant advice had not been so good, based on trust of justice from authority: with this authority you could not be sure of that. Now, true enough, she would find few to believe her.

Gerard, stiffening and cold in the bought woman's bed. He wondered if Gerard had found out the answers to life—if there were any; if he was at peace, after all his strivings and woundings. And it came to him, apart from everything else, that it was he who would have to tell Margaret. If she had had any feeling for Gerard—

"Jemmy, don't you see? I've got to get away! You know how they are. There was that shoemaker and his wife they said plotted to betray the city and bring in the Americans—just poor folk, it wasn't so—they hanged them, didn't they? Murder's worse, and they'd say it was murder—he's right there in my bed—"

He wouldn't doubt a British military court would call it murder. But—

"Jemmy?" She lifted the candle, looking up at him. For the first time something in his expression seemed to take her attention from herself. "Jemmy—there's something the matter for you too, isn't there? You look—"

He said abruptly, "I'm leaving New York tonight—now, and for good. No, never mind why. Enough that I'm going, and you see I can be of no help to—"

"Take me with you, Jemmy! That's what I wanted to ask, if you'd help me get away! I've got all my things, I knew I couldn't stay there. Please, Jemmy, I don't care where you're going, anywhere out of New York—"

"But, Gay, you'd not want to—I can't," he began helplessly.

She clutched him tighter. "I mustn't stay, after this! Don't you see, Jemmy? Please let me come with you—"

He owed Gay something from years back. But just briefly, vaguely, it touched his mind with irritation: Why do they always come to me, why am I the inevitable receiver of the responsibility? And he could answer that himself: Because you always reach so eager to take it!

"Yes," he said. "Yes, all right, Gay, I'll take you."

He had accumulated only a modest wardrobe here, and managed to get all his possessions into two saddlebags. But Gay had three bandboxes and a couple of valises, all stuffed full—actresses! It was a nuisance. He left her waiting in the entry passage while he went to collect his horse, telling the stableman a hasty tale of an unexpected journey to allay any suspicion for his setting out so late.

Gay was no help with the baggage; she was beside herself with panic. But his proposal to leave the valises behind restored some of her self-possession. "I will not! I'd never get them back, and wherever I go I've got to have all my things!" There was no time to argue. Grimly he unhooked the curb rein from the bridle and used it to tie the valises to the saddle.

He took the unfrequented streets, northward, holding to a trot lest the noise of galloping rouse curiosity. The weight of the pistol in his pocket felt strange. MacDonald had made him carry it; he wondered if he would have to use it tonight, for the first time. Gay had delayed him; it was more than an hour since he had run from Rivington. They might suspect that he had a tried route for leaving the city, but they could not know anything to lead them to the farmer Groot and his raft.

But he underestimated Rivington—and Rivington's influence with the Army officers. Once out of the city he urged the horse to a gallop, and within thirty minutes was turning into Groot's farmyard. It occurred to him that rousing Groot at this hour, to betray urgency, would probably raise the ferry charge, but that could not be helped—and then he heard horses galloping behind.

In the half-second as he turned to look, he knew. Rivington, that canny man, had persuaded some subtlety into the heads of the British officers—no mean feat in itself. Knowing Bethune must have an escape route, they had hung back and followed as secretly as possible, to catch any accomplices in a trap as well as Bethune. He caught a glimpse of several horses, off the road now in the trees; the men had seen him turn into the yard, and were reining to a halt.

"Jemmy—what is it?"

"Nothing." They would wait until he had roused the farmer, until the raft was afloat, before coming to nab them all in the act. That was just as well, the cold part of his mind told him, since Gay was encumbering his right arm now and he could not even reach the pistol.

He reined in and dismounted unhurriedly, lifting her down, and gave her the rein. "Listen," he said evenly. "Go round the back and down to the river bank. Hurry, but don't run. For the love of God hold on to the horse."

"Jemmy—" She was trembling.

He sounded almost savage to himself. "Don't be such a little ninny—help me, Gay! Go now. There is a raft on the bank down there. Wait beside it and don't scream, whatever happens."

She moved off obediently, leading the horse. Bethune went up to the house door and knocked, not too softly. After a little he knocked again.

There were sounds of movement, and the cautious voice of the farmer. "Who is?"

"Bethune. Open up."

The bolt was drawn back, protesting. "You want to cross in

de dark," Groot was grumbling. "An extra five shilling for de trouble I have."

"More trouble than you expect. There are British soldiers after me—up the road there, watching us now. I apologize to bring them down on you, but I never saw them until a minute ago. Have you a pistol or musket?"

Groot grunted, whether in surprise or anger was impossible to say. A stout vague figure in his night rail, he surveyed Bethune in silence and then swore in Dutch. "Bad luck it was I ever take your money in de first place. Maybe t'ree pound altogedder I get, and now you lead de damned English at me, to put me in prison or shoot me also, and anyway I lose my farm." He growled and hunched his shoulders. "You are a damned fool."

"Very possibly," said Bethune, "but there it is. They cannot hear us, of course, but as soon as we make for the river they'll be coming at a gallop to arrest us all. I should say that I have a young lady with me, who is waiting by the raft."

Groot called mildly on heaven. "No ears you have, maybe, to hear dem chasing you? Maybe too busy you are hugging de young lady? And sure, we get off across de river, all fine for you, but what about my farm? What for would I want to stay in Jersey? Dis war, it is a big damned trouble to farmers. How many Englishmen are out dere?"

"I think three or four." And Rivington? No—he was sure of that; Rivington was not a man of action. He would set the hounds on the trail, and then wait comfortably to be told of the kill.

Groot said, "I will get my guns and tell my woman to stay quiet." Within a few minutes he reappeared, having wrapped a heavy coat round him over his night rail; he carried two ancient muskets, upright in both hands. "Two is better, de time it takes to charge de damned t'ings. I am not going to lose my farm. All of dem we must shoot, and make a job. Come." They walked round the house in silence. The barnyard sloped to the river bank; Bethune made out the horse, and Gay beside it. There was some light here, reflected from the water.

"Oh, Jemmy—"

"Now," grunted Groot, ignoring her. "You take de first two, I take de rest."

Bethune primed the pistol and cocked it. He thought he and Rivington had that in common, at least, that they were not men of action. He was annoyed because his hand shook. But he had to get away. How much was depending on him!—MacDonald, Gay, the *Courier* itself. "Gay," he said, "get down on the ground, right down flat. And don't scream!" Perhaps she was too frightened to make a sound; she crouched down at once, still clinging to the rein. He hoped to God the horse was not gun-shy.

The waiting British had seen them leave the front of the house. Now, from fifty yards up the road, they burst out of the trees at full gallop and swept down on the farmyard. There were four of them, Bethune thought, as well as he could count in the half-darkness; and they were not expecting trouble from two civilians and a woman. They all pulled up suddenly, nearly on top of the raft, and one shouted, "Stand, in the King's name! You are all under—" Bethune's shot took him in the stomach, much to Bethune's surprise, though it was very short range. The officer toppled from the saddle, clawing for his pistol, and fell.

Bethune fumbled to prime and reload; his hands shook, and he was slow. There were two precise cracks, one after the other, from Groot's muskets, and the two men just dismounting went down.

The fourth man fired at Bethune; he felt the shot go by, then cocked his pistol, raised it, and fired. Too quickly; he missed, and the man came off his horse recharging his gun. Groot fired again, but almost immediately a bullet spat at Bethune from another direction, as the man moved—so Groot had missed too. He heard Groot grunt in disgust at himself. Then another shot raked fire across Bethune's right arm, above the elbow, and involuntarily he dropped the pistol. Groot was no longer beside him.

He dropped to the ground, hunting frantically for the gun. He heard mysterious panting and struggling not far off, and retrieving the pistol, ran toward the place. Groot rose up beside him.

"So. Now we see are de rest dead too." On the ground the fourth man lay still; from the way Groot was rubbing his hands together Bethune suspected he had strangled the fellow. The first man lay beside his horse as he had fallen; pure luck, that shot had been, the first Bethune had fired in his life. Groot's first two had never moved from where they'd dropped.

"Shooting practice I get," said Groot complacently, "at de birds after my corn." Methodically he collected the horses, which had stood under fire as trained to do, and led them into his barn. Bethune waited quietly; he was shaken and slightly ashamed— not of missing his second shot, but for feeling still some exaltation at the success of his first one. It was no matter for pride to have killed a man.

Gay was dithering at him in fright, now that it was all over; soothing her brought back some of his self-possession. He felt blood running down his arm, but did not think the wound was more than a scrape; he could move the arm well enough.

Groot came out of the barn. "Maybe not such bad luck, Mr. Bethune. Good horses dey are, I can use dem." He prodded the nearest corpse with one foot, thoughtfully. "And de men, dey can go in de river. Downstream from me. Nobody will know, and I stay on my farm."

"I doubt if anyone knew the direction they took, that's so," agreed Bethune. "But one never knows, and if anyone comes asking questions—"

Groot shoved the raft to the water with one powerful push. "Me, I'm only an old stupid Dutchman, and I don't know de English good, if dey come asking. Dere's not'ing for anybody to see." He spat into the river. "I don't take sides in de damned war, but I don't let de damned English take my farm eider. All right, Mr. Bethune, bring de horse on."

"Oh—yes," said Bethune. He smiled to himself in the dark; he'd been thinking MacDonald should meet Groot. MacDonald would never say again that James Bethune was the most unexcitable man he knew.

CHAPTER 35

HE WAS TIRED when they came into Newark in the middle of the morning. Gay was asleep in the saddle before him, head drooping on his shoulder. She woke only partly as he lifted her to the ground. Haagen, coming out for the horse, stood open-mouthed.

"All right, Willem," he said, "only an actress, not a mer-woman." He supported her into the parlor, carrying the bags she'd loaded them with.

MacDonald laid down his quill and said mildly, "God's teeth, Mr. Bethune and his women. He picks them up like stray kittens."

"This one is full-grown." He deposited her in a chair; she sat up and yawned, like a kitten: an innocent little black kitten. MacDonald was intrigued. Dorcas came to the door. "Dorcas, you'll see she's fed, will you, and has aught she wants?" He said brusquely to Gay, "Go along."

"Yes, Jemmy." She went off obediently.

"Your arm should be seen to," said MacDonald. He nodded after Gay. "Not another addition to our somewhat bizarre household?"

"God forbid. I've burned my bridges in New York, we shall have to get on as we can without the extra money." He told the facts briefly.

"The little actress—I recall. An officer, you said. Any I would know?"

He shook his head. "Only a British officer." And remembered, and rose up in sudden alarm. "Is Margaret here?"

"I think in the kitchen."

It was Sunday; she would not be at her school. And Gay, artless, never keeping her mouth closed.

"What is it?" asked MacDonald.

"Nothing." He sat down again. "Women," he said. "Complications." It was too late now to do anything about that. He smiled, and began to tell MacDonald of their narrow escape, and about Groot.

He did not see Margaret until they sat down to dinner. She was serene as ever, only a trifle pale; her eyes slid past his, not stopping. She was polite, and to Gay, friendly. Gay chattered, MacDonald studied her dispassionately, the scientist examining a new insect. Dorcas stared at her plate. Haagen only stared.

"Do you hear from Darcy, Jemmy? Such a nice boy, I always liked Darcy. I hope nothing's happened to him. This awful war, everything changed for it. I don't know why they had to have a war. They turned everything upside-down in the theater, you wouldn't believe, those fool young officers. Playing *Othello* as farce—Nick was furious." Adapting herself to strangers, a strange situation, with the ease her profession—both her professions—had taught her. He answered her in monosyllables; no one else spoke except as needful.

He did not know what to do about Gay, or about Margaret. He spent a restless night. He would have to talk with Margaret— Gay would have let out Gerard's name, must have. He had to know what she felt. And what the devil was he to do with Gay? An actress, a courtesan, in a little place like Newark. And she would share Margaret's chamber. Call it a tangle! MacDonald looking at him so sardonically.

His arm, as he had thought, was not bad; Dorcas bandaged it for him. It had bled a good deal, and looked worse than it was, but should heal soon. Meanwhile, it was an uncomfortable nuisance.

He did not see Margaret in the morning; she had gone to her

work when he rose. Gay rose much later; she wandered in to him where he fidgeted about the parlor, MacDonald having gone out to the printer's. She looked charming, but exotic, in a gold-trimmed black house-gown he suspected Dorcas had ironed for her. "Morning, Jemmy. I've not had a chance to talk to you. Who are these funny people and why'd you bring us here?"

"You'd neither listen nor care if I told you," he said a little crossly. "What had you thought to do away from the city, Gay? We'd not be inhospitable, but—"

The little smile on her mouth died. "And I haven't asked any charity. I won't stay if you don't want me."

"I didn't mean— I'm sorry, Gay."

She came and touched his arm; he looked down to her pert, pretty face, where the lines began to be traced under cosmetics. She smiled at him. "All right, Jemmy. I know—I've got eyes. It's this woman here, isn't it? She's nice. I expect she's right for you. She was nice to me, and women like that usually aren't. It's her, isn't it? I saw you look at her."

He asked rather bitterly, "Is that all you needed to do? She doesn't find me so transparent."

"You don't want me about, making it awkward."

He was ashamed and sorry. "I don't mean to—"

"All right, Jemmy." A little pat on his arm. "You were always so nice to me. She'd be good for you—you're awful easy to manage. She wouldn't take advantage like a lot would, with a man like you. Tell her? Well, I guess I did talk a bit, I slept in her room. But you needn't worry, not for that. She's no silly young thing, she wouldn't think much of a man who never had a doxy. Don't worry for anything, Jemmy. I'll go."

And he looked at her, remembering, thinking of Darcy taking him to her all those years back, of the time they had known one another, the changes it brought. He said helplessly, "Oh, damnation, Gay, I don't know what to say to you. If I can help you—"

"Nothing to fret about. I'll look to myself, always have. I don't reckon I'll stay here—go on to Philadelphia, I suppose, I know people there."

"If you're sure—money—"

"I've plenty of money, thanks, Jemmy."

She changed her gown; he walked uptown with her, carrying her bags. They told him at the Unicorn, the post inn, that the stage would leave for Trenton in an hour's time. She said gaily she was in luck. "Don't wait about, Jemmy, I hate saying good-by to people anyway."

"Gay—" He could never say what he felt, when the feeling went beyond the surface.

She stood on tiptoe, there in the street before the tavern, and took his face in her hands. "Don't you bother, Jemmy—I know. We've had some good times together, haven't we? Tell you somewhat, I liked you better than all the rest, always. I hope that girl's good to you—you deserve it, but you're awful easy hurt and people never think it, you so quiet all the time. We'll just wish each other luck and let it go. My nice Jemmy—thank you, Jemmy—for everything." She kissed him quickly and turned away for the tavern, holding her skirts from the street puddles. She did not look back, and when she had gone inside he came away.

He never saw Gay again.

That late afternoon he walked across the town to the place where Margaret taught her classes. The dame-school occupied a tall old house, once a mansion, at the edge of the town. He did not know about her hours of work; Dorcas said she came back to the house around five of the afternoon. It was half after four when he took up his station across the road, but he waited nearly an hour before she came out, and then she was not alone.

He thought there had been some event at the school; a number of carriages waited in the drive, and when the house door opened, it emitted a dozen matrons and their offspring, all clad obviously in their best clothes. They stood about exchanging bows, leisurely detaching themselves to seek their carriages. When she came out it was in the company of a pouter-pigeon female and a little girl with an enormous pink bow in her hair. And she wore the gown made from the silk he had given her. He was absurdly pleased about that. She stood talking with the woman; she had her shawl and reticule, ready to leave, and he was afraid she would accept an offered ride, so he crossed the road and went up to them. Her smile grew fixed when she saw him, but she had to introduce him. The woman gushed.

"Perfectly charming, Mistress Thurstan, we are so fortunate to have you, and I'm sure the Misses Chester feel the same. I know my little Hermione adores you, don't you, dearest? And the costumes—so pretty and sweet." Her eyes were speculative on Bethune: was it possible quiet Mistress Thurstan had a beau? She went off at last, and the difficult time began of being alone with Margaret.

He did not know how to begin. "You like your school?"

"Oh, yes. Very much." They started slowly down the road toward the town; she was smoothing on her gloves. "I like children, and fortunately it doesn't seem to matter that I've forgot most of my own lessons. They're mostly girls, and only to ten years old, so it's nothing very studious. Music and drawing and polite manners. We gave a little play this afternoon for the mothers, and tea afterward, that's why I'm late. How is your arm?"

"Oh—quite all right. It was not serious. . . . It made a very charming gown."

"Oh—thank you."

They walked in silence; she looked straight ahead, her eyes remote. He said abruptly, "Well—you know why I have come. I had to talk to you. Gay is gone—she would not be a nuisance." Margaret had known, of course, that he had once had a liaison with Gay: he remembered the day they had met in the street, Gay letting it slip out so innocently. But, as Gay herself said, that might mean little to Margaret, who was no simpering innocent after all. He was embarrassed to have her know it, but what did it matter? Perhaps he could have more hope if she did mind about it, to show she felt something for him. No, it was the other thing he worried about—that Margaret had any feeling for Gerard's death. "I understand she told you everything," he said.

"Yes. I rather liked her. Yes, she told me."

"Margaret, I—"

"I don't know if I'm glad or sorry he is dead. It doesn't seem to matter greatly, and I don't know if that's strange or not. I was never close with him—I think I hardly knew him."

"I'm sorry," he said with difficulty. "Perhaps if I had gone to see him, that morning, something could have been done."

"That's silly. It was an accident, the kind he was bound to have, I suppose. You can't hold yourself responsible." She was suddenly a little angry. "I believe you'd accept responsibility for the original fall of man if someone accused you. It's ridiculous. I've been away so long, more than four years now. And the war— I don't feel to be the same person, I've grown past all that. I've a new life now, a life I like, and all my own. I've found something to do I like doing, and earn a living at it."

"You'll stay here."

"Yes, certainly. Very likely the rest of my life," she smiled.

He said absently, "After the war we shall move the *Courier* back to New York."

"And what concern is that to me?" Her voice was hard. "You may go or stay as you please, here or New York or—or Africa. We've nothing to do with each other."

"I have got to try to tell you. I don't know how. I never meant—I don't know how or why it happened, but Margaret, if you'd listen—" It sounded fumbling, he had not the right words or any words; it sounded wooden. There was no way to tell her how seeing her after absence was like coming home; how lovely she was in the blue gown that matched her eyes; how he ached for her.

"No, I won't listen," she said almost briskly, still not looking at him. "I know you, James. It was odd, meeting again. We never really knew each other as children. But I've got to know you these last years. Your conscience—enough of it for three men. And that dreadful sense of responsibility. Don't you think I know what you're trying to do? You want me to feel you're responsible for me, because you feel you are. And there's just one way I might be made to feel that. I shouldn't think you had the courage to pretend it, but that's what's in your mind."

"No. You don't—"

"But I do. How could I believe that? It is worse than ridiculous."

"I know that. But it's true."

"Never. You are trying to take responsibility you think you shirked fifteen years ago. Well, aside from the fact that there is no need, I'd never let you. How could I? I've some pride left." They were walking up to the house; she stopped and faced him, head up, and her smile was taut. "I think I've come to believe in destiny, James—that what happens to us is none of our choosing or causing. I've not had an easy life, but a great deal easier than many women, I know that now. I've got over any bitterness I ever felt. And whether it is destiny or my own doing, I've made a life for myself I'm content in, in spite of everything. And now you come hanging about mourning over a thing that happened half our lifetimes ago, deliberately plaguing us both with your martyr's guilt, and expect me to sit back and accept what you give. To become a kept woman because it is the only conventional way you might support me."

"I never—"

"But you would have, don't deny it. The oddest part is that I really cannot feel very angry with you. Your intentions are so good, if you do go about them the wrong way. No, I'm not angry, only exasperated. I like living in this house, James, I like Mr. MacDonald and Dorcas. But now you're to be here day in, day out, if you persist in plaguing me with this I shall find somewhere else to live. I am quite independent, you know, and I intend to remain so. I find it's a pleasant feeling."

"Perhaps that is more than I expected," he said, watching her pull off her gloves. "That you'd even consider living in the same house. Thank you, Margaret."

She retorted unexpectedly, "Don't sound so humble, for heaven's sake!"

"I'll try not to bother you again."

She gave him a sudden friendly smile. "That girl. She was yours once, wasn't she?"

"Yes. For a little while. You knew that, of course." He was beyond reticence with her.

"She really is extremely good-looking. Which is another reason, if I needed another. When your taste is so good, you'd surely not consider me. I have seen mirrors, you know." She tucked her gloves into her reticule. "Come along in," she said. "We are late, and Mr. MacDonald likes his dinner sharp at half after six."

After all he did not see her often, usually only at the evening meal. He settled in to the round of work again, after that New York interlude; he was rather surprised to find how relatively solvent the *Courier* was after the low water of last winter. It was not all due to him: it was a turn in the tide; his winnings could not provide subscribers. The stay-at-home patriots had apparently grown used to the notion that the war would be much longer than anyone had thought, and they wanted to read about it. The *Courier*'s regular circulation rose gradually to nearly eight hundred, and they also supplied shops in several places which were persuaded to buy in lots and take their chances of selling over the counter. But even increased profits posed Bethune some problems in wartime.

There were only two editors in the colonies who earned any respectable profit: Rivington and Gaine in New York, who, as the most powerful mouthpieces of the Loyalists, were readily supplied with materials shipped from England. The *Gazetteer,* printed sharply black and neat on heavy-quality English paper, the trim edges of the letters, the even margins proclaiming the new type used for it, the English ink! He broke the appropriate commandment whenever he saw a copy. Such fine work, all to print four pages of lies each week.

And distribution: the British Army had drawn its lines straight across the old Royal Mail route from north to south. Now patriot newspapers here, if they attempted to sell in the south at all, must send copies by way of Philadelphia or Trenton, or take their chances in shipping. And all the carriage fee must be paid, for who could tell in advance what it would amount to, with prices fluctuating and delays the normal thing? Profits, yes, but slim, the price of paper being what it was, and all too little to

be had. It was small comfort to reflect on the printers' strike in
New York, which forced even the stingy Rivington to pay unprecedented wages of seven shillings a day per man.

CHAPTER 36

THEY HAD NEWS out of New York, across the river there so
near. There was some smuggling across the lines, and now
humbler people were leaving the city when they could. And some
of the conditions Bethune had seen for himself, doubtless wors-
ened now for the French blockade.

The blunder of the supply ministry in London sent the fleet
which brought supplies to the Army in New York up the river
to Philadelphia long after that city was evacuated, and lucky for
New York that blunder was, for the fleet did not return there
until the French admiral, D'Estaing, had weighed anchor and
departed northward to support the Americans under Sullivan at
Newport. That supply got in to the army in New York, but sub-
sequently the French took heavy toll among the shipping headed
for New York Harbor. The city then was almost entirely dependent for food on the farms roundabout and in upper New
York; that was barely sufficient.

With the arrival of the French fleet, the war became a naval
one, a war between pirates in more truth. American and British
privateers preyed on each other all down the coast between Nova
Scotia and Georgia, and, as for any advantage to either side,
came out in stalemate. But now New York merchants grew rich
and fat on the proceeds; the war brought them prosperity and

few inconveniences. There was not enough food for all in the city; it was they, and the military, who could pay and took the lion's share.

How could Bethune help but feel bitter, thinking of Susan there in New York? Likely her investments were earning more than ever. She would not be contributing to charities either, but sitting tight on her money, if he knew her. For there was a little charity left in New York. Even the most rabid Tories were horrified at the open secret of conditions on the prison-ships *Whitby, Good Hope, Scorpion, Jersey,* anchored in the harbor; there was a detail nearly every morning to bury the new dead on shore, in graves so hasty and shallow they were often dug up by beasts the same night.

Even when it had been possible to bring money out of New York, he would not have asked Susan for a copper. All the money she must have now! Paper had gone to fourteen pounds the ream, when it was obtainable. However, even with a fortune at his disposal he could not have bought all they needed, all they wanted. New presses—there was not one, he thought, in America, or new type.

He had no head for figures, but he had to work with them these days. They needed to reckon close; the profit was barely enough to keep four people. The printers' strike spread to New Jersey that winter, and none would work for less than seven shillings a day. The *Courier* could not afford to pay for the use of three presses besides its own, in Newark's one print shop, and four printers as well. Bethune drew a contract for the use of one other press and the team to operate it, and an apprentice to work with him at their own press, MacDonald setting the type. Thus saving the wages of three men and two boys, he and Mac-Donald printed one page of the *Courier*'s two each week, taking two days for that.

Even the smallest materials. . . . Quills. Those they had had been sharpened so often they were worn to half the original length. New quills were not to be had except rarely. They could not waste new paper for manuscript, but there they were served by one of the difficulties publishers suffered: the locally made ink faded so rapidly that they could save other papers until the print was almost illegible, then use the pages for composing their own articles.

"It's a pity," MacDonald observed, "that the *Gazetteer* is supplied with such good ink. I'd take almighty pleasure in using it for manuscript—or a homelier purpose."

"My God, sir, don't remind me we ever used paper for that. Reams of it!"

After nearly five years of war, the colonies were feeling the pinch. Lucky he had never been a dandy. He could not pay a pound for a new shirt; Dorcas mended and remended both his and MacDonald's, and there would eventually come a time, he thought, when they would be forced to go without body linen entirely. Their outer clothes were as threadbare. The horse was a luxury become a necessity: as the winter died and the spring of 'seventy-nine came in he had to scour New Jersey for paper and ink, and he carried copies himself to Elizabeth, Plainfield, Passaic, Perth Amboy, even New Brunswick, to save the carriage fee.

"We shall both be growing beards, Mr. Bethune." MacDonald felt his jaw. Bethune had brought two razors with him when he left New York; they had been dulled and sharpened so often it was scarcely worth while to shave himself. Fortunately he had not a heavy beard or a dark one.

He came out to the kitchen one evening bearing their only shears. "You've had practice trimming Mr. MacDonald's hair, Dorcas, I'll ask you to cut mine. I've just realized I look like one of these lap dogs the city ladies fancy."

"Well, sir, I don't know that I'd—"

"I'll do it," said Margaret coolly, putting down her mending. "Here, give me the shears. You're quite right, you look disreputable," as he pulled off the queue ribbon. "Sit down here in the light, and sit still." He could not help moving at the touch of her hand on his neck. "Have you a comb?"

"Half of one." He produced it meekly.

"Mm. What shall we do with him, Dorcas? I think a Hessian

crop would be suitable. We could use what's cut to stuff a pillow." Her hand was cool and light. "Will you sit quiet? I'll be cutting your head off if you jerk so."

"No tricks," he said. "Leave me enough to club and tie, young woman." If she could be so casually intimate, so could he.

She clipped carefully. "A pity it is so straight, a woman would appreciate such thickness. The queue needs pressing. Have you another? I daresay one of us has a scrap you may use. There, it is the best I can do. You look a bit more respectable at least." He stood and she surveyed him critically. "Yes, it'll do." And under his eyes she suddenly flushed and turned away.

"Thank you."

"It's no matter." He could still feel her hand on his head; he wondered why she had flushed and thought she regretted her brief intimate nonsense. He wondered if one day a long way off it would cease being so painful to love Margaret.

There was plenty of news to speculate on, but the most was rumor. He stopped trying to reckon up all the battles; it was pull devil pull baker, even with the French now aiding Washington. But he tried to track down every detail of an engagement when Greene's command was involved, hoping for some news of Darcy. There was never any mention of a Captain Darcy Trevelyan—and why should there be, among so many?—never any certainty about the news they had. Every newspaper still published (always excepting the confident *Gazetteer*) was full of cautious phrases—it is alleged, a rumor is circulated, by all available report, it may be hazarded. If there could be some regular, official source, available to all editors! Of course that was an impossible dream. News of a skirmish would come by a peddler who had it from a farmer who had it from someone who claimed to have seen the action. Whose command? Well, the American uniform was green, or it might have been blue, would that be Wayne's cavalry?

He had got paper at Elizabeth for some months, but in the fall that mill shut down for lack of supplies. He knew of no other in New Jersey, except that near Camden.

"We can write to ask," he suggested doubtfully to MacDonald.

"God knows the price they're asking if there's any to be had there."

"By the time a letter gets there and is answered, we'll be out of print for want of paper. I think we'd do better if you go yourself. And get as much as possible."

They collected every copper they could spare; for a year they had done without all but the necessities, putting the majority of the profit into paper, the most expensive single item they required. It amounted to three-hundred-twenty-odd pounds; he carried it in a belt under his clothing for fear of attack on the road. These days travel was uncertain in more ways than one.

He left Newark in early September. The fall rains had been heavy, and the roads were bogged in mud; he could have got on better riding, but must take the cart to fetch back any paper he succeeded in buying. It was a miserable trip down to Camden, ten days of it. He had to go out of his way twice to avoid British troops; since the defeat at Germantown the British commanded the Delaware. When he came there he found the mill still in operation, but asking fifteen pounds the ream.

It could not be helped; it was the only paper to be had. He asked a contract, twenty reams the quarter-year. "I'll guarantee the carriage to Newark—"

"Man," said the manager with weary good humor, "nobody could guarantee carriage to Newark. Who knows when there'll come a battle line between? I can't accept any commitments. I've fifty reams on hand now I'll sell, but guarantee anything a month from now I cannot."

"I've money only for twenty-one or two. I'll take those."

The man studied him, shrugged. "Well, Mr. Bethune, I subscribe to the *Courier* myself, I can appreciate your difficulties. Look you, I'll make a bargain. You and your editor are no fly-by-nights, you've been in publication a long time and intend to remain in business, by what you say. I'll let you take the whole fifty reams for three hundred cash and a note of hand."

Bethune could have kissed him. "I'll give you that gladly, sir, and thanks. I'll see it's paid within twelve months. Is that satisfactory?"

"Entirely. You'll be needing more by then, or sooner, of course. I wonder now—well, it's worth a try. You might stop by Cookstown on your way. There's an old fellow there by the name of Christopher Sower—used to live in Germantown—not too steady upstairs from what I've heard. He was always fossicking around with printing presses, and he used to be one of our regular buyers. It's possible he's some paper on hand he'd sell private-like."

Bethune could not afford to forego any chance, however slim, of acquiring all the paper possible, with the outlook for six months from now so poor. God, this war dragged on and on. He went out of his way over roads deep in slush and mud, to seek out Christopher Sower, who was a little mad and who lived in Cookstown.

It was a pleasant neat house with a flourishing garden, and old Mr. Sower—who still called himself Mr. Sower, Junior—was not mad at all. He was the sanest man Bethune had met in years. He was much impressed at receiving an actual newspaperman; he brought out some real brandy and opened his mind and heart with it. "Oh, Mr. Bethune, 'tis a pity, a great pity, this war. Such a fine place I had in Germantown. The destruction! One army as bad as the other. Set printing and publishing back a quarter-century in the colonies, it has. A crime it is. I was almost ready to begin the actual building of it, but workmen are unobtainable now, and the few one could get quite untrustworthy. I still have the plans—"

"To build what, sir?"

Mr. Sower hitched his chair closer. "The press," he said, dropping his voice reverentially. "The press. I believe it can be made to work—it may need a few adjustments, but once I have a model to work from— A press, Mr. Bethune, a man may operate with one hand!"

"What? But how would it be possible?"

"A wheel, that is the only innovation, a wheel to pull it around. I am positive it can be made to work."

Bethune was fired by the idea; they talked of it until Mr. Sower's sister came to bid them to the table. "You printers and your presses! I vow, a body would think 'twas the only thing of importance in the world!"

"But it is, my dear, it is. Ruling the modern world, not too strong a word, ruling. Why, when we consider, Mr. Bethune, what wonders might be accomplished with such a press! Perhaps it would be possible to print five thousand copies of a newspaper in half a day! With reading matter in wider distribution, the number of readers must increase. It is not too far-fetched to anticipate the day your newspaper might be read by ten thousand persons!"

He would rather doubt that, but it was a grand dream. He was sorry to bring Mr. Sower down to practicalities.

"Paper, Mr. Bethune? Oh, ah, yes, I know it is in short supply. I have a few boxes about somewhere. What size were you want-ing?"

Bethune smiled. "That does sound prewar, sir. We're not particular these days." The *Courier* had always used half-sheets, ten by six inches, as did most papers; the *Journal* had once experimented with larger pages but found the cost cut down profit. Now publishers took any size they could find.

"Well, I dare say I can find a box or two for you. I do little printing now. A labor of love with me, you know. Since my experiment with casting type—oh, yes, like our eminent Dr. Franklin I made the attempt. Not too satisfactory—I have several sets I can show you to illustrate the difficulty. The dies must be cut from wood to begin with, and we have not the right alloy; English metals are needful—"

"You have *type?* Mr. Sower, I'd offer to sell my immortal soul for a set of new type."

"I fear 'tis scarcely new, Mr. Bethune. I've used all my type several years."

"The *Courier*'s type was new when the present King was crowned. I hardly dare ask what price—"

Mr. Sower raised a hand. "As God please, I manage well enough here, with my little savings and my garden, even with the war, sir. It is you and your fellow newsmen do a great service for your profession, these difficult perilous days. I have several sets of type I have made myself, Mr. Bethune—it will be my pleasure to make you a gift of one."

"But it's too much, I can't accept!"

Mr. Sower patted his shoulder. "Busy, you are. For a little payment, if you ride this way again, stop and talk with me about my press. I will yet build it."

So Bethune started back with more precious a load than he had ever expected—fifty-three reams of paper in four boxes, and a set of nearly new type. Faulty as it might be with too much lead, new type!—a thousand times better than the blurring old dies they had. He was impatient to show MacDonald, and also, because it was drawing to winter, he wanted to be home before any threatened snowfall. He pressed on as fast as possible and drew into New Brunswick the second night after leaving Cookstown; another two days should see him in Newark, but he had to circle a British camp, and only reached Westfield the fourth afternoon.

He stopped there for a meal at the tavern; he was tired, but the horse was reasonably fresh. It was only another four or five hours' drive with luck, and he knew the road. He decided to go on, and left the town a little after six o'clock. There was not much between in the way of villages, and once he had left Westfield he was committed to go on to Newark.

He had driven nearly half the distance when it began to rain. The storm came on with little warning; he would never have left Westfield if the sky promised rain. And it was no passing shower, but a steady downpour.

He drove on for a little through it, increasingly anxious, hoping it might slacken. Finally he pulled up the horse and got into the back of the cart, feeling the boxes. They were dripping—God grant the mill had made them stout—but his probing fingers in the dark found wide cracks in the top panels. Wood was scarce, like everything, and dear; the boxes had been hastily knocked together out of old lumber.

The paper, all the precious paper . . . not again a thing like that at Kingston . . . all that paper lost. The type was no matter, it would dry safely—of course the type was in a stout oaken box. There was no cover on the cart, he had a couple of strips of canvas over the boxes but it was soaked already. Desperately he flung off his cloak, his coat, his shirt. He tore the shirt into strips, stuffed them along the cracks his fingers found; the cloth would absorb better packed close. He spread the coat over two boxes, his cloak over the other two, pushing them as far as possible under the seat for further protection. He climbed back to the seat and whipped up the horse. He did not know if he believed in God, he had never been inclined to take anything on faith alone. But so far as he knew how, he thought he prayed that night, driving through the dark with the icy rain beating down on his naked back.

Not Kingston over again, please God. He had had nightmares about Kingston long afterward. It was as near a prayer as he could get, perhaps. Not all that good paper lost. For the first time in his life he laid a whip to a horse's back. He had ten miles to go—less, surely? He did not feel the cold and rain; he was busy praying for the paper.

CHAPTER 37

MARGARET'S CHAMBER was at the back of the house. She heard the cart pull into the yard. It must be very late; she had been lying here sleepless a long while. The kitchen door was fumbled open. It was raining hard; likely he had driven through from morning and would be tired. She thought there was a little coffee left. She got out of bed, hastily pulled on her dressing gown, went out to the kitchen.

He was staggering in from the yard, pushing a box before him, a box too heavy to be lifted. He was clad only in his breeches, the rain running rivulets down his chest. He looked up. "The paper—help me get it in—"

She knew what it meant to them; she did not even exclaim. She was out in the yard with him, in the rain; they wrested the last box down, half carrying, half pushing it in. He stood panting, legs splayed, knelt, and began feeling the boxes anxiously. "I think it's all right—perhaps a few of the top pages, but—" She saw he had covered the boxes with his clothes. "The horse, I must—"

"I'll call Haagen. Sit down, you must be exhausted. Your paper is safe." But he would not; he went out again, for another smaller box from the cart, while she lighted a candle. Haagen, hearing her call and coming sleepily to answer, stared.

"*Gott,* Mr. Bethune—"

"See to the horse," she said sharply. "I'll look to him."

"The horse," said Bethune numbly. "Yes. Willem, see he's rubbed down. If there's any bran left—deserves it—"

"Sit down, James. Such a foolish thing, you are soaked—" He sank down heavily in the nearest chair, head drooping, eyes closed. She did not know what to do for him; her heart knocked on her side and not all for the exertion. After a moment she fetched a towel, went and knelt beside him, began to dry the rain from his body. He did not seem to know she was there. How far had he come like this, she wondered. He had got so thin now, but the work at the press had hardened the muscle in chest and arm. In the little light of the one candle on the table the few gold hairs on his chest glistened.

"I'm tired," he said, suddenly, childishly, without opening his eyes. "I'm very tired."

"Yes." She thought he would fall asleep in the chair, upright. "Get up," she said distinctly, "stand up, James. I'll help you." She got his arm over her shoulder, guided his stumbling steps to the nearest door, the door of her chamber. He was not quite up to the bed when he collapsed forward and lay sprawled across it. "Oh, James—" She pulled at his limp body until he lay more or less straight, then stood panting. "Your damned, damned paper," she whispered. "Think of nothing else—no sense whatever." She pulled off his shoes, settled the blanket round him. Wet—cold— he would be ill.

He was sound asleep; he must be tired. A little timidly she reached under the blanket to feel his arm; he seemed to be warmer. She stood indecisive with her heart like a drum, and then quietly she lay down beside him close, lying straight and still, feeling his slow unaware breath across her temple.

Just for a little, to pretend. She must not sleep, he might wake and find her. Haagen, the others, they would think— It did not matter what they thought. Just a little, only to pretend for once that it was true, that it could be true, and he really wanted her. Missing him so these three weeks. Pretend he had come back to her, not just to his *Courier*.

He slept for fifteen hours. It was quite safe after all; no one knew. She was in the kitchen when Dorcas rose. He had just wakened when she returned after her day's classes; he came out to the kitchen passage as she removed her cloak, her gloves. "I was a trouble to you last night, I apologize. Dorcas said—"

She gave him a polite smile, friendly. It was easy to do that now. "Not at all. You could not have got to your own chamber, I think, you were exhausted. A foolish thing to do, I hope you'll not take cold."

He answered a trifle constrainedly, "I'm all right. The paper is safe. But where—that is—"

"Oh, it was late." She turned to begin laying the table. "I sat here in a chair, I was quite comfortable." She had grown an accomplished actress, she mocked herself, this last half-year.

Worse than ridiculous, she had said to him; and much use to acknowledge it! She could not remember how it had felt before, all that time ago, loving Bethune. She had known nothing real about love, and the time between had been empty, so she knew little more now. No matter whether it was only Bethune, she loving him since, or two utterly different people and she loving him again; either way it was just as painful, just as impossible.

And she was much too old and staid to be loving anyone like

this. Little use to think that either. She thought if she had not known him so well, it would have been possible: if she did not know that he felt her a duty. It would not have mattered that he did not love her, if he really wanted her; it would not have mattered that he had a wife. But he was Bethune; she knew him and could not believe him, because of the one thing between them.

She was grateful for her work these days. She would likely remain here. The old Chester sisters who owned the dame-school were kind; she enjoyed her classes, the children. The war, if indirectly, had brought her here to partial haven. It was very wrong to hope it would go on a long time, to keep him here; and sometimes she wished passionately it would end tomorrow, that he would go and leave her in what peace she could find without his daily presence.

And she was still unable to feel the smallest anger for him, for the male stupidity of his trying to make her believe. As if a child would not have known, the halting conventional phrases. Perhaps it was because she wanted so much to believe him that she did not dare.

She knew he cared deeply for nothing but his work. He had buried himself in that; it was the one thing for him. No sacrifice, no effort too much for him to make. And MacDonald was the same. Men!

They both claimed a healthy cynicism toward the war, but whenever there was an American victory to be reported there was much excitement in how they went about it, she noticed. She felt sometimes that she had spent this time since they left New York together with five, not four, companions—the four of them and the *Courier*. And the *Courier* dominated the household. Men!

And ever afterward she was to place the important events of that war by the *Courier*'s extra editions. Is it worth or not worth getting out an extra for? they would ask; and if it was, the entire household was disrupted until it was done.

When Bethune came back from Camden with the new paper they were prodigal with extras for a little. He carried copies to the nearby towns twice a month; the very week afterward he returned from Elizabethtown, flinging himself from the saddle, rushing in. "There's been a sea-fight—a victory for us! Two weeks back, but—two warships sent scuttling! What? Oh, the *Bonhomme Richard* it was, under Jones. I thought—"

"Yes, yes, an extra edition by all means! Let's hear the details." And both of them waved away any mention of dinner until the thing was written. They printed an extra edition for the attack on Staten Island. The American Army had never been so near; Bethune rode down to Elizabeth to see it—but did not find Darcy Trevelyan with any unit—and watched the embarkation. From Newark they could see the glow in the sky of the American fires on the island, and once or twice heard the guns. She had been afraid, not fearful of the firing, but thinking, now perhaps the British will come here. She wanted to stay here, at her peaceful work in the school, with the children, the two placid old sisters.

But that was in November, and nothing happened that was worth putting out an extra for until after that Christmas of 1779.

The children . . . that was the other thing she must not, must not dwell on. Never a November passed, she never touched one of the children—the little girls so prim with pinafores and ribbons, the little boys so untidy and dreadful things in their pockets— without wondering. It was no use, only more pain.

She would lie there in the dark with that in her mind—and Bethune. And she would rise in the morning, dress in one of her neat shabby gowns, brush her hair to its braided knot, pinch her cheeks to make them less pale, and she was neat, quiet Mistress Thurstan, with all the realness of her bottled up until she should be alone in the dark again.

If anyone had asked her, she would have said she was not at all brave. There were different kinds of bravery; it had taken her five years to gather the courage to leave Oliver, and she had been more frightened to leave England alone than that time in Kingston when the British had come and burned everything. She was more frightened of betraying herself to Bethune than of anything else, now.

This had been a severe winter, most rivers iced solid, and it had been difficult for some days even to walk across the town. The heavy snows had delayed all post riders, and many *Courier* subscribers had canceled until the spring should make regular delivery possible. Bethune said that used to happen even in the city, before the war. Everyone said it was the snow that kept General Washington from attacking New York—troops could not move in such weather. But the British had moved; they had crossed the rivers and made a series of raids upon Elizabeth and White Plains, not attempting to invade, only destroying and looting. Perhaps in the spring they would come in earnest, or Washington go to them.

But today was clear and there had been no snow this week. Haagen had taken MacDonald out in his chair to the print shop, and Bethune was hunting for firewood—they were low of supply and he thought a farmer near town still had a supply he might sell. Likely the man would claim lack of laborers to cut it and Bethune and Haagen would need to do so. He jested, saying though he was not a soldier the war had forced him to develop a few muscles.

When they heard the first shots and shouts she and Dorcas sprang up and ran out to the street, with no need to be told what it was. At a time like that all the surface things vanished. She said to Dorcas, "They're raiding, as they did the other towns, they won't stay. They may not come here but we must stay in case they do and the house is fired—rescue as much as possible." She said it very calmly, very reasonably.

Dorcas said, "Yes, ma'am. In case the house burns. He's in the town, I don't know where, only that Dutchman— I'm going to find Robert, I've got to find Robert—"

And the panic knocked at Margaret's own breast, not for herself. He would be shot, he would be hurt, perhaps bleeding to death somewhere alone, she had got to find him. So having said the reasonable thing to one another, they ran into the town to find their men.

It was only a small British force and they could not have been in Newark an hour; supported by a few cavalry, they fired several buildings and a field or two east of the town, scattered the crowds with volleys of shot. When she and Dorcas came to the street where the print shop was they found the soldiers had been before them; a draper's several doors down the street was burning briskly, and two men lay in the street, one groaning and one still. Mr. Ellsworth peered from the door of his shop still clutching a wet, freshly printed page.

"I don't know about Mr. MacDonald, ladies, he had left. But they did not *care*," he kept saying, puzzled. "They did not *notice*. Women in the street, children—they came in like a flood, all shooting—only God's mercy there wasn't a woman hit! Mr. Bergman'd only come by for his week's *Courier*, and never harm he did any—lying there dead—they did not *care!*"

"I've got to find Robert," whispered Dorcas distractedly. They ran into the next street; a low branch caught Margaret's hair and tumbled it about her shoulders. There were a dozen British soldiers in the street; they had set fire to old Mr. Holmes' smithy, and were now firing their muskets at random. One of them slipped and fell on an icy place and his musket went off, shattering an upper window, and a woman screamed. Not many people about— they had all run—but a tall man came running around the next corner, right into them, and several of them fired at once. She thought it was Bethune and she ran panting, flung herself down beside him. He was a stranger, with blood filling his mouth and his eyes wide with surprise on her; his blood spattered her throat and gown. The soldiers had vanished. Somewhere a bugle sounded.

She lost Dorcas and ran alone, up this street and that, some deserted, some crowded with frightened people. She could not find him anywhere, he was dead, he was lost. Men were rushing up with hand engines to fight the fires; she dodged them frantically, running. She came back to the last street where she had seen Dorcas; at least she could find Dorcas, someone. She stopped, leaning on the wall because she could run no farther, and saw a man's legs sprawled in the mouth of an alley ahead, and ran there.

The heavy chair had overturned and spilled MacDonald out on

his side. Haagen lay face-down half across him. Dorcas was struggling vainly to pull him off. "He's dead, he's dead—Robert—"

"No," she said. She knelt to add the little strength left in her.
She pulled at Haagen's arms, turning him, dead weight. Yes, it
was Haagen who was dead, the same surprise in his wide blue eyes
on hers.

She was not quite such a good actress, when he came in at last.
He was dirty, soot-stained, his shirt in rags; he had been helping
to fight a fire somewhere in the town. It did not matter then that
she felt tears on her face like rain to see him, gasped his name,
reached to touch him. He never saw her then, as a person. Someone had told him about MacDonald and he barked, "Tell me!
Where is he, what—"

"The surgeon—in his chamber."

He was gone from her at once. She leaned on the shut door,
fumbling for a handkerchief, fighting for self-control. Because
whatever happened, come whatever destruction or change, he must
never know, he must never know.

CHAPTER 38

BETHUNE APPROACHED the bed almost timidly. The still figure
seemed scarcely to lift the blanket. He was realizing again
how MacDonald had aged, his hair all white now and thinning;
he remembered how shocked he had been for a glimpse of the
wasted legs, scarcely thicker than a child's. He stood quietly by

the bed; presently he found the bright dark eyes focused on him.

"But—not so—worried, Mr. Bethune," said MacDonald in a tired whisper. "They don't kill me—so easy."

"I had not thought so, sir. I'll give you another thirty years, and then put an extra-heavy stone over you."

MacDonald showed the ghost of a grin. "That I'll need."

"I put out an extra edition for the raid. There were six buildings burned flat, another dozen damaged. Twenty-odd wounded and five dead." He did not know if MacDonald knew about Haagen.

MacDonald shut his eyes. "Four dead, and Willem. Poor Willem. Did his best for his *baas*. Maybe his ball was meant for me, eh?"

"Don't try to talk, sir."

"Damnation—talk if I want. The type—"

"I've got it safe, I brought it home when the edition was printed."

"Good. Must save it. No telling—get any more."

"Don't worry for anything, sir, I'm looking to it."

"See you do," said MacDonald. He was silent so long Bethune thought he slept and was about to depart quietly, when he added in a stronger voice, "I meant to tell you. Decided—may as well add your name—co-editor. The bold-face type. Tell Ellsworth, eh?"

"Yes, sir. Thank you, sir, I will."

Co-editor. It was less than the fact, as that year wore on.

The ball had taken MacDonald in the side, penetrating one lung, the surgeon thought. He had lain between life and death a week and then begun to mend, but slowly. The raid was on the second day of January; it was March before MacDonald was out of bed all of each day, and writing for the paper again. "We'll find a strong lad to be with you in the day." "None like Haagen, Mr. Bethune, not the same." Of course he was right. The farmer's boy Bethune found was willing, but clumsy, and after a little they let him go. MacDonald got out very seldom then; he seemed content to stay indoors, writing or drowsing at the parlor fire. Bethune remembered him in their first days together, the eager terrier of a man, never still, poking into every corner of the city after news. This had aged him, the privation and discouragement and illness. Two days a week, that summer of 1780, Bethune took him to the print shop that he might set the type for their press; he had spent their saved money through MacDonald's illness, hiring the printing of the whole edition. But MacDonald was slower at the job, he saw, and the effort of concentration tired him, though he insisted stubbornly on doing it.

The subscription had picked up again, but these were not normal times when that meant increased profit; the costs outstripped the profits, all because of the paper, the rare and heartbreakingly expensive paper. He had struggled with the accounts since MacDonald's illness, and by the middle of the summer he found they were deep in difficulty. He still owed the surgeon twenty pounds —more than a hundred of these new dollars. With prices risen so high it cost four pounds fifteen each week to print the edition, even with MacDonald, a boy, and himself at one press. He owed the mill at Camden two hundred pounds for the paper he had got last fall, all of it used now. In April he had cut the edition permanently to one page, which saved a good deal of money, but they could not charge a regular rate for it. He had raised the subscription price to ninety shillings a year; that was cut in half for the smaller edition. He asked eightpence the copy at shops.

He felt added dismay to see how changed now MacDonald was: the spirit of him was still there, but he was an old man suddenly, slow, groping after memory, tiring easily. "If it is too much for you, sir, we could afford—" The mean little thought in his mind was that MacDonald would begin to err in putting up the type. "You attend to your news-gathering, Mr. Bethune, and allow me to judge my own capacities! I am not senile yet."

So once again there came a time when the decision must be taken: to go on or not? By all logic it was foolish to continue publication. The last six months it cost them more to publish than the sum of returns. He was inept at figures, but even he knew no business could survive under that. How long would this war go on? Five years and more now, and there seemed no end to it, no advantage to either side. He wished at times he had been in a good solid business dealing with some necessity of life—a butcher, a carpenter, a farmer—but God knew they were in near as great straits these times.

That very week there was definite news of a great battle at Camden, a defeat for the Americans under Gates, and he dared not bring out an extra edition, not even one page.

He remembered his interval in New York. What would he give for some of that easy money now! Probably money was not so free there now, not by a long way. And who this side of the lines had any to spare at cards playing and such fripperies? There'd been desertions right and left from the American Army these two, three years, because even the Congress had no money to pay the soldiers; the paper they issued would be worth more to the *Courier* if it were blank.

He would have hired out to Ellsworth as a press man; he was not a full printer, but he had been operating a press some time and printers were scarce; he could ask the trade wage, seven shillings a day. But Ellsworth, like most other printers, had few commitments now; the shop was not working full-time. He found work in the fields at harvest, and when that was done he took a job, the best available, at Newark's one tavern, where he had all the odd work to do from sweeping the floor to holding the post horses when the stage came in. He was paid thirty shillings a week, and that was the daily mainstay of the household; it bought their food and paid the rent of the house. Not a great deal of food or a variety, but enough, with several farmers nearby paying their subscription rates in produce. Margaret's five shillings toward the house rent helped; he was reluctant to accept more from her, though he suspected she gave Dorcas money.

The tavern keeper was a bully, pleased to have an educated man, a gentleman, in his employment. It seemed to Bethune he saved all the dirtiest jobs for him, pointing them out with obvious enjoyment. There were many occasions, the first while he worked there, when Bethune had to shut his teeth on tempting retorts, had to fix his mind grimly on the absolute necessity for that weekly thirty shillings. Because it was impossible to vent his anger by

complaining to his household, after a while he found an outlet
by inventing suitably insulting replies and imagining them spoken.

Not possessing an imagination of any sort himself, the publican
had no way of knowing why his jibes failed to reach their mark. It
was not to be expected that he would guess Bethune was occupied
selecting the right epithet to describe his physique, his sneering
voice, or his stupidity, even as he returned some mild answer. The
publican was all the more irritated at such outward meekness,
which afforded Bethune some meager satisfaction; but that scarcely
outweighed the unpleasantness of the job. Nevertheless, it kept the
household in food.

The *Courier* was another matter. He disliked being in debt, going
into more debt; but if it was the only way to publish— The mill at
Camden was shut down now, out of business. He wrote to Holt in
Poughkeepsie asking his source of paper now and a recommenda-
tion to the mill that supplied him. So he took another burden on
his conscience, one that kept him sleepless many nights, for he had
no guarantee at all that the *Courier* would be solvent ever again,
and if the war went on he doubted it would. He was using the
good faith they had established in contracting debt.

Holt's friendly reply only increased his feeling of guilt. "I have
the most of my paper from a mill new-founded in Hudson Falls,
well behind the lines and thus far quite satisfactory, thought it is
not the quality we saw before the war, but that goes without saying. They are charging twelve pounds the ream, manufacturing
only the one size, the small half sheet. Carriage, of course, is at
extra charge. I have written to the owner as you request."

They would save a little if he went to fetch it himself, but such
a journey was impossible in late fall. By the time he wrote to the
mill and had the news that they would accept his note, on Holt's
word, for fifty reams, it was December and the snow deep. He
could not expect the paper in Newark until spring. All through
the first months of that year they brought out one-page editions
twice monthly. And that was a tax on MacDonald. It was signifi-
cant that he made no attempt again to oversee the accounts. "How
do we, Mr. Bethune? Out of the wood still?"

"Yes, sir, quite. Nothing like prewar profit, but we manage."

"Good, good. When we receive the new paper we shall be able to bring out full editions again, and weekly. If it continues you can give up your outside work, it will give you more time."

"Yes, of course, but until then—" Later he would have to think of some excuse; they could not do without that steady pittance. He worked at the tavern ten hours a day, seven days a week, with second Thursdays free—he had stipulated that. On those Thursdays his hours were longer. They got to the shop by seven, MacDonald put up the type, and he started work with two boys, all they hired now, printing the front page. The five hundred copies were done by three, and all dried by the time MacDonald had the back of the page set up; it was generally ten or after when they were done. Two sides, five hundred copies: all they could afford in paper, ink, and sweat. The boys had three shillings a day, shocking wages; in New York they had got delivery boys for two shillings a week, and the printers' apprentices had only three. But it could not be helped.

They brought out only one extra edition that fall, for the incredible news of Arnold's plot to betray West Point to the enemy. By that December, Arnold was leading British raiders in Virginia. It was news that kept him sleepless again; if an American general was so certain the war was lost as to change sides at the last minute—! Partisan to the rebels, yes, but a trifle shamefully he knew his first concern was for how a defeat would affect the American newspapers. The Americans' success at Cowpens in Carolina was counteracted by their defeat at Guilford. As it had for the more than five years of this war, it came out in stalemate.

They returned from the print shop after ten one Thursday evening, a chill clear night in late March. He was finding belated respect for dead Haagen; the chair was awkward to maneuver, though MacDonald weighed so little. At the top of a slight incline toward the house he stopped to catch his breath. There was the dark figure of a man leaning on the house gate. He seemed to watch them; as they came up he stepped forward.

"Can I give you a hand, James?"

Bethune stopped dead at the voice.

"Darcy. Darcy, man."

"Evening, Mr. MacDonald," said Darcy politely. "I see you're still yourself if James has lost his tongue."

"I thought you underground years back," said Bethune. "The British are poorer shots than I thought." In the dark their hands met warmly.

"Or I a faster runner. They caught up with me at Camden." His hand, thinner than Bethune remembered, stayed and gripped a moment. "I'd not shock you in the light—I left an arm there."

"Ah, Darcy—" But the left, he thought. "That's bad hearing." They started up to the house.

"Otherwise, Mr. Trevelyan?"

"Oh, I don't kill so easy, sir, as I hear you don't. Better an arm than a leg. I can still run—from British or jealous rivals! And never mind that bastard Arnold, we'll beat them yet."

In the light they clasped hands again briefly. Darcy looked older—so must he. Bethune felt it by a thousand years, from that day nearly four years back when they had last met. Darcy's left arm was gone from the elbow; he said cheerfully, "The bone shattered, but it would have healed except for the gangrene. But you'll be surprised how handy I've got—damnation lucky 'twas the left. I'm invalided out, though I wager I could still fire a musket. And how does the *Courier*?" His gaze was searching.

"Fine," said Bethune. "We've not even rum to offer you, Darcy, I'm sorry."

"Talk will do."

They made enough of that. Darcy refought all the battles for them; it brought the real war clearer to Bethune; most of the accounts they had written from had been at second and third hand. War had built a man of Darcy; perhaps it was kill or cure in war, you grew or died. If it had killed the vestige of youth in Darcy it left the spirit and courage. "Desertions? My God, there were always desertions—good riddance to them, it leaves the Army unriddled with fainthearts! It is but a question of time."

Bethune was ashamed to recite their small, niggling history these four years since he had seen Darcy. Nothing, nothing, against what Darcy and the rest had done, had suffered.

He did not mention Jacquetta until they were alone, and then not until Darcy did. Darcy had come out of hospital camp to his uncle's house, and Rafe Trevelyan would have told him. He claimed to have written several times, the letters miscarried or lost. It was Darcy's secret what he felt, not to be discussed like the war. But presently Darcy broke a little silence, after Mac-Donald had left them. With a very slight smile, unhumorous, he said, "It is safe, James. I will not weep on your shoulder if you mention her."

"I was not sure, you used to be much given to that. I'm sorry."

"No one's blame," said Darcy to the low fire. "Love—it's a reasonless thing. Maybe the war, maybe only myself, I don't know. I've got past any bitterness for it now."

"If you want my opinion, you're lucky it was not a legal marriage."

Darcy shrugged. "Will I want to marry? I don't know that either."

It was late. Bethune said, "I'll make you up a bed."

Darcy's hand on his wrist stopped him. "Not yet. I want some straight talk, James. You don't do so well, do you? Mistress Thurstan told me somewhat before you came in."

"What do you want me to do?" he asked, sitting down again. "Walk off and leave all the responsibility?"

"Well, I understand the *Courier* is not supporting itself these days. What responsibility is it?"

"Women," he said. "I should not have talked to her." But he was grateful Darcy showed no disposition to ask questions about Margaret. "While I'm able," he said, "while it's possible at all. I don't know why, any more than you about Jacquetta. My job. My fight."

"You're a damned fool," said Darcy. "You will kill yourself. Working eighteen hours a day! You can't keep that up."

"Did you reckon work-hours in the Army?" he countered bitterly. "Who would look after MacDonald if I did not? As to the *Courier*—well, call me coward as well as fool, I deserve it."

"And I might have said so once. Now I just say fool. I want to know how things stand, James."

"Cards on the table? Well, it's easy enough told."

They talked until dawn. At the end Darcy said, "I'd stay—I could be of some use to you here—but it would make another mouth to feed and put the balance against any help I'd give. I've not a penny, I've been living on my uncle's charity. My mother left nothing. I don't know what I'll do. I cannot but feel the war must end soon; afterward, or even before, I must find something to do. As it is, I could not even help you at the printing," and he touched Bethune's arm. "If I'd five shillings a week to pay my keep I'd stay. And I will stay if you want me. I could help with MacDonald—he looks to need much care now, I was shocked. I don't like living on my uncle. If I could find work here—"

"I'd work another six hours a day to keep you, you don't know what a relief it would be. So much you could do. The delivery—the proofreading—but damnation, Darcy, I can't spare any wages for you."

"And I'd not live on your charity either, damn you!" Darcy grinned at him. "Look you, I'm quite fit aside from the arm. There must be some work I can do here. I'll look for it. I've been lying about Elizabeth for a month growing mad with boredom, until they said I could ride this far. If I'd known you were making a galley slave of yourself I'd have come sooner. Nonsense, man, that's what it amounts to! And tell the truth, my uncle's not so well off these days, with all he's contributed to the Army and investments tied up in New York. I'll find something. We'll see it out together from now on."

Never able to say what he felt, Bethune said only, "It would be good to have you here, you know that. But you must not feel any responsibility—"

"No, no," and Darcy gave him a sidewise grin, "no one's allowed that but James Bethune! I'll stay."

CHAPTER 39

HIS BURDEN was lightened enormously by Darcy's presence, and not only in material ways. He could be stolid in the face of hardship, but Darcy as always could be cheerful. He found work, against Bethune's private expectations; he was taken on as assistant to the town clerk, the office recently having fallen vacant. "But I'm set for life, I've only just realized it! All I need do is show my arm and murmur, 'Camden,' and they fall over themselves to find me a job. My God, after the war we shall have every rear-line brevet corporal whose single injury was a case of French pox claiming he's a crippled hero! It's too easy." Bethune might have laughed at the notion of Darcy Trevelyan, that New York blood of other days, working for twenty shillings a week, but those other days seemed part of a former life.

Darcy laughed at himself. "I've seen the time I squandered a pound on an after-dinner liqueur! I wonder if they still serve that French green-cream at Fraunces'?"

"If it was to be had they'd charge more than sixteen shillings a glass. When I was there in 'seventy-eight Roubalet's restaurant was pricing dinner at four guineas a plate, without wine. I saw a British colonel hand over two hundred pounds for a party of six one night—that was including wine, of course."

"I don't believe there's that much coin left in America."

Bethune said, "I wish to God Congress would stop appropriating paper to print money. We could use it better without all that pretty engraving. After the war? We may be worse off then."

But that phrase was heard oftener, more hopefully, as summer came on. After the war. The fighting now was all, or nearly all, in the south, and from the reports it did not sound encouraging —the Carolinas overrun, Charleston surrendering. Darcy knew the Army; he'd seen fighting, and he said Charleston meant little. "I don't give a damn for the numbers, we move swifter. Washington is bound to catch that arrogant bumbling old Britisher into a trap soon or late. You wait, we'll see it."

Darcy's twenty shillings made a difference. Somehow Bethune did not feel the same about Darcy's contribution as about that Margaret made. He let her pay a small share of the rent, what she would pay in any case to hire a room; but he had caught her out giving Dorcas money for food. That he stopped, when he could. You never knew with women; they conspired. It made him uneasy that he might be eating food she had paid for. With Darcy it did not matter. The extra fifteen shillings a week Darcy insisted on contributing was a godsend those months when prices went up again. Darcy had taken to a pipe, Bethune thought as an excuse to share tobacco, which he had not afforded for two years. "Here, have some of mine."

"It would likely make me sick after all this time, I'm better off without it, I dare say." But he accepted all the same. There was something relaxing about a pipe of tobacco; he went to bed these nights more at peace with himself after desultory talk with a friend. The debts were still on his conscience, the astronomical debts. He could do nothing about them. It was useless to brood on it; he had taken them on with eyes open. The surgeon still was unpaid, that was the least of it. Thirty-four pounds was owed to Ellsworth for ink, four hundred and ninety-eight pounds to the mill in Hudson Falls. And they would need more paper by December. There was no hope of paying, and likely they would not sell him more until the debt was partly settled at least. He had not four hundred shillings.

Darcy helped in other ways. He was much his own master at

the town hall; so long as he accomplished his work his hours were his to arrange. He took over some of the deliveries Bethune had been paying a boy to make, and saw to the dispatching of copies to subscribers outside the Newark area. Occasionally he assisted in making up the accounts, shaking his head over them, looking at Bethune quizzically. "Talk about damned fools. You, or I should say we, are working like madmen to support a business that failed two years ago."

"I'm quite aware of that."

"MacDonald thinks the *Courier* is earning its way. What will you tell him if he ever asks to look over the journal?"

Bethune stared at his pipe. "I don't believe he ever will, you know. He has failed greatly since he was wounded so serious last year. The surgeon was a little surprised he lived then. All the interest he seems to have now is working at the edition. You've noticed how slow he is at setting the type."

"Yes, that's so." Darcy looked at him curiously. "It is partly MacDonald with you, isn't it, James? The reason you feel it so important."

He had never tried to define it to himself, separate the *Courier* from MacDonald. "I don't know, Darcy. I owe him a great deal." He saw MacDonald sitting at his table in the Merchants' House, the MacDonald he had been, vigorous, black-haired, keen-eyed, quick of talk: It's a fact the Bethunes are an old sept-family to Clan MacDonald. God, it could not be but was—eighteen years back.

"Don't you think the debt is paid by now?"

"I don't know that. Do you think the debt between friends is ever paid, to balance out? But you needn't put me down as a martyr, Darcy. If he were dead I'd likely be doing the same. Being a damned fool. It's my job."

"If you don't mind my asking, your wife owns two-thirds of the *Courier*. You'd not—"

"What is there to the *Courier* to own these days? Three counts, Darcy—she could not send money out of New York, she would not if she could, and I'd never ask her."

Darcy grunted, filling his pipe one-handed, gripping the stem between his stump and the chair arm. "Well, I can't say I blame you there."

The first light flurry of snow came on the fourth day of October, and with it a post rider from Maryland. It was late afternoon; Bethune had just come in from his work when Darcy came bursting in from the town with the news. "I told you! We've got them at last! Washington has the British penned against the coast in Virginia, under siege! The rider said five days ago—and they expect the French fleet in from the sea!"

"That's promising news, Mr. Trevelyan. Where? Is it the whole British force, you think?"

"Every unit, under Cornwallis. Oh, some small coast place, Yorktown, that's the name."

"That's on the York, at the mouth, on Chesapeake Bay," remembered Bethune. "The fleet's to come into the bay then."

"Likely it's there now. We have them at last; there's only unimportant numbers elsewhere outside Cornwallis's command."

But they might yet slip out of the trap. And news so slow to travel! It did not seem possible the war's end might be in sight; and would it mean much after all? What price their precious independence, the agreement Congress had drawn up five years back on perpetual union? It would doubtless be years before there was any stable economy, and if there was to be no trade with England—of course manufactories might be founded here. He was tired of the war, and ashamed at every reminder that he had stayed home while Darcy and the other thousands had gone to fight. He was not a fighter, only a damned fool.

They settled down to wait for news. All that came into Newark was reiteration of what they knew—the British under siege at Yorktown. Ten days, two weeks, and still no news.

He argued to postpone the printing of that week's edition, and not wholly because they expected news out of the south. The weather had turned bitter—chill and wet—and MacDonald had taken cold. Bethune had occasion to lift him now, and thought he weighed no more than a child; a breath of wind might carry him off. But—"There is no excuse for postponing, Mr. Bethune, the siege may go on another month for all we know. I am quite all right—nonsense. We can always bring out an extra—have you written the mill about another shipment of paper?"

"I—no, not as yet, I will."

"Do so." He had not because he knew what reply he would have: a dunning letter for what he owed. Yes, at times he wished he had been in the mill business instead of at this end. And what would happen in November, December, when their stock ran low? Would he throw himself on Holt's mercy—or the mill owner's? They were not in business for their health's sake. Only he was in business as—what had old Mr. Sower called it?—a labor of love.

They went out in a downpour of rain to print that edition. He had never felt the lack of a fire in the shop, for he worked hard enough to keep wet with perspiration all day. But MacDonald, sitting inactive with only a shawl about his legs, was coughing and shivering when they came back to the house. Dorcas never scolded him, but scurried about fetching blankets and a hot brick, and got him to bed; she rated Bethune fiercely for having him out in such weather. "You know how he's been since last year, sir, you did ought to know better!"

"What could I do? He would go."

"The newspaper! Times I hate it."

She woke him from heavy sleep some time in early morning. He started up to find her bent over him shivering, a little ghost in her night rail, all that lovely brown hair round her shoulders. "Mr. Bethune! Mr. Bethune!"

"Yes, what is it?" Darcy was sitting up in the other bed.

"It's Robert, sir—he's an awful fever, I wish you'd get the surgeon, he's bad. I'm afeared—"

Bethune was out of bed, groping for his clothes, at once; Darcy cursed, trying to strike a light. As he came out to the passage struggling into his coat Margaret was there with a candle, his heavy cloak. "Put this on, it's raining harder than ever."

"Thank you. Margaret—"

"Nothing is going to happen until you return, I'll be here. Go along, hurry." She gave him a little push. He felt her hand on him all the way across town to the surgeon's house. When he got there, and Dr. Lockyear's wife said he would be down in five minutes, and he waited dripping in the front hall, he found himself thinking he had been wrong. It was not only himself in business for love, not money. Medical men, too.

It was Margaret prepared meals for them the next couple of days; she asked a week from her school, being needed at the house. Dorcas did all MacDonald's nursing. Dr. Lockyear came every day; on the Sunday he stayed two hours, came out looking grave. "I don't know, Mr. Bethune, you had best be prepared. The congestion appears to have increased."

Bethune went to the tavern next morning as usual, but only to ask excuse from work that day; he did not want to leave the house. The publican was surly. "What's your affairs to do with me? You go off today, you needn't come back tomorrow, and whistle for your thirty shillings. Not that you've ever been worth it. When the war's over your sort'll be two a penny. Stay or go, it's all one to me."

"Very well, damn you," said Bethune, "I'll go." He did not know what other work he could find, but at the moment he did not care. He felt they were coming to the end of something and nothing mattered much that had mattered before. He went back to the house and sat in the parlor, waiting. Darcy was out at his work. Presently Margaret came to the door, saw him there, and went out and fetched him a cup of mock coffee; the real thing was not to be had, but the Indian-weed coffee was at least a good rich color, and strong, and the heat was comforting.

She sat quietly in a chair opposite, sewing. She comforted him immeasurably more than the coffee, being there. She did not say any of the things another woman would have said, the right things. You think a deal of Mr. MacDonald, I know. You have been with him so long. Such a pity, he is only sixty, not really a great age. I know you feel badly over it, and of course I am fond of him too. She only sat there to be with him, and he was very grateful for all she did not say.

The afternoon darkened to early dusk, and Dorcas called her

in a frightened voice and she went away. They had not let him in to see MacDonald at all; of course there was nothing he could do. He was still sitting there in the dark when the front door opened and Darcy came in. "James!"

"I'm in here." He fumbled for a candle on the table. As the wick caught Darcy came up, dripping rain on the floor. He gripped Bethune's shoulder; his eyes were bright but his mouth a grim line.

"James—it's all over. Finished. There was a rider came into town just now, from the south. Cornwallis has surrendered, three days ago, on the nineteenth. The war is over."

"Well," Bethune said. His mind groped for what it would mean, what he should do about it. Important news. Cornwallis had surrendered and the war was over. He said, "I must tell MacDonald." He went slowly to the door of the chamber, opened it.

Dorcas was sitting alone by the bed in the light of one candle. She half-rose in protest, but he came up to the other side, quieting her with a gesture. "I've something to tell him—if he can hear and understand me. Mr. MacDonald—"

MacDonald lay flat and still in the bed; every slow breath he drew seemed a little battle of its own, loud in the quiet room, irregular. Bethune laid a hand on him gently.

Dorcas said, "Please, sir—no, the surgeon said—sir, I'm awful afeared—" She looked as ghastly-gray as MacDonald, as near death.

"Mr. MacDonald—sir."

Another difficult breath filled the struggling lungs. He found the dark eyes on him vague and clouded. It was suddenly very important that MacDonald should hear and understand. "Mr. MacDonald—do you know me?"

Slow impatience, a little humor, crept into the eyes. "Surely— Mr. Bethune. Not—senile—yet."

"I've come to tell you—listen, sir—it's finished. We've just heard the news, the war is over. Cornwallis has surrendered his whole army to Washington."

A tired triumphant smile just touched MacDonald's mouth. His eyes shut again; he could not speak at once, but fought for another shallow breath. "Good—news—Mr. Bethune."

"Yes, sir. I knew you'd want to hear directly."

The struggle for the next breath was harder; but when the words came it was in a suddenly stronger voice. "Mr. Bethune. We will—you hear me? We must—bring out—an extra edition."

"Yes, sir," he said. "I know, I'll see to it." But he spoke to a man who no longer heard him. That was an extra edition MacDonald of the *Courier* would not write.

PART FIVE

CHAPTER 40

BETHUNE CAME BACK to his town in that spring of 1782, alone. There had been an end, and he was so tired he thought he could give up and die, but he had not. There were things to do even after the end, and he had done them, and now must go on to the next meaningless design in the pattern, and the next after that, until it was finished and he could die and know nothing forever.

He left all he had in Newark until he should have found how it was in New York: the press, the type. He had run out of paper in January. All he brought with him was the account book and MacDonald's will.

Dorcas: little Dorcas. Neat, quiet as ever, only paler, with a lost look in her eyes. "He said to give you this, sir. He had it a long time, since we came away from Kingston. When I'm gone, he said, give it Mr. Bethune." In the darkened parlor after the services, polite, a child repeating a lesson.

He did not look at it for three days. They had been too occupied hunting for her. They had dragged the pond, and hunted the countryside over. Margaret said they would never find her, poor little ghost with no one to haunt. "It is no use, James—and she wouldn't want it. They'd been together so long, she'd looked after him so long. She's just gone."

"But not to know if she's alive or dead—"

Margaret looked at him strangely. "She is dead, James. Whether she's somewhere, moving and breathing, or not. She is dead. But it's prying to hunt her. Her own life, to do as she pleases. She had no one ever but him."

"You want just to—let her go, and not try to find out?"

"Yes, please. Not to pry. If she's gone into the river, it's no affair of ours."

"All right," he said. "All right, Margaret, we'll leave it." And it was then, absently, his hand came on the paper in his pocket and he split the seal and found it was MacDonald's will and that he'd been left all MacDonald owned: his one-third interest in the *Courier*, and that worth nothing.

He crossed over by the Point Hook ferry, only now in operation again. He must go out to the house and see Susan, but first he wanted to see New York, what they had done to her, what she was now. He was not fifty feet up Partition Street before he knew New York was a city in panic. This was April; they'd had the news in March that the Crown decided officially not to pursue the war further. The few Tories left elsewhere had flocked here for safety of numbers; but where next? And in the face of defeat, the military still in nominal charge, all rule was shattered at a stroke; it was a city without law.

He went to look at it, after four years away: after five years and more of British rule.

There had been no attempt to rebuild where the great fire had burned, and its path through the city was traced by weed-grown emptiness, the shells of blackened houses. Here and there someone had planted over an empty space, and a few rows of Indian corn or wheat nodded, incongruous. Elsewhere the poor had erected their tents, their huts, where houses had burned. Tents scattered the Common; it had been dug over for trenches, for latrines, for a little planting; there was not a blade of grass left on it. Many houses had all windows broken, smashed either long ago—and left because replacement was impossible—or recently by returned patriots. When he came to Cherry Street he found the house still standing, but emptied of the very floor-boards. The little furniture they had left was gone; someone had taken the doors, torn up the floor for firewood. Other empty houses would have suffered the same. There had been a new street for fine large houses along Gramercy Park—the Dutch *krom mersche,* the "crooked marsh," where the swamp was filled

in; most of those had been left by patriots, and the British army
wives had occupied them as tenements; the washing was spread
on the bushes, and children played in the high-weeded carriageways.

He stopped in at the Merchants' Coffee House; its old proprietor, Cornelius Bradford, had recently returned and taken up
its management again. A fat burgess sat at MacDonald's table
drinking watered Madeira that was six shillings the glass. "Three
dollars for a pair of shoes, it is outrageous! What's to come I dare
not think. Fixed prices—bah!—we've learned about fixed prices.
All they could think of as a cure, and a damnation bad one
it is!"

The rivers and the harbor were crowded with ships, all British,
all merchants except the great prison warships swaying at anchor.
And there was activity at the water fronts: already those who
could afford the passage were fleeing America.

The Bowling Green, empty of Sears' tall Liberty Pole, was not
green now, but brown and bare. The British colors still flew over
Fort George and the Battery. The shops were stocked with
luxuries at prices hard to credit, and no tradesman was doing
anything but cash business: tomorrow was too uncertain. The
theater in John Street was closed. The pleasure gardens called
Ranelagh, at the upper end of Broadway, where young ladies and
gentlemen had strolled to watch the displays of fireworks, had
been put to use as horse lines for the troops. The fine mansions
facing the green, Philip Livingston's and Rafe Trevelyan's among
them, quartered officers and their wives, but the lawns were weed-
grown, the carriageways uncared for. The City Hall at Wall and
Nassau Streets, near where there had been the new public
library, was ruined: the military had pulled down all but the
first floor and had left a shell of a building.

But, panic-stricken or not, the city was alive and pulsing. It
was still New York of the islands: now islands of Tory Americans, newly returned patriot Americans, British military, British
civilians, and the great golden island of merchants who were and
had been neither Loyalist nor rebel, but only merchants.

He went into the City Tavern on Broadway for a meal. The

dancing room where he had escorted Susan on that ill-fated evening was closed off. He was brought a meat pasty on a plate, the size of his palm, and a pot of coffee very hot and good, the first real coffee he had had in four years; they charged him eighteen shillings. At the next table sat two middle-aged men shabbily dressed, who drank coffee and eyed his meat pasty with eyes abstractly envious.

"There's a saturation point," said one. "Prices can rise only so far. Business? I've done ten thousand pounds' worth of business the last four years, and most of it on paper, and most of it with British. If they leave soon I can whistle for my money."

"You're well off," said the other. "I'm not such a fool as to think I'll receive compensation for the burning of my warehouse. Sent from colonel to brigadier to general and told, 'Eventually.' "

"And what is to happen when they leave? Washington is requesting Clinton to set a date, I understand. Likely the Americans will call all debts contracted during the occupation to be canceled, and where am I?"

"Sitting amid your imported wares the Americans have no money to buy."

When Bethune left there he walked to the old office. The building was there, the door and windows gone. He went in; the floor boards were left, at any rate. His steps rang hollow in the bare rooms. Someone had chopped the middle section from the counter where he had copied so many advertisements; in the second room both tables were gone, the cupboard, the chairs. Only one thing was left, and queer that no one had taken it for fuel; perhaps it had been missed, standing flat to the wall in a corner: the old sign. Its lettering had faded and was all but illegible. THE NEW YORK COURIER, PUB. G. SHIELDS. He looked at it and thought how very odd it was that this had survived all death and destruction and change.

The house in Greenwich Road looked very much as he had expected: the front garden tall with weeds, the curtains pulled.

He got no immediate answer to his knocking, and the door was
locked; when at last it was opened to him he faced a tall, keen-
eyed, elderly man in the decent city garb of a gentleman, who
repeated his name with lifted brows. "Mr. Bethune. I trust you
can prove your identity—you have seen my advertisement in the
Gazetteer?"

"I beg your pardon, I don't understand. This is my wife's
house—"

"Come in, sir. You are fortunate to find me here. I was
attempting to make some inventory. My name is Barlow, I am
your wife's lawyer."

"Where is my wife? I thought—"

"I see you do not know." Barlow looked distressed, embarrassed. "I think we'd best come in and sit down. This is an
unpleasant duty. Indeed, I scarce know how to— You have
been away from the city some time, I know."

They went into Susan's parlor, but it was not her parlor; he
looked about in bewilderment. The carpet was gone; the only
furniture was two plain kitchen chairs and the shabby velvet
hangings. He listened to Barlow, but he did not understand at
first. It was like being told black was white. He had imagined
Susan sitting here across the river on her father's fortune. All the
merchants with capital in shipping had stayed prosperous through
the war, especially here in New York.

"I understand Mrs. Bethune's former man of affairs, Mr. Carruthers, had advised her to convert some holdings into gold,
before he left for England. Unfortunately she had not decided to
do so until much of it had dropped in value—and on the whole,
she would have been better advised to keep certain of the investments. The mortgages on warehouses, for examples—for of course
such holdings rose again eventually, with the British occupation."

"But I thought—a fortune," he said.

"Fortunes in wartime—" The lawyer shrugged. "There was
the shipping—the majority interest in the schooner *Essex*—"

Bethune rose and went to the window, looking out to the bleak
garden. "I knew nothing of my wife's investments. She managed

her own affairs. I think I had best tell you that my wife and I were estranged. I've been out of New York more than four years. It is a shock, of course, but—"

"I see, I see. Perhaps that makes my task a trifle easier. I should like to assure you, Mr. Bethune, that I had no remote notion how it was with her. When I took over her affairs, that would be in the summer of 'seventy-seven, she had been very ill, with smallpox, and as perhaps you know—"

"Yes, I know. She kept much to the house after that."

"Entirely, sir. She would have me come and sign proxies when necessary. The capital was in a tangle then. If only she had held to those mortgages! But she had some return on it, and she gave me to understand she had converted much into gold, before I had the management. I was most distressed to hear she secreted it in the house—so foolish, with all the soldiers about; there were a number of most shocking assaults and robberies. But you understand, I'd no reason to believe she lacked ready money, even when the holding under my control commenced to—ah—melt away. I did my best for her. I hope you do not think otherwise."

"No, of course not, sir. There was—nothing—at the end?"

"Nothing whatever. Mrs. Bethune had some capital, a respectable amount, in tenement property. The larger part of the inhabitants had fled New York early in the war, and the—ah—women attached to the military, the military themselves, as well as the ordinary citizens who flocked in later, simply took over the property, and the city commandant made no ruling upon rent collections until last spring. You would not believe what hardship that alone brought those who owned rental property. When the law was passed, those living in abandoned houses and tenements—living there rent-free, for years, mind you!—either moved off or simply refused to pay, and really, litigation over it would prove more costly than the sum due if it were won in court. The military—extraordinarily difficult to deal with. I sold the property for her at the time; it fetched next to nothing. But I had no notion she'd nothing left. I've some common humanity. I understood she lived upon the capital she'd converted. It may not have been as much as I thought. Your wife was secretive some ways, she would be too proud that anyone know."

"Yes, I know."

"It was doubtless then she commenced selling her possessions, all that would fetch any price." The lawyer looked thoughtfully at the page in his hand, where he had evidently been listing the few contents of the house. Bethune stared out to the gray April sky. After a silence Barlow said, "She was quite alone in the house, there'd been no servants for some time. The physician said—insufficient food, and it was a bitter winter. Firewood went to twenty pounds the cord. A shocking tragedy, shocking, poor lady, all alone. I do asure you, Mr. Bethune, I arranged suitable services. At St. Paul's. I can bring you to the place—"

"Yes. Thank you, you've been very good. I should offer," he said with slight effort, "it was kind of you, but I am responsible—"

" 'Twas forty-three pounds," said Barlow promptly, "with the sexton's fee. Such a tragedy, and no one at all seemed to know of any relative. She had mentioned you, but I'd no clue to your whereabouts. That is why I advertised in the newspaper. Naturally you are the legatee."

He turned. "I understood there was nothing."

"Very little, very little. But what there is must be properly disposed of, sir. There is this house, the ground—as you can see for yourself, much depreciated in value. There is a bed and a chair or so upstairs, a few kitchen utensils. The one holding of Mrs. Bethune's I had nought to do with was the interest in the newspaper. I had understood from her that business had failed, but I believe you could tell me—?"

"I could tell you," said Bethune. "The *Courier* is still in business, Mr. Barlow."

"Ah? Then your inheritance amounts to somewhat after all; you come to the share in that. We can go into it better at my office."

Bethune was patient, listening to repeated sympathy, explanation. He made a note of the location of Barlow's office in Division Street. He was rid of him at last, and went upstairs.

All the rooms quite bare, save the one; it had a plain bed, a chair, a wardrobe—all formerly in a servant's chamber, worth nothing. The fine tall beds with their hangings, the upholstered chairs, the highboys, the Turkey carpets, the carved ladies' tables, the mirrors, the silver candle holders, the silver cutlery, the English-china dinner service, the silver tea service, the damask cloths, everything sold piece by piece.

He would not have wished her anything like that: Susan Shields dying alone in a servant's bedstead, of cold and starvation!

No, that he wouldn't wish for anyone. But Margaret—any woman—had instinctively more charity; she had been sorry for Gerard. It was only now he could find it possible to be sorry for Susan. He knew now another reason he had wed her: because he had seen in her something that was also in himself. All she had wanted was to be loved. If she tried to have it the wrong ways, she was not alone in that. But that is all any of us want, he thought.

He had not, however, told Barlow the jest; he should share it with someone. Susan Shields they all thought he had married for her father's fortune. A bed, a chair, an all-but-worthless house. And the *Courier*. He owned the *Courier*. All of it. The press, the type; the debt to the mill; the debt to the printer. And he must not forget he owed Barlow forty-three pounds—including the sexton's fee.

It was an excellent jest. He laughed at it alone there in her chamber. And remembering stout, brisk, belligerent George Shields, when he was all a man, he thought Shields would have appreciated it too.

Suddenly curious, he opened the wardrobe. It was empty save for a threadbare dressing gown and a lady's hatbox. He never knew what made him touch the box. He opened it because it seemed heavier than a hatbox should be. It was filled with gold coins.

He looked at them a while before counting them. He would never know if she had forgotten the money was there, or if at the last she had preferred the gold to food. No one would ever know.

But this was one item that would not suffer Barlow's lengthy legal proceedings. Least said, soonest mended.

He counted the money; it came to twelve hundred forty-eight pounds, all in gold.

CHAPTER 41

So HE WENT on pilgrimage back to Newark, before Darcy arrived in New York from his uncle's house in Elizabeth. He had found the Merchants' Bank open again, and arranged to pay the mill in Hudson Falls what he owed. He had paid Barlow his forty-three pounds. When he came to Newark he paid Ellsworth and Dr. Lockyear. Then he had no debt on his conscience whatever, except the one he could never pay.

She had moved from the house to hire two small rooms in another, nearer her school. He waited in the street for her; when she came, all of him went to meet her, Margaret walking proudly, the independent lady. He waited where he was, hat in hand, until she saw him.

"James. You're back."

"Only for the day, I am afraid. I want to talk with you; may we go in?"

She hesitated; she guessed what he would say; but her chin rose a little as if she said to them both, Very well, let us have it out and finished once for all! "Certainly." He followed her in silence into the house, where no family was evident at this hour, up the stair to the first of her rooms which was furnished as a tiny parlor. "Sit down, will you not? How did you find the city, and your prospects there?"

"I don't want to make polite conversation," he said. He sat in the chair opposite hers and told her about Susan. It sounded bald, flat, as when he tried to tell her of his love. If all that was in him for her could be let out in words, she would know—she must believe. But something dammed it inside.

"I'm sorry, that is—dreadful."

He did not comment. He sounded reasonable, stolid. "I want you to come back to New York with me. I want you to marry me. I cannot offer you a great deal now, there'll be much to do, but later—"

"So it is changed," she said pleasantly. "It can be a legal responsibility now. Upon rather sudden notice."

"I never cared—you know how it was. I was sorry, but—"

"Oh, yes, I know that. What I do not know is how you have the courage to say this to me—to think I would consider it. Do I need to tell you my answer?" She spoke rigidly, as if suppressing anger, and could he blame her?

"I don't know that myself. It's even a little laughable—but I love you." And even that sounded lame, and he thought suddenly, sickly, but that was why it happened at all. I remember: I wanted so to tell her and had not the words, and that was why it ever happened.

She sat back and folded her arms. "I have got away from all of you. I've a happy life here, I want to keep it. It was only accident we ever saw each other again—and queer we came not to mind. But I can't have this. Difficult enough to feel—friends."

"Do you think we could ever be friends?" he asked to that.

She moved sharply, turned away. "No! You are quite right. There is nothing at all, for either of us. Can you tell me honestly, if you had not known me when we met again, never connected me with Margaret Thurstan, you would be sitting there asking me to be your wife?"

"Now that I don't know," he said heavily.

"Of course not. But it is a waste of time to suppose it, for we both know, and that is why it would always be impossible. I wish you will go, and let us never speak of this again, please. You know how I feel."

"Yes, I know." He stood. He dared not ask if she meant he might not come again, only to see her. He thought she was more beautiful each time he saw her. "Margaret—"

She turned on him fiercely. "Will you go—please go!"

"I'm sorry," he said. He took up his hat. But at the door he turned again. "Margaret, if you ever need—if there is ever anything I can do—you would not hesitate to—"

"For God's sake!" She put her hands to her face. "Will you go and leave me in peace!"

He went out without another word.

It was no longer cold determination in him, or the anger he'd felt after Kingston. It was just the next thing, and the only thing he knew to do. He went back to New York and began it. He had six hundred odd pounds left after the debts were paid. He wrote to the mill asking a contract, three hundred reams the year to begin; he had a satisfactory reply, the promise of fifty reams by next month. He found a print shop in Chatham Street that would give him a decent rate with the use of his press and type, two hundred thirty pounds the half-year's weekly editions. He had hired a room at the City Tavern, but when a carpenter had fitted doors to the old office, repaired the counter, and made new shutters for the windows, he moved there, with a makeshift pallet in the second room.

His new paper arrived in the first week of June, and he published an edition the week after that, the day before Darcy came. Rafe Trevelyan was a cautious man; Darcy was to look over the property and inform him if it was possible that he return to New York. Many former residents, who had lived out the war behind American lines, had assumed they might reclaim their property at once; they gave up what lodgings they had and returned to the city, only to find their houses full of British military and the Loyalists who had appropriated them, with no legal redress whatever.

"The city's been robbed blind," Darcy said. "You must come and see the house, you'd not believe it. There are officers quartered there, six of them, two with wives and families. I was allowed to examine it—kind of them—but no one seems to know when there'll be a general evacuation. And try to get any satisfaction from the military! 'Some of the furnishings are missing? The silver service, the best carpets, the tapestries? What a pity, Mr. Trevelyan, vandals before we took over the house, likely, no responsibility can be assumed.' My mother would be wild. They have let the children hang on the curtains, they're shredded, and one of the women has an odious little spaniel with no manners at all. Yes, just as well Mother does not live to see it. My uncle has a more philosophic mind."

"Multiply that by five hundred houses. I'm surprised they were that polite."

"And they dislike the necessity, but orders have gone forth." In that month upwards of two thousand Americans had returned to New York, and it became a city of brawls. It was impossible not to feel some sympathy for the British commandant who, as the only nominal authority in New York, was expected to bring order from chaos overnight. Sir Guy Carleton, who had taken over from Clinton when that worthy was haled home to explain certain of his failures, had little stomach to do more than was immediately necessary, aware that the Americans would eventually assume control and probably reverse all his decisions. By the same token nothing he did would satisfy the Americans now.

Besides the returned patriots clamoring for restoration of their property, there were newly come Loyalists from other colonies, some of whom desired to go, others to stay, and the majority of them were destitute. "Speak of fair play!" Bethune grimaced to Darcy. "The Crown has given them a hand dealt under the table, right enough." For by the terms of the provisional armistice, the Loyalist Americans were not accepted as British subjects; they did not call themselves Americans, and the Americans wanted nothing to do with them, yet England would not have them. After a good deal of bitter talk it was decided to ship these refugees to Nova Scotia, those who desired to leave; meanwhile the commandant granted them pensions to live.

Carleton was further plagued by the prevalence of crime. The military police force was useless against it; with so many destitute in the city, laws in abeyance, and violence a lesson well learned in six years of war, a man took his life in his hands to walk a dark street alone.

And the ranking military had the job of suitably entertaining Prince William, third son to the King, who visited New York by royal condescension. Ironically, the stout young prince was popular, even among the Americans. They had just fought a war to escape the Crown, but they were agog with interest in royalty. "Damned yokels," said Darcy, adding vulgarly, "He uses a chamber pot same as anyone else, and I scarce believe it's gold-plated—though with a German I'd not be surprised at anything."

Bethune remembered MacDonald and smiled. The German in Whitehall had had his sound beating, but none of them would ever admit it. The bland arrogance of these British officers! And that not so different from Rivington. The insolence of the man, in his recent article defending himself! "Accused of the wildest enormities, I do protest to all I have but done my poor best, serving my profession and my country through the late grievous conflict, by printing the truth as reported to me." And going on to claim a circulation of thirty-six hundred readers! No newspaper in the colonies ever had that, or would for years to come, if ever.

There was enough news to write. Bethune wrote it, and published it, with Darcy's help. Darcy succeeded in August in ousting the inhabitants of his uncle's house. Darcy and his uncle lived quietly there in the ruined mansion; they pressed Bethune to accept a room in the house, but he refused, preferring to be alone. He would not be in debt to any ever again, if he could help it.

He went at the work without enthusiasm. It was comforting to see the *Courier* begin to earn a little profit again. The circulation built up gradually to eight hundred, counting a couple of hundred subscribers in other colonies. The Boston subscribers commenced to come back to the fold. Paper was down to nine pounds now, a relief. Holt of the *Journal*, who had returned to New York in January, planned to reopen his own mill; he was running a contest among his subscribers for which could contribute the most old cloth, and offered a prize of twenty pounds.

One circumstance that increased circulation and sent up all newspaper profits in those months was the unprecedented number of advertisements. Darcy had to refuse many each week, the space being filled. Nine of every ten Loyalists were leaving America, and selling possessions right and left—everything from extra garments to houses. Some, having obtained passage sooner than expected, sold off in haste for any price they were quoted; some valuable property changed hands that way.

Once, last year, he would have been in high spirits to see the paper flourishing. Scarcely at a prewar level, but earning profit: paying him and Darcy sufficient to live on. Now it was just a thing that happened, the next thing. Perhaps he was growing toward middle age and had lost capacity for enthusiasm.

"You're sickening for something, James. I said forty-eight pounds nine shillings fourpence. In a week."

"I heard you. Quite good. If prices continue this high it must do better than that."

"Never satisfied. After the way the journal looked last year it's a pleasure to open it these days. Which reminds me, we should settle a wage for me, we can't go on simply dipping into the till indiscriminately."

"Very well, but it's no matter, Darcy; we both do the same amount of work. How is five pounds to start with? What is that in dollars? I can't figure it." Darcy shrugged, went back to the accounts, looked up to ask if he had the headache. "No, I'm quite all right."

"I expect it's the war ending. Everything let down all on a sudden—no more battles to fight."

He said, "I never fought any."

And Darcy equably, "Oh, didn't you? Unlike a few men I know—have you seen Hector Kennedy swanking down Broadway with that pair of grays?—I've learned a little sense with age. Tell you something, James. It doesn't need much courage to go galloping off at charge with a hundred other men. It's over and done, dead or alive, in a trice. Needs the devil of a lot more to withstand all the niggling little nuisances day to day. I suffered more from mosquitoes in summer camp and boredom in winter camp than from the whole damned British Army. Inclined to think you had a harder war than myself."

"Well, that's a lie. I've both arms." No, he'd never lose that guilt either, that he had stayed home, left it to others, the winning of a war for (they said) all the fine words—freedom, independence, honor. And that was another thing he could be cynical about now. If New York was anything to judge by, the end of the war had brought only a thousand squabbles, a fluctuating economy, and confusion at all levels.

Was it that all the effort, the purpose, had been on Mac-Donald's account? Now it had dropped away from him, though the *Courier* was his. He looked at the sign over the door, trying to conjure in himself some pride of accomplishment. THE NEW YORK COURIER, JAMES BETHUNE, EDITOR. It said nothing to him, but there it was—a thing happened. Chance, like his first coming here, looking for work; like anything else that had occurred to him since. A man walked blind; and there came a time, knowing it, when he ceased to have great concern.

He returned to the office one day after luncheon at the Merchants' to find a tall country-looking young fellow standing outside, who called him by name. "Mr. Bethune. You don't remember me?"

"I'm afraid I—should I?"

The boy said a little shyly, "Maybe not, sir. I'm Will Clark from Tenafly. You said—after the war—I should come and see you, and you'd help me."

"Will Clark." The freckled, eager youngster, eighteen, nineteen now, still wide-eyed from his first look at New York. That was a little debt he had forgotten: young Will Clark had been the spur in his side at a time when he needed it, long ago. "I remember," he said. "You wanted to be a printer."

"Well, sir, I reckon—that is, I guess it was mostly the newspaper. I'd like to work at a newspaper—yours. I write a good hand, sir, the master said so, I worked at it hard." His eyes were still the eager eyes of youth. Bethune felt older than ever, looking at him.

"Did you? That's commendable. What d'you say to ten shillings a week?"

Young Will's face fell a trifle. "Well, sir, I—"

Bethune laughed. "Only a jest. Yes, you've a bit more sense than I had."

"Sir?"

"No matter. You shall have a pound."

"It's kind of you, sir, I'll do my best. Everyone said you'd never meant it, sir."

"Yes, yes. I'm sure you'll do excellently, but, Will—"

"Yes, sir?"

"Oblige me and don't sir me every other word. Not quite senile yet."

And he met Hugh Gaine, hanging about the edge of the new cricket field near the shipyards on the East River, where the royal visitor and his train condescended to join Governor Tryon and Sir Guy Carleton in watching the pick of the British officers play an exhibition game. Gaine was jotting down notes evidently about the prince's costume, admittedly lavish; he glanced up to identify Bethune and hailed him.

"Mr. Bethune! Your pardon. I know you hold no brief for me, but I would like to say I was sorry to hear of MacDonald."

Bethune looked him up and down; but it was the habit of contempt, not the real thing. "Would you, Mr. Gaine? I don't believe he'd be flattered."

Gaine looked at him with the old humorous belligerence. "So I'm still the traitor? Grow up to a man, Mr. Bethune. I never thought more of the British than you, but I had wit enough to see I didn't starve while they were top dog. That's the whole matter."

"I'm not sure that doesn't put you a step below Rivington—who at least did not change sides in the middle of the fight."

"Come," said Gaine, still good-humored, "it seems to me I recall an article in the *Courier* claiming that newsmen are not entitled to opinion, that they are the watchers to report impartially on those of other men."

"I'll not argue," said Bethune. "I'm not too sure I've any opinion on anything these days. Not a traitor for sacrificing your honor, Mr. Gaine—it's an empty word—but for sacrificing your integrity as an editor." And he remembered something, and smiled. "One day when you've nothing else to do, go up to the old churchyard at St. Paul's and look at John Zenger's headstone. Perhaps it will explain better than I'm able." Gaine was still shrugging and smiling as he turned away.

CHAPTER 42

ALL THROUGH that summer and fall of 1782 the troops came crowding into New York: the British Army from all directions, expecting orders home. They camped in the suburbs, quartered themselves on the city. That was one thing, the Loyalist volunteer militia another—nearly three thousand of them, still in uniform, seeming reluctant to disband. In September Burgoyne and his army came in; it was rumored Burgoyne would be held for court-martial when he was officially released by the Americans. A hand dealt under the table again! The same story as in the Arnold affair: Arnold free to go to England and collect his bribe, and the scapegoat John André, the honorable man carrying out orders, hanged for treason. Burgoyne's defeat was all Howe's blame; Burgoyne might be fool, not villain. But that was the Crown's business.

Bethune stopped at the little tobacconist's shop in Pitt Street one afternoon; waiting for service, he saw a lady before him and thought, But I know that woman. The Junoesque figure, the pure blonde hair—it was Johanna from Mrs. Wise's house. She gave him the familiar calm, radiant smile when he spoke her name.

"Why, Mr. Bethune, how nice to see you again. Of course I remember. I noticed you'd come back when I saw the *Courier* again in shops."

He gave her coffee at the York, again amused by her ladylike manner. "As a matter of fact we're worse off now than before the war ended—speaking of my job, you know. Dare say some other businesses are different. With all the officers here we got on wonderful in the war. I don't say I liked it overmuch, but you know you can't mix politics with my work. I liked your article about Prince William. Fancy that great fat boy coming here and lording it over us. But we get a different class of customers now, *Gott,* yes. And prices so high. New York's changed."

If he'd said it once to Darcy's questioning he said it a dozen times. "I'm quite all right, a trifle stale is all, don't trouble about me."

He was tired, that was all; sick and tired. He began to wake with a headache each morning; he had no appetite, and in spite of his tiredness, slept ill. There came a morning when Darcy suffered his irritability with only a narrow stare and said, "You're not well, James. Don't fob me off, you're damnation ill by the look of you." He came and laid his hand on Bethune's brow; Bethune jerked away. "As I thought, you've a fever. There's been small-pox about—"

"I had it as a child. I have a little headache is all." He was nearly blind with it; and he felt so tired he would be glad to lie down in his grave uncoffined.

Darcy went and fetched his hat and cloak, told Will to get a hackney. "You are coming home with me and will go to bed and let a physician look at you. Don't swear."

He did not. He let Darcy help him into his cloak, docile as a child. Like a child he felt ready to weep with weariness. They put him to bed in one of the chambers at the Trevelyan mansion and Darcy fetched a physician, who prodded him and asked questions and gave him a draught of laudanum for the headache. He slept and dreamed of Margaret, and woke with the headache gone but feeling weak and vague. It was an effort to remember his name. He cared about nothing, least of all Darcy, who came and asked if he was hungry. But he told Darcy to go and see what MacDonald wanted, he was calling somewhere near. "Yes, all right, James." He remembered that MacDonald was dead, and that seemed not to matter either. The laudanum took hold of him with a large soft warm hand.

A mumble of voices spoke over him. Fever. Rest. Quiet. Nonsense my dear Mr. Trevelyan a good bloodletting always nonsense yourself I know what's wrong well as you. The damned old leech.

I am ill, said his mind in alarm, very ill. It told his body to move, but the body would not obey. Dark shut down comfortingly and he swam away to a place where there was nothing, nothing, nothing, and he thought with sly triumph, I always knew death would be like this, black nothing, and I was right.

But he came back, unwilling at first; he came back to the bed in the tall chamber in Rafe Trevelyan's house, and a silent manservant attending him, Darcy looking in with his uncle, immensely relieved to have him back; to the view out over the Bowling Green and a gray October sky, to a low fire hissing on the hearth and the warmth of blankets over him, and a large ginger cat that sat on the bed and kneaded the blanket and watched him incuriously with great sleepy amber eyes. The cat knew all the secrets of relaxed acceptance: it was fluid life. He found it restful to watch her. But there came a day the cat was not offered half the food they fetched him, and his appetite came back and he began to mend.

"That damned leech," said Darcy in satisfaction, pushing the cat aside to sit on the bed, watching him eat roast beef. "All they can think of is bleeding. I told him what it was; your sins overtaking you is all. You worked yourself like a black for six years—and worried yourself to a rope's end into the bargain. It caught up to you, you needed a rest. Are you finished with that? I'll take it."

Bethune lay back on the pillow. "Dare say you're right. Though I never worked all that hard—only what was there to be done. Someone had to."

"You will stay where you are until you're quite yourself."

"I'll get up when I please," he said. "Tell me what you've done at the office." He was himself again now, only still a trifle weak when he tried to move about.

"We're getting on quite well without you," said Darcy with a grin. "News? Well, not much—still delays. They've set no date for the evacuation yet and we're more crowded every day. The estimate is over thirty thousand here now, if you can vision it. Most of the Tories and the military we'll be rid of sooner or later. The Prince is still here."

"The accounts," said Bethune. "I'll see them. Did you pay the physician? And has the paper come?"

"I'm looking to everything. Don't worry, James."

Well, he did not, in that sense. Doubtless he would again. He need not worry over the paper now, it was going on well. He was his normal self once more, the gray tiredness gone from him; he had concerns again with life. Propped in bed, he wrote an article for the *Courier* that week, from what Darcy told him about the crowded state of the city. It tired him, but it was natural tiredness.

That evening Rafe Trevelyan came in to visit him with his evening coffee. "You feel you are yourself again?"

"I feel I'm malingering now; I'll be up in a day or two. I should say I'm grateful."

"Ah, nonsense, we've been happy to have you! Alone as you are you owe us nothing, there's no debt between friends."

No, he thought; I said that once to Darcy in another way. No debt. But the other thing he had learned, lying here in fever—

How obtuse a man could be! A thing he should have seen years ago.

He got up the next morning and shaved himself and dressed, for the first time. The man looking back at him from the mirror, not much changed by illness—always thin-faced, the height of brow and cheekbone making him look gaunt—met his eyes almost as a stranger, as if he had seen no mirror in years. Almost twenty years. A tall fair man, unhandsome, the gray eyes having looked on life holding a little smile for it, a little sadness, a little resignation. James Andrew Bethune who, in three weeks' time, would turn thirty-six years old. A man should be able to look back from that many years and know some conviction gained, some truth learned. He had none. All he had learned was that there is no certain truth, that a man only teased at life and was teased by it, until at the last moment of it, whatever he had done or not done, he knew in panic, But I have learned, achieved, been nothing; and likely went into nothing and forgot even that. But it imposed duties on him if it offered no permanent reward.

So it came to him at last, the thing he should have seen so long ago, as if he had rummaged through a drawer long unstraightened and come on a note of hand he had forgotten.

It was not the kind of debt he had conceived. It was a material thing of pounds-shilling-pence. In all probability someone had assumed a responsibility which was his, and—twenty years or forty—he would have to find out and pay off the debt, and then he would be free. It was nothing to do with Margaret. When he had done that, he would be free to go on to the second half of his life.

He had thought it before: you could have one of all desires, no more. He had the *Courier*. He wanted to make the *Courier* a successful, important newspaper; he had all sorts of schemes and ambitions for the *Courier*. With enough capital ahead, he would like to start his own mill; and he must investigate the method and cost of printing these new humorous drawings sketching political opinion at a glance—ridicule was always a good weapon. He had in mind a series of articles upon the planned rebuilding of the damaged parts of the city. But all that, anything chance might bring him, must wait upon this duty left over from the past. He was impatient to know, and pay it, and have done.

In the second week of November he felt quite strong; he had remained at the house on Darcy's urging, but had been up and out to the office for several days. Business continued surprisingly good, stimulated by the number of people jamming the city.

There had been no word of or from the Isaacsons; perhaps he would never know. He wondered about them, harried little people. One day, if they did not come back, he would have the house repaired and sell it for what it would fetch. He would have no use for a house. He would sell the one in Greenwich Road too.

He looked over the accounts. Four-hundred-odd pounds in the Merchants' Bank; he owed the mill ninety-seven, would owe four times that by a year from now, but he meant to pay it quarterly, and there would be no trouble with that if the present profits continued or even if they slackened a trifle. Darcy said young Will Clark was proving reliant and intelligent.

"Do you feel capable of turning out a few more editions alone? I am going away for a bit. No, I don't know how long. Perhaps a week, perhaps a month. You know I'd not desert you for my own pleasure—it's a thing I can't tell you of, I'm sorry."

"Had I asked any questions? But you're only out of bed. You should not be starting off on a journey."

Bethune said absently he would be right enough. "I don't think I will be long; I'll let you know if I must be."

He drew three hundred pounds from the bank account: not enough, but enough to bind the bargain, show good faith. He left New York on his birthday, a gray cold morning, the wind off the sea, in the coastwise sloop *Hesperion* bound for Yorktown on Chesapeake Bay.

CHAPTER 43

"Y OU KNOW how it was," said the publican. His southern speech seemed strange after this long while. "The damned military—either ones—worse nor crows or weasels for thievery. Robbed us blind. You know Marion's bunch—"

"No. I was not in the Army."

"Ar? Stay-home or Tory? One bad as t'other. Y'read the newspapers, did you, mister? Know we just had a war?"

"I read the newspapers," said Bethune to his brandy. "I asked you a question."

"Ar. I'm tellin' you. You can go an' look, there ain't much left to see. I reckon you can hire a horse at Doyle's, up the street. Six shilling." Open hostility in the pale eyes. Bethune gave him the money. "Damned northerners come down here. Damned stay-home fence-sitters." Bethune smiled a tight smile to himself; a very good description that was. He got the horse at the hiring stable and rode out of the town northwest. It had seemed a much longer road that night when he was running away. It did not take him an hour and a half now. And he did not know why he went, if there was nothing to see.

There was a little: the tall posts and the iron gate brought all the way from England, sagging now on rusty hinges: the carriage-way still traced; the shell of the house—burned by the Americans, the publican had said, the British chasing them this way. Brick and stone would not burn, only blacken, but everything else was gone. The path marked, though, where the slave quarters had been, three or four cabins left, and Negroes there. A very old man came out of one, seeing him. "Mistah Thurstan, sah? He dead, sah, long time back—or maybe las' year. I doan remember. No, sah, I Jabez."

"You remember Mr. Thurstan's butler Shad? And Shad's wife Flora? There was a coachman Nego—and Abed and Billy—" There was a yellow girl named Zena.

"No, sah. Never b'longed Mistah Thurstan. They said we all be free atter the war, thass what they said. I was Mistah Haines' over at Taggarts' Chance over beyonder. Atter they burn, Mistah Haines run off an' leave us."

They had done that in the North, too: promised the slaves freedom after the war, and many had joined with the British as servants, camp orderlies, grooms. One of Carleton's headaches in New York now was trying to separate free from slave, restore the latter to their rightful owners. He gave the old man threepence and came away. He felt nothing in particular, looking at what had been Thurstan Hundred; it was just a place where he had been once; all that had happened to him since felt much more real. He rode on into the village. There was a new rector at the little church, who had not known the old one at all.

"You're looking for relatives? Any way I can help you, sir—"

"You might say that."

"Mr. Thurstan? He removed to Williamsburg after his house was destroyed. I heard he died there. I know nothing about the family."

Well, it was foolish to think he might find out without revealing himself, much as he disliked the necessity. A pure matter of business. He rode back to Williamsburg and sought out Mr. Wyeth's offices. The little, dry lawyer at least was still there. He looked at Bethune, this Virginia gentleman, this upright man, with distaste, curiosity, disapproval.

"I'm afraid I can tell you nothing whatever. Mr. Thurstan died some eighteen months ago. His wife had died the previous year, and his second daughter predeceased him also. The entire estate, such as it is now, was bequeathed to his eldest daughter, Mrs. John Collard, who is now residing in England. About Miss Margaret Thurstan—I should say Mrs. Gerard—I know nothing, she had estranged herself from her family."

"I'm not asking about Mrs. Gerard," he said patiently.

Wyeth shuffled the papers on his table, the distaste predominant now. "I really know nothing at all as to that aspect of the affair. It was a family concern entirely—naturally Mr. Thurstan never spoke to me. This late in the day, really, Mr. Bethune, it seems only morbid curiosity."

"I'd thought perhaps some legal provision—"

"Good God, no. No, most certainly not."

"I see." Foolish again, to think there might have been some small concern? He sat there silent, trying to think: trying to put himself in Thurstan's place, to guess what he might have done.

"I'm sure you will excuse me—I have appointments."

He looked at Wyeth. Well, yes, strait-laced: one man who might indeed be positive he had never got a bastard. Bethune thanked him and went out. They told him at the town hall that the orphanage was no longer in operation, for lack of funds. There was a Mistress Pollock who had been matron supervisor there. She now lived retired.

He found Mistress Pollock in a neat cottage outside the town. He wondered how to talk to a lady about this, but Mistress Pollock did not embarrass him; she was a tall, handsome old woman, direct as a man. She did not even ask why he wanted to know; he said vaguely it was a matter of inheritance.

"Indeed I remember very vividly, as I daresay many here would. There was a deal of gossip, as you may imagine. One of the wealthiest families roundabout, and I fear one of the most snobbish. A tragedy—no, no, not for the girl, pampered little miss, likely. The child, sir, the child! As if a few words not spoke by a rector could make a child evil of itself! Your pardon? Ah, but we never did, you know! I never heard aught about that. I should rather fancy, you know—" A suggestive pause.

"No," he said. "There was a child."

"Ah? I remember discussing it with several colleagues, we had wondered. But I never heard anything of it, in a professional capacity or otherwise."

"I see, thank you." Somehow he had expected that a few questions would end his search. He walked back the little distance to town and found a physician, to ask for Mrs. Williams, the midwife Margaret had named. The man had never heard of Mrs. Williams. "But I've been practicing here only a few years." The midwife he mentioned was more helpful.

"Old Bet Williams, sir? Lord, yes, I know her—been here donkey's years, old Bet. You'll find her at her granddaughter's, little farm south a ways, Ansell's the name."

The granddaughter was out. His quarry admitted him to a cluttered farmhouse kitchen crowded, on a day of streaming rain, with children of stair-step size, who made a staring circle. "I'm Mrs. Williams—what was it you wanted?" A little withered bird of a woman, bright-eyed, unholy curious.

"Could we speak private? It's scarce a matter for—"

She was interested, pleased. "I reckon." She shooed the children from underfoot and shut the door, set a chair for him. "Will you have a piece of my corncake, sir? Hot out of the pan."

"No, thank you. Mrs. Williams, what I want to ask—"

She was voluble enough, to a point. "Ah, that one. A nine days' wonder in society about, that was. When all's said an' done, a baby's a baby and a plenty of 'em come when they're not asked. They didn't want for the little lady to have it—that's a thing I don't hold with. He said, a hundred pounds and keep your mouth shut. Waste of time, 'twas all over the place a'ready, after the boy run off. Ah, I could've done that, reckon, but I weren't off to put it on my conscience, tell you straight. I told him 'twas too late, and it likely was so. Funny how they all be a little different —it must be a thousand I pull inta the world, and still a little bit difference to 'em all. That one, it come easy enough—o' course the little lady were young, and built right for it, oughta be good for a dozen more, I said at the time—but it was one as come lusty for life, just yellin' to take hold both hands, a handsome purty one too as love-childher usually be." But she turned suspicious at the repeated question. "Why d'you want to know? Sniffing round all this time after, what's it got to do with you? Maybe I've forgot. It's a long while back."

"I think you remember," he said. "You remember right enough."

"And maybe I don't intend to tell just for the asking. No, I don't mean that," she said as he put a hand to his pocket. "What trouble you off to make?"

"I don't want to make any trouble," he said. "It was myself. I am the boy who ran off. It's a responsibility I didn't take. I want to do something about it now."

She stared at him. "Well, Lord bless. That's a thing—it is indeed. A many bastards I helped birth but I never see one o' the men come back for it, even twenty years after. I don't know."

"I don't want to make any trouble for anyone. Only to—pay my debts."

After silence, her head on one side, she said, "You look that sort, sir. And it's a long time—reckon you couldn't make much trouble if you was a mind to it. Reckon I'd best say. Wed six, seven year they was, and no childher. Ellen, she wanted a fambly, and a farmer, he need a fambly. And they was going up toward Richmond, take up land, so no one need know 'bout it here. The Thurstan fella never asked an' I never told—reckoned least said soonest mended. Ellen, she couldn't hardly wait, they kept a'ready to go just as soon as—and I took it to her, same night, and they was gone in an hour and I never laid eye on any o' 'em since. That was the way of it."

"Where?" he asked. "Who? What was the name, Mrs. Williams?"

"Thought I said. Just up Richmond way, 'long the river, was all I knowed. Ellen Potter and her man—Ellen and Joe Potter."

It was a prosperous-looking farm. He sat on the horse in the road and looked at it before turning in the gate. It seemed a place kept by people who were forehanded with work and liked things neat. The kitchen garden at the side was weeded, the fences mended. There were five black-and-white milch cows in pasture. The house was logged, but had more than one room, and you felt the man would have raised a plank timber house could he afford the mill work; he'd got all the stumps out of his fields instead of plowing round, as lazy farmers did. There was a well-mortared stone chimney on the house.

He was not feeling nervous or curious when he dismounted and tethered the horse and went up to the door. It was a duty he carried out. From the first he had not felt it a matter involving emotions; in fact, now he thought, his mind had been so far from any such aspect he had not even troubled to ask the old woman —boy or girl. He had spent twelve days hunting these people, all the way up the James River, and he was rather tired and wanted to get back to New York and his *Courier*.

Yet something just stirred in him for the woman who opened the door. She was in the forties, with a pleasant round face, graying brown hair, young blue eyes. "Good day—sir," taking in his city man's blue broadcloth, his beaver hat. He asked if her husband was in. "Why, yes, sir, what was it?" The eyes doubtful: a persuasive peddler?

"It's a private matter." He was just realizing this would not be, after all, so easy. "I'd speak with both of you—it's a matter of business." That was all, business. The room she brought him to was a farm parlor, inhumanly neat, the room least used; she went to fetch her husband. Bethune looked about. One or two decent pieces of furnishing, an upholstered chair, a glass-fronted cupboard. Glass in the windows: a cut above the average farm family. There were returning steps and whispers; he turned. Potter was a big man near fifty, balding, shrewd-eyed, with unexpectedly bass voice. "Well, sir?"

He did not know, suddenly, how to begin it. He felt most damnably awkward, and so he was abrupt. Business, Bethune, business. He said, "I've come some way to find you, sir. I believe some years ago you and your wife took an infant born out of wedlock to a young lady near Williamsburg. 'Twas the midwife, old Mrs. Williams, gave me your name." He stopped there because the woman had gone white as death and the man's eyes were bleak.

"I don't know what you mean, sir," she faltered. "We never— she swore she'd never—all this time, nobody could—"

"You hush, Ellen. I do the talking. What's it to do with you?

Come fossicking around—nobody's business but mine, if we did. What d'you want with us?"

"I don't want to make trouble," he said. "Please understand that."

"Nobody shan't!" she cried suddenly, pulling away from her man's hand. "Nobody shan't have him—he's mine, he's ours! Nobody wanted him, they'd have put him out to die, all they cared—she told so! What do you want with my John?"

"Ellen. You let me manage this. —I'll not have trouble, mean to make it or no. I don't know what you be after but it won't take two o' me to toss you out so be you axe for it. Sit down, Ellen." But the man was breathing hard.

Bethune wasn't sure what he felt. He. John. He said quickly, "If you'll listen to me. I haven't come to make trouble—" He said it all like a lesson rehearsed. They listened; they did not believe; they were frightened. "It's a debt I didn't pay, that I owe you. You took the responsibility. I know, I know—you wanted it, it was your choice, but it was mine all the same. That's why I'm here. I owe you for it. I want it off my conscience."

They looked at him. The woman said, "You'd give us money? Bet said—a young lady. Gentry. They didn't care—they'd never ask if she drowned it in the river, she said. You want to give us money for John."

It just reached him now, it was not all cold fact—could not be. He, she said; John. He was panic-stricken at this sudden intrusion of personality. Let him pay what he owed and get away.

He began to speak rapidly. "I realize it is impossible to figure exactly. It was your choice, but all the same I feel it a debt I'm owing to you. I don't know how you're situated here. I've nearly three hundred pounds cash on me. I could manage somewhat weekly, or monthly, beside. I don't want to offend you. I don't even want to see— But if there is aught I could do for— Buy land, or education—"

The man said, "I don't reckon as you mean any harm. I got to tell you; I reckon you've a right. Be quiet, Ellen, he's the right if he be what he say. Seem to me he is. —The boy don't know. We never told him, wasn't no need. Never thought a soul alive'd know. We bean't important folk, what's it matter to any but us? Wanted a fambly but never had none."

Both stared at him so intently. Bethune wondered suddenly, trying to see resemblance—

The man said, "You don't owe nothing. If you don't want to make trouble, you get on your horse and go, that's all."

"But I can't leave it like this. Can't you understand how I'm placed? The responsibility—"

"You thought about that almighty late."

He said, "I was only sixteen." As if that were a valid excuse. But if they would not let him pay, if there was no way to pay the debt— "I never knew until a few years ago."

The man's eyes held brief scorn. "I don't give a Congress dollar what's true about that. I see you got a notion to do right for it—your conscience bother you, and well so it might. But you don't owe us nothing, nor John neither."

It was not a matter outside personalities, no. Bethune wondered that he had ever thought it could be.

"Look at it this way—fair exchange, you be so worrit 'bout the cash part, see. We do you a favor, but reckon you done us one to get the boy. He's a good boy. I ain't off to have him know, or have any talk about this atall."

"I don't want to make trouble." He wondered how many times he had said it.

"Wait," said the woman. "I guess that's so—you didn't know." She leaned forward, studying him almost wonderingly. "I don't reckon John's father'd be a bad man any way." She waved away her husband's flat words, a woman, going straight to the truth of it. "None of it's aught to do with money. Fair or uneven either side. Reckon we owe you more than we could ever pay, was it put in money. If you be what you say."

"All right," said the man grimly. "We said all there be to say. I won't take money from you on any count, I got no quarrel so you go off quiet and stay away and don't make trouble, that's all."

He'd get nowhere with this man. He stood up. It came to him that if they took all he had, if he had ten thousand pounds to give them or a hundred thousand, it was still a debt that could never be paid. That there was nothing he could do about it at all, ever. That all his searching and finding was a waste of time. People were not ciphers on a page.

He said, "Well. Then there is nothing I can do. I'm sorry. You needn't fear I'll talk of this or cause you any awkwardness." He took up his hat; he offered the man his hand. And as Potter hesitated before taking it, a door banged at the back of the house and a voice called. They had no time, any of them, to adjust expressions or speak before he came into the room.

"Pa, I saw Mr. Edwards and he said any day but Thursday, he's taking the bull over to Stedman's for a service. I told him—oh, I didn't see was anyone here."

CHAPTER 44

MARGARET'S EYES. That was the first thing he saw. Margaret's eyes, wide-set under the sharply arched heavy brows, and the curve of the hairline the same, the little widow's peak. The rest—it was only another person, not especially like or unlike. But Margaret's eyes.

A mutter of his name. A fierce look from the man. "Just a little business, 's all. Mr. Bethune's just going."

"Oh. Is anything the matter?" Puzzled, unsure, looking from one to the other.

He would not have such broad shoulders, such a span of chest, from himself, surely? Nineteen this very last month, November. All his growth, but the shoulders might fill out even more. The hair was dark as Margaret's, and with a little curl in it like hers. He

had a good deep voice, and the promise of a dark beard just showing.

"Nought's the matter. He were just going."

"That's right," said the woman in a frightened whisper.

Must be an inch taller than himself. There was the same
hint of auburn in the hair, like Margaret's, the same fair complexion, only burned red-brown except where a little V of white
showed below the open collar. He was quick, too: intelligence
showed in the broad brow, the firmly cut mouth. The hands were
broad, hard farmer's hands, but well-shaped, with the look of
integrity about them, independent hands, reliable. Nineteen, big
and handsome and confident as Bethune had never been; and Margaret's eyes.

"Oh. You from Mr. Fields in Richmond, sir?"

"No, he's not. Other kind've business, not the land. Don't matter. He were just—"

"Ma, you feel all right? I meant to say, it'll be five dollars for
the stud, Pa. You ride up from Richmond today, sir? Roads not
so good this season, we had a deal of rain." He was polite, making conversation; what people like these called well-raised. Manners.

"Yes," he said. "No. Have you?"

A little puzzled smile came into the eyes. He'd be a friendly
one—well-liked, warm with people; you could tell. The firm brown
young column of throat rising, the muscled brown arms; and yes,
something about the height of cheekbone, the straight mouth, that
was of himself—his, Bethune's.

"—Just off to leave," said the man loudly, desperately. Bethune
would like to reassure them, he ought to go, but he was occupied
with discovery: he could not look away. With discovery of the
truth, for there was truth. It was not all blind.

The silence had held to awkwardness. He cleared his throat. He
said carefully, "I came—because I thought I recalled owing a debt
to your father. He knew clearer than I. It was the other way
about, and he owes me—a deal more than I ever thought."

For this was the truth, the truth he had never believed in.
There was a pattern in life after all. No man ever walked alone—

he would never be walking alone again. There was a light in the darkness, a voice answering, a hand outstretched to meet the groping hand, and signposts pointing the way. It was not all for nothing—to nothing. A reason: this was it. The answer, the truth, the center force of the whole design. He had found it out at last, and he had never thought it was anything so fine as this.

He said, fascinated, "I have forgiven him the debt. The interest mounts too high—much too high."

Blind? But it was like—it was like the type. Jumbled, meaningless, upside-down, and one said, Nothing—there is no message. But if one knew the secret, there were the words to be read plain. The whole meaning: the secret of the whole meaning.

"Oh. Well, that's—that's kind of you, sir," said the boy.

"It's looking to come more rain." The man was near panic. Bethune could not spare him a glance.

"I am just going. Yes." He made himself look away. He put out his hand. "I'm very glad that we meet, sir. And thank you. Thank you for all you've done." His hand was dropped quickly and he gave it to the woman. "And you, madam."

She said in a pleading small voice, "Good-by, sir."

He'd said he was going; he ought to go. Really this was a most surprising and wonderful thing, utterly unexpected, a present from a stranger. The present of life and the secret of life. They were waiting for him to go, these good humble honest people who owed him such a tremendous debt. He must somehow get away. He looked back and the boy had his hand out politely. He took it—such a warm strong friendly hand, clasping the secret into his flesh forever like a brand. He did not know how to let it go.

"Good-by, sir." The man muttered thanks.

Somehow he let the hand go. He said, "Good-by." He dragged his eyes away again and walked straight out.

Into an entirely new world. Oh, indeed he had walked blind through life, never seeing, never knowing. Now it was as if a new pair of eyes showed him bright wonders never suspected.

It began to rain as he rode for the town, and that was a jest, and a little glorious too, the cold purity of rain on his flesh, the earthy smell of wet fields. There had been a night he came through rain desperate, frightened; he hadn't known then there was a pattern, a central truth.

It was a most extraordinary feeling. Being sixteen again, still believing in the good and true and right, but even better because he had seen the proof of it now. He would never walk alone down any road again. The knot in the chain had come undone, freed by a strong brown young hand, and he was not set apart any longer. The sin, if it was a sin, was cleansed by its consequence; the debt, if there was a debt, was paid the moment it was contracted.

He came into Richmond dripping and exalted; he took the horse back to the stable, and the stableman was his friend and brother and he gave him ten dollars.

"It only come to three and four bits, sir—"

"No, no, take it, I've no small change. Buy your wife somewhat —have you a wife?"

"Well, sir, I have, and a boy, but—"

"So have I," he said. "So have I." He went back to the inn and asked about a stage. There was an urgency on him, and it was a little nuisance that there was none down-river for two days.

But the publican was a brother—very fine, this feeling of closeness with all men—and he said, "Excuse me, sir, you be wet. Best you get dry and change clothes or you'll be taking cold."

"Oh, no, I won't do that. I must start down-river now, tonight."

"Well, sir, there's Jem Peabody's boat. He reckon to take them pigs down to Jamestown, start tonight, but I dunno—"

"I reckon he'll take me along, will he? You'll find out for me?" He went up to his chamber and they fetched him hot water and he bathed and changed clothes, unaware of chill. Standing there mother-naked in the hip bath, he felt the most powerful man in the world.

He came down the James with a boatload of squealing pigs. He felt fine, but something was driving him on. It never came to him what it was until he went to look for a ship making north, and the ship captain said to him, "I make out for Perth Amboy first off, but N'York after."

"That's where I want to go," he said. "Perth Amboy. That's good." He leaned on the rail waiting for the anchor to come up, and awe rose in him like the awe a devout man might feel in church. He was released out of bondage, and now he could say it to her. Now he could tell her and be believed. Everything dammed up in him was clamoring to come forth, and now he could let it out, he could say it all.

He must tell her about the boy, yes, that was important, but the other first. In one sense a release, but in another a forged link in the chain, they could never get apart from one another, they were halves of a whole and he could explain that now he knew, and she would know it too. Oh, now he could tell her; now he was set free to tell her.

It was a clear cold morning, three days before Christmas, when he disembarked at Perth Amboy. He hired a horse from a sleepy stableman in the town and rode out north through the bare, strong, winter country. He came into Newark about three of the afternoon, and then the urgency was hot in him and he almost ran up to the house door.

There was no answer to his knock. It was Sunday; she would not be at her school. He tried the door and it was unlocked; he went in, flung himself up the stair in a silent house to the door of her little parlor on the first floor, kept himself at once from bursting in, knocked. He leaned on the panel; she must be here, please God she was here, he could not wait to see her after this long while. He opened the door, went in.

She was there, just coming from the other room. He saw her as if in a burst of light, Margaret, his lovely Margaret, in the blue gown—a little shabby now—from the silk he had given her so long ago. She stopped dead across the room, seeing him. It was such a long way to reach her, and he could not wait to begin telling her. It came out of him in a torrent, all he had never been able to say, all that had been held inside so long. He could not stop the words, a flood-tide of words incoherent, shameless, unplanned, tumbling over each other in eagerness to be out and said. All he had never said, all he had wanted to say from twenty years back.

She stood looking up at him, her eyes wide and blank. Her lips moved to frame words unheard. "What are you doing here—I told you—" He could not pay attention to that. He was weak, breathless with the spate of words, and leaned on her still whispering urgently, Listen to me, Margaret, Margaret, all I never said, twenty years of words I could never say, Margaret, my darling, listen to me now.

Her hands pushed him a little away. She was looking up at him startled, and he had no more breath and stopped, her shoulders slim and warm under his hands. She said just above a whisper, "Why, it's true. It's true. James. I could not believe it—but it's true, it's real—you do.

A very little sanity returned to him, and he felt the push of her hands on him. He must not hurt her again. He tried for some control; he held her hands tightly. "Margaret, Margaret, yes, just that, all I'd ever ask, my darling, believe me, only tell me you believe me now."

The silence seemed very long as she looked up at him. Then she said, "It's real." Without violence she took her hands away; they explored up to his face, touching cheek and brow, the hands of a blind woman seeing him. "It's true," she said, very low. "James, James. Yes, I can tell you that now—I believe you, now I believe you. The thing I can't tell you, no words to say it—how I love you, how much I love you." But one moment they stayed motionless, and he was drowning in her eyes, before he bent his head and came home at last.

"James."

"Hmm?"

"Was it like steam in a kettle? All on a sudden having to come out? It would have been for me. It was. If you'd been near any longer. I don't know how I kept from letting you see, all that time. Like a nightmare."

He whispered against her, "Better when I was gone?"

She held him tighter. "No. No. Much worse. Never to see you again. Was it?"

He moved his head against her breast, negative. "Not a kettle. What a way to say it. No. Something else."

"Oh." There was a very long silence. "But all that time," she said. "All of it wasted. I thought, Keep my pride. Nothing to do with loving—but I never knew that either. I was very stupid. James."

"Hmm?"

"James." Just a thread of whisper. "I want to ask. Don't laugh at me. Please, James. I want—oh, God, all that time gone! I'm old, I'm too old, my dearest. But just perhaps—please, James, do you think we might—that I might—"

He began to laugh against the warm yielding flesh, into her hair; he drew her closer still, laughing, and of all the best moments of time this was the finest, right now, this space of time preserved only for them. "Oh, Margaret," he said, "yes, my love, I do—we will. I don't think we could do any better—but we might try. . . . My darling, I've something to tell you."

CHAPTER 45

BETHUNE LEANED on the back of Darcy's chair, watching the sketch grow under the quill. There was a flotilla of tiny ships in the harbor, all flying British colors, and in the foreground a motley stream of folk, with bags and bundles, marching down the wharf. All the bundles were embellished with the British flag to mark their owners as Loyalists.

"That's good," he said.

"Don't breathe down my neck, you'll make me spoil it. Never suspected I had such talent, did you?" Darcy blocked in the last beaver hat, retouched an expression, looked at it critically and added the caption below in bold-face letters: *Let the d—nd rebel rabble keep their unity!* Then, in a corner of the drawing, he sketched in the real point: thirteen little merchants, some fat, some lean, some in shirtsleeves, each labeled with the name of a colony-state. They waved their fists, shouted open-mouthed; New Jersey and Virginia were pummeling each other, Massachusetts sulked to one side, and a prosperous stout New York laughed at the lot. "That's very good, Darcy. We'll put it on the first page."

"Been down to the docks as yet? I heard there were more casting off today."

"Too old a story, no news. Will you see that gets to the printers? They always ask an extra day to do a drawing, a damnation nuisance. That is, if you're not otherwise occupied this evening." He wondered about Darcy and the Woods girl. She was only nineteen, much younger, but a quiet, sensible girl, and pretty; he'd like to see Darcy settle down.

"I'll take it, yes."

"Good. I'm leaving now." He got his hat, slung his cloak round his shoulders, glanced again at the sketch. "That's damnation good." In the front room he clapped young Will on the back. "How goes it?"

"I had to turn away a dozen advertisers, Mr. Bethune. More than twenty dollars just this afternoon."

"If that keeps up, we'll enlarge the *Courier* to six pages, eh? Not that it will—it's all the Tories departing. Once they're gone we'll see things settle down to normal."

"You heard aught about when the Americans are coming in, sir? Everybody's saying it'll be soon."

"We should hear this week—Washington has asked Sir Guy to set an evacuation date." Which was why the last of the remaining Loyalists were scrambling to get away. Poor devils, he was sorry for them. How many had left since April? Thousands—some sources said thirty thousand all told. Not counting the military.

And there was one poor devil he felt sorrier for, Gentleman Johnny under military arrest, setting sail for England with all his surrendered army for court-martial. The Hessians they had got rid of at the same time. Soon, now, the rest; and the Americans would come in officially.

Only officially. As he left the office and walked down Maiden Street to Broadway, he saw two new shop buildings going up, the workman chaffing each other good-humoredly. There were fewer uniforms among the crowds on Broadway, more people buying at stalls and shops. Prices were coming down. Paper was only six pounds the ream now. He stopped at a little shop near the corner where Fair Street ran up, to buy tobacco; there were newspapers stacked on the counter, and as he waited for service, two men came up behind him. "I'll have a *Courier*, sir—none left? Damnation, I shall have to subscribe. The *Gazette*? Good God, I'd as soon read Rivington as Gaine. Give me a *Journal* then." Bethune smiled to himself, pleased. As they sow, yes. It was a wonder Rivington or Gaine had the face to stay in publication.

He dawdled up Broadway. He would never get over liking to wander New York, his town, listening, watching. Since that first day he came ashore and fell in love with her, the eternal mistress. Changed? Yes and no. They were busy renaming the streets now, to make more confusion: in sturdy American independence doing away with Duke and King and Queen. Perhaps the new names would stay, perhaps not; people were in the habits of the old ones now. New York, an American city now, as easy and bland as if she had never been anything else; changed overnight again: where the British officers had driven with their ladies, a wagoner cursed a merchant's carriage, blocking the road. The British colors might still fly over Fort George, but New York had changed allegiance six months back when the returned rebels began to outnumber the Tories.

What price their war? They had not changed New York, the city of merchants. They never would. They would give her new streets and new buildings and new leaders—Sears and McDougall and their hurrah-for-liberty boys forgotten, the De Lanceys gone, and now presently Carleton and his staff of harassed officers. But others would come, of this sort and that. New York was not interested in them, except casually. He had the sudden fancy that New York was like himself, the stay-home fence-sitter, cynical for ideas, more concerned to get on with the job.

That was another thing. They talked loud and often, the Americans, of a war for their honor as well as their independence. And the first act they made as a nation? To overlook the agreement they had with France—a France who had so generously and eagerly sent men and ships to turn the tide of victory toward the rebels: a signed agreement that they would make no separate peace with England. They had made separate peace, ignoring the promise completely. Perhaps understandable? Everyone was eager for official peace, to have it over and done.

He would not soon forget one result of that. The news came to New York on the twenty-fifth of March, and still they had delayed—after eighteen months since Cornwallis surrendered!—until the sixth of April, when Captain Beasley of the *Ampheon* visited the prison ships one by one and read the proclamation of the war's official end. They had not believed it, the men released; they had come ashore from the boats—Bethune was there to see—hesitantly, men filthy, in rags, starved, whip-marked; and for a long time they had gone on not believing it. You could tell them in the street, even one given decent clothes, fed, with the pallor of the ship's hold giving way to brown—the way they would start and turn at a word, and back off to give wide berth to a British officer. But few had stayed; they scattered, trying to rejoin their old army units or get back to their homes.

He turned up Mulberry Street, and his steps quickened a little toward the house set back from a neat, small garden. The polished brass on the door shone—thanks to Greta; trust a Dutch girl to keep brass polished. He felt still a bit strange, master of a house-maid, if only one; but wages had dropped, twenty pounds a year was not really very high.

"Good afternoon, sir. Mistress is out, sir."

He was annoyed. She had no business to be out when he came in. He wandered into the parlor. The maid brought him a letter he had overlooked on the table in the passage, and it was a letter from old Mr. Sower—Mr. Sower, Junior. He sat down in his own deep armchair by the hearth where a pleasant fire hissed, and filled and lit his pipe, and read what Mr. Sower had to say in a spidery, old-fashioned script. The first models had been not too satisfactory, but some modifications had been made and the latest model worked well. Allowing for the ratio of size and weight, a full-scale press should be operable with a minimum of effort upon the part of one man, who would thus be able also to insert and remove the pages. It was too early to make predictions, but it was at least possible a wheel press might produce five hundred pages an hour, and all without straining a printer's muscles once. Only consider, Mr. Bethune, what this would mean.

Bethune was excited, and considered it. If MacDonald could have known! Would larger editions automatically mean more readers? Well, that they would find out; it was a gamble, but he would be willing to take it. He would never be satisfied, or feel quite safe, after those six years, until the *Courier* had its own shop, its own presses. He wondered how much a wheel press would cost to build, to buy. He must write to Mr. Sower—now triumphantly back in Germantown.

She came in so quietly he did not hear her. "Out to waste money on female fripperies," he said, not opening his eyes at her lips on his forehead.

"And you lazing here before a fire instead of out earning to support me." She adjusted herself comfortably across his lap. "James."

"Well?"

"I think you've quite forgotten it is your birthday."

"So I had. Is it? Have you a present for me?"

"You can't have it now," she said, her head on his shoulder. "Not as yet." She laughed into his shoulder. After a time she asked, "How does it go at the office?"

"Very well. Why?"

"Oh, nothing. You are still satisfied with your young clerk? You like him, do you not? I believe you are—what's the word?— grooming him to become a newsman, the way Mr. MacDonald did yourself."

"Well," he said. "Young Will's a good boy."

"Mhmm. You cannot have your birthday gift," she said, "until July. Next July."

"Well, that seems—Margaret? Margaret!" He turned her face up with one hand. She was smiling.

"Perhaps then—you'll not need to think of grooming young Will for your heir."

They were still sitting there close, no candle lit yet in the darkening room, when Darcy came in, having the freedom of the house. "Disgraceful," he said above them. "No decency in either of you, but the war has a sad effect on morals—I understand wars always do."

"Go away," said Bethune.

"We've not had tea yet, Darcy, won't you stay?"

"No, thanks, I've a dinner engagement and must get home to change. I only came by to give you some news, in the event you're at all interested. Carleton has announced they'll evacuate officially five days from now. Washington is to come in for formal possession the same day."

Bethune sat up. "Five days—that makes it the twenty-fifth. Next Monday. Damnation! Would you not know it! Now why could it not have been Wednesday? I wish they'd consult the editors before they set these dates. Right between editions!"

Shades of Sears and McDougall! Ironic? Well, not so much irony as farce. New York of the many faces! She had hung back in the war, thinking of her commerce; she had treated with the enemy, thinking of her commerce; she staged a grand welcome for the conquerors, thinking of her commerce. The British ships in harbor had scuttled away, more each day. It was the Americans' hour; so New York was American to the core, her citizens shouting patriots.

It was a cold, clear day; the city stirred early and broke out hundreds of American flags before every house and shop front. The streets filled with impatient, excited people awaiting the arrival of the American troops they knew were near. They were all ready to display their new flags and cheer for Washington. New

York did not care about ideas. Her harbor was crowded with merchant ships, and that was enough reason to celebrate.

Toward the middle of the morning the first American troops came in. They marched up the Bowery to Grand Street near the barracks gate of the fort, and there broke ranks. They scattered about, exchanging talk with the crowd, sitting on the grass at street-side, waiting for the British to get under way. They waited until past noon, when all the nominal guard remaining on duty at Fort George marched out in column with the fort colors at their head. All the other British stationed in the city, on Staten and Long Islands, had been taken off to waiting warships during the previous three or four days; these were the last in New York.

A little delay, and then the second advance guard came: General Knox with some corps of dragoons and infantry, artillerymen, a battalion of Massachusetts troops. They marched in, proud and gleaming as became the conquerors, up to Wall Street where they halted before Cape's Tavern and the officers dismounted and went in for a dram before the arrival of the commanding general. Knox sent a picked detail of troopmen to enter the fort and raise the American colors. That was where the farce turned to broad comedy.

The same mischievous spirit that had set off the feud between the redcoats and the Sons of Liberty over the Liberty Pole had prompted the British regulars, after hauling down their colors, to remove the halyards from the pole, knock off the cleats, and cover the whole staff well with goose-grease. There was a delay while one man after another tried vainly to climb the pole, treating the crowd to a fine lesson in military profanity. At last someone fetched a saw, a hammer, and nails, and one man, tying the halyards to his belt, succeeded in climbing the staff, pounding in cleats for foothold as he went, replaced the ropes, and got them on the pulleys. The American flag went up to the accompaniment of raucous mirth as well as cheers.

The new governor of New York had gone out to meet General Washington; they rode into the city together at the head of some picked cavalry, with an escort of influential citizens all mounted, and the crowds lined the way, cheering, and waving flags.

Bethune made one of the crowd; he had forbidden Margaret to venture out on such a day of excitement and noise, and the streets were iced. But he did no cheering or flag waving. He wondered what Washington was thinking as he rode along the streets of New York—the scene of his earliest, most disastrous defeat, the city that had denied him and now welcomed him in with such joy.

Over the heads of the crowd he saw the general, tall on a tall gray horse, eyes straight ahead, only occasionally inclining slightly to the crowd, as if their plaudits somewhat embarrassed him. A soldier, not a politician: a man no longer young, grave of expression, a trifle stern. Yes, what was he thinking? He had won their war for them—with the help of a France they had thanked by deceiving—and what would they do with the victory?

He thought about Darcy's sketch: thirteen squabbling tradesmen. He thought of MacDonald: The key word, Mr. Bethune, is 'unity'! Well, whatever they did or did not, whatever came after this, it would all make news for writing and publishing.

Washington and his staff officers were to stay at Fraunces' Tavern, where the governor would give a dinner party for Washington this evening, with everyone of influence present who could wangle an invitation. When they had all disappeared into the tavern and their horses been led off, the crowd straggled back down Pearl Street, reluctant to disband, and jammed the Bowling Green. Some commenced singing patriotic songs, a couple of would-be orators got up on boxes and shouted unheard. Bethune and Darcy had gone along with them; but it appeared the official ceremonies were done, and the mob was only working out excess excitement. At least it seemed amiable enough; there would be no riots as in the old days.

He looked about the mass of people, MacDonald's words again in his mind. An American city, sir, American! New York of the islands—here they were again: German, Dutch, Irish, Jewish, Negro, Catholic, Scot, English, Protestant—merchant, shopman, sailor, farmer, clerk. His town: his people, who made his news.

He laughed at the crowd; he took Darcy's arm. "Looks to be all over, or nearabout. I'll buy you a brandy at the City."

"Right." As they walked up toward Broadway Darcy said, "By

the way, James, I'm to wed Anne Woods. In the spring, we thought."

"That's good news, Darcy! A charming girl. Er—?" Old Woods had the reputation of being difficult: an impoverished gentleman, a fearful snob.

Darcy laughed. "Oh, no trouble at all! I told you how it would be—all I did was show my arm and murmur, 'Camden,' and I was the great war-hero, nothing too good. Not even Anne—which she is. Thanks, James. I thought—" He went on talking about a wedding journey, a house. Bethune listened absently. They were at the door of the City Tavern when Darcy shook his arm. "You've not heard a word I said."

"Oh, yes," he said. "Certainly. Only one brandy—I must get down to the office. It's not really late, only seven o'clock. We must bring out an extra edition. Two pages, I think. I never told you about old Mr. Sower's letter. He has got his press working. Can you feature it, Darcy?—five hundred pages an hour, he says. Five hundred!"

Darcy grinned at him. "You're blocking the doorway. Come in and tell me about it. Boy! Two brandies!"